ALIEN DECEPTIONS
AN ERICA JONES ALIEN HUNTER NOVEL

Written by: Tina Marie

Alien Deceptions

What would you do if you and you alone knew of a potential alien invasion that could destroy the Earth? Of a secret war waged among intelligent life forms, thought only in the imagination of Government conspiracies fanatics. Given a gift, rekindling the fire locked away in your DNA. Would you try to stop the invasion? What if you knew no one would believe you? Would you take it on your shoulders to save the world or quietly seek to go about your daily life without knowledge the end was near?

Erica Jones, executive secretary, athlete and a friend to many will make such a choice.

An ordinary woman, who happened to be in the wrong place at the right time or the right place at the wrong time, depending on your perception. A successful business-woman that had a close encounter with the truth that would eventually change her life, her beliefs, and the way she views life, death, and humanity.

An innocent vacation to the tropical island of Maui and a chance meeting, or so she thought, with a man that would forever change her life. An intimate romance with a secretive Government Agent, which eventually turns to the fight for her life and everyone on this planet's existence. Erica soon discovers that we are not alone on this planet and the enemy is closer than she thinks. A Far cry from the movies, these aliens have learned to use our way of life to their advantage. Their agenda, hidden beneath deception, secrecy, and lies extend to agencies far higher than that of the Presidency.

Erica must throw away her own beliefs and put her trust into the hands of a lover, entities not of this world and secret agencies thought not to exist. Millenniums in the making, she alone, given this burden to carry, will try to tip the scales in this ongoing battle the rest of us will never know about—Until it's too late.

A fiction book based on years of documented facts and files your Government doesn't what you to know about, at least not yet.

ERICA JONES ALIEN HUNTER

LOOK FOR THE NEXT BOOKS IN THE SERIES

COMING SOON

PROJECT DEEP CORE
THE SECRET GOVERNMENT PEACE TREATY

Also

VALLEY OF THE ORBS
THE UNSEEN TRUTH

ALIEN DECEPTION

Second Edition: October 2014

This is a work of fiction. All the characters, organizations, and events portrayed in this novel either are products of the author's imagination and/or used fictitiously. Any likeness to actual business, accounts and or person is coincidental.

Note: If you bought this book without a cover, be aware this book is stolen property; reported as "unsold and destroyed" to the publisher, and neither, the author nor publisher has received any payment for this "stripped book."

Jacket Cover Designed by: Tina Marie Entertainment

www.tinamarieentertainment.com

ISBN 978-0-9835010-0-8

Printed in the United States of America

Acknowledgments

To *Matt Coe*, my longtime friend, a special thanks for taking time from your hectic family-life to help edit this novel. You have always been a loyal friend and a positive influence on my life. May sunshine forever radiate on you and your family, even on the cloudiest of days.

Finally, to the members of Higher Vibrations Radio Show and The Las Vegas UFO Hunters. Thank you for your contributions, expertise, and outright support. Alex & Ron, your passion will someday reward you with the truth, sooner than you think.

In addition, I would like to thank the following two websites for their help in construction and translation of the English to Hawai'ian glossary. I have developed a deeper appreciation of the Hawai'ian language in part to your detailed websites. Thank you.

www.free-dictionary-translation.com

www.1800sunstar.com

Dedications

To my parents for their continued support even miles away.

Sean, I hope someday you will read this novel and be proud of whom you are and where you have come from….

Colby, our golden retriever and true inspiration behind Colby's character in the book. We adopted you, brought you home without knowing the impact you'd have on all of our lives—who knew.

Principally, to Kristine, my soul mate, my reason for life. Thank you for the continued support and encouragement each day I wrote; even on the days, I didn't want to. One day they will discover a word that equates to my true feelings, but for now, 'I love you' is the best I can do

ALIEN DECEPTIONS
AN ERICA JONES ALIEN HUNTER NOVEL

Written by: Tina Marie

Chapter 1

After what I saw and did last night; today starts a new chapter of my life. I wish I could erase the last few weeks, most importantly the last twenty-four hours, but those memories have forever singed my mind. It still feels like I've been living a dream or more fitting, a nightmare.

Didn't sleep at all, instead laid with my eyes shut trying to shake the pain that was rushing through my veins. I could almost feel the sun rising over the horizon. The warmth of day was a welcome change from the coldness I felt last night. Even in Vegas, January nights can be extremely cold. They always say that for every end a new beginning begins. I think after what I have been through over these last few weeks, makes me wish I didn't know the ending.

The bright blue neon of the clock reads 6 a.m. I turn my head on the pillow lying here wishing I could sleep. The alarm clock went off fifteen minutes ago and I can smell the fresh morning coffee percolating in the kitchen. Who set the coffee? Who cares! How long can I lie here and listen to that annoying beeping? How long since I've slept longer than a couple of hours. I rolled over; hit the snooze button, almost smashing my hand through the plastic. Rolled back, cuddled, next to the one friend who's consistently been there the last few years, but especially the last few days. I pulled the blankets up to my neck, looked across at those big brown eyes and snuggled into his neck.

Colby's not your typical golden retriever. I mean that in a good way. I adopted him from a soldier on his way to Iraq for an extended tour. Not knowing his future, he wanted to make sure Colby went to a loving home. A co-worker had introduced me to him, knowing I'd lost my golden retriever of fourteen years. I didn't know if I was ready to take on another commitment, but after meeting Colby, the bond was instant. I've had Goldens over the years, but Colby at times acted human more than dog. He always sensed my emotions and just loved to snuggle. What could a single woman, with no kids and pushing thirty-five ask for other than a good man! Somehow, though, I don't think a man could ever be as loyal as Colby.

Colby turned three a few months ago, but still acts like a puppy. He weighs in at just over ninety pounds, half that being fur. On a cold night, he's the perfect warm blanket, with those deep brown eyes always looking at me without the slightest regret. Colby's the closest comparison to a child I'll experience in my life. Many times when talking, from the way I describe his unique personality, people always ask *how old your son is.* I think only a true dog lover, especially a Golden Retriever lover, would ever understand.

I turned over and buried my face into his fur, hoping that I could just stay in bed. The coffee was calling like a mother trying to get her kid up for school. Just five more minutes I kept telling myself. I could smell the baby-powdered freshness of his fur. He smelled like the security blanket I had as a child. For a second, I felt displaced, craving the simplicity of my youth, as today on, my innocence, lost forever. One couldn't witness as well as discover what I had and still have the same optimistic hope for the future.

Colby leaned over, put his head on my shoulder, looked me in the eyes, and gave me a modest lick on the nose as if to say, *everything will be alright.* How could he know, I mean, he is just a dog. He licked me again as his tail began to wag. He had a tail that forever seemed happy to see you. I knew what he wanted and it wasn't coffee.

I gingerly rolled out of bed, still clothed from last night, too drained to shower or even change when I got home. How did I get home? I managed to remove my boots, but was too sore to take off my jeans and tee shirt. I usually try to put my hair up before bed but that never happened. Catching a reflective glimpse in the mirror, horrified by the image as my brown silky hair looked like a dreadful toupee. I must have driven home in the convertible, top-down, trying to stay awake, because my hair was paying the price this morning. Then it occurred to me, I didn't take the convertible. I was going to go comb it, but the smell of coffee in the house was too strong and Colby was craving his breakfast.

I never tire of watching him do his doggy dance in the morning. He's a hefty dog, with a ballroom dancer's grace and the appetite of a tapeworm. Colby, from time to time, shakes his butt so hard his tail acts like a whip, knocking everything down in his path. I've learned to position items in the house above waist-high to avoid repercussion from this whirlwind.

I gradually leaned over, still in a daze and in pain, fed him, gave him fresh water and made my way to the coffeepot. As he ate, I fixed myself a cup of coffee. I had switched from decaf to regular a few weeks ago, not by choice, but of necessity. I should switch back, but maybe tomorrow, if tomorrow ever comes.

It's funny how you can be a never-ending optimist until a tragedy happens in your life and then that cup begins to look half-empty. Speaking of half empty, I need to refill the cup. That first one went down oh so fast. My normal routine is a pot of coffee before work, but only after going for a morning run. Lately though, I drink coffee as if I own the company. Note to self, buy stock in *Hillcrest Coffee*.

Every morning, until the last few mornings, I ran ten miles a day with my friend Tracy. I knew Tracy wasn't going to make it and I didn't have the stomach, after last night, to hit the road myself. I enjoy the solitude of running alone. The time gives me a chance to reflect on one's inner soul. However, I'd already spent much time over the last week reflecting and wondering about the future. It was depressing; the future I mean, unlike before when I knew it—What laid ahead now was a blank slate waiting for an inscription.

I turned to the fridge to add creamer to my coffee not realizing I'd drank the first cup black. Its bitter aftertaste, sufficiently wiped the cobwebs from my mind. How people drink black coffee I'll never understand. I gave up adding sugar to my coffee about two years ago while training for a marathon with Tracy. Now, it's just low fat hazelnut creamer. I know, sugar wasn't any more in calories, but a woman still needs her vices; coffee black was not one of them.

I grabbed for the handle on the fridge momentarily stopping in my tracks, on its surface, a picture of Tracy and I in Hawai'i. We'd just crossed the finish line of a marathon held a few weeks prior during our second vacation together. This year's trip was Hawai'i, predominately the island of Maui. Tracy thought, running a marathon while there would be fun. I strongly suggest never trying that unless you have ample time to recuperate. We had run the next to last day of the vacation and with a six-hour flight back to Las Vegas. Let's say I spent a good portion of the flight soothing and massaging the cramps out of my legs.

The vacation was extraordinary, and unfortunately our last. It was tough seeing the smiles on both our faces, hands extended over our heads in glory as we crossed the finish line together. Tracy was a faster runner than I was, but she ran the last six miles encouraging me all the way to the finish. What always amazed me was how she finished races barely having broken a sweat. I later found out why! I crossed looking like I just showered with my clothes still on. Maui is awe-inspiring, but the tropical humidity doesn't make for great running weather. If I recall, it was ninety degrees that day with eighty-percent humidity. Tracy wanted to go back and do it again next year. It is painful to think that after last night that'll never happen.

I removed the Maui magnet, slowly removed the picture, and cradled it in my hands. I could feel my eyes welling up and watched as a tear fell onto the picture. Colby came over and nuzzled his head into my thigh. I told you he always sensed my emotions. I wish I could've ripped the picture up and thrown it out with the morning trash. I longed to erase our friendship formed over the last few years, but couldn't. This feeling of nausea came over me; the knees went weak as I used my hands and Colby to stable myself.

He knew what to do and walked me to the sink. I wish I could've thrown up, at least that might've helped. Instead, I took a deep breathe, wiped the tears from my cheek, and took another sip of coffee. *Damn it! Black*, I'd forgotten to add the creamer. I slid down to the floor and hugged my only true friend I had left.

However, ten minutes had passed, before I gathered myself. Finally adding creamer to my coffee before beginning to write the story I could never tell, at least not for now. Sworn to secrecy, never to reveal what had happened over the last few weeks. I knew that would age me more than the reflection I already saw in the mirror every morning, but knew, if word got out what had happened, the world's future would change for good. I should say for the worst. Society, presently, wasn't ready for the entire truth.

I never had cops interrogate me, but understood that I'd better get my story straight. It was only a matter of time before they called, requested a statement, and begin asking me *a few questions*. I was never a good liar, but learned how to perfect the art over the last few weeks. I also learned how to read a liar better than your universal lie detector.

I no sooner finished the thought than the phone rang. There comes a point after having liberal amounts of coffee that you can't get any more jumpy. I'd arrived at that point a week ago, unflappably reaching for the phone.

"Hello, this is Erica how can I help you?" The response was automatic from years of experience as an executive secretary.

I could hear sirens in the background as this deep voice replied, "Erica, this is Detective Wilson again, do you know a Tracy Miller?" It wasn't much of a question, but as an aimed fact.

"Yes, she's my best friend." What could I do? Currently ill-prepared for questions, I had to find a way to stall. "Why?" I replied. The detective took his time responding, as if waiting to see if I'd give away any information. "Hello," I said. "Detective, you still there?"

"Yes. Sorry, I was checking my notes." I knew otherwise. "Miss Jones, something has happened to Tracy Miller. I wonder if you'd come down to the station for a statement."

I hesitated for a moment. I was expecting this call, just not so soon. Did he notice I was stalling? God, say something. "I was about to jump in the shower, can it wait till after I get out?" This was good, if it worked. I needed the additional time to get my story straight.

"I'll expect to see you around one sharp, this afternoon, at the station!" From the tone in his voice, that was not a request but an order. I heard that tone enough from my boss to know the difference.

"Yes, fine, 1 p.m. Detective Wilson." I wrote his name down on a sticky note so I wouldn't forget. How could I.

"Okay Miss Miller, 1 p.m." There was a transitory pause before the line went dead.

I hung up the phone and stared at the picture of Tracy. It hit me. What was the detective fishing for, did he know? *Oh my god,*

I never asked what happened, if she was even all right, what friend forgets to ask? It was human nature to ask. You don't ask questions about events you already had the answers to. God, I just gave myself away! I looked; the clock now read 6:30 a.m. I needed a shower and time to think of a believable alibi the detective would buy. My heart was pounding, harder and faster than when I ran. I'd grown up a lot over the last few weeks, seen, and done stuff that no one else could imagine.

I seized one last sip of my coffee and headed for the shower. A long hot shower would clear my mind or at least stimulate it to come up with a good story. The truth wouldn't work. It would get me a one-way ticket to a mental institution or worse—a death sentence. I wondered where my new friends were now. Clearly, not here; truthfully, probably still not on this planet. God I already hate my new life.

Chapter 2

I love my bathroom! I mean I bought this house for three reasons; the backyard, open with much privacy; the large walk-in closet; the oversized master bathroom with Roma tub. What woman doesn't love those features in a house?

Being an executive secretary has its rewards, especially in the pay department. However, because of recent events, I'll have to rethink my career path. All right, enough worrying, time to relax for a few moments and challenge myself to forget the night's events.

This wasn't a bathroom of choice for people self-conscious about their body. Everywhere you looked, there were mirrors. At thirty-three, a size two, plus an athlete, I didn't have to worry about that right now. I loved the fact my outfit-adorned body was viewable from any angle in the room.

A few years ago, thanks to Stacey & Clinton of *What Not to Wear*, I became extra aware of how clothes fit my body. Being petite does have advantages with some clothes, but at five foot eight, almost all my pants and skirts needed hemming; too tall for petite and too short for the tall section. Luckily, my breasts had stayed in proportion to my size. I never saw the excitement in having large breasts, although many women I worked with had undergone breast augmentation. Training for a marathon and a size larger than B—not my idea of fun. Being taller than most women did have advantages as well, especially dealing with men. At least when they stared at my breasts it wasn't as noticeable.

I turned the lights on, started water running in the Roman tub; the centerpiece of my bathroom. It had fourteen powerful massage jets and today I needed every one of them. The gold plated fixtures, purchased upgrades after closing, gave an exceptionally rich feel to the tub. I lit a few candles and added lavender bath oil to the water. I needed to relax and the smell of lavender had a way of making me feel as if floating on clouds.

I took a long, hard look into the mirror and hoped the rest of my body didn't appear as ghastly as my arms and face. This was going to be a hard sell to the police looking like I went a few rounds in an FCC cage fight and although closer to the truth, authorities couldn't know what happened, at least for now.

There were still blood droplets on my favorite pair of jeans. Why is it when you finally find a pair of jeans that look great on your butt they never last? I should have picked up two pair! I gently removed the tee shirt, which hurt as soon as I tried to pull it over my head. I stared at the mirror—the black and purple bra blending with the bruising around my ribs and shoulder. At one point last night thinking, I dislocated it. I can still see extended finger marks that started on my back shoulder and protrude down to my waist. You wouldn't think such gentle fingers could inflict that kind of collateral damage. Then again, she wasn't your typical woman.

After seeing the bruises, I feared removing the pants, but the bathwater ready and hating it cold, I had to try. I slithered out of my pants like a snake shedding its skin; the pain intensely prevalent. My legs hadn't swollen, but did feel tighter than normal. The removal, not without causalities, as a few nails broke back. However, if this were the worst injury sustained today, it'd be a good day.

I opened the door under the sink disposing of the jeans and shirt. Mysteriously, they would need to vanish before the police showed up with a search warrant. It was liberating removing my bra as the straps had started burrowing into the skin, irritating the bruising. I stood in the mirror looking at myself, a poster board for battered women. I was enlightened my body would heal faster than normal, but then again, define normal.

I walked over; popped in a CD of the latest Hawai'ian music I had picked up almost a month ago. It's remarkable how the sounds of the islands can put you in a superior mood; must be that Aloha vibe. My toes dipped through the bubbles into the scalding water. Half the tub had filled with bubbles and with every pop, the air filled with the warm scent of lavender. It took only minutes to settle into the tub, but well worth the wait.

The tub effortlessly fit two, not that I'd know, having never got the time or chance to find out. I, a speck, forever lost in tranquility as the next half an hour was all about me having given myself a well-deserved time-out. I closed my eyes and let the sounds of *Over the Rainbow/What a Wonderful World* by *Israel Kamakawiwo'ole* engulf my mind. It took me back to the beaches of Lāhainā on Maui, the warm surf, the romantic sunsets and the feeling of tranquility. Maui, one of those islands you just couldn't shake from your mind once you've been. I tenderly ran my hands over my body hoping the power of Reiki would help heal my wounds. No serious cuts, just massive amounts of bruising.

For years, I'd taken Judo classes, partly to stay in shape, but mainly because being a single woman in Vegas had some disadvantages. Guys, in general, think if they're bigger than you are, they wield the power. The truth, in a fight, the larger they are the more force they produce which you can use against them.

I used this knowledge only once, before last night, to protect myself while at Planet Hollywood's new Club opening, Prive. It was a Friday night, a few of us from work decided to let off a little steam. The real motivation to visit Prive came from my boss who silently invested a sizable amount into the club and wanted our opinion. It was the Strip's new meat market, although what club wasn't. I constantly felt out of my element at these places. The smell of smoke, beer, and desperation was a genuine turnoff to someone with an above level IQ. In addition, the appeared secretary-convention looks a magnet for the dredge of society. I mean, what's up with guys and their erotic fantasy about secretaries. Do they honestly believe we act like the women in those porno movies?

The club, without a doubt, high-class, as the higher echelon of the Vegas elite surrounded us. Even the working girls who managed to tip their way in the door were on a totally different pay scale. In all likelihood, they made more a year, working fewer hours than I did, morally not for me, but legal in Nevada. Anyway, as women, it's always smart to travel in packs at clubs in Vegas. There's something to be said about safety in numbers.

As Colleen was about to buy the next round of drinks, two guys approached our booth. I always find it interesting the number of pick-up lines guys come up with to impress women. I should write a book or at best, pick-up the book these men use just so I can cross off the ones I've already heard.

First impressions sometimes are obvious and this was no exception. The first guy, a former co-captain of the football team, I'm so into myself, emblematic jock. He was cute, roughly six foot four, pushing two hundred-forty pounds, with blue eyes the color of the deep blue sea. The eyes you could hopelessly lose yourself in if you weren't careful, and he knew it. He wore jeans tight enough to tell his religion, a royal blue short-sleeve shirt, which he left untucked with a white tee shirt underneath; the bright white setting off his bronzed tan. The white luminance of his ideal straightened teeth smile, lit up his dimples—A definite sun worshiper. He couldn't have been much older than twenty-five. Considering the average age of the women at the table was forty he must have been having cougar fantasies.

"Hi, I'm Troy. Could I get y'all a drink?" His hands proudly rested on his oversized cowboy belt buckle, waiting for a response.

From the southern accent in his voice and his demeanor, he wasn't local. In fact, adding a cowboy hat would have made him the stereotypical mold of a good old boy from Texas. Probably grew up on a farm, bred with the notion that women should stay home and be barefoot and pregnant. Heather instantly became attracted to him; course, Heather rode anything with a pulse.

"Who's your friend?" Heather asked, while licking the whipped cream off her straw.

"This is Ryan," Troy replied, his powerful arm falling to rest around Ryan's shoulder.

Ryan was the committed yet marveled wingman for Troy, but truthfully uninterested in his current environment. Looking at him next to Troy, he failed to compare in size. If I didn't know better, I would have pegged him for gay. Although short, his thick reddish-brown hair, appeared newly cut. He had a light-pink button down shirt that washed out his ghostly paleface. Most straight men don't wear pink into a nightclub, although he was pulling it off nicely. His black straight-legged dress pants fell off his absent hips, maybe because of the lack of a butt compared with Troy, but appeared almost the wrong size. The white eighties high-top sneakers were a definite taboo with that outfit. A gay man would've never made that mistake. Ryan was along for the ride, or at least he gave off that impression, as his disinterest in our table was blatantly obvious. Although, many guys intimidated easily around women. His raised hand scarcely acknowledged us before continuing his cerebral scanning of the room.

Heather invited them to sit down while the rest of us gave her the look only friends can do. You know the one that says, *what the hell are you thinking!* She shrugged her shoulders as if to say, what? After a few minutes, Troy and Heather disappeared for the rest of the night on the dance floor. Thank god, because although he was cute, he had the IQ of a floor mat. Ryan had intelligence, but in a club environment, it was all visual presentation and Ryan displayed the smallest package in the room.

We closed down Prive and in Vegas that meant 4 a.m. as Heather and Troy exchanged numbers. After peeling Heather away, we began the long walk from the club to the garage. Even walking through the casinos, knowing there are eyes in the sky, you still have to keep vigilant. Heather had parked next to me in the garage, while Tracy and Amanda parked valet. That's what you get when you sleep with the boss. You'd think our boss would've paid for valet, but then again we weren't sleeping with him. Some services I can't see paying for—valet, one of them.

As we approached our cars, hairs on the back of my neck began standing on end. You know when you think something bad is going to happen moments before it does. Then within seconds, I found myself pushed to the ground while Heather screamed. It was Troy, but I couldn't see Ryan.

Heather moved like a rag doll in Troy's arms. We tried to get her to come to Judo with us, but she wanted nothing to do with violence. I bet she was regretting her decision now! I shook the cobwebs from my head, brushed off my hands, and approached Troy.

"What the hell is your problem?" I needed time to survey the situation! Where was Ryan? How long before security arrives?

Heather clearly wasn't as interested in Troy as we thought, having given him a wrong number. She didn't think Troy would try calling right away. Maybe he was smarter than we gave him credit for or unfamiliar to rejection and expected more than what he'd gotten in the club. It always amazed me that men equate dancing with foreplay.

Those once blue eyes now glazed with an evil blackness. "This bitch gave me a bullshit phone number. Do you think I'm stupid?"

I wanted to answer, but felt this wasn't the right time to be sarcastic. He grabbed at her arm even harder, pulling her into him. I knew we couldn't wait for security—'cause when alcohol joins the mix outgoes reason and logic.

"Troy you're going to break her arm!" I said searching for help. "Where's Ryan?" Maybe if he answered it would buy us more time.

"I told him I'd meet him at the tables." He then tried kissing Heather.

Good, this meant if I took him on it would be a one-on-one confrontation. You practice hundreds of times in class, but I'd never tried this in a fight. My heart raced as the adrenaline pumped. Could I manage this in a skirt and heels? I couldn't answer, but was going find out. I had to get Troy to focus on me and let go of Heather. Men have the attention span of kids when they start thinking with the one-eyed monster. They want what they can't have and I had to make myself untouchable to him.

I screamed the first thought that came to mind, "Sorry, we don't go for short-dick men!"

There's something about insulting a man's penis, especially size, that makes him need to prove something. He threw Heather to the side causing her to bounce off a car and triggering the alarm before hitting the ground. I was hoping that would've been enough to scare him off, instead he focused his attention towards me with a sense of urgency.

I was ten, twelve feet away and knew I had a small opportunity to get this right. I didn't have time to second-guess if I could take him, instead let instinct and training take over. He was taller and outweighed me by well over a hundred pounds. I knew I'd have one-shot and one-shot only, so as he approached, I focused on the weakest point of his body—his kneecaps.

You want to attack the knee of the person's dominant writing hand. My instructor stressed that if you're right-handed, your left knee is the strongest, so attack the right. I remember watching him write with his left hand earlier in the night. It's startling the useless information one recalls in stressful situations. It took fewer than two seconds for him to make his way towards me, but time had stood still. I took aim at his left knee with all intentions to hyperextend the kneecap straight back as he stepped forward. If I could drop him to his knees, I'd now have the advantage.

I set myself, "Don't do this," focusing only on his left knee.

Before finishing my thought, a charge of power unleashed through his knee. We learned not to strike the knee, but instead a focal point just beyond, allowing the power to extend through the delicate joint. I'd never heard a bone curling snap like that before as Troy hit the ground. If he had a football career, I just ended it with one kick.

"You bitch!" He said dropping to the ground clutching his dislocated knee.

I don't know what hurt him more; being dropped like a napkin by a woman half his weight or the genuine pain in his knee. He tried to stand, but couldn't, instead crawling towards me, attempting to grab at my ankle. I retreated out of his reach en route to Heather. She was still crying, yet more shocked at my destruction.

"See I told you Judo would pay off," grabbing her hand to help lift her off the ground.

Finally, bike security arrived and had a hard time controlling their laughter while taking my statement. I knew they'd go replay the tapes and have stories to tell in the weeks to come.

Heather, being too distraught to drive, wanted me to take her home. She didn't want to go to the hospital, although I knew she was going to have a large bruise on her arm.

The realities of a distant ringing phone quickly replaced my daydreaming. Apparently, I'd fallen asleep while in the bath. I looked at the clock, it had been only fifteen minutes, but felt like hours. The most sleep I've had in days. I let the answering machine pick-up figuring if it were important, that I could always get back to them. I turned the jets on high and settled down for ten more minutes in the tub.

I wanted a little more me time before getting out and coming up with an airtight alibi. The bruising, lessened significantly from an hour ago, and healing extraordinarily fast, faster than normal, but was this normal? My life was anything but normal and this phenomenon wasn't any different.

I closed my eyes, drifted to my neck in lavender suds, and wished this had been a bad dream.

Chapter 3

I wrapped myself in a robe, still feeling the effects of the lavender essence and hot water. Colby, my three-year-old golden retriever, who always thinks it's playtime, brought me his ball. How can you say no to deep brown eyes, a wagging tail, and a slime covered tennis ball? He dropped the ball at my feet as his drool hit the top of my foot as well as the floor. "Okay, just one toss," throwing the ball towards the master bedroom. I could never say *"No"* to Colby. No matter how dreadful my day, week, or year, he always brought a smile to my face. After last night, I'd need him more now than ever.

Colby ran out of the bathroom allowing me time to get to my walk-in closet. You can learn volumes about a woman by her closet. Most men don't take the time to understand; otherwise, they'd be able to tell compatibility right away. Of course, I haven't had a man over to the house since moving in three months ago. In fact, I haven't had a live date in over a year. Most of the men I've met over the years weren't stimulating. Okay, with several, the sex was good, but mostly they had nothing upstairs. I didn't care how good you were in bed, if you couldn't bring me to orgasm with your mind you're not worth the long-term commitment. *Make note to self…social life.*

I had doubled my wardrobe over the last few months on an irrepressible spending spree. Since moving into this home, which now provided larger closets, had only encouraged my poor spending habits. For most women few vices work as an aphrodisiac, although for me, clothes shopping and chocolate were weaknesses. I was unemployed or soon-to-be, shopping as well as the fate of all my business clothes in question. What I had experienced the past month, offered me little doubt that returning to my job, as executive secretary, was going to be a viable choice anymore. Maybe a bodyguard or hired hit man. I mean hit-woman. However, there isn't much call for a hundred and thirty pound feared killer, especially if you happen to be a woman wanted by the United States Secret Military.

Colby returned to my side as I mulled over fashion alternatives for the police station. From watching countless episodes of *CSI*, what you wear can speak volumes of whom you are as a person. Go in wearing a suit, they'd mistake that for a power trip. Especially when dealing with male cops who have enormously exaggerated egos. Go in excessively casual they think, some dumb brunette, and would try to grill me in hopes I'd slip up during interrogation. At this point, I didn't care; geared up for any confrontation they sent my way.

I chose my second favorite pair of jeans. They sat ultralow on the hips, but fit like a second skin. I put on a spaghetti strap black tank that ended at my natural waist displaying bright red words; *"Have you seen my—"* The shirt, just below the last line, had the deliberate jagged cut-off appearance. I know, for women like me over thirty this was a *"What Not to Wear"* moment. However, I spent the last two years getting my body in shape. I ran everyday and for the first time in my life I had tight abs, was at three-percent body fat, and felt good about myself-image. Hell, I had only a few good years left, might as well show off the goods.

I made my way to the shoes having to peeling Colby from my side. I spent many hours running in sneakers and the thought of putting them on, as casual wear, didn't conjure pleasant thoughts. I grabbed the most comfortable pair of black ankle boots I had, slid them on and zipped up the sides. They had a two-inch block heel with a small pointed toe. I knew that later in the day, I'd regret wearing them, but they absolutely completed the outfit.

I threw Colby's ball into the bathroom, following to make my way to the mirrors. Taking a profound stare, I quickly noticed this shirt wasn't going to work. The hibiscus tattoo that horizontally extended eight inches on my lower back coming to a V at my spine was a smidgen too exposed. I loved the vibrant colors, artistic representation of the Hawai'ian Flower and its overall professional design. I had it done in Hawai'i at this local shop in Lāhainā over a month ago and it was healing nicely. Friends thought I was having a midlife crisis and trying to regain my youth. Older women called this a tramp stamp, yet in the 60's and 70's, when they got their tattoos it was socially acceptable as enlightening times. The shirt's biggest problem, it exposed my bruising shoulders as well as the recessed scratches down my back. If I went to the police station like this, I would be spending the night or longer in jail.

It was at that point Colby stopped, dropped his ball, and stared into the bedroom. The hair on the back of his neck stood up as he slowly began to growl. This was odd behavior, as I'd never seen him do this before today. I had a weird feeling inside my body someone was watching me. Colby's reaction mimicked my anxiety.

I cautiously made my way towards the bedroom. Each time I took a step, Colby took one too. He always stayed slightly in front of me as almost to say—*If something is going to happen, let it happen to me first.* I turned the corner into the bedroom and felt warmth. I could almost feel my body's temperature starting to rise, having felt this sensation before, but not dressed and definitely not alone.

Colby directed his concentration towards my black purse that was lying on top of the bureau. The closer I got the heat further intensified in my hands and chest. I felt a heavily orgasmic feeling that every so often you experience during passionate sex with a lifelong partner. I'd felt this once before, weeks ago with Russell in Hawai'i. Was he trying somehow to contact me or was I still in the bath dreaming?

Colby began barking repeatedly at the purse and as I approached, I started to experience the warmth emitting from within. The bag began to glow incandescent blue, almost blinding. I grabbed the purse, began to open the zippered compartment as a placid bliss suddenly rolled over me. I noticed Colby had stopped barking and now stared at me, awaiting my next move. Suddenly, I had a flashback, remembering the purse's content and confirming this wasn't a dream. Sometimes, amid tragedy, our mind forgets; willingly protecting us from embedded suffering. Some call it a temporary amnesia.

A friend, who'd fallen off a roof when he was younger, breaking his back, battled this exact condition. To this day, he remembers only seconds before falling, missing the first three of the twenty days, spent in the hospital. Although he talked to us and was awake, he doesn't remember those three days. The doctor told us someday he might remember, but for now, it was his body's way of dealing with the accident.

I reached apprehensively into the purse's open compartment, sensing somehow that it was all right. In all likelihood, a reaction most wouldn't have considered logical. I had to turn my head from the blinding warming radiance of the crystal that now glowed like a super nova. I remembered Russell gave me this in Hawai'i saying it had healing powers.

Pulling it out of the bag the crystal came across as fragile, as if something you'd see displayed in a high-end jewelry store, sitting on a pedestal, surrounded by security. Although I figured it for nothing more than a trinket, something sold in a psychic or tarot card shop. The glowing dimmed, but not the warmth as it sat cupped in my dainty hands—a geological wonder unlike anything of this world. Russell was not forthcoming with its origin only explaining that ancients believed the crystal, in the right hands, had healing powers. At times, his ambiguous beliefs shadowed that of Ancient Stone Hedge Paganism.

Covering the crystal with both hands, I walked back to the bathroom mirrors needing, for myself, to bear witness to its dominance. The warmth emanating intensified, nearly too much to take, but my grip tightened fearing it would drop and break. It felt like someone dropped a lit match into my hands. Russell said, *"This crystal is made of energy, as are we all and only a person of faith shall receive the power of its healing energy."* I wasn't into faith having lost all credibility with religions years ago, at the displeasure of my devoted Catholic family. I hated wasting energy on ideas without solid scientific facts to back them up.

The last few weeks taught me, if anything, how manipulated facts held as much credibility as so called faithful believers. I had a hard time still believing in faith, but what the hell. Colby had followed like a shadow. I turned to thank him, as he gave me a nudge with the top of his head, as if to say—*It was all right*. If you can't trust a dog, who can you trust?

I held the crystal taut in the palm of my hands unsure of what awaited. I struggled to clear my mind as vibrant flashes of Russell appeared; his face, his eyes, and the softness of his voice. I was going insane as my thoughts intermittently entwined. The light began pulsing from a deliberate steady blue to fiery red. The brightness danced similar to an evening campfire in the park. The heat ascended and so did the luminosity, gradually finding its way up my hands, arms, until the warmth engulfed my entire body. My body's reflection appeared on fire, with a surreal glowing red aura. The heat released became nearly unbearable and I feared that at any moment I was to explode into a heap of ash.

The luminosity morphed from a fiery red to cool crystal blue as an icy Arctic calm flowed through my veins. The bathroom's fluorescent brightness dimmed as my eyes squinted, struggling to adjust as if I'd come in direct from the sun to darkness. My dilated pupils struggled to focus in on my body's reflected image. Little by little, my eyes normalized taking in a long breathless gaze as the bruising received the night before had vanished. Somehow a magician had waved his magic wand and said, "*Be gone*" and they were gone, every last cut and bruise. The crystal at this point had stopped emitting light. The coldness and warmth replaced with a climate controlled sixty-eight degrees. I tentatively opened my hands and laid the crystal down on the sink. Was this really happening? Had this tiny crystal healed my entire body?

I gradually lifted my arms, as they no longer hurt. My legs no longer felt swollen. I turned around; all the bruising on my shoulders now replaced with soft, blemish free skin and appeared years younger, as if I'd bathed in the fountain of youth. Had I found faith or deceived by false representation? Deceit had revealed itself many times to me over the last few weeks. Whatever the answer, it wasn't scientific in origin, only instantaneously pure powered energy. My core beliefs teetered on change or not!

I sat for a moment on the floor patting Colby, recalling my time spent with Russell. He was the first person I'd ever fallen in love with, of course leave it to me to pick a nonhuman, or so I thought. Russell had given me this crystal at the end of my week with him in Maui, pleading for me to keep it private. Heck, I didn't even remember it until just this very moment. I hadn't seen Russell since early this morning and even then, those images seemed distorted. I always felt as though he was watching me, every minute, somehow protecting me from what lay ahead. He was uncertain if I could handle what they asked of me, but last night proved my loyalty. I questioned the full understanding and scope presented to me, but it was bit by bit becoming *crystal* clear.

Chapter 4

I headed to the sitting room, neatly tucked away off the kitchen's back wall. It was a relatively large room with windows encompassing all three sides, which extended the two stories of the house. The view of the Strip was breathtaking, especially at night. Although Vegas is known as "Sin City"–from a distance, it is exceptionally beautiful. The room had plants located all around and resembled a nursery. An interior designer, who's a friend of mine, helped me with the design. I never had great luck in keeping plants so half of them were artificial and sometimes even I forget which ones.

I stepped in the middle of the room with the warmth of the intoxicating sun highlighting its features. I closed my eyes, spun around hugging myself as it felt awkward not being at work. I, on no account, took days off, except for the occasional vacation with Tracy. It's probably why my boss liked me so much. Come to think of it, I don't think I'd ever taken a sick day in my life.

The house had a built in speaker system acoustically designed for every room; as I said this was a truly nice house. I walked over and punched up the Hawai'ian music from the bathroom. Now, all that I needed; tropical bird sounds, a cascading waterfall and I'd be back at the floral gardens on Maui.

That the first places Russell took me when we met in Maui. He said there was a hidden energy within the plants that no one could see, unless you opened your mind. My eyes closed again making an effort to experience the plants in the room thinking I could now hear their voices. I missed Russell, but knew he was watching, somehow he was watching.

I sat in my wicker chair made from genuine Curly Koa wood. Next to my bed, it was the most comfortable piece of furniture I owned. Russell sent it to me as a gift straight from Maui, somehow having it delivered and specifically positioned in this room on my return from Maui. Russell was intelligent and mysterious, but a hopeless romantic.

Colby sprawled out next to me on his giant pillow, also a gift from my new boyfriend. Russell understood the easiest way to me was through my dog. Colby increasingly attached himself to Russell and the frequent spoils that came with a new boyfriend. Colby, impatiently wanted to snuggle, but knowingly eyed the designed-for-one chair from the floor; not like it ever stopped him before.

The next few hours, I had to write clearly in detail what occurred over the last month. The journal was not for the cops as much as it was a needed form of personal therapy. In my life, I'd endured sessions of psychotherapy to distinguish what worked and what was a waste of time. I reached for one more sip of coffee, took a deep breath, knowing how complicated the next few hours were going to be. However, needing to face the past, as well as what the future held, I grabbed my laptop, opened *Word* and began to document the previous events.

December 26, 2009

I stared for minutes, but it felt like hours, at that first dated line. I recognized that if these events ever went public they'd change the way we humans perceived life. I nowadays lived by a different set of ideologies and equated it to a person who's told they have cancer with only months to live. Some, allowing their days silently to fade away, while others cherished, forcefully grabbing, and living to the fullest their remaining essence. From today on, I'll be one of those people who treasure this rock we call Earth.

I took one final glance down at Colby, who was already sleeping; his snoring acted like white noise and helped focus my thoughts. I consoled myself, "start from the beginning", as my eyes closed taking in one last deep breath while the warmth of the morning sun engulfed me with hope...*now type*.

Chapter 5

The day after Christmas was unforgettable, as it elatedly declared the start of our Hawai'ian vacation. Tracy and I made plans to take ten days off and visit the islands of Hawai'i. We also made plans to race a Marathon in Maui while we were there. We had different bosses and worked for two different companies, which shared the same office space. In Vegas, commercial office space cost a premium and if you could find a way to split the overhead even better; although neither of them worried about finances, both well-established millionaires.

Tracy was executive secretary for one of Vegas' most powerful real estate agents. I say powerful because, one third of all property transactions, residential and commercial, came through this office in some form or another. Every neighborhood displayed at a minimum one sign on its front lawn—Jim Charleston Real Estate. In fact, I bought my house from Jim. His current million-dollar deal involved one of the old Freemont Street Casinos. He wouldn't disclose the hotel, but said his vision for a new state-of-the-art, billion-dollar theme was going to revolutionize the way the industry noted entertainment.

He was a pleasant older man, late fifties possibly early sixties, but didn't look a day over forty. He barely towered over five feet four with a slight weight problem. His fundamental nature belonged in the frame of a Norman Rockwell painting; constantly well-dressed, following the strict standards of the power hungry executives that graced *GQ Magazine*. His thinning silver hair dressed a head that would appear good bald. His car of choice was an old 1966 Ford F100 with over 300,000 miles. He bragged this was his first and only car he ever owned; outdating most, if not all, of his employees. He was rich, the Bill Gates kind of wealth, although he never flaunted his success. His money, neatly tucked away in multiple offshore accounts, partially because of government taxation, which he constantly complained about—all the time! He'd recently married a year ago someone half his age, with no prenuptial, yet still enjoyed the occasional taste for the erotic. The office girls silently referred to him by his nickname, *dirty old man*, but never to his face.

Tracy had been working for Jim for nearly seven years. She always said he'd give you the shirt off his back, if he liked you. He was letting us have access to his home in Hawai'i while on vacation. A six-thousand square foot oceanfront house on Keawakapu Beach with every amenity you could dream up. It was a recent buy for his new wife as a honeymoon gift for the punitive price tag of eighteen point five million dollars. I viewed the pictures and couldn't wait to be on its sandy beach. I told you he was generous! It was Jim's persistence and friendship with Mr. Grant that got me the job. I only met Jim a few times, a golden retriever lover, whose dogs on occasion I walked, but he took to me right away.

My boss Gerry Grant was a born and bred "Ivy League" hard ass. A product of a wealthy family, yet still wanted more; born with a silver spoon in his mouth and before he spoke his first words, had bought the matching knife and fork. He reminded me of Michael Douglas from *Wall Street*. You know, *"Greed is good"*. I believe he had a picture of him on the wall signed with that exact saying. Don't get me wrong, he was a great boss to work for, you just didn't want to be on the opposite side of any deal he was working on.

He held two degrees, a law degree from Harvard, and a business degree from Oxford. A lofty level of intelligence, only dwarfed by the enormous industry contacts, allowed him to know what you were thinking even before you did. His favorite hobby was to buy stocks in soon-to-be bankrupt companies; pay off their outstanding debt, thus creating an extremely hostile takeover environment. At that point, change management with friends he trusted, hold the company for a year or two, and sell it off for a huge profit to the highest bidder. The last big deal was a casino in Atlantic City. He bought the company for twenty-three million dollars, a steal in today's market, and then invested twenty million in renovations and new attractions. All his Hollywood acquaintances often visited, thus increasingly adding value to the business and in under a year, sold it. The sale price was two hundred and seventy million dollars; a two-hundred and twenty-seven million dollar profit. Let's say, that even the great Donald Trump has called him for counsel over the last few years.

Gerry married a beautiful supermodel and truthfully, I do mean stunning. She has posed for many magazines, but to him, her most famous; last year's *Playboy* centerfold. She was years younger than Gerry was, but loved money, probably more than even he did. I don't want to say she is a gold digger, but we have had our share of confrontations over the last year. She was regularly jealous of any woman who spent extended time around *her Gerry*. I endlessly had to explained, Gerry was categorically not my type.

This Christmas break, the first, the two bosses shut down the entire office, thus giving us all a seven-day vacation, eleven with the weekend and holiday plus a substantial holiday bonus. I think they both had a good year, but I'm sure the wives had something to do with the decision. You have to keep the wives happy or your checkbook may become less profitable.

Tracy and I made plans to leave the day after Christmas and fly direct from Las Vegas to Maui. I asked Tracy's boss if bringing Colby was going to be a problem, thrilled, when he confirmed it wouldn't be. I worried though, Colby, never having traveled on a plane before, cage below in the cargo hold. However, my boss, as a Christmas present, offered up his private jet to take us to Hawai'i and back at no charge. I told you; sometimes it's rewarding to be an executive secretary. This meant that Colby could travel on the plane with me, first-class.

Colby and I arrived at the Executive Airport in Henderson at 6 a.m. I live only a few miles from the airport off Seven Hills. The flight wasn't leaving until eight, but I wanted to make sure Colby had enough time to do his business and acclimatize him with the sounds of the airport. Delighted he was coming with me and not staying home, but the thought of him relieving his bladder at fifteen thousand feet, well you know what I mean. I didn't trust leaving him with anyone while I was gone. Tracy arrived around 6:30 a.m. and I almost didn't recognize her. I've seen her in sweats for running, at work in a suit but I don't think I'd ever seen her in jeans.

Tracy was a few years older, roughly thirty-seven, but never asked. Women, at any cost, avoid discussing birthdays, but principally, their age. I knew her birthday was July 20, only because her boss, religiously, brought her an arrangement of flowers on that day. She wore designer jeans; ones costing more than most people's paycheck, with a matching Prada shirt and bag. I love Tracy, but if it wasn't a designer label, she refused to wear it. She had never graced the fluorescent isles of Wal-Mart, as the idea alone would've killed her. Her purple Oakley sunglasses pushed atop her head, the model with a built in mp3 player, and a matching pair of purple open toe sandals that laced up with white gladiator style strings. She had no intent to do laundry, unless there was a housecleaning service, as her additional luggage, stacked four high, rolled behind her on the tarmac. I was on vacation, not going to a fashion show. Hadn't she checked with her boss? There was a butler, or as Jim put it, a property manager.

We boarded the plane around 7:30 a.m. with a chance to meet Captain Martin, and Co-Captain Welds. This private jet comfortably seated twelve and we had it all to ourselves. I'd never flown on a small jet, but had heard horror stories from others. The Captain reassured me there was nothing to fear and the skies appeared clear all the way to Hawai'i. Where was Captain Sully just in case?

I strapped Colby into a chair with his own puppy seat belt harness, fidgeting, unaccustomed to wearing it, even in the car, having free run; this would be interesting to say the least. I fastened my seat belt and before the safety clicked Colby's head was at rest in my lap.

Tracy smiled at me as she clicked her belt, "You ready?"

"Can't wait!" I replied. The desert landscape passed slowly through the cabin window as I set my hand on Colby.

The Captain's voice echoed over the speakers, "Okay ladies and dog, we're next in line for takeoff. We'll be traveling at an altitude of 15,000 feet. Please keep in your seats with seat belts on until I give you the okay." He no sooner finished, as the plane's rushed force pushed us back into our seats as it accelerated off the runway into the dry Nevada air. This was going to be a great vacation, Hawai'i, my best friend by my side, and my friend Tracy.

Chapter 6

We arrived at Kahului International Airport on Maui at 2 p.m., sorry noon with the time difference. The flight was great, no turbulence, and right on time. The sun, even in the late-morning, felt warm through the plane's windows. Colby snapped to attention, after sleeping a good portion of the flight, when the wheels touched the runway. The pilot's voice broke through the speaker telling us the temperature was already a balmy eighty-five degrees. You have to love paradise! We taxied passed a distant line of palm trees on way to our terminal, having received special permission ahead of time from Hawai'ian Airlines. My boss received the clearance from his friend, CEO Mark Dunkerley; a first-class trip all the way. I'll have to call Jerry and thank him when we get to the house.

The aircraft gradually came to a rest and we waited for the okay to disembark to the tarmac. Tracy, while waiting, called Jim's caretaker to confirm the limo's arrival. She was a stickler for details and punctuality. I hurried to exit Colby before he christened the plane since his pee-pee dance had increased in intensity. Not something I would've wanted to tell the boss. The pilot noticed, kindly let us off and promptly pointed me to an area of grass alongside the plane.

The co-captain at the bottom steps managed a brief tip of his hat as Colby dragged me by, "Hope you ladies had a good flight. Thanks for flying Rigil Air. Have a great time on Maui. Aloha."

"Thanks we will," I said.

Colby pulled at his leash, stretching down the tarmac as if he was going to explode. I took in the warmth of the sun allowing Colby a chance to explore the trivial patch of grass. Tracy waited by the luggage cart as the handlers stacked our collection of bags, or should I say hers. Colby didn't take long to finish and we were shortly on our way to find the limo.

I love flying into tiny airports as their condensed terminals offered the convenience of rapid luggage claim. It was a quick skip into the terminal through double doors, then baggage claim, and finally, out to Frontal Road by another set of double doors. Lines of black limos stretched the curb, and somewhere amid them, ours.

"Tracy, did they tell you what limo we're to look for?" I asked.

My eyes patrolled up and down in search of a driver with our names or a limo boldly displaying *Charleston Real Estate* on the door. Jim, having real estate licenses in Las Vegas and Hawai'i, over the many years invested, on the various islands, in residential and commercial property. He anticipated a tiny loss now, but the upside returns in years to come; too good to pass on. He had convinced a trio of local investors from Las Vegas to form CHARA (Coalition of Hawai'ian Area Residents Association). I thought it a bizarre acronym, but he had raised over three hundred million dollars in which to buy hundreds of foreclosed properties throughout the islands. So what do I know!

"No, the driver was told to look for two women and a golden retriever." She grabbed her phone redialing the house's caretaker.

Colby was uncharacteristically barking at an approaching gentleman. It wasn't an aggressive bark, as much as an attention-getting festival of excitement barks. This was my first encounter with Russell. He walked with a wave of confidence and grew taller with every approaching step. He wore a charcoal gray, white pinstripe, Giorgio Armani suit custom-tailored to fit his muscular body. Nothing is more attractive than a guy wearing a great fitting suit. He was gorgeous, although, he would've made plaid look good. I couldn't help but ogle, mentally undressing him with my eyes as he advanced.

"Colby, Stop…Sit…Good dog."

Colby sat next to me, his tail whipping left to right in excitement, as he approached. Colby sensed my attraction to him, but showed no signs of competition to be the only male in my life. Russell gently reached down to Colby, extending his hand, patting him on the head then rubbed his ears. Colby loved every minute of it.

"Hi. I'm Russell Hamilton." He looked up with a smile that sent chills down my spine. If he had proposed to me then I would've said unequivocally—*Yes*.

"Hi, Erica Jones. And this big guy is Colby," returning the smile.

He grasped my hand, with a handshake that said *I'd love to get to know you better*. His hands were soft, but in a masculine way, with freshly manicured nails. He probably never worked a hard day in his life. A loving power extended up my arm penetrating all over my entire body. I've heard of love at first sight, but never experienced it myself. His eyes, an emerald green, which sparkled like fiery crystals thanks to the sun's reflection, his long, straight black hair flowed with every movement, an almost, "Fabio" effect, that was hypnotizing. Clean-shaven, perfectly proportioned facial features, flawless sun-kissed skin, and the most perfect teeth I'd ever seen. Put him on a beach in a white, button down shirt, with his exposed pectoral muscles and I swear he could've been the jacket cover for any romance novel.

"I hope you don't mind, but I absolutely love golden retrievers. I lost mine a few months ago." Russell responded.

He rubbed Colby in all the right places, as if he knew what the dog wanted. I wondered if he could do the same for me. *God I'm bad*. It's been excessively long without an intimate connection.

"No. Colby craves attention, sometimes too much," I laughed.

Tracy looked over smiling, knowing I hadn't been with a man, even on a date in months. She put her phone down for a second, motioning, *get his number*, with her hands and mouth. I turned away, in fear I'd start to blush. Too late!

"Is that your friend?" Russell asked, simultaneously motioning a friendly hello towards Tracy. She returned the gesture, before quickly returning to her phone.

"Yeah, we're looking for our limo."

He had nearly a half-foot over me, standing at 6'3". At that height, I got a good glimpse at his chest, which appeared restricted in that white silk button down shirt. I imagined one intense breath and his shirt would've ripped off, or maybe I was hoping it would, *God what was I thinking*. Around his neck was a priceless red power-tie. A reflective gold flash from a Rolex watch hinted from underneath his cuff while real Italian black leather shoes flawlessly displaying Colby's image. I understood enough about high-end fashion being around my boss and his clientele that Russell was an extremely thriving professional or had a generous expense fund.

"So what brings you to Maui?" I asked never much good at small talk.

"A little bit of business and a little bit of pleasure." The word "*pleasure*", lingered on his voice as he smiled as he cocked his head in my direction. His captivating voice put me in a hypnotic trance as the hairs stood on the back of my neck.

"And you…business or pleasure?" Again, that word "*pleasure*", lingered on his lips.

I'm horrible at relationships, especially long-term, which is self-evident being single at my age; however, I can still distinguish flirting from conversation.

"Here on vacation and to run the Maui Invitational Marathon." My eyes broke for Tracy with hopes she'd save me from awaiting self-embarrassment.

"What a coincidence, my company, Dynamics Aeronomics, is sponsoring the marathon this year." His eyes casually marveled up and down in admiration before refocusing his attention on my eyes. Nothing speaks volumes more of a man than when he spends most of the conversation gazing into your eyes. It shows he's interested in you more than just as a piece of meat.

Tracy finally reappeared through the crowd saving me from the awkward moment of silence. She always wore emotions on her sleeve and it was a valued trait as a friend always knowing where you stood; but for those unaware, she came off as a royal bitch. She rejoined us, her face clearly pissed.

"The limo driver got a flat on Highway 350. It'll be an hour before he gets here."

"Tracy, this is Russell Hamilton, his company is sponsoring the marathon." Tracy reached out her hand eyeing him up and down. I couldn't tell if she was sizing him up for herself or seeing if he was good enough for me. She'd done that with numerous previous acquaintances; so far, none of them met her approval.

"Hi, Tracy Miller." Her face went from frustration to bliss while shaking Russell's hand. I guarantee she was thinking exactly what I was thinking, but we had an unwritten rule, neither would date nor steal the others' man. I hoped she identified my lusted interest and retracted her hooks. We never had a problem before, but Russell, easily the manly specimen who could warrant a change.

"You're cute, are you single?" Tracy asked.

Tracy teasingly flicked her hair back, before turning in my direction. I told you she wore her emotions on her sleeve. Her surrendered eyes were for my viewing, a white flag that declared *he's all yours*. Others might've stumbled, blushed, or felt threatened by that line of questioning but it didn't phase Russell.

"Actually," turning his attention from Tracy to me, "Thank you for the compliment, and yes…**I am single**." He flashed a smile towards me, the sun's rays catching his green eyes again and they sparkled like an engagement ring. If this were a movie, The Bells of St. Peter in Rome would've rang in the background. "It sounds like you need a ride, maybe I can help. Which hotel are you staying at?"

Before the words in my mouth drafted a response Tracy quickly replied, "We're not staying in a hotel, but at my boss's private house out on South Kihei Road down by Keawakapu Beach"

"No problem." His eyes turned, motioning to his driver five cars down. "My company's house is up the road from there, near Wailea Blue Golf Course."

"Really." Tracy replied with a whimsical look on her face as she turned towards me. "How convenient. Isn't it Erica?" I knew her evil intent.

Russell's driver arrived before I'd rallied enough courage to ask him on a date.

"Aloha, Mr. Hamilton," Nohea interrupted.

Nohea looked like a kid in his late teens or early twenties, probably trying to make enough money to pay for college; decked out in a classic Hawai'ian tee shirt, jeans, sneakers, and dark blue tinted sunglasses that hid the true color of his eyes. The only facial feature missing, a mustache, and then he could've passed for a younger Magnum P.I. I highly doubt he would've understood the reference being the show was older than he was. He screamed, homebred local through and through, part of the Generation Y. Based on Russell's appearance, I expected a more professional exterior than this from his driver.

"Ladies, this is Nohea. He knows the island better than anyone I've ever met. If you need anything and I do mean anything, all you have to do is ask. If he can't get it, no one can." From that one statement, I figured if he was that valuable, a difference in dress code wasn't a big concern. "These ladies are going with us," then Colby barked, "Oh I'm sorry, Sir Colby too."

"No problem Mr. Hamilton," Nohea firmly stated.

"Nohea, what does that mean in Hawai'ian?" Tracy asked. Tracy, knowing she had no chance with Russell and always having a thing for younger men, clearly was redirecting her interests.

Nohea made his way to the cart while making sure to draw eye contact with Tracy. "It means handsome…," he replied with a childish grin.

Before we could commence a *thank you*, Nohea had already taken our cart and pushed it towards the limo. Russell, well mannered, extended his hand forward, guiding us now to follow Nohea. It was gratifying to see chivalry wasn't dead. We walked towards the car, side-by-side, grinning uncontrollably like schoolgirls, with Russell pulling up the rear; clearly not enough room on the sidewalk for two women, a dog, and a clear-cut gentleman.

It took less than a minute to advance down the sidewalk, but the entire time I could feel Russell's presence and his eyes watching me. There was an unequivocal chemistry; I hope that I'd find the nerve to act on it. Russell opened the door for us while Nohea loaded the luggage into the trunk. Colby immediately jumped in pulling me in as well, followed by Tracy, then Russell. The limo easily held twelve and I felt nearly lost inside but it was the nicest I'd ever been in; and my boss rides in them all the time.

Hawai'ian music was already playing on the stereo and although the words were foreign, the beat was catchy.

Russell attempted to sit next to me, but Colby got there first. Sir Colby, the prince, accepted his conquest with a majestic bark then waited for his carriage to take him to his castle. Tracy journeyed to the furthest part of the extended limo, sitting with her back to the driver's tinted privacy window. I was unsure if she hoped to talk to Nohea or was giving me time alone with Russell. She continued to examine the dry bar on the right as Nohea climbed into the front of the car. He rolled down the dividing window and turned slowly towards us bringing his sunglasses to rest at the tip of his nose.

"Help yourself to the bar and if you need anything else just pick-up the phone," pausing while looking down to change CD's. "You'll like this better, it's Hawai'ian, but in English," redirecting his attention towards us again as the music started. "I hear we're going to south Maui, South Kihei Road, right?"

"That's right. The girls are staying at—," Russell paused waiting for the blanks to fill.

"1534," Tracy replied putting down her drink long enough to look it up on the phone.

"1534 South Kihei Road. We'll drop them off first." Russell reiterated.

No sooner did Russell finish his statement than the darkened window returned. The car pulled forward, away from the curb, off to our new vacation house somewhere on the southwest side of the island. I considered could Russell be, *"the one"*? Regardless, this was going to be the best tropical vacation ever; my dog, friend, and man of my dreams. I could not ask for more!

Chapter 7

We left Kahului airport en route to Jim's private house out on Keawakapu Beach, also known as *"the sacred or forbidden harbor"*. Nohea estimated the drive would be roughly forty-five minutes, occasionally pointing out landmarks as we drove south down the middle of the island on Highway 350. Nohea's knowledge alluded to a long life as a native. He explained driving here was pretty simple since there were only a handful of major highways that extended north to south and east to west. Apparently, you can drive the circumference of the island, however tourist guides strongly advised against it without four-wheel drive. Being our first time in Hawai'i, my senses were in overdrive from the island's majestic scenery.

I rolled the window down trying to take in everything, as there'd be plenty of time later for pictures. Keawakapu beach was on the west side, opposite of Haleakalā's dormant volcano. The west side of the island, created by an extinct volcano known as Pu'u Kuku, and its isthmus running between the two landmasses. Travel books said, the view from the summit of Haleakalā at sunrise was breathtaking; something to experience at least once in your lifetime. Nohea explained that many referred to Maui as, *"Valley Isle"*, but to locals, No Ka 'Oi or merely *"the best"*.

Tracy turned, looked out the front window while simultaneously engaging Nohea in small talk. She occasionally returned, interested only to steer the conversation towards the topic of Russell. She can be extremely pushy at times. However, he seemed more preoccupied surfing his emails on his phone and honestly, I was too busy, basking in the profoundness of being in Hawai'i.

We passed an array of pineapple plantations, sugarcane fields, and ranches that blanketed the semi-rolling countryside. Nohea offered, if interested, us a tour of a pineapple plantation his dad owned on the other side of the island near Hana.

Colby was enjoying the ride but demanded a better look as he advanced to compel his furry head out the window. Nothing is funnier than seeing big floppy ears dancing in the wind, but the cascading drool flying in off his lips—not so cute. I ignored his uncontrollable ability, since it was our first time here with both of us planning to have fun. Russell finally peeled himself from the phone, and without hesitation, Tracy began the personal interrogation.

"So Russell, what do you do at Dynamic Aeronomics?" Yeah, just your run-of-the-mill icebreaker question as she was only trying to encourage a conversation, uninterested in his response.

"Well, promotions mostly, like the marathon you're running in next week." Russell's response was as formless as her question. Maybe he felt awkward talking about this with strangers.

I finally gained enough courage to ask my own question in an attempt to join the conversation. "I take it this isn't your first trip to Maui?"

Russell swayed his attention towards me with a soft smile that made me melt. The goose bumps on my arms by now proudly displayed and it wasn't from coldness, not when it was eighty plus degrees outside—and getting even hotter inside. He had noticed, as his eyes wavered from my arms, deeply up into my eyes.

"Actually, I grew up on Maui most of my life. I only go to the mainland a handful of times a year." He paused, interrupted by a vibrating text, and then returned one more chilled flash of a smile. "However, I'm considering making a move to the West Coast in the months ahead."

I glanced towards Tracy wanting to tag out of the conversation. She smiled, attempting to busy herself on the phone, leaving me to fend for myself. I discovered later she was busy texting little one-liners to my phone. However, like a little schoolgirl with a crush, I never noticed the flourish of activity filling my text inbox.

"Why would you want to leave such a tropical paradise?" I asked.

"My company has a branch in Las Vegas and the old CEO is moving on, they've asked me to fill the spot."

"Wow! Vegas? That's where we live." My heart pounded through my chest with excitement. Did he say Vegas? This was divine intervention stepping into my boring life. "Where in Vegas?" His eyes were so captivating, my social fear, as well as this surrounding tropical paradise, melted away like a New England spring day.

Colby had decided he had enough of the open window, again pushing his way between us, plopping down on the seat, and putting his head in my lap.

"They have a small office off Industrial Road. I believe it's located somewhere behind the Strip, but I've never been. However, I'm making a trip in the next couple of weeks. Maybe I can look you up?"

I couldn't let this opportunity get away and before pausing to think, the words ejected from my mouth.

"I'd like that. My number's 702-645-7734." Colby's head turned up and tilted at me as if to say—*What!* "I know, I know," my hand went to his head and scratched his ear.

Russell feverously finished entering the numbers in his phone then looked at me. "What did you say?"

"Nothing, I was talking to Colby."

"From his reaction I think he understands you." He leaned to rub Colby's head. "Don't you?"

"Did you want my name?" Here I am giving out my number and not even sure if he'd remembered my name.

"Already got it, see." His phone displayed an unflattering picture, or so I thought, of Colby and me at the airport. God did I truly look that bad from the flight. My hair was a mess, but on the good side, Colby looked great. He had my name in his phone, both first and last. Wow was he good. A guy that can remember your name after only one meeting was worth keeping.

"What's that?" Pointing to what looked like words in Hawai'ian next to my name.

"Elika. Which is the Hawai'ian equivalent to Erica and a native Hawai'ian name for you Ka'iulani, which means *'the lovely sacred one'*."

I avoided looking him in the eye knowing the blush now glowed bright as neon on my cheeks. Instead, I directed my attention to the passing mountain scenery over his shoulder through the open window. I should've asked at the time why Ka'iulani, but wasn't thinking.

"I didn't embarrass you did I? That wasn't my intent. I just find it easier to associate names and faces with a visual in a language I'm accustomed to," Russell apologetically replied.

How could a woman not fall for a guy like this? Either he was the sweetest guy I'd ever met or extremely good at PR work that it naturally carried over into his personal life. We suddenly found ourselves at that awkward conversation stage again. I needed to steer this exchange into a different course calling attention to the vast mountain out his window. You could see the rugged emerald color terrain even from this distance.

"Is that mountain in the distance Haleakalā?" I asked.

"That's Haleakalā. It's not a mountain as much as a dormant volcano." Russell's head reluctantly turned wanting instead to prolong eye contact.

The sky was an ocean deep blue, broken only by the occasional wandering white cloud, as the volcano dominated the scene with its summit extending into the earthly heavens.

"It's beautiful."

"That it is. Even better at sunrise." Russell's eyes found their mark once again. "Nohea wasn't understating the sunrise from there was breathtaking. At the summit is also one of the world's best observatories. I have a friend that works there. If you like star gazing I could take you." There was a slight pause. "I mean both of you. If you'd like?"

"That sounds like it could be fun."

I turned to Tracy for confirmation. She silently turned her head, smiled, nodded agreeing then returned to her conversation with Nohea.

Russell continued, "There's even a great botanical garden halfway up with nearly every native species to these islands, even some which are not. The volcano is one of only a few that has five distinct climate zones."

Russell briefly turned to admire the natural beauty before evaluating my facial reaction for interest. His voice was so intoxicating, I could've listened to him talk all-day about anything. I literally had to pinch myself to keep from daydreaming about being intimately alone with him.

"I'd love to go to the garden," my voice pitched, "I have plants throughout my house. Maybe I could pick-up some seeds to plant."

"Okay, we're pulling onto South Kihei Road right now, what number am I looking for?" Nohea shouted back from the front, halting Russell's impeding response.

"1534," Tracy yelled! "You were saying, Russell?" She flashed me that devilish smile.

"If you're free tomorrow…I mean both of you…I have time after lunch to take you to the garden," Russell replied.

I unquestionably wanted to go, but did come here with Tracy and didn't know if she had made plans for tomorrow. Knowing how organized she was, even on vacation, I'd said yes. I wanted to reply agreeing immediately but instead turned to Tracy.

"Why don't the two of you go. Erica, it would be fun. I'm going to hang on the beach for a while. I'm not much of a flower person anyways."

I knew she was lying, not because of her facial expression but because of her history; although her ability to lie convincingly was a skill. Forever raving about the flowers her boss would get on her birthday. In addition, Tracy from her own private backyard garden handpicked many of the flowers in my sitting room.

"Okay we're here." Nohea again yelled.

I was ready to commit to a date with Russell when Jim's house, our house for the next ten days, appeared into view and suddenly I was at a loss for words.

Chapter 8

We had barely enough room to pull the limo off the road as the front bumper set inches from the gate as a six-foot wall, on each side, extending the length of the property. The house appeared inviting from the road although the security boldly said—**Keep Out**. The bold gold initials, JC, stood out, dividing the gate on a black matte finished shield. Nohea reached out the driver's side window, pushed a button, and waited.

"Can I help you?" An elderly sounding voice asked.

"We have Miss Miller and Miss Jones." Nohea replied.

The gate, shortly after that, opened into a lush tropical retreat. In every direction, vibrant foliage extended to the house. The narrow dirt driveway separated perfect blades of grass, the greenest I'd ever seen and seemingly disappeared into the sultry jungle. If not for the gardener mowing the lawn, you would've sworn it was artificial. Most golf courses strived for such perfection. Hard to imagine fewer than four hundred feet from the gate on the other side of the house was the Pacific Ocean and a golden sand beach. The first floor was barely clear, but the house's roof had a clear visible line, as it challenged to poke over the top of the palm trees while we curved around the horseshoe driveway. A clear-cut modern design, but with an aged oriental twist, at least from the visible sections I could make out. The palm trees lined the driveway, escorting us to our final stop as we rolled past a disabled limo. I assumed this was our original chariot that had already found its way back home. The driver, tinkering under the hood, turned on seeing our car, shut the hood, and went to the front. Joining him, as if by magic, an elderly man emerged from the foyer, and I could only guess it was Jim's caretaker, Pakile.

Nohea came to a gentle stop in front of six exceptionally large sculptures; the two men positioned themselves to the front of the foyer. I noticed Russell's attention abruptly drew towards the outside, but didn't bother to ask why. I impatiently waited for Nohea to get the door, opting to open it myself instead and made my way around the vehicle to our awaiting reception. Colby excitedly took the lead from me, or maybe he just had to go pee, again. Tracy nonchalantly made her way around to the back of the limo while Nohea began unloading our luggage.

"Aloha, ladies. I'm Pakile the caretaker of this property."

Pakile was a Hawai'ian elder, although it was hard to define his age. His George Hamilton tan seemingly altered his true emerging age and he had a softness about him, even when talking. He was of average height, not much taller than 5' 6" with slightly receding gray hair; his eyes the color of black Onyx, and had a grandfather's warmth. He was wearing a bright blue and white, floral print, Hawai'ian shirt, the kind shelved in every downtown store. His khaki shorts showed the frailty in his legs from years of picking pineapples while the flip-flops screamed local comfort. Jim, in all likelihood, didn't pay him much, though he had the money, but for someone like Pakile to live in this house was a distinct reward.

Tracy spoke first, weaving around the newly stacked luggage, "Aloha Pakile, Tracy Miller," extending her hand towards Pakile, "and this is Erica Jones."

Pakile, tenderly shook my hand. His hands, covered in calluses from years in the fields, had found revived softness in his new position. "I apologize for the mix up at the airport."

"No need, it worked out." I replied.

"This is Lulani our driver," he gestured. "He'll take you anywhere you need to go while you're our guests. However, if you choose, there are a couple of cars in the garage for your use. The keys are always in them."

Lulani, smiled '*Aloha*' then whispered back to Pakile in Hawai'ian. I will have to try to learn this beautiful language. Pakile brought back from the statue's base next to him three of the most beautiful leis I'd ever seen, assembled from native Wild Orchids. The lavenders and the whites danced in the sunlight, interlaced together between dark brown Kukui nuts that remind you of highly polished beads. I remember reading about them on-line before the trip. The Kukui nuts hard-shell, cleaned out and meatless, needed no special care. Lulani approached us; leis in hand, slightly bowed, raising the leis above his heart, and began describing their true meaning.

"It's custom to give the spirit of aloha with leis when arriving or leaving the islands. It's a symbol of affection and love. Never discard the lei, instead return them to the earth or you'll be throwing away the love of the giver. The lavender and white symbolize the love of the Hawai'ian Islands. There are eight nuts, each one representing a major Hawai'ian Island. The dark white one of the eight symbolizes your first visit to the islands. Each time you return, a new white nut will replace one of the darker nuts. Once you have achieved all eight white nuts you will become an honoree Hawai'ian."

Lulani approached me first, bowed slightly again, raised the lei to his heart and with his eyes motioned me to take the lei from him. I unhurriedly place it around my neck taking a moment to admire the beauty, weight, and quality of the work. The Orchid's aroma, intoxicating and incomparable to anything I've ever experienced. To this day, the essence of lavender still brings me back to the islands.

"Thank you, it's absolutely beautiful." I gestured.

Pakile followed closely behind Lulani, "In Hawai'i, mahalo means thank you," leaning in kissing me slightly on each cheek then smiled.

"Mahalo," I smiled back.

Lulani went to Tracy repeating the same ritual.

"Mahalo," she spoke with a gitty excitement.

Pakile approached Tracy, gave her a warm hug, and then kissed her on each cheek. There was closeness to the greeting, almost a grandfather's fondness, but she hadn't met him before today. I didn't think of it at the time, other than a respect for finally putting a face with months of detailed communications.

Pakile stopped in front of Colby and gazed down. Colby was sitting, watching and with every move, his tail wagged creating a dust storm around his back paws. Pakile gingerly bent down and patted his head. "This must be the world's greatest dog I've heard so much about. Sir Colby, aloha to you to." I took the lei, placed it around Colby's neck, and quickly took with my phone the cutest picture I'd ever seen. Colby rose on all four legs and shook his head side to side, as if to play as the lei swayed. I thought for sure it was coming off, but a brief full body shakedown and he proudly stood motionless. One of the many great features about Colby was the ability to dress and position him any way you wanted for a picture, never moving—such a ham.

Pakile struggled to rise from the ground as he directed his attention to Russell. "I'm sorry sir; we were only expecting three guests. And you are?"

I felt like such an idiot forgetting to introduce Russell. Here we get a ride from this great guy and I forget to introduce him. I cut Russell off as he was about to speak, "This is Russell Hamilton. He lives nearby and was kind enough to give us a ride."

Pakile extended his hand in gratitude as a seemingly underlying tension transferred between the two. Was Russell so wealthy he felt servants were beneath him? I couldn't put my finger on it, yet it troubled me. Great, I finally found a flaw.

There were six stone statues around the foyer entry sidewalk; sitting fifteen-feet from the front door, standing roughly four-feet tall, with no hard edges and made of a unique stone—the likes I'd never seen. They looked tribal, but with a soft marble beauty. They greeted you, but not with open arms, as their eyes followed your every move. Neatly landscaped, floral plants grew generously around the bases and were an array of rainbow colors. A designed set in walkway, made of enormous four-foot slabs of perfect granite separated them from the rest of the house's foliage. The lying grass, cut to perfection, as if someone painstakingly had taken the time to cut each blade by hand.

Russell finished shaking Pakile's hand, walked past him towards the statutes, mesmerized, as if he'd found the Lost City of Gold. I wonder if this was what caught Russell's eye as we pulled up the driveway. He'd expressed, during the long drive, his love of art, especially for local artists working on the island, but for some reason these pieces intrigued him.

"Pakile, are these made from a local artist to represent a local tribe?" I questioned. Trying to show an interest or subconsciously wanting to score points with Russell, not that it was necessary.

"These aren't local, but came from a distant land. They're from a tribe, but not of these islands," Pakile, followed Russell's examination of each pieces, before returning his attention to us, "Come, you must be tired from your trip. Let me show you the rest of the house and to your rooms."

Lulani and Nohea had already made their way in with some of the luggage. Pakile turned, making his way to the front door. I watched as Russell discreetly snapped off a few quick shots with his cell. Tracy noticed as she passed, rolling her eyes in disgust, before turning to following Pakile.

"Well thanks for the ride," I said. It took him a second to break his fascination from the statues before refocusing on me. However, I could tell the pieces were still troubling him.

"Oh, I'm sorry," he slightly paused, turning for a last look at the nearest statue, "You're welcome, I'm glad I could help."

Then came a moment of awkward silence; the kind after the first date, when he walks you home and you're unsure if he's going to kiss you. He leaned in, as my heart raced, only to give me a quick hug. I wasn't expecting that…perfection. A hug that said, I'm interested, but we've just met. A true gentleman. I couldn't wait to see him again.

"Are you coming in?" Tracy reemerged from the foyer, "You've got to see this house!"

"Yeah, just a second," I said impatiently barking back!

"Are we still on for tomorrow?" Russell asked, bending down to pat Colby. Colby's response was simply a big lick on Russell's face and his patented drool mark swipes left upon his pant leg.

"Oh, I'm so sorry," glaring down at Colby and his dirty work.

"No problem," he laughed. "Well what about tomorrow?" He was being serious.

Russell was referring to his invite tomorrow afternoon at the floral gardens up on Haleakalā. I couldn't turn him down, could I? He was the first guy who gave me goose bumps and made my toes curl. "Yes, absolutely!" Did the excitement show in my voice?

As a woman, you wanted to appear interested, but make him feel he still had to put in the effort.

"Great, I'll call you tomorrow with a time," Russell expressed.

Nohea, winded, returned from carrying Tracy's entire set of luggage upstairs. He wiped his brow, opened the back door of the limo, and waited for Russell. I watched Russell vanish from view as the door closed and was at a loss for words. A part of me hated to see him go. I thought, this is what true love felt like and I was truly beginning to enjoy the sensation. The dark tinted window, leisurely rolled down exposing his charming face, while Nohea made his way around to the front side drivers' seat.

"Aloha Miss Jones. Until tomorrow," He smiled the entire time.

"Aloha Mr. Hamilton." Chivalry wasn't dead.

The window rose, transferring his image to a reflection of my own, before finally pulling away. The car rolled down the extended driveway, seemingly forever. Was it too soon to be missing him? Colby barked his approval, as moments later it disappeared through the majestic gated walls. Colby was missing him too.

Tracy was impatiently waiting at the front door. I grabbed my purse, Colby's leash, momentarily stopping while turning for the house, and glanced at the statues. What did Russell find so interesting about these pieces? Why was Tracy so disturbed with Russell taking a few pictures? Determined to learn more, but right now, my vacation awaited.

Chapter 9

The aroma emanating from the house's front floral growth was amazing; reminiscent of my local flower shop on Valentine's Day. No one dominant scent, simply an intricate combination, strategically arranged to heighten the arrival experience.

The two, great dark Koa wood entry doors, each weighing hundreds of pounds, swung effortlessly open as if cushioned with air. Centered directly in front were a dark, handcrafted, and maple table with six beautifully arched abstract legs. It appeared insect like, with an elegance only an expert craftsman could design. Its centerpiece was a polished wooden vase with a large planted arrangement of Birds of Paradise. The species, native to South America, but many associated its uniqueness to Hawai'i. The flower's unique name, stemmed from the uncanny likeness to the actual bird of paradise; with petals spreading like an open fan and the color of a bright orange sunset. Sporadic bright blue plumes completed the flowers dramatic appearance; the entire arrangement framed within the distant blue of the ocean that protruded through the bordering rooms' all glass walled windows.

The openness of the entryway highlighted to the left an obvious feature, a stunning light Koa wood staircase extending to the second level. Pakile motioned us to accompany him to the second level but the view of the ocean was too insatiable to resist. We continued past the arrangement into a large living room through Roman style pillars used as an interior-dividing wall. They were wide enough apart to allow the light and breathtaking views of the room's windows to spill effortlessly into the foyer. This room alone dwarfed most loft apartments. Your feet, greeted, by a cold warmth, as the beige Italian Marble floor extended in and underneath you from the foyer. The outside wall, made from panels of pure glass, extended its entire width with an unobstructed view of the outside covered patio. In the backyard, were large crescent shaped palm trees basking in the sun shielded from the ocean by a fortified wall. The visual, overshadowed by the daunting sounds of the crashing surf against the golden-brown sands of Keawakapu Beach.

The full-size, glossy black, Baldwin piano to the right was a trademark centerpiece; an elegant white orchid floral arrangement, similar to the flowers in our leis, centered on top. Built into the far-right wall, a mahogany bookshelf, completed by a centrally divided, granite fireplace of modern design. Ordaining the shelves were classic, first edition books, and an array of genuine Hawai'ian priceless collector pieces. An onyx, highly polished, marble inlay floor spanned directly in front of the fireplace; separating it from the rest of the room, while two off-white, modern sofas, mirrored across from one another on the inlays' outer edges. My body instantly drew to a larger, almost Egyptian looking artifact, flawlessly displayed atop the mantel. It was a bizarre, circular relic, with detailed etchings that resembled a family crest with three partially lit candles on each side. It felt like a shrine or altar and I found myself having to restrain from physically wanting to touch the piece.

The left side corner of the room included another beautifully built table with a resting Birds of Paradise arrangement similar to the foyer. Encircling the table were four oversized white wicker chairs with floral print cushions. At first glance, I thought this must be the dining room, but the single framed door adjacent to the table told me otherwise. It had modern recessed lighting throughout the room except for a hand-blown glass lamp, which seemingly hovered over the tables' dark mahogany surface; although the room's natural light was more than sufficient. The morning sun was overhead and couldn't wait to meet the watered horizon while the windows readied to frame a miracle of Mother Nature—A Hawai'ian Sunset. No wonder the price tag. You know the saying, "location, location, location."

I wanted to step out onto the patio, get a closer look at this breathtaking view, but could hear Pakile persistently calling for us from the second level. The only extra item in the room, also just as impressive, hung behind the piano and I couldn't believe I missed it the first time. Apparently, the magnetic draw of the artifacts as well as the call of the ocean had clouded my visual perception. A six-foot by eight-foot original Christian Lassen wall mural, built into a black glossed, shadow box frame, with a deep purple velvet inlay. The remote dimmer lying on the piano controlled the specifically designed track lighting, heightening the painting's features.

I recognized his work from the frequent trips Tracy and I took to his gallery in the Las Vegas Forum Shops. Tracy also had given me a coffee table book as a housewarming gift, although the book did an injustice to his work. The painting, a virtual snap shot from the patio at sunset and on closer examination, revealed hundreds of small diamonds, embedded in the crests of the crashing waves. This wasn't a print, but instead an original, signed by Lassen himself. I could only fathom the price, knowing originals one-tenth this size sold for hundreds of thousands of dollars. I bought a signed, limited edition, lithograph of 'Hawai'ian Dawn' for my house. That piece cost me about a month's salary and I make damn good money.

We'd gotten lost in the intricate brush strokes of the painting, finally pulling ourselves away to join Pakile. At the top of the stairs were a loft, extended railing to the right, and four wall-to-wall glass panels to the left. The two middle panels slide open revealing a large study and an awaiting Pakile. Again, the far wall was a clone of the living room's glass wall, except for a single sliding door that opened to a balcony that overlooked the backyard and beach.

The floor transitioned from the down stairs marble into a dark-rich hardwood, in the center, a thick creamy-white open area rug. Two oversized, bench like, blood-red couches rest only a few feet away but gave enough room for reading and walking. To the left and right sides of the study and walled floor to ceiling were custom built-in bookshelves. Hundreds of books littered the dust free shelves, fiction on one-side, and non-fiction on the other. There was even an entire section alone on the history of Maui as well as the other Hawai'i islands. Cleverly cloaked within these units were doors leading to the two master bedrooms.

"Miss Miller, this is your room," Pakile pointed to the right. "And over here, Miss Jones, is yours," he paused. "You'll find your luggage is already in the rooms."

"Mahalo," Tracy said making her way into the room.

"Oh, Mahalo, Pakile," I said. Gathering from his expression, my pronunciation was off, but I had a week to work on it. Right now, I couldn't wait to see my room.

"I'll be down stairs waiting to show you the rest of the house once you're settled." Pakile's softly spoke. His voice was an afterthought as I entered the bedroom, but I figured he'd understand.

The room's floor, a continuation of the study's dark hardwood, where an intricately detailed, Oriental rug sat like a magic carpet under the bed and I assumed it was as expensive as everything else was in this house. Apart from the rare top of an adult palm tree, the two oversized windows framed an excellent view of Keawakapu Beach and the Pacific. A dark cherry, four-poster, queen-size bed, set above the floor, higher than most with two small ottomans at the foot. Colby may need the ottoman, if he wanted on the bed; this might apply to me as well. In anyway, putting a blanket down to protect the rich red velvet cushion tops was going to a priority. Matching cherry nightstands to the left and right had identical blown glass lamps and directly across from the bed, a built in armoire. A rocking chair visually pushed into the window's corner, with a modern, stainless steel, three-bulb lamp, that arched over the chair like stadium lights. I pictured myself, curling up at night to a book, drifting away, while ocean sounds played in the distance. The ceiling rose to a gradual center point with huge beams of glazed Koa wood extending from each corner, and at its peak hung a hand-blown glass fixture that resembled a Japanese lantern. The room had no ceiling fan, but with the ocean breeze, who needed one? Finally, to the right of the bed's nightstand was a doorway to paradise, the prized bathroom.

The highlight of the room, for me, was another Christian Lassen original, 'Maui Magic' that centered over the top of the bed. A simple sunset with waves crashing over a small rock cove and with only a glimpse of palm trees leaning. The purples, oranges, yellows and whites a perfect combination. The room's contents were most likely greater than the price tag for my entire house.

I glanced at Colby, "Don't you dare chew, scratch, bite, or pee on anything! You got it?" He immediately hit the floor, head

47

between his paws, expressing one of those small-whimpering wines, as if to say *well there goes all my fun.*

My centerpiece at home was the master bathroom. So eagerly, I stepped through the door less frame, to see what a half million-dollar bathroom looked like; it didn't disappoint.

The room, enormous, was appearing more like a walk-in closet than a bathroom. The bedroom floor extended in, surrounding the great jade granite topped island, with its two incredible dropped in seamless sinks and matching sterling silver fixtures. The island's underneath storage had a surplus of built-in drawers and cabinets. To the right of the room, a spaciously designed open closet for hanging clothes, plus plenty of sliding drawers for the storage of hundreds of shoes. The few pairs I brought for this trip were going to seem lost.

In front of me, across the island, was a full-size drop-down mirror and to its left, extra storage for clothes, jewelry and more shoes. The whole left side of the room, a continuation of the same, minus an interrupting, door-sized pair of oriental panels. At first glance, the oversight of a shower and toilet had me confused. However, on further investigation, I found the remainder of the bathroom secretly hidden behind those panels. I gently parted them, revealing the room's true size as they opened, displaying another room; which had a built-in glass door, tiled shower, a small Roman tub with jets, and to the left a lavatory neatly disguised behind a door. A single window rested on the rim of the tub overlooking the side yard. However, if you sat in the tub, your head resting, you still had a decent view of the ocean. Impressive! Okay, I was more than impressed.

I ran over bubbling with excitement to see Tracy's room. It was identical with mine, except hers had a different Lassen painting over the bed called '*Secret Reef I*', a lifelike painting of dolphins. We both stood like schoolgirls in the middle of the room holding hands, jumping up and down; truthfully too old for that behavior, but what can I say, you needed to be there.

"Okay, I need to go unpack," I said. "Then we should call Jim to say thanks."

Tracy just shook her head in agreement. "Did you want to go for a run or are you hungry?"

"I'd rather go for a run before I eat and then maybe see the rest of the house. If that's alright?"

"Sounds good to me," Tracy said walking towards a small LCD computerized panel positioned next to the bedroom door. I never noticed if my room had one. "This controls everything from music, lights, temperature and no matter where Pakile is on the property you can communicate with him," she pushed a button on the screen to talk, "Pakile."

"Yes Tracy," Pakile's voice flowed through the room's recessed surround sound system.

"We're going to unpack and then go for a run. We'll eat and see the rest of the house when we get back."

The entire time, mobile in the room as she spoke, I wondered where they had hidden the microphone.

"Okay Miss Miller. The front gate key number is 5465. I'll keep an eye out for you in case you forget." His voice's amazing clarity appeared as if standing in the room with us.

"Mahalo," Tracy replied. She returned to the panel, touched the screen but this time Hawai'ian music began playing throughout the room. Then she faced me with a big impressed smile. "Okay then, let's unpack. I'll meet you in the foyer, let's say, thirty minutes."

"Works for me."

I returned to my bedroom, unpacked, but not before finding my own panel and adding music to a play list. I knew it was going to take Tracy at best thirty minutes to unpack, but for me, more like fifteen. I looked forward to a run, needing to burn off some of this excitement. Colby already made his way to the top of the bed and was sound asleep, snoring, and unphased by the music and my unpacking. I wasn't afraid of leaving him alone, it happened all the time at home, but this was nicer then my home. If I unpacked, changed, I could take Colby out to do his business with plenty of time to spare waiting for Tracy.

About forty minutes later Tracy finally made her way down stairs apologizing. Of course, I expected it from her.

"Ready," She reached for the front door.

"Yeah." I had spent the last ten minutes stretching.

"We'll head down South Kihei about three miles and turn around. That should allow us a chance to get the feel for the humidity."

Vegas air was drier with little to no humidity. It could be a hundred twenty degrees, but you wouldn't feel it per se. Today's temperature, eighty-five, but I already felt sweat beading on my forehead and we were only to the front gate. Tracy typed in the code and moments later the doors swung open. I was looking forward to running, but couldn't wait to return and explore the rest of the house.

Chapter 10

Glancing up from the pages, I checked the time. It had been almost two hours, my writing hand cramped and as much as I hated to admit it, my mind was drained from reliving the past. It was evidently clear; there wasn't time to note down everything this morning. Detective Wilson would be expecting me soon at the police station, but I worried the clarity of the images was going to fade overtime. They wouldn't completely go away, that was for sure, but I didn't what to forget even the most minuscule details for future references.

During my texted flashback, Colby had transferred himself to the kitchen over my shoulder almost certainly bored from hours of neglected belly rubbing. Since last night, he hadn't left my side. I decided to take him for a brisk walk, needing a break physically and mentally myself. He sensed my fear, decisively volunteering to protect me the best he could.

The fermenting smell of lingering burnt coffee met me as I returned to the kitchen; not thick enough to stand a spoon in, but strong nonetheless. Strong coffee was better than no coffee and I needed that last cup. Colby's eyes followed my every step, although his head never moved. I took a sip, trying to swallow, but had to succumb, finally spitting it all into the sink. All right, strong coffee wasn't always good. After dumping the balance into the sink, I grabbed a bottle of water from the fridge and made my way to the closet door next to the pantry. Colby instantly jumped to his feet, dashing excitedly to my hip with an understanding, the only time bottled water came out was when we walked. Energized would've been an understatement, if you could've seen him attempting to open the closet door with his paws.

"You want to go for a walk?" My voice vibrated in a goofy high pitch tone while opening the door enough for his head to pop in and grabbed the leash.

He franticly shook it, rubbed next to my leg, and then headed towards the front door. I took that as a yes, grabbed a light jacket, keys, attached his leash to his collar, and made my way out the door. A little fresh air was going to do us both some good.

We made it halfway down the driveway, almost to the sidewalk when Colby froze in his tracks. Something spooked him, probably the identical feeling that was causing my neck hair to stand on end. A Cadillac Escalade, black, dark tinted windows, solid flat black rims, and no visible chrome had parked directly across the street. I'd never seen this before and coming from a small suburban neighborhood, everyone knew everything about everybody, especially when it came to your choice of transportation. The whole status thing and this screamed—*I don't belong.*

We crossed Palm Drive openly in front of the truck. Partly, because the bike path's locality across the street, but mainly to get a decent look inside the truck. Colby always pulled on his leash until we reached the bike path, but today, opted instead, to stay close. His midsection attached to my right hip, walking stride-for-stride with me, eyes vigilantly focused ahead, with the occasionally sneer towards the truck until we passed; as if expecting an ambush. My entire body tingled, as if death watched from within its black opaque tinted windows, as every piece of glass, including the front, masked its impossibly seen interior. No front license plate, illegal even in a liberal state such as Nevada, but somehow I didn't think who or whatever owned this obeyed by the same laws. If someone watched from within the truck, you wouldn't know it; clearly, that was the whole idea. The lifting warmth emanating off the hood meant someone had recently driven it but now it sat waiting in stealth.

After crossing, we turned to make our way down to the bike path, both of us periodically checking over our shoulders until the entrance. Then a click came from the truck's ignition, a thunderous roar, even at our distance you could feel the horsepower from its modified engine push against your back. My nerves synapses firing as we trekked our way down towards the path. Colby stopped halfway, turned back, and began to growl. The truck, having moved forward, stopped just short of the path's entrance and if not for the yellow security poles, might have followed. Someone was definitely following and watching us.

"Come Colby," pulling his leash with all my strength.

We reached the end of this section of the path, looked back to see the vehicle as it slowly, almost gracefully, coasted forward. We hurried across Plant Street, almost jogging to the paved path's extension. To the left, immediately up the street, another black Escalade. No way was it the same truck, as again its engine revved and gingerly rolled forward. This part of the trail had no street access for the next mile, only the gated backyards of half vacant rental properties. For the time being, I felt somewhat safe, although paranoia was quickly sneaking into my mind.

I'd seen similar Government-Issued trucks about a week ago patrolling the desert out at Groom Lake, home of Area 51; identical make and model, but their color of choice—white. The occupants were adamantly refusing to reveal themselves. Why were they following me? Did it have to do with last night and what happened? My mind raced as I walked faster, constantly checking for any signs of sudden movement.

Moments later, further down the path, as if out of nowhere, a woman appeared running towards me. Colby started growling again, something he never did to strangers, especially while we were walking. She wore sunglasses, not unusual for Vegas, but it wasn't that sunny and I felt a little bit paranoid at her drastic emergence. Although she ran toward me at a good pace, I was still able to get a good mental image of her.

"Good morning," trying to elicit a response as she passed.

With no facial emotion, she ran by, not even acknowledging my greeting with a smile. She had one of those customized wrap around headphones in her ears, so maybe she didn't hear me. Correction, only her left ear had a headphone. Noticing the absence of a right one should've sent up red flags, but it didn't. She continued toward Plant Street, pivoted in my direction, but only for a second after she passed. I did a quick double take as only moments later she had vanished; no one was that fast.

Was she an alien? No, I kept telling myself your mind is only playing tricks on you. Scenarios like this don't happen. A month ago, convincing me of that would've been easy; but now with the newfound knowledge of extraterrestrial life, it was comprehendible. My pace quickened from a walk to a slow jog. Colby intermittently turned back at me, with tired brown eyes, unfamiliar with this swift of a pace. He was trying his best to keep up, his tongue dangling out the side of his mouth, while long strands of thick drool waited to launch, like projectile missiles, with one good headshake. He reminded me of Hooch from the movie *Turner and Hooch*.

The pavement ended merging into a desert trail. I stopped, hesitated, and pondering pressing forward. Normally it wasn't a problem, but if someone was following us, this path's section became further desolate; a perfect place for a surprise attack. Stopping gave Colby a chance to catch his second wind as his head shook in approval, with drool airborne in every direction, including mine. Great, I'd require a wardrobe change before heading to the police station.

While traversing back to the house my apprehension gradually dissipated. Was my concern even justified? Could my sleep deficiency be manifesting itself into an outward appearance of psychotic delusions? That question answered itself halfway home, as an exceedingly brawny male appeared leisurely jogging towards us; too laid-back of a pace for someone so athletic. Again he passed by my left. The sudden appearance of another woman seldom intimidated me; however, males elicited a different reaction as my body tensed into defense mode. This time, there would be no initiating a cordial greeting, simply, an unyielding gaze. For the second time today, someone passed wearing the identical earpiece and sunglasses. This time his glare was deliberately obvious, as if wanting me to take notice, before continuing down the path; this wasn't a coincidence. I waited a few seconds before rotating my head to get one more glimpse, once again, like a magician's assistant; he had vanished into thin air. Inconceivable on this section of path, with no place to hide a man of such volume, the situation increasingly became vexing. As if my nerves hadn't exceeded their limits over the last twenty-four hours, now I'm seeing phantoms.

We returned to the intersection of Plant Street, looking both ways, before progressing gradually across. The second Escalade had moved further down Plant Street; its rear now faced our direction with its engine still idling. There was no license plate, not even Government-Issued. Ahead of us, within a few hundred feet, Palm

Drive, as the original vehicle little by little inched its way past the trail's entrance heading towards my house.

Colby, now defiantly agitated, as we cautiously made for the end of the path and our house. One of the SUVs had boldly parked straight in front of the house, while the other gradually advanced down Palm Drive, keeping its distance. I now had my mace in my hand, armed, ready for deployment, but no cell phone. I hoped that if something went down, my excessively observant neighbors would call the authorities. That's if they weren't already here. The remaining SUV finally passed, deliberately in front of me, as it positioned itself on the opposite side of my driveway. No one exited, but both vehicle's engines simultaneously fell lifeless. I hesitantly, but vigilantly, walked between these suspicious pillars, expectantly waiting to discharge my mace on anyone or anything.

I made it to the sanctuary of the front door without a confrontation, key in one hand, mace still in the other, with Colby unyielding in his barking. He smelt something, continuously scratching at the doors edge, while I fumbled with the lock; it was however, already unlocked. Colby always entered first; today it was with an urgency and a varicosity never seen. I had a feeling this wasn't going to be good, attempting to restrain his lunges and frightened to let him go. Suddenly his persistence broke the collar away from the leash as his feet struggled to gain traction on the granite floor. A million scenarios raced throughout my head, pushing the door open, and then intentionally leaving it ajar in the event of a rapid retreat. Colby, now a blur of golden fur, swiftly bolted towards the kitchen, nose to the floor as he had picked up a scent. I was being considerably more cautious. Moments later, without explanation, Colby's barking stopped and should've been a sign to run, but not without my best friend.

Turning towards the kitchen my attention suddenly diverted back to sounds of the closing front door. A mammoth beast of a man now eclipsed the front door and my only escape route. Wearing black from head to toe including his sunglasses, except for a hint of white in his button-down shirt and had the curious appearance of a mortician. His face, dressed in a lifeless expression, as if death itself was staring you in the eyes. He didn't advance, obviously his role was simple, avert any escape, and he was doing a stunning job.

I made my way to the last direction Colby headed, still no sound, even calling his name, and I became increasingly concerned. Entering the kitchen, I noticed a new man, again in a black suit, sitting in one of the dining room chairs. Neighboring him, another person in black, who appeared female, and knelt next to Colby before taking her position alongside this man.

"What the hell did you do to him?" I surveyed the situation, but my rage was blocking my judgment.

"A mild tranquilizer. He'll be fine in a half hour." The woman replied, without remorse, as she exchanged glances between Colby and me.

"Please, Erica…Take a seat." The older male sitting at the table motioned.

Odds unquestionably not in my favor, terror inched up my spine as my only means of escape blocked. Who knew the countless others waiting in the trucks? The only weapon I had on me was mace. Russell had supplied me one last night, but it inconspicuously hid in the bedroom. With no real alternative, I gradually descended into an opposing chair, paying close attention to the man-in-black sitting across from me while occasionally glancing at Colby hopeful he was alright.

The man was late fifties from the mannerisms in his voice, but the outward appearance screamed midlife crisis. Unlike the others, dressed entirely in black right down to his silk shirt, the top two buttons intentionally left open, exposing his dark tanned, clean shaved, chest. The sunglasses took away from his face, but the blonde from his long flowing hair seemed to glow like a halo against the black. You might've thought he was on a date. If so, I wasn't interested!

Over the last few weeks I'd become acclimatized to trust no one whose eyes I couldn't see. Minutes seemed like hours as he sat motionless across the table, his hands crossed and as still as a mannequin. I refused to talk first feeling a slight bit stubborn, but as time gradually rolled by the silence was getting me agitated. They had broken into my house, tranquilized my dog, and sat expecting tea? I tried to relax, focusing on the rhythmic deep breathing emanating from Colby as well as the tick of the clock behind me on the wall.

"What the hell do you want?" blasting back from my seat!

Again he sat, staring intensely at me with a sightless expression, my tiny face neatly framed within the reflective surface of his glasses. If he wouldn't talk, maybe the woman next to him would.

"Is he always this social with the ladies or does he prefer guys?"

There was no response, no expression, not even a cringe from either. *Okay, insults weren't going to work.* Then the man slowly released his hands, reached for his sunglasses, and took them off laying them directly in front. A microscopic, LCD screen, set in the lens, reflected off the freshly polished table, these were unquestionably not commercial grade. His eyes were a deeper blue then the sky, with the iciness of the ocean, and as lifeless as Deep Space.

"You have been a troublesome little lady for us Miss Jones," speaking softly.

I snapped back. "I'm sorry, do I know you?" firing back again, before he reacted. "Just who the hell are you and what gives you the right to break into my house?"

"Who I am is no concern to you right now and as of last night; you no longer have any rights." The seriousness in his voice toned.

"Last time I checked, this was still America, and I still have Constitutional Rights."

"Miss Jones, we don't operate on the same laws as you perceive to believe exist in this, how should I say it, country. You should be grateful that I am at least giving you this meeting. The consensus was for you to be terminated, for security reasons of course."

"Well then, maybe thanks should be in order."

The concern for my life, greater than last night, which I didn't think was possible, while emotion lit his face, as if the reaper himself was staring across at me.

"Miss Jones. You've stumbled on to something, *we*, aggressively have protected since the early part of the 1950's. Whether you like it or not your life presently hangs in the balance. I nod my head, and you're dead before the image even registers in your tiny little brain. So I suggest you sit, put your hands on the table where we can see them and keep your pretty little mouth shut!"

"Who is, *we*?" I asked, while slowly putting both hands on the table, remaining motionless, not chancing he was bluffing.

"I will ask the rest of the questions, if you don't mind," his attention dropped to a side briefcase.

I knew he wasn't jesting and if I didn't take part willingly, he would have me exterminated. I had read a lot over the last month on UFO's, aliens, and Government Cover-Ups, including Above Top Secret files about Area 51 and these men had to be part of the *Men In Black*. The brief literature I witnessed was vague and the Internet had even less with few valid sightings. However, the consensus was, they weren't to be taken lightly as some reports suggested individuals that made contact, mysteriously disappeared. God, I wished Russell or any of his associates were here, I could've used backup.

He leisurely pulled three pictures from a manila folder and placed them in front of me on the table.

"I'm going to ask you a few simple questions. Your answers will control your future. Do you understand?"

"Yes," I replied.

I would keep my answers diminutive, uncomplicated, on spot and I hoped, correct.

The first picture was of a General, but couldn't make out the uniform, maybe Navy, adorned with more embellishments on his chest than a Christmas tree, plus an unfamiliar pattern of stars balanced out his shoulders. If he was a general, I'd never seen one so youthful in appearance. I made an effort to commit his face to memory, knowing if he was significant to them, then somewhere down the line our paths were going to cross.

"Now Miss Jones, do you recognize this person," pointing to the picture.

"No!" I looked to be sure. "Really, I haven't seen him before."

After a slight pause, he sat back in his chair evaluating me. I don't think he believed me.

"She's telling the truth." The woman standing next to him said.

Okay, that was eerie even after seeing a fair share of telepathic powers over the last few weeks. *Was she reading my mind? Could she read facial expression like some poker players? Did I have a tell?* I didn't dare test her, but after a peeked glimpse of the last picture, well let's just say I was going to experiment on this next picture.

"Miss Jones, we'll know if you're lying, so let us not play games." He leaned forward pointing to the second picture. "Have you ever seen this device before?"

"No!"

The truth was, on the mantel at Jim's house in Maui sat a similar model. It appeared ancestral, maybe a Mayan family shield, not encased in gold like the photograph, more sandstone, or a clay terra cotta. It had the twelve astrological symbols rotating around a small sphere shaped object with a crest of some sort in its center. However, recalling its likeness in my head, there weren't twelve symbols, instead thirteen, which now seemed bizarre. It's humorous how the most microscopic details from weeks ago crammed my psyche with such significance now. I rechecked the photograph; it too had twelve symbols, but missed the thirteenth and center seal.

Again, silence from him, as he sat back awaiting my answer in the chair.

"She is lying." The woman said.

"Are you sure?" His eyes never broke focus on me.

"Yes!"

"I'm not going to play games, Miss Jones!" He slammed his hands on the table with enough force the vibrations echoed with authority all the way to the floor. It made me jump, even though I saw it coming.

"No," I repeated before pausing, "I mean I've seen something similar, but not precisely the same piece. What I saw, was more an artifact than a device. It had an extra centered symbol, plus was smaller."

He sat back again, this time interlacing his hands and brought them to a point to his lips.

"She's telling the truth," the woman stressed.

"If she can read my mind why do you even need me to answer?" stalling before he went to the next picture.

"I'll ask the question here today," leaning forward.

My answer bothered him, not quite sure why, but it was a good thing. It was the first bona fide emotion in his body language that made him seem on edge.

"What did this thirteenth symbol look like? Can you draw it?"

"No, I really didn't get a good look."

I was telling the truth. I remembered there were thirteen symbols; however, its image remained undefined in my mind.

"She's telling the truth."

"Where did you see this item?" he asked.

"On Maui at a friend's house."

"Does this friend have a name?"

"He's a real estate broker here in Las Vegas. His name is Jim Charleston."

It bothered me giving up Jim's name, but I knew they'd get to it eventually. Plus, the fact he didn't make a note led me to believe he already knew the name.

"One last question, and no games, do you know this man?" pointing to the third photo.

It was a photograph taken of Russell or a close likeness from a distance using a telephoto lens. He was wearing a military issued uniform that resembled Special Forces or maybe Air Forces. The shorter hair, without doubt military issued, taken from the side, as he stood in front of what appeared to be an Area 51 or the S-4 facility hangar. A base I became intimately familiar with over the past month, but I'm jumping ahead or not keeping up depending on your definition of space and time. There was no way from this photograph I could've make a positive identification.

"Maybe," pausing, "He's vaguely familiar but it's hard to tell from this picture."

"She's telling the truth."

I'd given a candid retort, purposely not elaborating, in hopes this telepath couldn't see the discrepancy in details. Maybe her ability was limited to yes or no answers, and hoped my ambiguous answer would satisfy their curiosity. We were about to find out.

"Who is he and how do you know him?"

Well so much for that, the man removed a notepad and pen from his jacket waiting for my response.

"His name is Russell Hamilton. He works for Dynamic Aeronomics. I met him about a month ago in Hawai'i on vacation and we've become emotional involved. You know kind of a boyfriend girlfriend thing."

"She's telling the truth," a waver hinted in her voice.

Great, she couldn't see anything beyond true or false. My mind's particulars were still intact. As long as they didn't press on with specific questions, I'd be okay. I didn't want to endanger Russell's life or my own; yet still questioned why I was a target for such interrogation.

The man spoke again, "When was the last time you saw Russell—," looking at his notes, "Hamilton?"

"Not that long ago. He was out here on business for a few days and stayed here with me."

"When do you plan to see him again?"

"I really don't know. I wish I could see him for dinner tonight, but don't think that's going to happen."

That was the truth. He had some loose ends to clear up and thought it safer for me not knowing. He was correct.

"She is telling—," she stopped as the gentleman raised his hand.

He leaned back in his chair, tucking his notepad back in his pocket and removed a phone from the other pocket. He sat in anticipation, staring at his phone and me for less than a minute until finally the phone rang. He never said *Hello*, or even responded, just listened while never removing his eyes from my direction. I knew my existence rested on the contents of this exchange. The conversation, if you could call it that, only lasted a couple of minutes. It was the longest two minutes of my life. He closed the phone and returned it to his inside pocket. He was in command of this task force, but someone else higher was pulling the strings. I only hoped they contained the capacity for human compassion.

He motioned for everyone to exit the room, leaving me with him and Colby still motionless at his side. I contemplated taking him, but wouldn't do any good if others waited in the next room. I felt like a criminal waiting for the judge's verdict, either life without parole or the chair. Freedom, I didn't believe, was a viable outcome.

Once everyone exited, he patiently gathered all the photographs, returning them to the folder as he lifted his briefcase from the floor and deposited them inside the top pocket. The fact the case remained open on the table as his mind pondered wasn't reassuring. Its internal contents intentionally blocked from my sight while his hands delayed removal only helped intensify the sentiment of a firearm. My life flashed before my eyes.

He finally, emerged from behind the case, this time grasping a blue folder, and placing it in front of him. He closed the brief case, returning it to the floor, and then pushed the new folder towards me without hesitation. I went to retrieve the folder from the table but his icy soft hands overwhelmed mine halting the retrieval. He glared through my eyes into my soul and I could feel him setting up shop.

"What's in here?" hating to ask.

"Miss Jones, what I'm going to say to you will be kept in extreme confidence. Your existence depends on it and I do mean that literally. From this moment on, we will record and monitor anything you say or do, with or without your permission. Within this folder, you will find two items. First, a list of personal possessions we need from you; some now, others in the future. You have no choice but to comply, failure to do so will mean immediate termination. Second, there is a prewritten statement requiring your signature, which is for your visit with Detective Wilson this afternoon. I would advise you study and commit it to memory as the truth."

His hands, warmed from mine, released, allowing me to open the folder as he once again leaned back in his chair.

On top was the statement to Detective Wilson that read:

Detective Wilson:

In response to your query about Tracy Miller and her demise, I offer the following testimonial. Tracy was a close personal acquaintance of mine over the last few years. However, after returning from our vacation in Hawai'i we had a falling-out.

Although working directly together in the same office, outside work we had no contact, especially over the last couple of weeks. On my whereabouts last night, I believe a General Samson spoke to you earlier this morning.

For National Security and my Q Clearance Security Level I am bound by law not to discuss the circumstances in any more specificity without counsel or General Samson present.

Attached is an epistle from the Secretary of State and C.I.A. Director. The order is for you to dismiss me from any further exploration regarding Tracy Miller. Any breach will constitute as an intrusion with the Federal Government's National Security, thus placing you and anyone else connected under arrest for treason.

Sincerely,

Erica Jones

I took in a deep breathe now realizing I was in way over my head. On the surface, I was afraid of plunging deeper into the abyss, questioning my friends, acquaintance, and the integrity of the Federal Government. How I wished never meeting Russell a month ago as there seemingly were more to him and everyone else involved than I originally thought.

"Miss Jones, for now you may call me Orion," handing me his pen.

Taking the pen, I continued to sign my name on the statement then began to glimpse at the inventory of sought items on the following page. Most being medical procedures, including giving them blood, plasma and DNA samples. My attention promptly diverted to the bold footnote declaration on the bottom page.

GOVERNMENT RESERVES THE RIGHT TO REQUEST ADDED INFORMATION AND/OR COMPLIANCE FROM YOU IN THE FUTURE. FAILURE TO COMPLY WITH ANY REQUEST BROUGHT FORTH FROM THIS MOMENT ON WILL RESULT IN INSTANT TERMINATION FROM THE PROGRAM.

To what program were they referring? I was trembling thinking about *The Program*, and it visibly showed in the pen's movement across the paper.

"Does this mean what I think it means?" looking at Orion.

"It means you're allowed to stay alive as long as you act in accordance with our requests."

"And what if in the future I can't help you?"

"We'll never seek anything which you can't provide. However, if you choose not to help...," he paused, "Accidents happen all the time. Know what I mean?" He leisurely reached for his sunglasses, giving me one more glance with those shimmering eyes before masking them again with the glasses. As he rose from the chair, two men reappeared from the kitchen wearing white lab coats and hospital masks that disguised most of their face. Their hair, comparable to Orion's, was long and blond, but with eyes that altered in luminosity as they moved through the light. Orion walked toward me, put his right hand on my shoulder, picked up the pen with his other, turning his hand palm up he revealed the pen motionless in his hand.

"Do you see the pen?" Orion explained.

"Yes."

"So can everyone else on this planet," pausing for effect.

He detached his right arm from my shoulder raising his sunglasses just enough for me to see the radiance emanating from his pupils. Although mesmerized by the view, I drew my concentration back to the pen in his hand. Within seconds it levitated, glowed a blinding whitish-blue before imploding on itself as it vanished from his hand.

"Now you nor anyone else on this planet will see the pen again. Do you now understand the gravity of the situation?"

He gracefully lowered the sunglasses, returning his right hand to my shoulder once more, almost as if to stabilize himself. I swallowed hard in complete understanding of the demonstration.

"Although I would like to stay, my core is running low and I must depart. These men will obtain your blood work and other vitals. It was a pleasure to meet you, Miss Jones. You have an exceptionally welcoming home and a courageous dog. I'm sure we will meet again."

He unhurriedly strolled out of the kitchen, stopping briefly to admire my décor, turned, and returned a half smile. After hearing the thud of the front door, I redirected my attention to the men with lab coats swarming around the table.

I wanted to rush to Colby, but the lab techs already had my arm prepped for blood work. The entire procedure took less than five minutes, but I couldn't wait for them to leave my home. They never talked while going about their business, only checked off from a list, labeling vials, before returning the collection to a bulky white case and leaving as suddenly as they had arrived.

I wanted to dart, lock the door in their wake, but realized if they'd got in before they could get in again. I instead fell to the ground alongside Colby as he awoke from his induced slumber, gradually opening those huge brown eyes. There was sadness, a sense of unsuccessful protection. I knew given a second chance it would be different, but for now sat, with his head in my lap, rubbing his ears, trying not to cry, encouraging him it was going to be all right.

Orion and I would meet again, including the rest of the *Men in Black*. Nevertheless, I fearfully considered what would happen in the future if I chose not to consent to their requests. *Why the concern over Russell? Who is General Samson and what Project? What's so important about this artifact that spooked Orion? Why did they need my blood, plasma, and DNA?* Colby let out a deep sigh; this wasn't going to be the last time I sat comforting him for trying to save my life.

It took Colby about fifteen minutes to recuperate, sitting with him the entire time, now more than ever motivated to document the past and future events. Thinking if the story went public, they'd have a tough time trying to make me vanish without controversy; it might be the only way to save my life. Although, if any government organization could execute someone, it would be the MIB's as secretly they have been removing threats for years.

Making my way back to the sitting room with Colby in tow, I sat down and continued to archive the past. I wanted to call Russell, but knew without doubt by now they would record my conversation. They wanted to get their hands on him and I wasn't going to be the connection to his detainment; not that they could hold him, but I'm still learning about his secrets, our Government and all my new 'friends'.

Okay, where was I. Tracy and I had gone for a run…

Chapter 11

We ran six miles, but it felt longer in the humidity with my legs feeling lethargic and my equilibrium off from the flight. I looked forward to eating something, anything, along with seeing the rest of house. Tracy barely broke a sweat; of course, she wasn't running at her normal tempo, only keeping pace with me.

Returning to the house, we entered through the secured gate, walked up the dirt driveway towards the house and stopped at the stone figures aligning the access to the front door. Russell seemed particularly interested in them so I wanted a closer inspection. *I wondered why?*

"Tracy, are you familiar with these sculptures?" exhaustedly speaking.

"No, but I could check with Jim when I call him later," Tracy replied, "Come on, don't worry about them, we're on vacation."

I walked around examining their features, each one special, but with similarities, especially with the scrolling typeset that intersected the focal points of these large sculptures. The language boldly not English and it didn't appear to be Hawai'ian. *What could it be?*

Tracy had seemed hard pressed to change the conversation. At the time, thinking it was her impatience to take a shower and wanting to head to Lāhainā.

Writing this now I recognize what was her true intent.

As if on cue, before I could press her for any more questions Pakile opened the door to greet us.

"How was your run ladies?" he asked.

"Good," Tracy replied heading for the door.

Making my way around the nearest figure's backside, I noticed an emblem, which I'd seen before. However, for the life of me, I couldn't remember where; it had to have been Vegas. Staring a little longer, hoping to jog my memory as a sense of déjà vu engulfed my mind. Tracy was right, stop worrying, for this was vacation. If I got an opportunity I'd check on-line, but right now, I desperately needed a shower as well as food. Pakile closed the door behind us as we headed up stairs.

"Are you ladies hungry?"

"Yes!" Simultaneously Tracy and I turned and answered

"Then I'll have something prepared when you come down."

Pakile then disappeared, I assumed heading toward the kitchen. Tracy headed for her room and I mine, she turned quickly before vanishing into the doorway.

"I'll see you in a half hour. We can eat, see the rest of the house, and maybe take the drive to Lāhainā for sunset."

"Sounds like a plan," I replied.

Tracy, seemingly always on the move even on vacation, but I did look forward to seeing Lāhainā.

Entering my bedroom, Colby was right where I'd left him, still lounging on the bed dead to the world. He, too, was enjoying the vacation. Jumping on the bed next to him he quickly perked up demanding to lick the sweat from my arms. I figured the kisses were part, '*I love you and I missed you*', the other part being he treasured the salty tang of the sweat on my skin. God, I needed a shower.

The water felt great cascading down my bare body, so I took a longer than normal shower, knowing Tracy would allow me the time. I focused on what to wear, not this evening, but tomorrow, with Russell; my so-called 'date'. The image of his face was still vivid in my psyche. Closing my eyes, I fantasized him naked, in the shower making passionate love to me, my hands mimicking his, exploring the softness of my skin. The entire time I wondered was my imagination doing his physical body justice. I hoped an answer would present itself before vacation's end.

I finished, toweled off, and felt more than reenergized. Tomorrow's outfit could wait, as I needed one for tonight. I knew just what to wear which was extraordinary for me considering for work, I'd spend at least an hour the night before switching out pieces to get the perfect ensemble. I, by no means, was good at putting together outfits except with jeans; my outfit of choice.

I bought, prior to the trip, an informal purple strapless sundress, with an off-white shawl and white sandals. The shoes, Tory Burch Crisscross Wedged Espadrilles, with a reserved two inch heel; exceptionally comfortable for walking and the best way to experience Lāhainā was walking. I hoped the heels, if crowded, would lessen my claustrophobic sensation. Plus, the outfit tied together agreeably with the lei Pakile gave me earlier.

I finished getting ready, Colby's eyes shadowed my every move, and aware, he'd subsequently have the room once again to himself. I wanted to take him to Lāhainā, but unacquainted with the local leash law, decided against it. Moreover, if we felt like browsing through stores, it wouldn't have been practical. With time to kill waiting for Tracy, I inspected the library's books, settling for one on the history of Lāhainā. The balcony, which overlooked the backyard and the beach, called with thunderous ferocity. I pulled up a wicker chair, which had cushions so soft they felt like you were floating on clouds. I only glanced through a few pages before Tracy reappeared shortly in my wake tapping me on the shoulder.

"You ready to eat?" she asked.

I turned, the afternoon sun highlighting her unblemished skin tone. Her appearance was one of a cover model for *Hawai'ian Tourists* magazine. She wasn't Hawai'ian, at least not that I knew, but could just about have passed for a local. She wore a small wrap around white skirt revealing her curves, with a very short white top accentuating most of what God had endowed. A few years my senior, with the body of a twenty-year-old and she proudly displayed it. I, a bit more reserved with my clothes selection in public, not that I didn't have a great body, just not the personality for being a public exhibit.

We made our way down stairs, two single women ready to hit the town after a little nourishment. Colby must have smelt the food as well, as a blur of fur passed us halfway down the stairs. Then it hit me, I hadn't brought Colby's food from home and it was closing in on supper, Pacific Time. I swear that dog had his own built in alarm clock.

We headed left off the stairs, then another immediate left down a small hallway towards an open door with an adjoining room. We passed, along the way, another bathroom to the left, while on the right displayed another Lassen. On entering the large rectangle room, you couldn't help but notice the centered hefty black table that seated ten. Its settings were elegant, white with red oriental trim patterned China, crystal, and sterling silver utensils.

Pakile entered behind us, "Please, sit anywhere you'd like. Dinner will be ready in just a minute." He pointed to the adjoining veranda through the glass slider, "However, if you prefer you may sit on the veranda."

The dining room was remarkable, filled with natural light, its all glass windows encompassing from the left around to the front slider, peeking out to the amplitude of foliage around the house. There was a blend of plants, flowers, and palm trees with the ocean as a backdrop. I assumed these palms highlighted my room windows upstairs. The right side of the room had an enormous painting, a portrait of a surfer riding a wave, displayed over a waist high bar shelf. Its realism captured to perfection. On the shelf were three medium size blooming plants in green hand-blown glass vases. The bouquet in the room altered with every step, truly amazing. Although a stylish room, we decided to eat on the bordering veranda with the ocean as our backdrop.

A gentle wind with the lingering scent of the ocean hit us as we made our way through the glass slider. Italian marble flowed from the dining room to the veranda flawlessly. A small modern square table with four chairs in light oak finish lay in its center. Pakile must have assumed we would opt for dining outside as an editable fruit arrangement awaited on the table's center. As if the ocean view wasn't enough, a miniature heated saltwater pool extended off the veranda. It appeared like a transparent extension of the marble floor reaching to the adjacent green grass of the backyard. A lone stone figure, similar to out-front, acted as a fountain spraying a fine mist over the water's surface. I reached my hand in testing the temperature and it had to have been at least eighty-five degrees. This was the perfect place to host a house party.

We sat down while Pakile served us something to drink. A yellow looking frozen cocktail garnished with a piece of chocolate covered pineapple and whipped cream, as if I needed the cream or the chocolate. I hesitantly tasted this guilty pleasure.

"That's a fresh pineapple smoothie. My own receipt. If you prefer something else just let me know," Pakile muttered.

My taste buds immediately agreed. It was heavenly and I had never tasted something so smooth that made my senses come alive.

"Tracy you have to taste this, Oh…My…God."

Tracy took a small sip, then a larger one. "Wow!"

Pakile then placed in front of us a bowl of salad with freshly cut greens, vegetables and grilled chicken, along with his homemade ginger dressing.

"Tracy called down saying you might be eating in Lāhainā so to fix something light. If you'd like something else…,"

Pakile waited for a few seconds for a response. I'd never had a servant before and felt awkward asking for anything.

"No this is great," I said. "Pakile, do you know where I can get dog food? I forgot to bring Colby's."

"No problem Miss Jones, just leave me the brand. Lulani is heading to the store in a bit nonetheless."

"Oh, thank you…I mean Mahalo."

"If you'd like, leave the feeding instructions and I'll make sure to attend to him the entire time you're here."

"I don't want to be a bother."

"It is no bother. I've had dogs for years and understand their needs."

Colby danced with excitement as he expected to eat supper now. "You still have a couple hours," then remembered he was still working on West Coast time.

We sat for about an hour, enjoying our salads and watching the waves roll into the shoreline. In the outlying waters, faint images of surfers trying to seize the last perfect wave. The waves on this side of the island failed to compare with O'ahu's North Shore this time of the year. The tiny inlet of rocks extending left and right off this private beach, plus the shallow ocean shelf, kept the waves to a minimum inland. On low tide, I imagined you could walk three or four hundred feet offshore and be no higher than your knees in water.

Although a private beach, Hawai'ian law allows access to all beaches, including privately owned. However, you'd have to climb a few jagged rocks from the northern and southern sides to take real advantage of this part of the beach. The house was extremely secure with a six-foot perimeter stone wall that divided the beach from the back lawn with a narrow, coded gate for beach access. The wall served two purposes, first acting as a barrier holding back the ocean during a typhoon or god forbid tsunami, second an unspoken fortified security. The cameras, lights, and motion detectors concealed within the palm trees and walls were barely noticeable.

The veranda was about two hundred feet from the ocean and sat ten feet above sea level on a raised plateau from the backyard. Huge stone steps cascaded their way down to the lush green grass, botanical gardens, and palm trees. To the right, a gathering of outsized palm trees, and strung between two of them an oversized hammock. I imagined sleeping beneath the stars with the placid sounds of the ocean playing softly in the background.

The sun was making its way downward towards the ocean displaying one of nature's most beautiful spectacles, especially in Hawai'i. If we wanted to make Lāhainā by sunset, we'd have to leave immediately, considering it was about a half hour drive north. Being unfamiliar with the drive, we didn't want to chance hitting traffic thus missing the show; of course, it would repeat tomorrow night.

Pakile offered the limo and Lulani's service but we decided to take one of the cars. The rest of the house could wait until tomorrow or later tonight. I felt bad leaving Colby again, but Pakile returned to the table, this time with a treat for Colby. A tennis ball, one of his favorite of course.

"I'll entertain Colby in the backyard while you're gone, Miss Jones," Pakile teased Colby with the ball, "Colby can have full run of the house. No worries." My concern wasn't Colby, as much as for Pakile, with Colby likely outweighing him.

"I'm fearful he might break something that's all," I said.

Colby was a gentle giant, but after seeing parts of the house, images of a bull loose in a China shop played in my head. Especially, when excited, his tail whipping in the wind, his uncontrollable urge to jump and spin as if trying to buck a rider. I gave him a quick squeeze and he returned the embrace with a gentle lick before he chased Pakile down the stone steps to the backyard. I watched for a few moments as he played fetch, or more like keep away, with Pakile.

Tracy and I headed to the garage, unsure which of Jim's cars to drive; unacquainted with our choices. Lulani met us at the garage and opened the doors for us as the two cars sparkled like showroom display models. They looked new or else Lulani was unbelievable at detail work.

The first car was a jet-black Ferrari. It didn't fit Jim's profile unless he was surreptitiously trying to recapture his formative years. The second, a vintage fire-engine-red, standard five speed Mustang Convertible. Yes, that screamed ladies night out Hawai'ian style. Tracy needed to drive because I couldn't handle a stick shift. Just my luck.

The newly replaced black leather interior gave this Classic that new car smell. The keys were already in the car so Tracy started her up. Even with just over 75,000 miles, the finish and interior had no signs of mileage, as if time stood still on this vehicle. The black top rolled down, as we turned up the Alpine stereo in search of just the right Hawai'ian station for the drive.

Lāhainā was a relaxing half an hour cruise except for the roar of the engine, which was a little was distracting. However, the Island's beautiful Pacific West Coast to our left, along with the Hawai'ian background music more than made up for it. The road to Lāhainā was by means of Honoapi'ilani Highway as the landscape of Maui was awe-inspiring with no traces of man-made structures larger than a palm tree in all directions. We turned on to Front Street, the main drag for Lāhainā, opting to take a whirl in the car up and down the boardwalk, checking out the views before parking.

Lāhainā was once a small whaling village, until banned, now a hotbed tourist attraction. There was much history here, maybe a venture for another day. Most of the original buildings stood, some modernized to meet new local codes. The overall sense was small-town surf shops that lined the boardwalk pedaling local tourism merchandise, just what a couple of young women needed. The center of town filled with expecting tourists waiting for sunset. The majority, if not all, of the locals now made their wealth from tourism, but this place to them still held a spiritual significance. The streets were restricting, with hardly enough room for the flow of traffic as tourists spilled off the sidewalk. In the background harbor boats prepared to depart in time for sunset. The boardwalk filled with local attractions and the sounds of live Hawai'ian music. We decided to park next to the Mala Ocean Tavern and trek the rest of the way by foot, as it was getting harder to sightsee and drive in this congestion.

Chapter 12

The overcrowding of the sidewalks reminded me of the Vegas Strip on a Saturday night. However, the ambience with the sounds of the surf and allure of storefronts filled with local merchandise made it a unique experience. We must have stopped in every store along the way and I was glad I didn't bring much money 'cause it would've been easy to blow my entire budget in one night. Additionally, I was relieved Colby had stayed home, for this was not canine friendly.

The local art, jewelry, and music were so striking as well as the assortment of art galleries, which alone was impressive. We headed north on Front Street, galleries everywhere you turned, some such as Wyland and Lassen I recognized, others I didn't. Then I caught a glimpse through the crowd of a memorable face, Russell's, exiting an art gallery called Sargent's. Its store window filled with authentic paintings, jewelry, as well as sculptures made of stone and wood, all from the island locals. Nudging Tracy, I smiled and intentionally bumped into him leaving.

"Oh I'm sorry," I said.

It took him a moment to wipe the intense focus from his eyes. His thoughts preoccupied.

"Erica. Tracy. Funny bumping into you here," he replied.

"Well, it's a small island," I tried to be witty.

"Yeah, you're right about that," he laughed.

Russell flashed one of his heart stopping smiles as Tracy looked around for an escape, her face said it all, *third wheel.*

"You guys talk," Tracy interrupted, "I'll meet you over there in the next shop," pointing to an adjoining high-end jewelry store.

That definitely was her cup of tea.

"Okay…," attempting a response.

However, Tracy swiftly exited while my focus returned to Russell.

"So shopping for some art?" I asked.

"You could say that," Russell answered, a little hesitant at first to respond.

"This has something to do with those figures at Jim's house, doesn't it?"

I didn't like meddling in other people's business, only trying to make conversation and hoping he wouldn't take offense, or worse, cancel our date tomorrow.

"Well, actually, it does," he grabbed my hand pulling me under the front window's awning away from the sidewalk's tourist traffic, "Erica, what do you know about those pieces or the owner, if anything?" He had an uneasiness in his tone and expression.

"I don't know…I mean…I noticed a symbol on them today I thought I recognized, but couldn't wrap my mind around from where. The owner, Jim Charleston, is Tracy's boss in Las Vegas. A nice older gentleman. I've known him for a few years. Why? Are they stolen or something?"

Russell's head pivoted around the crowd as if he had some big secret but didn't want anyone else to hear. The mass of walking pedestrians were surely more engrossed in the setting sun than our conversation.

"No they're not stolen, I don't think so, I mean…," pausing. "Let me do a little more exploring and I'll talk to you tomorrow when it's a little more private," his apprehension for full disclosure apparent.

"Okay," I replied.

Unsure if I should worry, panic or just be suspicious.

"We're still on for tomorrow, right?" He said with a smile.

"Absolutely!" Relieved to see my lacking social skills didn't affect our date.

"Okay, I got to run," he leaned in close. "Do me a favor; just don't mention anything to anyone about this until we talk tomorrow."

He waited for my assurance as the magnitude of the situation crawled over the fine lines of his eyes.

"Yeah, no problem."

Approaching my personal space, he embraced me and I returned the gesture. Perhaps it was the scent of his cologne or the shampoo used on his long silky hair that spilled over my face, but I wanted to snuggle into him; maybe I'd get my chance tomorrow. He gently broke the embrace and whispered in my ear.

"Please tell no one, and be careful."

Pulling away, my eyes looked in his briefly, then he turned, disappearing down the street as the crowd engulfed his escape.

Please be careful. That was a strange way to say good-bye. Great, I finally meet the guy of my dreams and he is a **Conspiracy Nut.** Well if that was his single fault so be it, his physical characteristics would outweigh it unquestionably.

I joined Tracy in the jewelry store with the thought, *Please Be Careful,* still echoing in my ears. He told me not to discuss this with anyone, but Tracy was my best friend and I'd just met Russell. Maybe talking to Tracy would help eat away at this feeling of a conspiracy. She was at the counter experimenting with a pair of pearl earrings that looked great on her; then again, everything looked great on her.

"So what do you think?" she asked.

"They look great," I replied.

"You should get a pair."

I scanned the display case of diverse sizes, colors and styles for something simpler, more my taste, finally settling on a smaller cute pair with an imbedded pearl and surrounded by a gold star cluster.

"Can I see these?" I asked the clerk.

Setting them in my ears I gazed into the mirror with astonished at how great they looked.

"Nice. You should get them," Tracy encouraged.

She was waiting for the attendant to come back with her pricey purchase.

"I don't know. How much?" asking the attendant.

"The price is on the bottom of the box," she replied.

The number resembled a serial number more than a price.

"Ouch!" I said returning the box to the counter.

"What's the matter?" Tracy asked.

"A little out of my price range."

"That's too bad they look great on you. So what did you and lover boy talk about?"

"Nothing much," returning the earrings to their box. "He inquired again about the sculptures at Jim's house. I think maybe he was looking to buy some."

Russell didn't what me to discuss this with anyone, but it was bothering me. I thought telling my best friend wasn't going to be a major concern. However, Tracy's expression soon went from gossip girl to an intrigued investigator pumping me for information.

"What did he say, exactly?" She asked.

"Not much. Just asked if I knew anything about them or about Jim," being caviler about the whole conversation. "I asked him if they were stolen."

"They're not stolen," she abruptly cut me off.

Her hasty, self-protective retort distressed me a bit. If the items indeed were stolen, I thought; *would she even know?* She was Jim's right hand man or woman for the company.

"I didn't say they were. I only asked him if they were and he didn't even give me an answer."

"Well, they're not stolen," with an intense seriousness on her face, "Anything else?"

"No. He said he'd have more information tomorrow."

"Are you sure?"

"Yeah…," pausing, "Well…"

"Well, what?"

"Well after giving me a hug he whispered in my ear to be careful. Kind of weird, what do you think?"

"Anything else?"

"No. He took off down the street in a rush."

"Maybe you should cancel your date with him tomorrow. He's sounding a little creepy."

Funny, a few hours ago, she was planning my wedding, convincing me to go out on a date and now she thinks he's creepy.

"I don't know. I think I'll sleep on it."

The smirk disappeared from Tracy's face, replaced with serious apprehension. It's nice to have someone looking out for my best interest, but he was just too damn cute to let go of…at least not yet.

We spent the next hour making our way up, then back down Front Street, stopping briefly in each store. The nightlife atmosphere felt like Mardi Gras. We decided to get a bite to eat at the Mala Ocean Tavern before heading home. The backside deck overlooked the ocean and we'd made it just in time for sunset. I've seen sunsets before, but this was truly amazing as the warm colors reflected off the rolling ocean while the intoxicating sounds of crashing waves hit the rocky shore of Lāhainā teasingly beneath our feet.

Tracy didn't chat much the rest of the night, even during dinner, except for the typical small talk. She was clearly displeased with me for not taking her concerns for Russell seriously. I didn't want to push the matter considering we'd recently arrived in Hawai'i with our whole vacation still ahead. I refused to be the one to ruin this trip, especially over some guy.

The drive home with the top-down was breathtaking, the distant not quite full moon illuminating the road. Perhaps it was the island's remoteness or the lacking city light pollution, but the amplitude of stars, overwhelming, in the sky above. In my lifetime, I'd never seen so many stars. Looking upward, I felt drawn to them the same way I felt drawn to Russell. His cologne still lingering on me as the tepid sea air blew through my hair giving me goose bumps. In the morning, I needed to take assessment of the possibility of canceling our date, but for the moment, I was enjoying my vacation.

Chapter 13

We returned to the house shortly after ten, exhausted, still working on West Coast time as Pakile once again met us at the door. How he constantly knew we were home was getting eerie.

"Miss Jones, flowers arrived for you just after you left. I put them upstairs in the study."

"Thanks, Pakile."

"Miss Miller, your boss called for you. He said to call him when you got back no matter the time," closing the door.

"Mahalo, Pakile," Tracy replied.

Her familiarity with the Hawai'ian dialect was impressive. She'd been silent on the way home and I hoped we'd chat before bed and try to clear the air.

Just then, a cherished reverberation erupted from atop the staircase, starting with a high-pitched whining, then into a full grunt as it appeared from the second floor. Colby, on hearing my voice, had darted down the stairs, his momentum, as he slide across the marble trying to stop, almost knocked me to the floor. I'd never seen him so animated, maybe it was the fresh air he received playing ball with Pakile.

"Okay, Okay" I shouted while he jumped up resting his two front paws on my shoulder, uncontrollably licking my face. "Did you eat?" half expecting a response.

"Yes, he did," Pakile, explained. "Lulani went out and bought him food shortly after you left and it's in the kitchen pantry. He also bought bowls for his food and water. They too are in the kitchen. Now, if there's nothing else. I'll do my final walk of the grounds and see you ladies in the morning."

"Thank you, Pakile," my voice raised as he rounded the hallway to the right responding with only a simple wave of his hand.

"I'm going to call Jim," Tracy stated.

She made her way up stairs as I followed with Colby attached to my hip. We entered the common study that connected the two bedrooms. I made for an empty couch with Colby at once following, jumping directly onto my lap. I hadn't spent much time with him today and decided to have a little *us time* before bed. Tracy vanished into her room without saying a word. I expected she was going to call Jim in private as well as she was still irritated with me about Russell. I treasured our friendship too much to quarrel on vacation, particularly over a guy I'd only recently met.

While waiting for Tracy, hopeful she'd reemerge from her room, I reconnected with Colby. I scratched around his neck, left ear, and noticed a tiny bump. At first, I thought it was a piece of knotted hair. He was notorious for those, his long hair extended well beyond his ears, seemingly doubling their size. He could have somehow scratched himself leaving a scab. However, after closer examination I didn't see a knot or even a scab. It wasn't much larger than a quarter inch, but you could unquestionably feel it beneath the skin surface. I considered the possibility it was a calcium build up, trying to convince myself it wasn't something worse, like a cancerous mass. I'd have it tested when we returned to Vegas. It didn't appear to bother him so I wasn't going to lose sleep over it, unless it started to swell over the next few days. Tracy emerged from her room ten minutes later, still on the phone chatting to Jim or so I assumed, but appeared happier than she was an hour ago.

"Jim wants to know how you like the house," pausing as she walked towards me. "Let me put it on speaker," touching the phone, she placed it on the table in front of us. "Hi Jim. Can you hear us…we have you on speaker."

"Yes, loud and clear," Jim replied.

His voice was deep, clear and seemed almost like he was in the room.

"The house is absolutely gorgeous. Thanks for letting us stay here," I responded quickly.

"You're more than welcome. If you need anything, make sure you ask Pakile. That's what I pay him for."

"Okay," we replied collectively.

I debated asking about the sculptures, not wanting to sound rude, being how I was a guest. However, something about them bothered Russell and Jim's clarification could help in my decision to go on tomorrow's date.

"Jim, those sculptures on the front lawn, can you tell me about them?"

Tracy twisted her face bluntly at me, her facial expression hiding nothing from what she was thinking. This earnestly was becoming an unpopular subject matter. *What was so out of the ordinary about these sculptures that had everybody spooked?* Maybe Jim would shed some light on their origins.

"Jim, are you still there?" Tracy beckoned.

A brief silence came from the phone's receiver while we waited for a reply.

"I'm sorry," Jim replied. "What do you want to know about them?"

"I don't know. Where did they come from? Did they come with the house? Anything really?"

I didn't want to charge our host with stealing considering there was no proof. Then Tracy piped in before Jim could respond.

"The gentleman I mentioned from the airport was inquiring about them."

"They're primordial tribal pieces that Pakile purchased for me from a local art dealer in town. I had only seen pictures by email before I bought them. They seemed fascinating and flowed well with the themed landscape of the property. You can check with Pakile tomorrow, maybe he can give you more information."

Jim's retort was vague and ambiguous, not what I was expecting, but they didn't sound stolen. Maybe Russell was crazy after all…great! I'd have to check with Pakile tomorrow. Right now, I was exhausted.

"Anything else ladies?"

"No. Just thanks again for letting me stay here and for bringing Colby," I replied.

I now felt guilty bringing up the subject; damn you Russell Hamilton for putting conspiracy thoughts inside my head! At least Tracy appeared relieved with Jim's reply.

"No problem, Erica," Jim paused. "Tracy I need to talk to you about C.H.A.R.A. if you have a second. Erica, have a great vacation!"

"Thanks Jim, I will."

With that, Tracy took it off speaker, returning to a private conversation with Jim as she progressed back into the privacy of her room. I wasn't trying to eavesdrop but her voice was carrying through the silence of the night. There was several *Okay's*; *I'll do that*, and *no problems*. From the sounds of it, Jim wanted Tracy to do a little work with C.H.A.R.A. while here on vacation.

I wanted to talk before going to bed, waiting for her to get off the phone, which didn't take longer than fifteen minutes. By that time, I had made my way to the patio. The moon was almost full; the white crests of the diminutive waves hitting the beach while the sounds of the approaching surf soothed my mind. High tide crept up like a resilient army and the beach nearly lost to the ocean. The motion sensor lights on the palm trees lit up, startling me, as Pakile's figure appeared beneath, walking the grounds. I wanted to go and talk to him tonight, but knew it could wait until tomorrow. I wondered if someone tried to enter the property would Pakile really be an obstacle at his age, unless of course he was Mr. Me Aggie. I privately laughed as that picture played in my head.

"Is this not the life?" Tracy asked, joining me on the patio.

"Yeah," I agreed, this was something I could easily get accustomed to. "Jim wants you to do a little work while you're here?"

"Kind of. He's having difficulty getting some information from the C.H.A.R.A. branch out of O'ahu and wants me to make a trip over in the next couple of days to see if I can inspire them a little."

"Was Jim annoyed with me asking about the sculptures?"

"No. He wants me to keep him informed of what we find out about them," she paused. "Between you and me, I think he's a little curious as well."

"So we're good about me seeing Russell tomorrow?"

I was still going to see him regardless of her answer, but tensions would be less on edge living together if she agreed.

"Yes, go have fun," she replied.

She had a different attitude than beforehand. Did Jim and Russell's curiosity regarding the sculptures have something to do with the transformation?

"So we're cool?" I asked.

"Of course," she reached over to give me a big hug. "Sometimes I act too much like your big sister. Sorry."

She was right, she did act like my big sister, but I didn't mind, seeing how I was an only child with vague memories of my birth parents. My adopted parents had died a few years back. At that point, I tried to get information on my real parents or any living family members, but had no luck. Tracy, truthfully, was the closest thing to family I had left, next of course to Colby. I was trying to hold back the tears as those memories flooded my senses.

"Thanks, sis," I said.

We must have sat there for another hour; listening to the sounds of the waves hit the shore, not saying another word except *goodnight* as we made our way to separate bedrooms. I was looking forward to a goodnight sleep and it was well past my bedtime.

I got ready for bed in less than five minutes and opened the windows so the sounds of the waves would rock me to sleep. The bed was high, even for me, the box spring, mattress and eight-inch Tempur-Pedic foam hit me at the hip. My body descended into the mattress like it was a cloud, the silk sheets caressing every layer of my being. Colby pushed his way to my side by means of the ottomans, plopping lifelessly down before putting his head ever so gently on my pillow. I hated to share my pillow, but this in all honesty wasn't my pillow and he knew it. I think he knew I'd let it slide. I was going to dream of Russell tonight; don't know why, just a feeling. I wrapped my arm around Colby like a body pillow and was dead to the world in no time.

Chapter 14

December 27, 2009

Last night was the most tranquil sleep I'd had in my life. It could've been the bed, the sounds of the surf or my intimate dreams of Russell. Either way, I stretched out in the bed, drifting in and out of consciousness late into the morning and didn't care. I should say late in the morning for my standards. Even Colby slept well. Usually, up by five looking for breakfast, it was now seven and he's still snuggled by my side, sound asleep.

Outside, the surf beckoned me, but unsure if Tracy or anyone else was awake, I tried to be quiet. Colby dashed for the closed door quicker than I could roll out of bed. Swiftly putting on sweats and sneakers I made my to the bedroom door before Colby woke the entire house with the whipping excitement of his furry tail.

I managed to make it downstairs without waking Tracy and although the house appeared soundless, it still felt wide-awake and breathing. I didn't want to call on Pakile. If I happen upon him fine, but if he was sleeping, I didn't want to rouse him. The kitchen, I guessed, had to be within close proximity of the dining room. Sure enough, to the left, through the dining room's entryway hid the doorway.

The kitchen, of modern design, indeed, the most technologically advanced room in any house I'd ever seen. I expected a bigger space based on the house's size, but its small-scale was because of its economical design with everything organized and neatly arranged. I swear, it appeared never used as the stainless steel appliances showed no sign of wear, as if delivered yesterday. It had a cold, futuristic, unlived feel compared to my kitchen, which had plants and pictures littered everywhere. I couldn't even find a calendar, picture, or even a clock, which I thought odd for a kitchen. Above the middle island's granite top with dropped in double sink hung brass pots. Across the island, on the far wall were two dark-panel sliding doors, which I assumed was the pantry Pakile mentioned. Sure enough, upon opening the doors, there was Colby's food. Although, I will say for a pantry there wasn't much consumable food inside. Maybe they had another kitchen I hadn't seen yet in the house. By this time, Colby had already found his bowls on the other side of the island. He sat, licking at his chops to the point of blowing saliva bubbles as I measured out a two-scoop breakfast.

The entire time, a feeling crept into my subconscious, as if someone watched, causing the hair on my arms to rise. Grabbing the water bowl, I began filling it from the island; once again, my neck hair tingled as if someone had gently blown on it. At that moment, two large beeps came from behind breaking the silence of the kitchen. I dumped the water in the bowl, spiraling around, planning to use the bowl for security. It took me a second to realize the origin of the sound; an automated coffeepot had started. I was getting excessively jumpy for a vacation, I thought. Then smiling, hoped it was decaf, and returned to filling the water bowl.

As if on a sick perverted cue, Pakile entered from the only other kitchen door, a screen door leading to the side yard and for the second time in under a minute, I jumped.

Colby was too preoccupied with swallowing his breakfast and never even heard him. Usually, the mail carrier can't even get to the end of the driveway before Colby barks frantically.

"Good Morning, Miss Jones. I didn't mean to scare you," slowly closing the door behind him.

"That's okay. I'm just a little jumpy this morning, sorry."

I finished filling the bowl and returned it to a patiently waiting Colby.

"Would you like some coffee?" Pakile asked, as he pulled coffee cups from an above cabinet.

"Only if its decaf." I turned with anticipation, as it smelt heavenly.

"Yes, it's decaf. Kona Coffee, from The Big Island. Only the best," he smiled removing an extra-large travel mug. "I figured

Colby needed to go out and you might join him so I got you a travel mug. Is that alright?"

"Yes, great."

This was getting weirder by the day, too many people seemingly reading my mind. I started to question that many coincidences in such a short period of time.

"How do you take it?"

Pakile asked while grabbing creamer from the double door stainless steel fridge.

"Just a little creamer. Hazelnut if you have it."

Before my comment even finished crossing my lips, he had turned back to the coffee raising the creamer, Hazelnut, even my brand. Seeing we were alone, this felt like a good time to inquire about the sculptures as Jim had suggested last night. Colby was already heading to the door, but I figured he could wait a minute. Taking my coffee from Pakile, I took a deep inhalation of the scent and a small taste. It was pure heaven.

"I talked to Jim last night. He said you purchased the sculptors out-front. What do you know of them?"

"They're from an ancient tribe. I bought them from a local art dealer." He avoided eye contact, which bothered me. Jim had said the same thing last night. He then tried to regain control of our conversation. "Why do you ask?"

"A friend of mine's interested. He's thinking about getting one for his backyard."

I knew this was an outright lie, but would he recognize it? I just wanted a genuine answer. This was quickly becoming a complex enigma and I was unrelenting when it came to solving puzzles, sometimes downright compulsive.

"You mean your friend Russell, don't you?"

Turning, his once black glossy eyes had morphed into a lifeless flat black as they met mine. I honestly can say now, that scared the hell out of me.

"Yes, I do mean Russell," refusing to let my fear show, but somehow he knew.

"Miss Jones. I understand you're a guest of Jim's, but every so often, some things are what they are. If Jim didn't explain them to you, I am not obligated to discuss them with you either. Sorry, but that is how I feel." He turned to return the creamer to the fridge.

It was bizarre, Jim said he didn't know and here was Pakile telling me differently. *What was the big damn mystery?* Afraid to push the matter further, I'd wait, at least until after talking to Russell to see what, if anything, he'd uncovered. The few moments of awkward silences finally broke when Colby began whining at the door. Pakile busied himself with preparing breakfast as if I wasn't even in the room. Suddenly Tracy entered the kitchen making me jump for the third time this morning.

"Morning everyone." Tracy cheerfully shouted. She was tremendously peppy in the morning, even before coffee.

"Morning," I replied with a noticeable apprehensive voice.

"Did I interrupt something?"

Her eyes toggled between Pakile and me.

"No, Pakile made coffee and I was on my way to take Colby for a walk on the beach."

I didn't want to get into it, as it was too damn early. Maybe Pakile was right, hinting to the fact I was just a guest. I mean, if Jim and Pakile didn't want to discuss the sculptures I should just forget it, right?

"Great, let me have breakfast first," Tracy replied. "Then I'll join you in bit."

She sat down and instantly Pakile put a delicious looking omelet in front of her. Although the image was mouthwatering I wasn't going to bother to ask Pakile for one at this point, the coffee would do for now.

"Okay. I'll see you down on the beach shortly," I replied.

I opened the door as Colby ran down the two stairs into the side yard. I couldn't have got out of there fast enough. Something was becoming troubling in regards to this trip, including the behavior from some of my cohabiters. Those words from Russell,

'*Please be Careful!*' echoed faintly in my concerned ears more than it should have for a vacation.

Colby and I trekked through the backyard, small security gate, and out on to the beach. It was early, but the sun's rays already warmed the soft sand. Dislodging my sneakers and socks from my feet, I could feel the soft white sand melting between my toes. I've been to the beaches in California, Florida, even the Cape in New England, but this sand felt like balls of cotton caressing my feet with every step. Colby ran to the shoreline, hopping back and forth, as if playing tag with the incoming waves that abruptly returned to the horizon, as low tide replaced high, thus doubling the size of the beach from last night.

The beachfront for this private cove wasn't long. Although beaches in Hawai'i are all public, the real beach for Keawakapu started on the other side of the bay's lava rocks and extended for miles, lined with hotels, condominiums, and other private houses. I understand the house's pricey value as its illusion of isolation gave it a tranquil appearance. Kneeling down I tested the water with my hands, it had to be in the low 80's and felt like bathwater. I glanced up towards Colby, having a blast chasing a small crab back into the water. As soon as he saw me up to my knees in the water, he decided it was okay to take the plunge. I do mean that literally and within seconds, a watered downed version of him came abruptly towards me in the water. He appeared like a dolphin leaping through the crashing waves. I ran out from the water, which only encouraged him to pick-up speed. I knew what he wanted to do to me and I didn't have a towel.

"Stop! —Sit!" I yelled putting my hands out while he stared at me, slowly inching closer, like a game of Mother May I. "I said sit!" As he crept within arms-length, I swear he smiled and without hesitation transferred half the ocean from his fur coat to me. It felt like a tsunami. He stopped, putting his butt in the air, his two front paws in the sand and wanted to play. I just wanted a towel.

"Need a towel?" Tracy's voice called from behind.

"Yeah, you could say that."

I answered, while wiping the sand and saltwater from my face as Tracy handed me one of the two towels brought down from the house. She mentioned last night wanting to lie out before the sun got too hot in the afternoon and must've already had her swimsuit on under her clothes in the kitchen.

"I talked to Pakile. Don't worry he isn't really a morning person," she comfortingly expressed.

"I didn't mean to upset him, but Jim...," unable to finish.

"Yeah, I know I told him. He said he'd have some information for you around lunch."

"Great." I was trying to sound positive but wasn't sure how much information, if any, Pakile would offer to me.

"By the way," she laid her towel on the sand. "I'm leaving for O'ahu just before lunch. I'll be gone till tomorrow morning."

"Really?" A part of me, disappointed.

"I figured seeing how you have plans with Russell in the afternoon...hopefully tonight too," displaying a devilish smirk, "I'd booked a flight for today. However, I couldn't get one back until tomorrow morning. I have a dinner meeting with the directors of C.H.A.R.A. tonight."

"No problem."

I was a little apprehensive being in the house with Pakile alone, even for one night. There was something about him that screamed secret serial killer. They say it's always the quiet ones. Maybe if things go well with Russell I'll invite him to stay the night.

"You want to stay and get some sun?" Tracy asked, as she finished putting on sunscreen

"No, I was thinking of going for a run before lunch." Running in the morning motivates me for rest of the day. "Did you want me to wait for you?"

"No, go ahead. I'll run on O'ahu."

She put on her sunglasses, rolled over onto the towel and turned up her iPod. She looked like a Goddess lying on the sand; glistening with lotion, I was envious of her never-aging body.

"Okay."

I called Colby, while making my way up towards the house. There was no way he was going into the house until he dried off. I figured I'd head upstairs, get his long leash, and tie him to the palm tree outside. I told him to *"stay"* then made my way into the kitchen. I worried about seeing Pakile, but figured I'd apologize if I saw him. It was like trying to stay mad at your grandfather; you can't do it. He wasn't in the kitchen so I continued upstairs to get Colby's leash and within seconds found my way back into the foyer. About to turn left towards the kitchen when down the adjacent hallway my ears heard sounds of an animated exchange. A bizarre light illuminated from under the far right hallway door. I approached, figuring it must be Pakile and Lulani talking. I thought with at least Lulani there that I wouldn't be so nervous confronting Pakile. We hadn't seen this side of the house, but I assumed it must be either an office or even Pakile's room. I knew Lulani didn't live at the house.

The radiance from under the door changed constantly from a day glow blue, to a cool white to a fiery orange. Never had I seen colors like this emanating from any light bulb. Trying the doorknob it felt warm, in addition, locked. The hair began standing on my arms as a strange sensation of fear slowly crawled up my spine until it entered my conscious mind. Voices were communicating on the other side, but I couldn't clearly distinguish whom. Gradually, I placed my ear to the warmth of the door, unable to establish if the voices were male or female, which I thought was strange. What a great houseguest, first I insult the host, then the help and now I was eavesdropping.

I wish I knew Hawai'ian, had a recorder or even my cell phone, which was upstairs. It didn't sound Hawai'ian, not enough vowels. In fact, it didn't sound like any dialect I'd ever heard. This trip was getting weirder by the day. I debated whether to knock, but decided against the intrusion and proceeded to remove my ear. Colby then startled me, his unfathomable directional barking emanating from outside as if something had spooked him to the likes I'd never heard. Immediately, from behind the door, the conversation terminated, the lights disappeared and the hallway became considerably quiet. I turned abruptly, quickly tiptoed to the kitchen, and made my way outside to attach his leash. I had all I could do to hold him back from entering the house. He moved towards the stairs barking at the door, the hairs on his back spine standing, and strands of thick salvia dangling from the corner of his snout. I've seen him do this around other dogs, but not to this extreme and there wasn't another dog on sight.

It took all my strength to return him to the enlarged palm tree's base, barely able to wrap the leash around. He kept barking, pulling, trying to break free for the house. It took minutes to distract him enough from whatever spooked him. He slowly calmed down, finally resting at the foot of the tree. His eyes followed in apprehension as I returned to the kitchen door to fetch him some water. I entered to a now sitting Lulani at the center island having coffee, Pakile, again getting creamer, this time with a tension that strangled the surrounding air and I only imagined the look my face projected. Interesting, as a few moments ago, they were nowhere to be found, and yet here they sit as if they'd been here the entire time.

"Do you want a refill?" Pakile asked. His tone had completely changed from our earlier conversation as if it'd never happened. Maybe he did only need his morning coffee.

"Yeah, that would be great," I responded.

I walked toward Pakile, who slowly filled my cup while Lulani watched closely trying hard to disguise his glare with the bottom of his coffee cup.

"How was your walk on the beach?" Pakile asked in an attempt to create small talk.

"Great, Colby got a little wet. I should say, really wet. So he's outside drying."

I walked towards the door to confirm he'd calmed down. He was half-asleep on the grass sunning himself, but you could see his limited brown eyes fixated on the door. Lulani piped in after putting his coffee down.

"If you'd like, Miss Jones, I've a family member that does mobile grooming. I could have her stop by later while you're out with Russell."

I only mentioned my date with Russell to Tracy, yet everyone in the house clearly knew my plans. I hadn't even confirmed them myself. If I did go with Russell, at least I'd be gone for a while so it couldn't hurt.

"Yeah that'd be great. What does she charge?"

I walked from the door towards Lulani aiming to appear a bit more social. Colby's coat had a dusting of beach sand and he'd gradually started to dry in the sun so a bath wasn't a bad idea. I always liked the smell of Colby after a bath; his fur was fluffy and felt like a Down Pillow.

"No charge, Miss Jones. A friend of Jim's is a friend of mine," Lulani voiced before inhaling another sip of coffee.

"At least let me leave some money for a tip."

I was insistent and hated people who didn't tip for services, just a little pet peeve of mine.

"Sure, that'll be fine. Just leave it with Pakile."

Lulani tossed back one last mouthful then pushed it toward Pakile for a refill. I wasn't going to ask about the exchange behind the door. I was sure it was the two of them, and from their expression, they knew I knew. I brought water out to Colby, and then lingered in the kitchen another ten minutes finishing my coffee while engaging in small talk with the two men. The entire time, a feeling of wrongness engulfed my soul as if they were waiting for me to admit my guilt. I was an adult, not a kid. Mommy hadn't caught me stealing from the cookie jar. I felt in the wrong for having escaped prosecution or so I'd thought.

Chapter 15

A strange feeling dropped around me while making for the bedroom. I felt like a witness to a mob killing, the mob knew, and there was no way the government was going to be able to protect my life. I tried to shake the feeling when my cell phone rang. I rushed to the bedroom to answer it with no concern who was on the other end. I desperately needed to find a way to take my mind off the last half an hour and a good conversation was the cure.

"Hello, this is Erica."

There was no displayed name or number on the caller ID. Odd, as it usually showed at least the words "private" name or number, instead of absolutely nothing.

"Erica, this is Russell. I've been trying to reach you all morning."

I looked down at my phone, three voice mails. I'm amazed, for I always carried my phone. Being on vacation, you start to forget routines, and over the last day, I guess its been a bit uprooted. It was comforting to hear his voice, although it sounded anxious.

"Sorry. I was out on the beach with Colby."

I didn't dare talk about what just happened or what I thought I'd seen, 'cause for all I knew it might be nothing, and no sense scaring away the first real love interest in years.

"Not a problem," then a pause, "Is everything okay?"

I think he could hear the minor pitch variation in my voice.

"Well," contemplating the right response, "I'll tell you later when you pick-me-up."

How do you respond? I wanted to tell him, but wasn't sure of his reaction, plus at this point wasn't sure if someone was listening in on my conversation. God was I getting paranoid but if it was true this so wasn't my idea of a vacation.

"Okay. So, we're still on for this afternoon?" I asked.

"Yes!"

"What time?"

"I'll pick you up around one. Is that alright?"

"Yeah, one would be great!"

"Okay, one it is. See you then."

No matter what, I looked forward to seeing his face and basking in his warmth and as quickly as his voice appeared it became lost to the distant dial tone. I wanted to check his messages, knowing you can tell many things about a guy from his phone etiquette but they could wait. Besides, I was going to see him in a few hours anyway.

Having a few hours to kill I chose to go for that quick run. After settling on doing only a couple of miles I decided to take Colby along. He loved running with me, for a hefty dog, he was an excellent runner, graceful on his paws, and he needed time to dry anyhow. I quickly changed, but the idea of crossing the kitchen with Lulani and Pakile made me slightly apprehensive. I decided to go out the front door and around the side of the house to get Colby. He already had his leash and it would allow me to avoid them both, so far so good. I was sure it was just my lack of sleep or overactive imagination getting the best of me. All those sci-fi thriller novels I liked to read. A relaxing run might offer a chance to clear my thoughts and get in the right frame of mind for my date. I considered it a date but, wasn't sure if Russell felt the same way, I could only hope.

Colby was thrilled to see me, having conditioned him to the sight of my sneakers; he knew we were going for a walk. We lightly jogged to the front gate with Colby leading the way. He never pulled faster than I could run and was always a great short-distance running partner. His limit was four miles before he tired and for today that was fine with the plan to keep it under three.

We took a right out the front gate, south down Kihei Road. On the map was Parking Area 3, less than two miles down this dead end road. I figured Kihei, being predominately flat, would be a simple run down and back. It didn't take us long to cover the first mile stretch of South Kihei as the main road curved off to the left and the sign on the street said Okolani Drive. South Kihei continued forward with huge oversized signs that read *Dead End* and towered on both sides of the road. After this morning, the signs hit me to the core, although knowing they weren't referring to my plight. There was a parking lot at the end for public beach access and with cars passing all the time during the day, I felt somewhat safe.

I raced the short distance to the end of the street to a sparsely filled parking lot compared with the northern parking lots. I stopped at the fountain near the bathrooms for water and filled Colby's little portable plastic bowl. He inhaled it while I took in the scenic view, gasping for air as the humidity here was hindering my pace. I could only imagine wearing a fur coat and running and in hindsight, it probably wasn't the smartest idea to bring Colby. I decided to walk the rest of the way home giving him and myself a break.

It was clearly apparent from looking around the parking area, why many didn't make the journey to this section of the beach. Although lovely, it was secluded, even its beach access. Signs ubiquitously warned *Not Responsible for Damage or Theft to Vehicles.* Clearly, this section of beach was void of patrolled security, a sharp contrast to the other beaches. Scanning over the people leaving their vehicles for the shore, this was a clear-cut local's beach. The divers, surfers, and sunbathers were all Hawai'ian tropic locals.

As soon as Colby had finished his water and fully recuperated, we began the short walk back to the house. The gratefulness in Colby's face showed with each stride. As we started to cross the entrance to the parking lot, we stopped abruptly on the curve, and motioned the incoming car to continue into the lot. It ceased its progress, motionlessly idling. I motioned again with my hand, yet it remained frozen, seemingly waiting for me to pass. So I did, waving a heartfelt *thank you* to the driver.

The car, all black, an unusual color considering the island's dominating heat. Their windows tinted a midnight black making inside viewing impossible, even from the front. I figured it helped tone down the inside heat. In Vegas, that degree of tint is illegal, but I didn't know the laws of Hawai'i. I turned back as it passed behind me for one more quick wave. Compared to other cars within the vicinity, this sedan stood out like the only new car in a used car lot.

Continuing up the sidewalk, we picked up the pace to a brisk walk, almost a light jog, as I considered my ensemble for tonight. I hadn't packed date clothes. Go figure. Tracy and I were comparable in size, and she had packed half her wardrobe. Maybe I'd borrow something from her closet. I'd ask her if she wasn't gone when I got back. If not I figured she wouldn't mind anyways. I mean, she was the one trying to set this date up in the first place.

Colby stopped halfway from the house to do his business. I always brought a disposable bag when we walked, but being on vacation I'd forgotten. I didn't know the town's policy for cleaning up after your pet, although it's a common courtesy and the last thing I needed was a ticket. However, even with no security in sight, I figured I'd at least clear his mess from the sidewalk with something. As I searched for a stick to use, out of the corner of my eye I spotted the identical sedan. It was a hundred feet back and coasting slowly forward. I abruptly turned towards the car and it stopped. Something felt off, as my pace quickened to a steady run the rest of the way home, intermittently looking over my shoulder for the black sedan. Little by little, it crawled forward, never getting more than one hundred feet within my vicinity. My heart pounded in fear with each running step. Thoughts and images of the darkest tossed around in my mind. Thankfully, steady streams of walking traffic on both sides of the sidewalk helped to relieve those fears.

I finally arrived at the house, entering swiftly, quickly locking the gate behind. I watched as the sedan's eerie crawl passed by the house and stopped briefly. I could feel the eyes of its occupants watching me from within. Colby turned, growling, sensing something wasn't right, as the hair on his back rose for the second time today. The car's tires painfully screeched as it sped up full force down the street. I tried getting the car's plate numbers so I could report it to the local police, but there was none.

This day kept getting better and better every minute.

Reflecting back, I truly believe it to be my first encounter with the so-called *Men In Black*. Which ones, to this day I can't say, but the awful fear instilled in me that day I'll never forget.

Chapter 16

Colby was asleep on the bed, nice and dry from his run. I left the shower's comfort wrapped in a towel around my naked body. I went to the balcony wanting to take in the gentle wind that rolled off the waves. A welcome relief, as the slow rising humidity had returned. Today's forecast called for upper 90's with a clear blue sky. Tracy had already left by the time I'd gotten out of the shower. I never heard her leave, but she did text my phone saying it was okay to borrow an outfit.

Making my way to her room, I snuck a quick peek at the clock. Great, still forty-five minutes before Russell arrived but I prayed he wasn't one of those people that always had to be early. Tracy brought ten times the clothes that I had, even some business suits as if knowing ahead Jim was going to need her to work. I'd never borrowed anyone's clothes before, especially someone whose taste was on a different price scale than mine. Trying to select an outfit, not knowing our plans, complicated, but I finally settled on a light beige cotton, high wasted pencil skirt, with a yellow silk short-sleeve displaying white hibiscus flowers and a matching pair of beige gladiator sandals. I was going to bring a white button down Cashmere sweater with me in case it got cold later. I was never big on make-up, especially when hot, so I tried to go as natural as possible. Thankfully blessed with my mother's good skin, or so I'd been told. Standing in front of my bedroom mirror, I double-checked my ensemble, fidgeting with everything. Even at my age, when the right guy comes along you still get nervous.

I returned to Tracy's room for jewelry that would complete this outfit because nothing I had worked. I didn't need much, just a little something to tie it all together. I randomly searched the drawers in her bathroom not knowing where she had stashed all her jewelry. As the third drawer slid open, a folder labeled C.H.A.R.A. ejected, hitting the floor, and spilling some of its contents. In hindsight, I shouldn't have opened it, but somehow drawn to its contents, I did.

Upon opening the folder there were pictures of people I'd never seen, and attached to each picture a yellow sticky note. The strangest thing was the text written, in an unrecognizable form, on the notes in Tracy's handwriting. It wasn't English, Hawai'ian or even shorthand and the unique symbols at the bottom of each note reminded me of ancient hieroglyphics, but they weren't Egyptian. Finally, there was a three-page letter written in the same text, on C.I.A. Government Letterhead, signed only by MJ-1, and dated less than a week ago. Why did Tracy have a letter from the CIA? Then suddenly, Pakile's voice came over the intercom as clear as if he was standing next to me, making my heart skip for the fourth time today.

"Miss Jones, Mr. Hamilton has arrived and is in the entryway."

Startled, I quickly closed the folder returning it to its original spot. Not remembering how to work the intercom to respond I decided against the jewelry, did one last check in the mirror, grabbed my purse, and gave Colby a kiss good-bye on his head. He was sleeping, snuggled like a ball, exhausted from his run and awaiting the groomers to do their magic. I continued down to my dream date, planning to do a little magic of my own.

Russell was standing next to Pakile, seemingly making small talk. I wondered about what, but had a fairly good idea. Russell had exchanged his Armani suit for a pair of perfectly fitted jeans, a white silk button down shirt, his black hair pulled in a ponytail and sandals. Even casually dressed, his manliness touched me with a hotness, the likes of no other. I made my way down the stairs with his eyes locked on mine and knew he was undressing me with his eyes. To be honest I was doing the same thing to him. The cosmic energy of attraction between us was intense and drew us together like magnets. At least that's how I felt and hoped I would find out this afternoon if he felt the same.

"Miss Jones, are you going to be late?" Pakile asked.

It was all he could do to make eye contact with me as my eyes probed Russell for an answer unsure of his plans.

"I don't know."

"Sometime after supper," Russell responded, looking around me to Pakile.

"Then I'll feed Colby later," Pakile humbly returned, "Lulani's friend will be here in the next hour to groom Colby. So, go enjoy yourself and take your time." He quickly turned, returning to the hallway of the earlier strange lights.

"Thank you, Pakile!" raising my voice. "Colby's upstairs in my bedroom."

And with a quick wave, he vanished around the corner.

"You look great," Russell, voiced. "Ready to go?" He opened the door like a perfect gentleman.

"Yes." Walking through the threshold as my cheeks filled with a natural blushing glow. "Is Nohea here?"

"No. I gave him the night off."

I wondered what a man, accustomed to limos, drove for fun and before I finished considering that thought the answer revealed before me in the driveway. A Chrysler Sebring convertible, my car of choice, except his was the newest model. What's the odds the man of my dreams drove the same car as me? I believe the word is astronomical.

"I hope you don't mind the top-down. It's such a nice day," Russell asked while graciously getting my door.

"Not at all. I have the same car just not as new."

I couldn't stop undressing him with my eyes as he walked around the front of the car. Somehow, I think he knew, making sure to extend the experience. I was definitely going to hell with these thoughts. He lowered himself into the car's seat, his muscular mass engulfing the driver's seat as it molded to his frame, his physically powerful hands dwarfing the steering wheel as he turned towards me for approval with only a smile.

"Are you ready to go?"

"Oh yeah."

The orgasmic excitement in my voice managed a return smile and I took in a deep breath trying to relax. This, the first real date I'd had in years, in one of the most romantic places on earth, and with the sexiest man on the planet. At least I thought so. The car turned north onto Kihei Road en route to the top of Haleakalā. I knew little of our date plans and even less about Russell.

"So, where are we going?" I asked.

"Kula Botanical Gardens. It's on the way to the summit of Haleakalā and pending traffic shouldn't take us more than an hour."

"Sounds romantic."

I couldn't believe that slipped out of my mouth.

"It can be," he quickly replied with a grin.

I wasn't much for small talk and didn't know if discussing this morning's events was fitting, but we were going to have enough time. I wondered if he'd found any information about the sculptures, not really a first date conversation piece, but it might break the ice and allow him to control the conversation. *Why was I so stressed? Come on Erica he's just a guy*, I told myself, but not convincingly enough.

"So, were you able to find out anything about those sculptures?"

"Why don't we discuss that later?" He turned with reassuring eyes and a calming voice. "Let's pretend we're on a real date."

"Alright."

My anxiety was obvious, but I didn't know what else say. There was a weird moment of silence then...

"Hi, I'm Russell Hamilton," extending his hand, "and you are?"

I laughed, "Erica Jones," playing along.

"Nice to meet you, Miss Jones."

He turned on a local Hawai'ian station and started to sing along in Hawai'ian. The song was so mesmerizing, even though I couldn't tell you the title because it was in Hawai'ian. I think anything, even if it were depressing, would sound beautiful in this language. However, it was the playfully deep tone in his voice serenading me that left a lasting impression. Nothing like a guy who can sing I always say.

The drive up to Haleakalā flew by as we laughed while making chitchat about our hectic lives. Russell controlled the conversation and was extremely interested in every facet of my life. He had a way of retrieving even those token details, things I had never revealed to anyone, including Tracy. His interest in my life, my dog, was unprecedented and as every minute passed, I felt increasingly content in his presence. We pulled into the parking lot of the gardens with a part of me wanting him to keep on driving just so we could continue talking.

The dark brown bungalow of the Kula Gardens rested on a small hill bordered by a slightly faded wooden fence. Its exterior, dwarfed in importance by the plant life nested about, it almost seemed out of place among the lush green jungle foliage. We traversed up an undersized, hand-built, winding wooden access ramp. At the top was a small white weathered door with a bordering window equipped with its own flower box. I gently opened the door as a miniature bell above us chimed our arrival. Appearing from behind a cheaply hung curtain was a dainty, older, island native women. She walked with the frailty of her age, the pronounced wrinkles around her eyes told stories of the island's history. She took one look at us with a smile.

"He ipo no ke po," she lightly muttered.

"Mahalo," Russell replied with a smile.

He then turned in my direction with this schoolboy goofy grin as if he had a secret. I gently nudged him in the ribs.

"So, what did she say?

"I'll tell you later," returning his attention back to the woman. "We'll take two tickets please."

If I continued dating Russell, educating myself on the Hawai'ian Language was going to be a priority.

The cost, only ten dollars for the two of us with no time limit; some might have misinterpreted this as frugal. I took it as an attempt to distance himself from any misguided impressions of his wealthy stature.

He opened the sliding glass door to the back of the house and I stood in amazement at the tropical paradise that lay before me. I tried to grab a brochure map that described the plant life, but Russell hurried me through onto the deck. We spent hours walking in the intertwined dirt paths that traversed the backyard. We followed a large Koi pond, then up through the small rolling hills, back across a wooden bridge, finally arriving back to the sounds of water running and the Koi. The five-acre retreat remained tucked back, unnoticeable from behind the frontage of the house and I wondered how many tourists drove by unaware of the serenity locked away in this garden.

Hundreds of unusual species of plants and flowers lined the passageways. Amazingly, as we stopped at each, Russell meticulously described them better than a tour guide did. On the return, we crossed again over the Koi pond's stretched arch bridge. At its heart, a waterfall, cascading down only feet away into the pond as the gardens seemed to vanish leaving nothing but an awe-inspiring marvel. The tranquil resonance of water on water along with Russell by my side was priceless. He reached for my hand while gazing deeply into my eyes. There are few moments in a person's life that reach such supreme perfection and this was one of them.

"So what did you think of this place?" he asked.

"Perfect."

"Not yet."

My heart pounded as he leaned in, sensing the energy in his hand as it flowed into my body. I was hoping, but wasn't expecting a kiss, at least not this soon. It seemed ideal, the perfect time and place to make a forever memory. A memory, which I hoped would last my entire life. His lips, soft and warm like the island sand. I swung my arms around his waist as he reciprocated, slowly elevating me off the ground like a magician. He was gentle but controlling and seemed to know exactly what I liked. There was no past, no future, just the moment, which I didn't want to end. It lasted only a minute, but time had stood still. As we released our lips, my eyes opened now lost in his, and I felt vulnerable in his arms. I knew he was my future and now knew he felt the same as our smiles lingered for the longest time. I willingly longed for another kiss, but instead basked in the memory that we created. He gently took my hand, slowly leading me across the remainder of the bridge towards the path for home.

"So, what did that woman say to you when we arrived?"

"She said, *a lover for the night*," as he kissed the back of my hand.

As we returned to the cottage, I almost wanted to thank her for planting the seed in his head. Then again, maybe he'd planned it all along. We made for the exit, when again the woman appeared from behind the curtain.

"Ho'amalu ia makou pauloa Ka'iu lani kamali'i wahine," she spoke.

She labored to make her way around the counter towards Russell and me. In her hands, a custom-made necklace with two diamond crystals the color of my birthstone; between them was what appeared to be shark's teeth. Bowing her head, she offered up the jewelry. I didn't know what to say so instead tried to offer payment. She steadfastly refused before delicately returning to the refuge of the curtains, disappearing, to the silent muttering of Hawai'ian. When we got to the car I was going to ask Russell what she had said, especially the last lingering repeating syllables *kamāli'i wahine*.

"What did that woman say?" I asked.

I stared at this precious gift while Russell started the car.

"Do you truly want to know?"

"Yes. I truly want to know!"

"She said, *Protect us all Sacred Princess*. The necklace she gave you has been passed down to generations of Warrior Princesses before they entered battle."

"I don't understand."

"You will, someday."

Russell put the car in drive as I sat confused and in love in the front seat and having one hell of a vacation.

"Are you hungry?" He asked.

"Yeah, I could use something."

"Great. I know this little café not too far from here."

He was deliberately trying to divert my attention. I was hungry, but also getting more and more confused. The conversation lulled on our way to town and in a way, it was a wonderful ambiance. I kept looking at Russell, the necklace and the view. I could still taste his lips on mine and I reached for his hand, grabbing it firmly, not wanting to let go.

Chapter 17

The remote town of Makawao was tucked away at the base of Haleakalā and set off Hali'imaile Road. The population was under a few hundred, but had traffic equivalent to any major city. This town was a stopping point for some of the bike tours coming down Haleakalā's crater. I only knew this because Tracy mentioned doing it for fun next weekend as she had already booked the tickets. We were going to see the sunrise from atop the volcano, before biking down the crater, stopping a few miles from here at the Ku'au Inn for breakfast before finally finishing at the ocean's edge.

We passed this little café as bikes and minivans lined the parking lot. For a small café, they must've done great business. Russell proceeded a little farther down the main street stopping in front of Hali'imaile General Store. The street was full of activity as tourists window-shopped while sporadically stopping for photos. Not wanting to question his decision, I exited the car and joined him on the curb.

"There's more to this place than meets the eye," he explained.

"I trust you."

"Maybe you shouldn't."

"What's that supposed to mean?"

"Nothing."

As soon as we entered the place, I understood. A high-end stylish restaurant, contrary to its implied name, it was definitely out-of-place for its locality. It had a total capacity of maybe forty people, which added to its romantic atmosphere. In the far corner, a local strummed away on his guitar singing the most beautiful Hawai'ian love songs. The exclusively set tables for two were a honeymooner's paradise. The room architecturally designed to be dim even during the day, lit only by the softness of candlelight penetrating from the centerpiece Hurricane Lamps. The hostess met us at the door motioning us to follow, which we did, past the entertainment, across the particularly small dance floor and to our table.

"This is really nice," settling myself in a chair.

"I thought you'd like this," Russell replied.

He eyed over the nearly empty room for other patrons; clearly, we'd beaten the evening crowd. Russell then ordered a bottle of wine before I had a chance to speak. I used to drink wine endlessly but had cut way back since training for marathons. I wasn't an alcoholic it was just one of the few cocktails that I found relaxed me after a long day's work. White wine was my preferred cocktail, but I'd drink red, depending on the brand.

"I hope you don't mind I ordered a bottle of Symphony Mele by Volcano Winery. A friend of mine owns the Vineyard on the Big Island. You can only get this wine in Hawai'i."

"You seem to have a lot of friends."

"I told you I spent most of my life on the islands and in my business I've made many more good friends."

"So what do you really do?"

Before he could respond, the waiter arrived with hot sweet rolls, fresh butter, and the bottle of wine. He opened it, pouring each of us a sample glass and waited patiently for our approval. I took a small sniff, and then a sip as the smell of peach, apricot, and lychee escaped leaving the lingering smell of grape. The ripened fruits had a lasting finish and a delicate sweetness. It was the finest bottle of wine I'd tasted. After giving our approval, the waiter removed himself, leaving the bottle that Russell was scrupulously browsing.

"Mele in Hawai'ian means song. This was a gold medalist in the 2004 Finger Lakes International Wine Competition," he read from the bottle.

He romantically raised his glass to mine admiring me like a work of art. Every minute I spent with him, I wondered if there was anything he didn't know. Soon after I realized he'd shifted the subject again. God was he good, but so was the wine.

"So did you find out anything about the sculptures?" I asked.

I wanted answers, now more than ever, and questionable pieces of this puzzle were coming faster than the answers.

"First, a toast," Russell raised his glass. "To an undetermined future, a perfect flower, and a princess who'd rival any *God*."

How could I resist? So I joined him in a toast. "To the man that rivals my dreams, an enigmatic man, and a passionate future."

Raising glasses, we clinked, and each took a drink. My toast didn't resonate as well as his, but the passionate future definitely had his attention. The waiter returned to take our order, which Russell placed for both of us without hesitation. At this point, I trusted him, but I still was seeking answers to at least some of my questions. The waiter rushed to the kitchen as Russell put his glass down, the trepidation in his face obvious. This was the first time I'd seen this in any man.

"What I'm going to tell you doesn't leave this place."

"Alright," I worriedly replied.

"What I'm going to say will change the way you view the world, me and your existence. Please listen with an open mind. I trust if you search your heart, a part of you will understand but listen to everything before you cast judgment."

"Okay, but you're kind of scaring me a little."

He took another drink of wine before continuing, surveying my facial gestures. This date was rapidly taking a bizarre twist and for once, maybe Tracy was right, he is crazy. I sure can pick'em.

"Those sculptures, at the house, are from an ancient tribe alright. I've not seen anything like them in over a thousand years. The material is not found in Hawai'i, in fact it's not found on Earth."

"What do you mean Earth?"

I about choked on my wine causing a scene as my mouth resisted the urge to yell *'Check Please'*, but I did promise to wait before making a verdict. The day started out strange and was only getting stranger. Maybe I was dreaming. God, please let this just be a dream.

"Those sculptures are from a race of beings called the Draconians. Originally, from the planet Alpha Draconis in the Draco Constellation, they have moved since then throughout the Galaxy. I've read about them, but personally never seen them. I had to corroborate they were genuine and not some form of reproduction. I don't know how or why they are in front of Jim's house. I'm still waiting for that information to come in. Maybe you can shed some light on them."

The seriousness in his face was proof of his honesty.

"Are you saying they're alien?"

"Yes, I am."

I always believed we weren't alone or at least, based on mathematics, thought as a species we had to be arrogant to think otherwise. My friend Scott constantly preached about such things, but I brushed him off as eccentric. I was going to try to keep an open mind.

"How do you know for sure?"

"You know how I said my company does several government projects. It has one client in particular, the U.S. Military. A majority of our business is done out at Groom Lake."

He vehemently scanned the room for prying ears while I sat puzzled.

"You mean so called Area 51?"

"Yes. My company is currently working on many top secret projects at the base…one in particular."

His voice stalled allowing the blurred information to register. I remember watching a documentary with Scott years ago about a former employee claiming reverse engineering of a UFO. For a while, Rachel, Nevada, which resided just outside Las Vegas, developed the title, UFO Capital of the World. While the world wondered, most of us locals wrote it off as a joke and the story soon died except for the real hard-core crazy UFO enthusiasts. My face echoed, *real crazy*, back towards him.

"You don't mean UFO's."

"Exactly!"

He wasn't joking as the seriousness showed in his eyes.

"If that's the case, won't you get in trouble talking to me about this? I mean many of those so called crazy's say whistle blowers have had their lives ruined. Some supposedly even killed for talking."

I tried calling his bluff, because dream or no dream it was starting to get a bit much.

"Erica, you're not dreaming," Russell paused for effect, "and yes, I can get in trouble. I also feel that your life could be in danger. So this is why I'm telling you." He grabbed my hands. "I do have feelings for you. I've had feelings for you since we first met although I cannot protect you 24 hours a day."

I felt the openness in his touch and saw my fear turn to love in his eyes for he was serious, deadly serious.

"What kind of danger do you think I'm in?"

"I'm still working on that. It'll take a few days, but have you experienced anything strange since you've been on the island?"

"This morning was strange."

I explained in detail what occurred earlier in the day. He grabbed a pen, then a napkin and started taking notes. He asked me careful questions and became more apprehensive with each response. I finished to a vibrating tone as my phone shook the table. Looking down a text from Tracy appeared '*how's the date*' and I quickly texted her back, '*great... story tomorrow*'. Russell was so preoccupied writing notes he didn't even notice the brief interruption. It was girl talk anyhow.

"So what do you think?" I asked.

He gathered all his notes, tucking them away in his pocket as the waiter arrived with our dinner. I loved fish and you don't get any fresher than here on the islands. He had ordered a local special, grilled opakapaka, spread over a large Greek salad with a light vinaigrette dressing. We silently stared at one another as the waiter grated fresh cheese over both of our salads before leaving. He couldn't have gone away fast enough.

"The car you've supposedly seen sounds like the **Men In Black**," he proceeded. "If they're paying attention to you than that's not good. As for the lights and conversation at the house, well without hearing the conversation I can't help you, it might be nothing. Then again," shrugging his shoulders. "Regardless, it's safe to say, you're going to need to watch your back while you're here."

"Great," I replied sarcastically. "That's not comforting."

I'd forgotten to mention the files in Tracy's drawer, but didn't think at the time it was anything. This day had been nothing but a roller coaster ride of emotions. One for the journal. We didn't say much to each other over the next half an hour, only enjoyed the meal, the companionship, and the atmosphere as our heads both went a mile a minute; universally concerned for my well-being. I'm just an executive secretary, I thought, but felt that was going to change sooner than later. Russell, wanting to salvage the rest of the evening, had motioned the local entertainment to our table.

"Do you know IZ's song '*In This Life*?'"

The local smiled, returned to his guitar, and waited for Russell's cue. Standing up from the table, he reached for my hand, pulling me to the center of the dance floor. Russell's sudden nod triggered the musician to begin serenading us from the stage. Briefly, everything melted away as we danced to this beautiful song. Although, Russell towered over me, he floated across the dance floor as if on air. He was a regular Fred Astaire. I followed his lead, which was tough. Thankfully, he could control me like a marionette and even though my life was getting outlandish, I didn't want this date to end.

Chapter 18

The sun was starting to set as we made our way out of the restaurant. Reluctantly, I wanted to hear more, but truthfully, I wasn't ready to go home. The car ride was quiet, but romantic. The car's top down displayed the true beauty of this island. It was still somewhat warm, the skyline lit with not quite a full moon as the stars moved with every turn of the road. With a new appreciation for what played in the vastness of space, I let my mind wander. We were almost home, when the recognition this date would soon end fashioned a sadness in my heart as well as more questions. I didn't know if I was prepared to hear the answers tonight.

Turning on to South Kihei Road, Russell pulled into a gravel parking lot on the north side Keawakapu Beach. The few cars parked belonged to the neighboring condominiums lining the shores, as well from people who were watching the sunset from the beach. I thought that maybe the night wasn't ending as the car came to a stop. Russell popped the trunk, headed to the rear of the car and pulled out a blanket. I followed, unsure of his plans, but hopeful for the best. Leisurely, we made our way down to the beach with the sand still warm from the day's sun. There's nothing like a romantic walk on the beach at night with the surf, the moon, and the distant sounds of Hawai'ian music playing from entertainment along the boardwalk. I wanted Russell to talk first, but was totally okay with his silence. Being with him, holding his hand had its own set of unspoken words. We made our way as far as we could down the beach to our own remote secluded paradise. He positioned the blanket on the sand far enough away from the lightly rolling incoming waves. A sea turtle lingered not far away, surveying our every action, but not bothered enough to move.

"Do you think he'll mind if we share this spot?" It was Russell's take on humor.

"I think we can outrun him," I said, smiling back.

I sat down on the blanket, laidback and took in the stars. The smell of fresh lavender emanating from the newly washed blanket reminded me of the Lei I'd received earlier in the day. Russell made his way down next to me and joined in the stargazing.

"Where are these aliens from?" I asked.

"You can't see their star from here with the naked eye. I can take you up to the observatory sometime and show you. If you'd like," leaning to his side in my direction. "So you believe me than?"

"I don't know what I believe," rolling in towards him.

"Just promise me you won't discuss this with anyone, for your safety and mine." He gazed severely into my eyes, all the way down to my soul.

"I promise."

With that, I rolled over on top of him trying to rekindle the fire from the kiss we shared earlier in the day. It wasn't long before an inferno engulfed my body as he fit perfectly against me and little by little, I gave up control. Kissing his neck, the smell of his cologne was an aphrodisiac, and only added fuel to the bonfire. He was alive, feeling the beat of his heart against my chest. He rolled over on top of me, gently nibbling at my neck as his pleasure grew in other regions. His body outweighed me, and the helplessness of being beneath him only increased my desire. I wanted him absolutely, body and soul, as our bodies grinded in perfect harmony. I'd never made love on the beach, especially with an individual I still thought a stranger, but the heat between us was intolerable. I wanted to rip his clothes off and give myself utterly to him as his hands explored my body in ways no one had ever done. My hands stroked the muscles on his back, barely able to reach the climax of his spine, and I felt myself quickly giving over total control. I ensued to show my gratitude when his phone rang. He casually peeked at the blue hue that danced at the edge of the blanket.

"I have to talk this call," he said.

My body was on fire inside and out, as the feel of my skin warmed from his full-bodied touch. He removed himself from the blanket only to walk a few feet away. The conversation lasted a minute, but the intense look in his face as he returned to my side said it all.

"You got to go, don't you?"

"Yes. I am sorry."

"Can you tell me about it?"

"There're things I can't tell you for many reasons, but mainly for your safety. I hope you understand."

"I guess...for now."

There was a remoteness in his eyes as I helped fold the blanket. He grabbed my hand, pulling me in for one last kiss before leading the way back towards the car. He saw the sadness on my face, not from his lack of disclosure, but for bringing me so close to ecstasy, and unable to fulfill my desires. Truthfully, I didn't care how complex his life was because I felt alive around him, like our souls were destined to be together. I couldn't wait for our next date. I looked forward to seeing the observatory and learning more about him plus this was getting thrilling. I wondered if this is how a spy felt like with all this hidden secrecy, maybe that's why everyone loved James Bond. I was falling in love with Russell. He was my own 007.

The gravel parking lot appeared too soon as most of the cars had moved on and so had the setting sun. My hand tightened around his as my feet slowed, attempting to linger in this moment. However, those feelings were short-lived as we got within range of his car. I directed Russell's attention to the parking lot's far corner to what appeared to be the identical car from my earlier encounter. Its silhouette stood out against the darkness while a nearby streetlight barely cast enough radiance for a detailed confirmation. My eyes were slowly adjusting from the darkness of the beach, but I was convinced it was the same vehicle. A similar feeling from this morning, one of ultimate fear, ravaged my senses.

"Russell, that's the car I saw earlier in the day."

"Are you sure?"

"Almost positive."

Russell dropped his hand from mine.

"Erica, get in the car now!"

"What's going on?"

"Just get in!" He demanded hastily.

The distant revving of an engine suddenly drowned the outlying sounds of crashing waves. The car's lights remained off, as if waiting to pounce on its unsuspecting prey, and I made, without hesitation, to the passenger seat. Russell watched the car intensely as I entered then firmly secured the door in his wake. Before my seat belt clicked locked, he was in the car, had started it, and began pulling away. The smell of burnt rubber from the spinning tires never hit my nose as the parking lot vanished. I managed to peel myself off the fabric, still trying to catch my breath. He sped up, continually checking his rear-view mirror for signs of life. We were two miles from Jim's house, but I felt the acceleration and urgency in the engine while sporadically checking to get a glimpse of our pursuers. As we crossed a brightly lit stretch of road, the faint, glossed reflection of the car materialized. It shadowed us at a secure reserve with its headlights still quenched. How they maneuvered on this street without lights was astonishing to me.

We arrived at the main gate, entered the code, and pulled in enough to allow it to secure safely. Russell patiently waited to see if the car would pass by the house. It vigilantly rolled past the gate, the same as this morning and then suddenly disappeared down the dark street. The street was a dead end so I kept an eye out expecting a possible return as Russell pulled up to the foyer. It didn't return, at least not yet.

Russell wanted to conclude the date as if nothing happened. His face was as calm and charming as when he first arrived. He chivalrously made his way to my door, opening it and helping me out. He walked me to the door, again eyeing the sculptures in passing, which now held a new eeriness for me. My heart rate had finally calmed down as the sounds of a high-speed chase once again replaced the distant sounds of approaching ocean waves.

"I had a pleasant evening Erica. I'm sorry it ended this way."

"You really know how to stimulate a girl in more ways than you know," I just smiled.

"You should see me at my best."

He gave me a gentle kiss, but seemed preoccupied, as he quickly returned to the car.

"I can't wait!" I called to him down the walkway.

"For what?"

"To see you at your best."

"You will."

I didn't know if I should take that as foreplay or a serious threat. Either way, it saddened me to see him go, as a part of me wanted to run to him, invite him to stay but then I remembered his call...

I became overly concerned for his safety as I watched him roll down the driveway, but somehow felt this was all in a day's work for him. He watchfully pulled out on to the street as if in anticipation of an ambush. The gate hadn't even closed before once again the black sedan dropped into his draft. There was a thunderous acceleration, a squeal of tires and burnt rubber smoke poured over the wall. I ran to the front gate, but too petrified with fear to open it. I lingered on the metal gate like a caged animal until the sounds of the chase had scattered in the distance. I peeled myself from the bars as the stench of newly burnt rubber began burning at my nose and eyes. I was hoping to go to bed with the smell of Russell's cologne still on me; instead, I'd have to settle for the wretched smell of rubber and tar.

Considering recent events, the house seemed more alluring to me right now. I couldn't wait to get into the house and lock the door behind me. No sooner did the lock click register when from atop the stairs came Colby. His newly groomed fur smelled of baby powder and the enthusiastic greeting was a welcome to the ending day. He was now the second love of my life, yet in many ways, he was still an equal. Pakile always met guests at the door, but tonight I wasn't going to complain as I ran upstairs with Colby in chase. I jumped on the bed and turned to watch as Colby made the leap. His legs, folded up underneath him like landing gear as he slid across the comforter on his belly right into my side. I didn't know how to take this day, as in some ways it was magnificent, however in others a pure nightmare. Little did I know that my perception of what constituted a nightmare was only just beginning.

Chapter 19

December 28, 2009 Early Morning

The following series of events I obtained from rechecking my journal entries and from the intermittent daymare flashes, which I still get to this day. I know there are still gaps in my recollections and I fear someday they'll present themselves. I've considered seeing a psychiatrist and undergoing regression hypnosis in an attempt to fill in those omitted moments. However, I fear those memories may be more traumatizing than was already consciously accessible. For that reason alone, I'm holding off chasing the truth. I wish for the strength to adequately cope and pray I don't suffer a psychotic collapse.

It took me a while to fall asleep, my body willing but the mind not. Images of Russell and I on the beach kept flashing through my head, intertwined with the images of an unanswered mystery. Colby had already fallen asleep at my feet and was snoring away. I tried relaxing my mind, calling on the knowledge of self-hypnosis and meditation gained years ago. Finally, from pure exhaustion, my body began gently drifting into a deep state of unconsciousness.

At some point during the early morning, I violently awoke from what I can only describe as a deepened dream state as an intellectual presence descended throughout the room. I felt awake, scanning the room in slow motion, but couldn't focus my eyes as everything appeared in a fog. Colby, barely recognizable, was still asleep at the foot of the bed. That much I knew. I thought it was a dream, but it felt genuine, as if a different plane of existence crossed into my reality.

Out of the corner of my half-awakened-eyes, in the darkest recesses of the room, I saw movement. Filled with fear, my heart began to race, as my mind overflowed with unimaginable images. My body was paralyzed, unable to investigate, as my deaf ears listened to a voice whisper through my mind. The tone of voice, although calming, wasn't mine and cautiously repeated, *'Everything was going to be alright'*.

I managed to rotate my head slightly towards the window, where a blinding blue incandescent light grew brighter by the second. The voice in my head repeated, *'Relax, we are here to help'*. The paralyzing terror and apprehension swelled around my chest, but somehow suppressed from coming to the forefront of my psyche. I had to be dreaming and wanted to wake, but I couldn't.

At this point, the external light became blinding. I closed my eyes and tried to realign my head with the ceiling. Upon reopening them, my now dilated pupils, tried to adjust to the light that currently engulfed the entire room. Colby remained motionless. Had it not been a dream, the light would've definitely awoken him, but the sensation of panic didn't subside as my heart unrelentingly raced and my breathing amplified. I thought I was going to hyperventilate and again tried closing my eyes. I was hopeful this was all going to go away, but it didn't, as the sounds of movement in the room only intensified these suspicions. I tried to look around the room as faint, out of focus, shadows moved freely around the bed. The immense light penetrated so intensely the walls began to lose their definition and I no longer could distinguish between the walls, windows, and blue light. At least three entities had manifested themselves at the foot of my bed. I call them entities, because the visible outlines were not of a human composition. My mind reached for answers, but rationally couldn't arrive at a conclusion, at least not a comfortable one. The panic was becoming even more paralyzing than the numbness my body already felt. I felt as if I was drowning on my last breath of air.

The tallest of the entities reached out, gingerly touching the tip of my toe and within seconds, the trepidation I felt was replaced with a recessed calm. An androgynous voice again repeated, *'Relax, we are here to help.'* The tallest one vibrated the quintessential embodiment of male. However, these entities weren't human, so was it truly male?

"We are not here to hurt you."

This time the voice spoke clearly but systematically and rung not in my mind but from the bed's perimeter. You would've thought their comments comforting. They weren't! Somehow, I knew they were controlling my mind or at least altering my sense of reality. They were removing my fear and replacing it with false memories. I tried to speak, even scream, but couldn't form the words, as my animated mouth was voiceless. This was, by far, the scariest thing I'd ever dreamed in my life. The best theory I arrived at, my subconscious was manifesting metaphors based on today's past events. I half expected Russell, any minute to appear in clarity, rescue me, and then make love to me.

"Russell is not coming, but we will take good care of you," intensely the voice clearly spoke.

Then a bizarre sensation passed throughout my body, as if each molecule began vibrating at an elevated frequency. The shadowed entities watched from the foot of the bed. Excluding the tall one, the others scarcely managed to rise above sheet level. Their heads dominating compared to their emaciated bodily features, but that was all I could distinguish.

I felt as if my essence was leaving my body and I wondered; *am I dying in my sleep?* I wanted to close my eyes but couldn't muster the strength. I even tried praying to God, but for the life of me couldn't remember the damn words even with all the years of Catholic school. I thought; *this must be God coming to take me away.*

"We are not Gods. Just relax."

A different toned voice clearly entered my head. I could tell, even without seeing their faces, it had originated from the middle entity.

I watched, as my body materialized slowly through the blankets like a ghost. In my ears, a faint pulsing sound echoed, as my body floated slightly above the bed. The room's bright blue light replaced with a warmer orangey-white glow as the shadowed entities had now shifted to the side of my bed. My body gradually began turning clockwise, as if an illusionist was levitating me on stage. However, I was no eager assistant at this point, but instead a vulnerable and powerless victim. My body floated above the floor with my head now facing the windows. I could see Colby still sound asleep. The pulsing sound weakened, leaving a vacuum as the sounds of the rolling morning waves vanished. They quickly were replaced with my quickening pulse, which painfully pierced my ears.

Once more, the pulsing returned, as my body passed effortlessly through the solid wooden wall of my room. Metaphysically I knew that wasn't possible, that this had to be a dream, but presently I knew I was conscious. My body was at this time hovering two stories over the grounds of the backyard. I was unable to focus on my surroundings as a bright white light illuminated above, surrounded by the intermittent circular flashings of a bluish violet outer halo. I tried catching my breath as the beach air vanished, as if someone or something had punched a void bluntly into the atmosphere. My body ascended towards the light like a dying soul. The entities departed as I conceded to the roofline of the house. Terrified of heights, a childhood phobia I was never able to vanquish, my eyes begged to close for fear of falling. I wasn't going to fall, I knew they wouldn't let that happen, it was just an automatic defense. The ionized air began to smell of burning flesh, which began to make me feel nauseous.

Time became irrelevant, as my body's raised essences became engulfed in the approaching luminosity. I wanted vehemently for my eyes to press shut in the hopes all this would go away. The whitish-orange, scorching light, that bore down outside on my now half-closed eyelids was slowly replaced with darkness. Then by a faintly dimmed room light. My body no longer levitated as the spine of my back felt a chillingly cold hardness. It definitely wasn't a bed, as it felt smooth to the touch, like a stainless steel slab. I wondered again if I had died and was laying in the coroner's office. I wanted wholly to open my eyes, but feared the picture that might manifest in display over me. My entire life passed from beginning to end in my mind with goals I'd accomplished, ambition I hadn't and aspiration I'd wished I'd done. I begged, *I don't want to die.*

"You are not dead. Relax. We are here to help you," the calming voice returned echoing in my ears.

I gradually opened my eyes, my pupils increasingly adjusting to the lower light levels. In this space, at least two entities now stood over me, and although different, there were odd likenesses to the entities from my room. They towered above me and I estimated their height to be well over eight feet. Their body mass, anorexic compared to the domineering features of their enlarged craniums. I blinked several times which helped to bring their faces into focus and as their bodies began to register within my brain, I felt compelled to scream. My mouth mimicked the action, but no voice, just a deafening silence. I unsuccessfully attempted to thrash about, as I demanded freedom from this paralysis. Conscious control reestablished over my body, but only enough to experience the controlled pain emanating from the restraints on my legs, arms, and chest.

"Please relax. We are here to help you."

A frail, cold, elongated hand rested on my forehead and again my fears subsided with the thought, *we are here to help*. In truth, that line was getting irritating. My nightmarish entities began to animate like something out of a B Rated Sci-Fi film. The light gray color, with just a hint of green, made their skin not quite transparent. Their heads seemed entirely out of proportion to their emaciated bodies, supported only by an extended skeletal neck. The nose, a minute raised triangle, was just about unnoticeable in the dim light. The mouth seemed nothing more than a vertical incision with no visible lips and the ears nearly fully recessed into the upper cranium. The lifeless black eyes conquered the facial features with no noticeable body hair. My sense of smell returned to a distinct foul stench emanating from their bodies. A sort of decaying flesh smell or maybe an unbathed odor but with a strongly sulfur undertone. I was about to gag, wishing my sense of smell hadn't returned, as again a simple touch to my forehead and the putrid appalling smell dissipated.

This phenomenon made it clear to me their obvious ability to control my mind surpassed my inferior understanding of the human body. I tried to inspect the room for some sort of reference point or at the very least, the orientation of my captives. My head slightly pivoted left to right as my eyes strained to focus. At this point, from my restricted mobility, I managed to make out no more than two large; I had to assume aliens, in this confined room. The room bowed in all visible directions and felt isolated, with no detectable suggestion of an exit. On the adjacent wall, a small panel of visibly pulsating, multicolored lights briefly caught my attention. This panel was set in a dark gray wall, which illuminated with a web of flowing whitish-blue light as if alive.

My surveillance broke as an enormously bizarre apparatus appeared over my head and gradually descended. The vibrating tone deepened and intensified as it lowered, hovering only feet above the heart of my body. A whoosh of white visible mist shot out, encasing my entire body and then at once dissipated. I felt as if my body had just undergone a form of decontamination or sterilization. I had lost the sanctuary of my clothes, but didn't' know it as beneath me the coldness of the stainless steel slab intensified. The naked vulnerability exceeded that of a gynecologist office, which I never considered achievable.

"This will not hurt."

The voice telepathically echoed in my head as neither of the entities mouths wavered. Extending from the hanging centerpiece, one of the entities had taken what appeared to be some kind of prehistoric drill attached to a clear tube. I watched the device approach my face as the tip emitted an orange glow while a strange fluid evenly flowed down the clear tubing. I struggled, trying to scream, but it fell on deaf ears. Gently, my head slanted back at an angle as I felt the device extend up my right nostril before forcefully protruding into the recesses of my brain. A warm liquefied solvent injected painlessly into my head as my skull felt as if it were inflating. I felt as if my brain wished to explode out of my scalp. I watched the tubing once again go clear and the device delicately removed.

The second entity advanced grabbing for another device from the centerpiece, slender in width but elongated with an attachment. My eyes focused, screaming, on the incoming hardware, "*No! Don't!*" They wouldn't respond to my thoughts as again my body became immobile. The attachment resembled one of those tools used to grab light bulbs from extended heights. As it approached my face, it opened and closed testing its mechanics.

"Relax. We are not here to hurt you," reiterated the psychic voice.

The tool then aggressively plunged back into my right nostril expanding it to double its size. A small, glowing, round orb at once yanked from my head attached within the grappling hooks. While the gathering entities examined their find they permitted me the experience of the uncontrollable dripping of this liquid from my oozing left nostril. The pressure in my head gradually normalized and my body again was free to struggle. I chose not to as my head unhurriedly rose revealing the nakedness of my entire body.

The fastenings around my ankles and legs had detached and I sought to kick the sons of bitches back, but conscious control hadn't returned from the waist down. My legs were slowly spreading as the shorter Grey reached for an elongated cable with a fairly long needle-tipped-end that penetrated the side of my stomach and within seconds swelled my abdomen. I had the outward appearance of being five months pregnant. The pressure on my stretched out skin was piercing. My uterus was expanding to its maximum capacity, which set off spasmodic and painful cramps mimicking labor pains.

"What are you doing?" I mentally asked.

I tried communicating my displeasure with the procedure, but there was no response. They continued, emotionless, and without concern for my well-being while from above they brought back yet another tool. This had an attached hose and again an unusual low frequency tone pulsed deeper as it approached. It reminded me of an embruosphaktes device from medieval times, yet with a futuristic sadistic twist. It came within reach of my inner thigh and I screamed within my mind as loud as I could.

"**NO!**"

Whether intentional or not, the throbbing, almost ripping sensation, extended through my lower regions. I wanted to close my eyes, ready to lose consciousness, unable to handle this nightmare any longer. I vaguely remember something retrieved from my body. I do remember watching in horror as my stomach returned to normal. Suddenly, unconstrained, a spontaneous impulse to vomit overcame my body as my sides uncontrollably cramped. I turned to my right in convulsions, expelling a dark, thick, black fluid to the floor. Lastly, my sides and stomach strained to the point of detachment as I reached the point of dry heaves. My eyes watered as the last of the repulsive fluid dripped from my mouth. Again, a hand touched my forehead opening my thoughts.

"You will now be returned. Thank you for your cooperation."

"Cooperation? You mean violation," directing my thoughts ruthlessly in its direction.

Before my thought was even finished, a serene sense of calm engulfed every inch of my body. Once more, whether it was the trauma of the event or their deliberate response, I quickly lost consciousness. I eventually awoke; somehow back in my bed with Colby licking my face. Morning arrived and the absolute horror of the night a not so distant memory. I tried to wrap my mind around last night's proceedings and recapture my bearings. This had to have been a dream. My tired body fought the urge to return to the pillow's comfort, afraid of a relapse into the nightmare. I laid in the bed, patting Colby, trying to recall specific details of the dream. It was vague and getting ambiguous by the minute. I sprang from the bed to write in my journal before all traces of this nightmare scattered. My stomach muscles convulsed as if I'd overdone crunches, dropping me to the floor, and I now questioned if it had been a dream. The alarm clock read 5 a.m. as the sun gently warmed the room to the beginning of another beautiful day. Rapidly, I put pen to paper to capture my fading memories as pages upon pages filled my journal. In time, the details rapidly dwindled.

Shortly after, I headed to the bathroom and stared at myself in the mirror with water little by little dripping off my chin. Again, I threw water on my face taking a deeper gaze into the mirror. This time catching the glimmered reflection of my now stopped watch. I turned to see the facial features directly and paused. It had stopped at 3 a.m. exactly, the battery clearly dead. I thought, weird I just had it replaced before leaving the mainland. I removed my watch, set it on the sink, and slowly examined the pain coming from my stomach. There was a small reddish scar on the left side of my stomach no bigger than the top of a pencil's eraser. I was positive the scar hadn't been there before last night. I could be magnifying the situation, but the truth was my abs hurt. If this experience was real, what the hell had happened to me last night?

I craved breakfast and felt famished as Colby entered the bathroom to remind me he was, too. It was official; I wasn't enjoying this vacation. What I thought should've been the trip of my lifetime had turned into the worst waking nightmare I'd yet experienced. However, that still was yet to come.

Chapter 20

Throwing on some clothes, I halfheartedly raced Colby down to the kitchen. Still a little dazed, the smell of the already brewed coffee was making me nauseous. My unrelenting need for a cup hastily halted by the greater need to get a bite in my stomach. Colby's food was already in his bowl, an evident sign Pakile was already up and about the house. Colby wasted no time devouring his breakfast while I considered mine.

Opening the refrigerator, I still questioned the certainty of last night and tried shaking the imagery from my head. What I craved was sustenance for breakfast as my eyes scanned the refrigerator. Everything looked enticing, but at the same time unappetizing. Finally, I settled on a plain bagel, void of any butter or cream cheese.

Pakile entered from the outside kitchen door, probably finishing his morning rounds of the property. I didn't want to deal with his *bullshit* this morning so decided I'd try to be pleasant. I greeted him in the perkiest voice my body could muster while waiting for my bagel to finish toasting.

"Morning, Pakile."

"You look tired, Miss Jones. Didn't sleep well?"

Although phrased as a question the underlying tone made it appear as if a factual statement. Great, we're already heading off on the wrong foot this morning.

"Actually, not feeling so hot," I gathered a fake smile.

If for some reason he knew anything, I wasn't going to give him the satisfaction of making last night's horrible experience known.

"Sorry to hear that. Perhaps a nice walk on the beach will brighten up your day. It's supposed to be another beautiful day in paradise."

There was that underlying tone again, this time accompanied by a coy smile, which struck me to the core.

"That's my plan," snapping back. "Right after I finish breakfast."

He approached me and the coffeemaker as his bitter sense of lifelessness turned my stomach. I refocused my effort on retrieving my bagel after quickly letting Colby outside. With my freshly toasted breakfast in tow, I sat down at the kitchen's island. Pakile promptly turned with a cup in hand.

"Coffee?"

The thought of taking a sip made my stomach turn, but he wasn't going to earn a sign of weakness from me, at least not this morning.

"Yeah, that'd be great."

The approaching coffee, with its freshly filtered smell, already agitated the backside of my throat. I needed to take a taste knowing full well he was watching as he hastily worked about the kitchen. The warm cup felt like lead as it rose to my mouth, taking in a small amount and swallowing. It was all I could do to keep it down.

"Good coffee."

He turned and smiled with his face expressing as much emotion as a corpse. After pouring a larger cup for himself, he continued towards the dining room stopping briefly, as he passed, as if forgetting something.

"If you need the limo, Lulani will be back shortly. He's gone to pick-up Miss Miller at the airport."

He then departed to my relief. Crap, that's right! Tracy would be home this morning. I wanted to copy the files I found yesterday in her room for Russell. I debated telling her about last night. I was unsure what had happened myself, however chatting about it with someone might help me establish I wasn't crazy.

I did a swift check on Colby, even thought he was securely in the yard, before immediately running up stairs. I grabbed the files from the drawer, making for the communal accessed computer and printer in the study. I fired up the processor hoping it wouldn't take long. Altogether, seventeen pages zipped through the scanner. I quickly returned the originals and hid my copy by taping the folder to the back of my toilet. I figured they'd be safely out-of-the-way, at least until I could get them to Russell.

I rejoined Colby, who waited patiently outside for his morning walk on the beach. My energy level gradually returned as the breakfast, little by little digested. Even the coffee in my hand became appealing. I'd brought my phone with me in the hopes of contacting Russell. Searching my recently added contact list, I clicked on his name, and waited as the phone rang.

"Yes," a female voice replied on the other end.

"Is Russell there?" I asked.

"May I ask whose calling?"

"Yes, tell him it's Erica."

"Erica who?"

"I'm sorry. Erica Jones."

"Just a moment, Miss Jones."

I hoped this wasn't his girlfriend or worse a wife; maybe he just had a service. It sounded professional, definitely a service. *Why do you always go to the negative, Erica?*

There was a short pause, followed by a familiar rejecting click then the dial tones emptiness returned. Did she disconnect me? I occasionally did the same thing when transferring calls for my boss. I hit redial. The phone rang about eight times, until an automated voice picked-up *'Sorry, this number is no longer in service'*. I hung up, checked the number, and dialed again only to get the same message. I was concerned now for Russell's well-being, as a million thoughts flared through my mind. Did the so-called **Men In Black** catch up with him? Did the Government learn about our conversation and terminate his employment? Maybe he had no intent of seeing me again. Questions kept piling up and I was no closer to the truth. Of course, I wondered what justified the truth and would I recognize it if I saw it?

After spending a relaxing hour on the beach, Colby and I made our way back to the house, entering through the kitchen. Colby had managed to avoid getting himself drenched and ruining his newly groomed image, which I took as a sign of good things to come today. Lulani had returned from the airport and was enjoying his coffee, while Pakile prepared breakfast. I assumed this was their daily routine and hoped to glide by them with minimum chitchat. I made it as far as the dining room door when Lulani's voice stopped me as his eyes refused to leave his coffee.

"Miss Jones. Miss Miller is upstairs. She wanted me to inform you…if you were up for it…she planned on making the drive to Hana today."

"Thank you. I'm on my way there right now."

I turned with no hesitation as Colby ran ahead, already making for the upstairs. I have to admit, the two of them were starting to creep me out. I wanted to speak with Tracy about my dream and get her take. Although Tracy is an executive secretary with an MBA, she minored in psychology, which came in useful dealing with her boss and his high profile clients. I didn't fancy being on a couch as someone psychoanalyzed me, but she was a trusted friend, and we shared everything, or so I thought. Colby announced my arrival and no sooner did I enter the study, Tracy appeared running from her bedroom to give me a hug.

"Pakile said you weren't feeling good," she looked me over; "You look tired."

I'd hoped I looked better than I felt; guess not. That's what friends are for….

"A little tired, but the walk on the beach perked me up. How was your trip to O'ahu?"

"Boring! A bunch of stiffs in suits. Who, I might add, didn't appreciate a power trip from a woman, but I survived," she dragged me to the couch, "So, how was your date with Russell? I want details!"

She was excessively peppy for me this morning.

"It was interesting. Let's just say he knows how to make a first date memorable." A schoolgirl smile engulfed my face as the thought of him reenergized me. "I tried calling him earlier, but the number says it's disconnected or something."

"Maybe you just wrote down the wrong number. I'm sure he'll call. I sensed chemistry between the two of you right from the start," enthusiastically she jumped from her seat, "so you're coming with me to Hana, right? And I want all the dirt from last night."

"Yes. I need a shower first."

"Okay, let's say an hour. I've got to brief Jim on yesterday's meeting anyways so that should give you plenty of time to get ready."

The excitement in her movement was obvious and I don't believe she would've taken *"No"* for an answer anyways. The thought of a hot shower sure sounded appealing as we embraced one more time before heading to our own separate retreats.

The road to Hana is an all-day excursion. I thought so much for running today, not as if I planned on it, at least not with my stomach feeling edgy. I wondered if Tracy had gotten her run in, knowing her, probably.

The path to the shower was next to impossible as Colby, attached to my hip, insistently sniffed by my sacred areas, obviously bothered. Dogs have a sixth sense or at least a heightened sense of smell and I didn't know what he was thinking, but wish I had.

I set the water temperature to the hottest my skin could take without scalding and as my eyes closed images of those beings flashed, paralyzing me relentlessly. I shifted focus on images of Russell and I on the beach trying to suppress the nightmares. It took a while, but at long last, Russell's manifested body was in the shower with me, his hands caressing my body and now I didn't want to get out. I heard his voice, *"Please, for your safety and mine; tell no one"*, it was as if he was here, in the shower. I opened my eyes, half expecting to see him standing across from me naked as my pruned hands showed signs it was time to get out.

I dried off, getting dressed in record fashion having lost track of time in the shower. Tracy always ran delayed by fifteen minutes so I still had time to check my phone. I had no messages. I again called Russell's number, no change, still disconnected. I came to the verdict I would keep Russell's history in the dark to Tracy. She'd hear about the romantic parts of the date, but I'd exclude as much information as possible without ruining the story. I further decided not to burden her with my dream, assuming that's all it was, a dream. Why spoil Tracy's vacation with such an outlandish narrative?

Tracy entered my room, knocking first, as I finished lacing my boots. There're many breathtaking waterfalls on the road to Hana based on our map, the only problem, most required a modest hike to witness their magnificence. Tracy had her boots on too, so I knew she planned the same thing.

"You ready to go?" She asked with great pep.

"Yeah, let me get my camera and purse."

I searched the room franticly for my camera while Colby watched with sadness from the bed. With everything we had planned, I was beginning to second-guess my decision to bring him to Hawai'i. It wasn't any different from the hours I worked, but still the look on his face was breaking my heart. I finally found my camera, apparently already in my purse, then gave Colby a great big kiss and hug.

"Okay, I'm ready."

"You want to drive or shall I?" Tracy asked.

It was a question, but she knew I couldn't drive a stick.

"You. I'll ride shotgun."

I was feeling better, thank god, being the drive alone was a couple hours each way not including the hikes. It was an awfully long time to be in a moving vehicle feeling nauseated. I made sure my phone was accessible, in hopes Russell would call. Since I arrived, I hadn't enjoyed much of the island or my vacation, however, I was determined to amend that; starting with this expedition.

Chapter 21

The road to Hana reminded me of why I sought to come to Hawai'i in the first place. The fifty-two plus mile ride, although long, especially on the return trip home, covered some of the most breathtaking scenery. We reset our odometer at mile marker sixteen, which officially began ground zero or the start of the road to Hana. The road narrowly traversed all the way through the tropical countryside. The six hundred plus curves, no exaggeration, and roughly fifty-six bridges, some only one lane wide, forced us to wait for frequent traffic. With elevations occasionally reaching more than a thousand feet with no visible guardrails, this was not for the faint of heart. If not for periodically stopping, my motion sickness would've gotten the better of me. The stops encompassed earthly waterfall features of biblical beauty only Mother Nature could present. The drive, as a whole was well worth it!

At mile-marker thirty-one stood the Hana Lava Tube. Tracy had pre-booked this engagement since they didn't allow walk-ins. Thankful I didn't opt out for the day, because to walk through this tube was like taking a step back thirty thousand years in time. That's how long in had remained untouched by man in this tropical rain forest. In a way, unfortunately this natural arrangement had turned into a popular tourist attraction, although it did educate you on the powerfulness of the planet. The extremely cold darkness of the underground bothered me slightly as occasionally the damp walls appeared to have eyes that followed us through the lengthened cavern. The periodic dripping of filtered water drumming the tubes' rock base only urged you to advance expeditiously. I would definitely not recommend the adventure to someone who was claustrophobic.

Wai'anapanapa State Park and its Black Sand Beach were one of the two attractions on my bucket list. The delicately crushed volcanic rock was a must, especially after witnessing it firsthand for myself. A local had shown us a trail leading to a freshwater cave that some considered a heiau. My body internally vibrated standing inside as if a higher reason entitled me to be here at that very moment. The reflected illumination on the water from the cave gave off the outward show of red blood. Legend had it, a Princess and her handmaiden hid in the cave from her wicked husband. After finding them both, he killed them in the water. When the water turns red in the cave, it's said to be their blood's essence returning, but it actually is millions of tiny red shrimp that breed in the waters of the cave. It was miraculous to view in person. I left feeling there was more to the hidden cave than met the eye.

The second, on my to-do list, was Waimoku Falls a spectacular four hundred and fifty foot waterfall, passively tucked away into the landscape. A modest, two-mile hike, from the Pools of 'Ohe'o on the Pipiwai Trail and in reality, a short climb to view such an impressive piece, one of Nature's true engineering marvels. Along the way, we also passed Makahiku Falls, which is a breathtaking view of a hundred and eighty-five foot waterfall. This region of the island seemed lost to the modern day technology but more resembled a panorama slide out of *Jurassic Park*. I felt an underlying magic as if I were home.

We ate lunch in Hana at this little café off a small beach, a single wharf extended into the endless ocean. I speculated it was easier, more cost-efficient to receive shipments by the wharf then from a delivery truck. The roads barely allowed a car let alone a semi. The population, although just under seven hundred, gave off a sparsely less experience. The neighborhood income consisted mainly from tourism and was thriving; it showed in their hospitality. Truly, to understand "Aloha", its expression and significance, take the time to visit Hana.

The drive back was an adventure; relieved I wasn't the one driving as every so often the road made abrupt turns constantly keeping you on your guard. One slip in concentration and you'd plummet hundreds of feet to your death becoming a permanent part of this island's topography. Tracy had no problem navigating the road as if she was a local, even with inadequate light replacing the day's sun. A majority of the journey home saw an absent of city lights, houses, or signs of civilization. Occasionally, emerging headlights ruined the solitude of the darkness. At times, emotionally in awe at our meaningless insignificance compared to the supremacy of the earth. If not for the music modestly singing from the car's radio, you might've imagined yourself at the island's birth; a new rising island, void of human inhabitants, with the wind, surf, trees, stars, and moon.

We returned home shortly after 10 p.m. both beat and ready for bed. I wasn't sure if I'd be able to sleep following last night's fiasco. However, pulling an all-nighter with the marathon days away wasn't the answer either. Colby and Pakile greeted us at the door. He wanted to play, Colby that is, but I sought the comfort of the bed.

"How was your trip?" Pakile asked, again aiming the dialogue towards Tracy, as I attended to the needs of one golden fur ball.

"Great. We got some spectacular photos," Tracy replied.

"By the way, Miss Jones. A Russell Hamilton called for you. He mentioned trying to call your cell, but kept getting your voicemail."

I'd forgotten to check my phone, or there had been no service in Hana. Maybe it was still on silent. I reached into my purse, scrolled the dozens of missed calls, each with no name or number, and assumed it was Russell.

"Did he leave a number?" I asked.

"No, I am sorry, Miss Jones he wouldn't give me that information," Pakile responded, "I'm heading out to do my final rounds, unless you are planning on going back out," he passed us on his way to the grounds.

"No, I think we're both exhausted," Tracy said.

Pakile removed himself from our presence, closing the front door without another word. I couldn't read him, sometimes a sweet old man, and other times a schizophrenic who'd forgotten to take his pills. Either way, I didn't trust him, only needing to tolerate him while a guest here.

The long day had distracted me from last night's sleepless torments and for that, I was grateful. We didn't run today, but the miles of hiking had made-up for it, just ask my legs, as we climbed the stairs to our rooms. I wanted to get one last hard run in tomorrow, a tune-up, for the marathon in a few days. A test to confirm my body could handle the change in humidity.

"So will you be up for a long run tomorrow?" Tracy asked, clearly on the same page.

"I was planning on it," scratching at Colby's ears, "how about before breakfast, after I take Colby for a walk on the beach? I'll use it as a warm up."

"Works for me," she replied, "Sleep tight, don't let the bedbugs bite," she whispered in my ear while embracing me in a hug.

Then almost sadistically, laughed her way to her room. Although a figure of speech and only kidding, after last night that was the last thing I needed to hear before bed. Colby had attached to my hip following stride for stride to the bathroom. I wanted to shower ahead of changing for bed; however, for me it would've triggered my body to become wide-awake. In hindsight, I perhaps should've taken the shower.

I climbed into bed, my body melting into the blankets while Colby did his typical habit, tucking himself into my side as I reluctantly contested half my pillow. I examined the growth on his ear, no change in size. That was good. I hoped it was a calcium deposit and nothing cancerous. Quickly glancing across the room the glowing neon reiterating what my body already knew; it was 10:30 p.m. and time for bed. I needed sleep, for 5 a.m. was going to come fast.

Again, the subsequent recollection came from my written journal the following morning. Unfortunately, my hand and body couldn't stop shaking while I wrote, as if a low volt electrical shock continuously pulsated through my body. When the quivering finally decreased, most of what I'd written visibly unreadable. Although I tried to decipher, even the few memories I had were becoming harder to recall with each passing minute. Again, there are time gaps and missed details that I can't account for. Maybe someday they will return, but I preferred they didn't.

December 29, 2009 Early Morning

I can't make out how long I was asleep, but it was the deepest sleep I had in a longtime. Once more, the tightness in my chest awakened me, as that utmost sensation of fear returned, stronger than the previous night. I tried sitting up, but again failed, only faintly able to open my eyes. Colby was still at my side, motionless as if frozen in time.

I had lightly dimmed the overhead lights, intentionally leaving them on to fight the darkness. However, somehow they were now off. The insensitive lights from outside my window called like the darkness as once again I felt an ominous presence. This was different from the energy emitted last night. It was primal, almost Jurassic Malevolence.

"Leave me the fuck alone," I screamed!

I wasn't going tonight without a fight, or so I thought.

"We are not here to hurt you. It will be different from before."

The voice resonated in my head, but I immediately accepted it as female. Did they think this was going to make a difference in my cooperation?

"I said leave me the fuck alone!"

I don't know how, perhaps my temper, their astonishment in my lack of cooperation or just plain luck, but I managed from under the blanket to move my foot, kicking one of them to the floor.

"We are here to help you."

Those words were the last audible communication before blacking out. I eventually awoke, in what I can best describe, as a laboratory. Unlike the night before, where I consciously witnessed my abduction, awakening with no recollections of how I got here. My perception of space and time was clearly distorted, and left only a vague representation of reality. I didn't know if this was unintentional or deliberately done because of my rebelliousness.

Gradually regaining consciousness, this time thankfully still clothed, lying on an oversized examination table. This time the table wasn't cold, maybe because of the clothes, but didn't feel like steel. There was a bright light emanating from the bottom of the table, and although unrestrained, I still felt powerless to move. Able to turn my head side to side I examined the room for signs of life. This was undeniably a lab of sorts, but I couldn't distinguish the specifics of any of the room's contents. The far side of the room was beyond my focus, but I heard sounds of sterilized utensils placed on a stainless steel tray, reminiscent of being in surgery. A short-lived blur stepped into my sights appearing as an elf in adaptation of last night's entities. My heart raced in panic not wanting for a recurrence of the previous night's procedures.

"This will be different," a female voice expressed.

The calmness in her voice penetrated my inner thoughts, reminiscent of a mother's love for her child, unlike the unsympathetic male's voice from last night.

"I don't what to be here! Why can't you understand that?"

I telepathically tried to respond to the woman's voice.

"You have been chosen. Please try to relax."

I heard a door, open and close, but couldn't distinguish the origin of the sound. Similar to the previous experience a hand stroked my temple, but this time it felt human. Trying to remain composed, I focused on my breathing with a set of deep meditating breaths. On my right, as if appearing from nowhere, a humanlike aide in a blue lab coat approached injecting a foreign substance into my arm. I quietly thought; *where the hell am I? Why were humans working with these entities? What the hell did they want with me?* Whatever they injected caused an immediate euphoric feeling of love and harmony over my entire body.

"Where am I?" I asked in a hallucinated voiced. There was no response, just the mysterious flurry of other entities bustling around with a sense of urgency. "Where am I? What's going on?" A kaleidoscope of blurred colors overlapped the reality I was witnessing.

"When the time is right, everything will be revealed to you. Please try to relax."

The woman's voice vibrated from my left side. I turned to address a distorted female apparition dressed in a white lab coat.

Although the picture seemed fuzzy, she appeared human, tall with a touch of oriental ancestral DNA, flat olive skin masked by the lowlight, and set off by her jet-black, straightened hair that fell well beneath her neckline. Briefly able, I focused in on her enlarged, glossy yellow eyes and blood-red vertical slit pupils as they implied an impression of being reptilian, almost snakelike. I wrote this off as a hallucination from whatever drugs they'd injected into my body. Attached to her coat pocket was a badge of some sort, with no recognizable name, with an implanted translucent orange square. An outline of a pyramid or inverted V came into focus with a singular line dissecting the middle as atop, two circular moons hovered both left and right. Quickly noticing my strained focus towards her ID, she hastily detached it with her jewelry free hand transferring it to her inside pocket. She resumed writing on an undersized digital clipboard while other techs cautiously waved a stretched illuminated cylinder over my body. This seemingly persisted for about five minutes. However, my sensitivity to time, whether it the newly introduced drugs or not, hastily fell dormant.

Supportively, they brought me to a sitting position before this woman, as I struggled to keep my balance. She handed her clipboard to a passing, childlike entity that dwarfed her own size while accepting from another a glass filled with a translucent odorless solution.

"Please drink, it will make you feel better."

"What is this?"

"Just drink!"

She politely asked, steadying the item amid my two hands. I was apprehensive raising the glass to my lips, not wanting to swallow this foreign liquid. Insistently they pushed it towards my mouth. Trying to impede the procedure, I sniffed the top of the glass for any resemblance of a familiar odor, and found none. After a little taste, it became obvious this wasn't water as the flavorless thickness, a consistency of gel, oozed down the back of my throat to the point of making me gag. However, within seconds of finishing, my entire body rejuvenated, internally vibrating to a higher level of consciousness. I wanted immediately to run, but to where I thought, knowingly deciding an escape would be a futile undertaking. So instead, I leisurely swung my legs letting them dangle off the table's edge. I was petite, and my feet hovered endlessly above the floor, maybe the raised slab was to accommodate their superior sized bodies.

I finally focused on my surroundings and its inhabitants, without limits; undeniably, this was a lab of sorts, and the table, its focal point. Many childlike Greys, similar to the previous night, and best described as the workers, occupied the room. They were no more than four feet in stature, vocally speechless, waddling throughout the room and working feverously, similar to bees in a hive.

At last, I noticed a single visible door to my left as a couple of the Greys exited. The hint of two intensely armed guards still detectable through the door's fixed triangular patterned glass as it closed. The uniform insignia was undetectable from this distance, but came across as Air Force, then again maybe Navy as they alertly stood in a hallway, *but a hallway to where?*

My thoughts interrupted as an older, more distinguished man in a lab coat rejoined the female to my side and for whatever reason his facial details were purposely being wiped from my psyche. Although, and this will sound ridiculous, it felt like Sean Connery. It wasn't, but in some way I got an impression, his demeanor and facial expression mimicked the actor. Maybe I've watched "*Hunt for Red October*" one too many times.

His hand seized a gadget resembling a revolver, three clear vials attached to its crown, each packed with three noticeably diverse fluids; one lightly translucent, another bubbling with a fluorescent green tint and the third a day-glow blue. He began sterilizing my upper left arm with a cotton ball and alcohol, the tang undeniable. I assumed it was an injection device, but before the thought registered, he brought the apparatus to bear on my disinfected appendage and fired. My arm ached intensely as the contents emptied into my blood. The chemicals mixing internally, burning to the nucleus of my cells, transfusing throughout my veins, until my body shut down from the pain's intensity.

At some point, I awakened from my induced coma into what felt like a hospital ward with makeshift beds extending along the wall to the point of infinity. My brain gradually regained control over my body allowing me to witness others from all different races, sexes, and ages. In fact, at one point, I vaguely recalled two small Greys escorting a male child out a door while holding his hands. He couldn't have been older than five or six, crying, and calling out for his mother. I wanted to sprint over, liberating him from his captors, and the nightmares he would have to endure, but what could I do? I was still optimistically praying this wasn't really myself.

Everyone in the room appeared in some form still unconscious or at least ignorant to my imminent movement. My inquisitiveness, someday, was going to be the death of me, but I felt the need to explore. Unobserved, I little by little made my way to the lone door that exited the end of this dormitory. I slide my face up its cool metal frame peering out an undersized tempered glass window to the hallway. Unlike the prior night, this was a structured human realm not alien in nature as the unoccupied hallway was void of guards or commotion. Maybe this was recovery and they hadn't expected me to improve so rapidly. At this point, I didn't care, gradually turning the lever down with my left hand until it opened. The snap of the lock echoed throughout the infirmary as an intense pain shot down my upper arm from the injection sight. I bit into my right knuckle trying to avoid screaming and upon examination noticed a series of three needle-sized, blood-clotted holes had formed a triangle with no visual bruising, at least not yet. I again tried rotating the lever with my right hand, this time with better results.

The door opened into a long thin corridor with accessible movement only to the left and under twenty feet away, directly to the right, was a closed steel door baring the resemblance to a submarine air lock. *Was I somehow under water?*

To the left, the passageway lengthened indefinitely on the way to darkness. Trying to focus on an end point, I hesitated on the decision to persist forward, knowing my depth perception had lost its credibility. With no signs of movement, I opted to embrace the wall, cautiously going on with my focus only feet ahead. The passage of just over a hundred feet took a lifetime. The corridor besieged with solid steel access doors and set in with foreign, if not alien symbols. I tried each door as I passed all with the same results, locked.

I advanced another twenty, maybe thirty feet before the concrete walls dematerialized having merged with the subterranean rock. The corridor still existed and extended ahead, but the walls became meticulously cut from stone, cold and smooth to the touch. Passing an implanted porthole, I glanced in as it revealed a modest visual of the occupied space on the other side. To this day, I can't recall even the faintest recollection of the displayed images. All I can say is my mind decided to suppress those horrifying images, leaving only raw emotions. Therefore, although I sense the experience, I can't describe the contents.

Another twenty feet and before me stood a four-way intersection. I peeled my head from the wall cautiously as voices echoed both from the left and right side of the junction. While lying on the floor I carefully inched my eyes around the left corner to the obvious sounds of an elevator door chiming open while trying to avoid detection. As the occupants entered, they turned momentarily, waiting as the doors began to close. I remember one dressed in what looked like a black jumpsuit, donning a red beret with a similar trilateral insignia as the doctors. The other, standard military wear, maybe Air Force, his chest adorned with hundreds of commendations. What stood out were the five stars that circled the far end of his shoulders and I assumed General. Odd, because I didn't think the military had honors that high. Also puzzling was the lack of facial recollection as if smudged with an eraser. As the doors closed, I heard the General specifically request Level 7. So, I knew I wasn't on Level 7, whatever that meant, still no closer to identifying my location.

Again, I heard voices, but this time coming from the right side of the hallway. I thought the female's pitch was recognizable but couldn't distinguish the other considering the uncomprehending dialect. What I'll explain next is my last recollection before struck by some sort of blinding lightning bolt.

I watched two beings appear within forty feet of me with unfastened flowing cloaks, hoods draped over their reptilian heads. The female dwarfed in height compared to the male who towered in a modest eight feet with a mass double hers. Their exposed skin best described as that of a crocodile. Hers a coffee color with what looked like dark green rims and his greenish-brown. Unlike the female, he had a definite pronounced tail that levitated effortlessly off the floor. Their face and hands displayed a reduction of pronounced scales in comparison to the rest of their body and the arms extending longer than normal with what looked like three fingers and a thumb. I didn't get a good look at their feet, but the nails were short as if rounded claws. The male's robe dangled open briefly, enough to notice his omission of a navel. They each had a somewhat conical shaped head with no appearance of a bridge between their eyes as their compressed nose had a visual V appearance at its tip. The hood blocked any visual assessment of their ears, but the mouth was bulky with no outward lips.

They carried on their conversation for a few minutes before noticing my presence. Within seconds, ear piercing alarms sounded along, with *"Security breach level 5"* blaring over the PA. I assumed this voice had clarified my detained level. As these Reptilians scurried towards me, their image flickered back and forth from Human to Reptilian. Prior to reaching me, they both had resumed complete human forms. I quickly identified the two images as the earlier humans in lab coats. Before the astonishment registered, I hastily sprung to my feet running for the elevator door. The last image I committed to memory was looking over my shoulder and the women pointing an object in my direction. Suddenly a burst of light energy struck my back, propelling me against the closed elevator doors with such force it knocked me out cold.

It was at that point I awoke from the bed screaming and trembling violently as Colby began barking uncontrollable on the bed in every direction. He sensed my terror but powerless to establish where the intruders were. I remember Tracy running into the room, but by this time, I had huddled in the corner, and was shivering in a cold sweat. She tried to comfort me, even tried to get a blanket around me to control the shivering, but Colby constantly blocked her access to me.

"No!" I screamed kicking at her "Leave me alone!"

I was experiencing a psychotic break but still aware as my grip on reality slowly slipped away. I was in my room, but for various reasons I wasn't registering it in my mind. Colby recoiled like a snake fending off anyone approaching my inner circle. I smacked Colby numerous times, involuntarily; not associating it was him, yet he in no way left my side. To this day his persistent barking, I believe, pulled me out of that mental state. I regained awareness of my surroundings, reaching for Colby my security blanket, holding him as tears streamed down my face with my heart about ready to explode. Tracy backed away, retreating to the bed, watching as Colby's bond inaudibly healed my emotional wounds.

I stayed in the corner well over an hour, holding Colby and gradually regaining my composure. Tracy went downstairs to make coffee and breakfast. While she was gone, I wrote in my journal all I could retract from my memories. By the time she returned, I'd finished writing, eventually making my way to a couch in the study. At this point, every light was on upstairs and it still felt insufficiently bright. Colby, still being protective, lunged at Tracy as she entered the room with coffee.

"Colby come," I barked.

He returned at once at my feet while Tracy sat at my side like a big sister, not saying anything, only trying to comfort me in any way possible. Colby, with the occasionally low-pitched growl, watched her like a hawk. I knew she wanted to know the particulars; it was human nature. When I was ready, I'd talk and she knew it, but right now, I was still trying to quiet the nerves.

The clock read 3 a.m. Had it only been a few hours? I was sure about one thing; there was no way I was going back to sleep tonight. This launched the string of my sleepless nights and my clear-cut switch back to caffeinated coffee instead of decaf.

Chapter 22

The rest of the night, I spent in a rocking chair looking out the window from the corner of my room, a caffeine IV drip close by, my eyes powerless to shut, Colby at my feet. I never again wanted to sleep. Eventually the shivering stopped and so too the cold sweats. Tracy reluctantly went to sleep, but not before setting me up with a portable coffeepot filled with high-octane caffeine. I wondered why, throughout all the commotion, Pakile never awoke, or at the least checked on me. This was peculiar behavior for someone supposedly in charge of security.

I fanatically glared at my phone, persistently expecting Russell's call, wanting to gaze up at his face, hold him, and take in his soft manly warmth. I was afraid to open my mind to any memories at the moment, even blissful ones connecting the features of his face. The hours until morning lingered for what seemed like days and I yearned for the comfort of my bed at home. I was doubtful I could've slept there either, sensibly wondering unless medically induced, if I'd ever sleep again.

Tracy pierced the silence of the room shortly after 6 a.m. to check on my status and see if I needed anything. I wasn't in the mood to eat breakfast and, assuming Colby wasn't leaving my side, Tracy had thoughtfully brought his breakfast up from the kitchen. Colby by no means missed or would wait past six for breakfast, however, this morning he vigilantly slept, lethargic at my feet, oblivious to his food. Tracy retreated to my bed in silence, struggling to find the right words to say. I reached for the coffeepot with my left arm abruptly plagued with a spine tingling numbness. There was no bruising, but the raised defined triangular mark on my upper arm was a souvenir signifying last night wasn't a hallucination.

"Do you want more coffee?" Tracy asked, dismounting the bed quick to serve me the last cup. "Let me make more."

"No. I've had more than enough."

"Do you want me to call a doctor?" She asked.

"No," I belted out, "I've seen enough doctors for one night, Thank You."

I reached for the mug with my right hand, unbearably shifting my weight back into the niche of the chair. Tracy sensed my need to speak, but I couldn't draft the words with my mouth as she returned to the bed, confused by my last statement. She sat, legs crossed, with a not-persuaded stare in disagreement with my prognosis, while she thought about making the call regardless. Reluctantly, I recovered my journal from beneath the chair, handing it to her while pointing out the past two-day's entries. She read, periodically stopping, asking for clarification to my deciphered scribble as her facial reactions expressed an excellent illustration to the past few days. The absolute dread and terror in her eyes cemented her sympathetic understanding. She couldn't finish the complete entry, instead gingerly closed the journal, holding it to her heart, and effortlessly wept, letting the tears roll down her face like a river. She wanted to embrace me, but we both knew what little comfort it would convey.

My phone rang, startling both of us, the residual droplets of coffee ordaining my jeans as the amplified jingle reverberated in the silent sanctuary of the moment. The caller ID registered no name or number. I normally would've let it go to voice mail, but in some way felt it was Russell. The hours of crying and recent tears ricocheted in my voice.

"Hello."

"Erica is that you?" Russell asked.

"Yeah," I was wiping the tears away trying to refrain from sniffling.

"Are you all right?"

"Just had a really bad night."

I fought to hold back the tears that should've run dry by now. Tracy could tell I needed privacy so she left my journal on the bed and somberly retreated closing the door in her wake.

"Where are you?" I asked.

The background roar of jets was drowning out his voice to an almost inaudible level.

"I can't tell you; your phone is probably being monitored."

"What? It is hard to hear you with all that noise."

I turned the phone's volume on high as his voice sounded like a man on the run, but on the run from what?

"Just listen to me very carefully. I don't have much time. Do you remember the turtle?"

"I think so."

"Meet me at the turtle 4 p.m. Tell no one, not even your friend Tracy and make sure you're not followed," he paused, "I got to go. I love you."

Those three simple words blanketed me with warmth as the phone went dead before I could respond to his coded message. The image of a turtle floated helplessly in my mind before finally resting on the beach of our first date. I whispered at the phone, knowing he couldn't hear me, but somehow felt he did.

"I love you, too."

From the sounds of things, we're both having an awful morning and I hoped we'd make it to the afternoon. I so wanted to say those words to his face. It had been years since I've said *I love you* to any guy. His apprehensiveness towards someone listening in on our conversation was not reassuring. Although, hearing his voice, knowing I was going to see him, displaced some of my fears.

Colby refused to eat his breakfast, no matter how hard I coaxed him. He had attached himself to my hip, my shadow and I knew there was no way to pry him away today.

Tracy was sitting out on the deck, deep in thought and I startled her by accident, grabbing for the seat next to her. The sun had barely risen but people were already congregating on the beach. How I wished for their life. At least today, for some, it would be another beautiful day in paradise. *Where had I heard those words before?*

"Was that who I think it was?" Tracy asked.

"Yeah."

She was still fighting back the tears as her bloodshot eyes matched mine.

"What did he want?"

Her response was sincere, but Russell voiced clearly not to tell anyone, including Tracy.

"Nothing, really. I think he was getting on a plane. We didn't talk long."

I couldn't look her in the face, hoping she bought this lie. I watched and wondered as the morning waves rolled in, gradually eroding the beach, returning the smallest granules back to the sea. Was this going to be my fate? The first of many deceits and deceptions I would soon weave, especially to Tracy. My soul, like the beach sand, with each wave of lies eroded, never to return to its original beauty.

We sat as friends, silently for hours. It saddens me as I write this now to think that was the last true moment of friendship we ever shared.

Chapter 23

It was midmorning as we sat watching the beach, the windsurfers, and the occasional cloud floating across the sky. I didn't scrutinize or ponder the past, present or future. Instead, I focused on the moment trying to keep my mind as negated as possible.

"So a priest, a lawyer, and a rabbi walked into a bar...," Tracy uttered with a smile.

Before she finished, we had both busted out, hysterically laughing, then started to cry again, finally embracing with a warm and caring hug.

"So you still want to go for a run later?" She asked. I knew she was serious.

"Right now, I'd be lucky to manage a walk," I replied.

"How about tomorrow...Are we on for the bike down Haleakalā?"

This meant a 2 a.m. wake up call so we could get to the top in time to watch the sunrise. I thought it was a good idea, seeing how I wasn't planning to sleep anyway.

"Can you give me till later this afternoon to decide?" I asked.

"Okay," she affirmed, "I think I'm still gonna go for a run."

My arm was still tender, unconvinced I could handle a bike for any extended length of time and the last thing I wanted was to go flying off a curve at nine thousand feet. She gave me one more squeeze while excusing herself from the chair and patted Colby on the head before returning inside to change. I wasn't in the frame of mind, physically or mentally, to do much of anything, although euphoric with thoughts of seeing Russell. I had more questions for him than answers.

I returned to my room, Colby in tow, wanting to lie down but not sleep. I curled up into a relaxed fetal position; Colby nudged his soft baby powdered puppy head into my neck, gently licking the underside of my chin. He sensed the trepidation to close my eyes and did his best to keep me wide-awake. My eyes watched the minutes tick by, dragging on and on with four o'clock not approaching soon enough.

Although snuggling with a puppy is one of my favorite pastimes, I desperately needed a shower; settling on a relaxing bubble bath instead. I soaked at length in the Roman tub while watching the surfers negotiating the waves along the beach. It was therapeutic. It gave me time to think. *Why did Russell want to ensure I wasn't followed?* I rehashed my pursuers from the other day playing out different scenarios. I wasn't in the spy business, so how does one avoid being followed? The only thing I was sure of, Colby was coming. One for protection and two, he wasn't willingly going to leaving me.

Tracy had gone for her run and returned while I was in the tub. She was leaving again as her impassioned conversation with Pakile over the intercom about the readiness of the limo noticeably carried throughout the house. She in no way entered the room, probably assuming my need for a little alone time. I declined to mention my meeting with Russell of course, by his request.

As four o'clock approached, I became more apprehensive about meeting Russell. I presumed it was the uneasiness of being followed more than the meeting itself. Colby showed little animation as I attached his walking leash, even as we headed downstairs and out the door to the gate. He was all business, his vigilant ears responding to each sound that emanated our surroundings. I had the finest protection a woman could want or need.

The first choice from the house to the rendezvous point would've been taking the beach all the way. However, with sections not particularly dog accessible. I decided against it. I did have concerns about walking the street, even with periodic streams of tourists, mostly because of what transpired yesterday.

Within minutes of leaving the sanctuary of the houses' inner walls, a sensation, as if hundreds of eyes were watching, overwhelmed my senses. No black cars, no men in suits, no helicopters, and no aliens, at least none I witnessed. I wasn't the only one, Colby was feeling it too as we walked, suspicious of every passing person. I was paranoid, insistently wondering if somebody was tracking us. If so, they stealthily blended in well with the locals.

I arrived without incident at the beach and gradually continued along the shore to where we'd seen the turtle. Our first intimate moment played in my head as I sat in sand and watched Colby inch forward, pondering attacking the approaching waves, but refusing to leave my side. Then his fascination fixated on two men playing Frisbee, his body twitching, fighting his instinctual urges to retrieve the round object from the sky. Checking my watch, 4 o'clock had come and gone. Russell wasn't the tardy sort. I endlessly inspected the beach for him, and worried I was in the wrong spot. I checked my phone, no call, and no way to reach him. I'd give him another half hour, until 4:30, before trekking back.

Minutes later, my distant focus broke, as a Frisbee relentlessly appeared heading my way. Colby snatched it from the air only moments before it hit me. One of the men was rapidly in pursuit to recover or try to recover it from Colby's mouth.

"Aloha," he said, kneeling next to Colby and me.

"Aloha," uninterested in chatting, but wanting to be friendly, "I don't think you're getting the Frisbee back."

"Don't worry about it, Miss Jones. Just listen and smile. I have a message from Russell."

He played his part well the entire time smiling and playing tug with Colby.

"Where is he?" I wondered, eagerly scanning the beach.

"Go to the far end of the parking lot. There you'll see a black BMW. Place Colby in the back and climb into the front passenger side."

"Where is Russell?"

"Please, Miss Jones, you don't have much time," eventually wrestling the Frisbee from Colby.

"How do I know Russell sent you?"

"Your nickname is Ka'iu lani;" smiling with a quick wink, "now please go!"

He tossed the Frisbee back to his partner, leaving as abruptly as he'd arrived, as if the conversation never happened. I waited a moment contemplating the authenticity of his demand. *How could he have known Russell's nickname for me? Was Russell in the car?* I had to see how this was going to play out, but to tell you the truth, the idea of getting into any black car, especially after yesterday, scared the hell out of me.

Within minutes, I'd made my way back to the far end of the lot with the car parked as described minus a driver. I situated Colby into the backseat, and then observantly made my way to the front passenger side, settled in while a small note addressed to me and taped to the dash caught my eye. Upon opening it, I instantly recognized Russell's signature at the bottom.

It read:

Ka'iu lani,

Please buckle up…Hit the horn three times…don't be alarmed. The driver will take you to me. Hold on tight…See you in a bit.

Love Russell

I did what it said and seconds after the third horn sounded, Nohea appeared as if out of thin air, casually strolling past the front of the car. Without a word, he climbed immediately into the driver's seat, ignited the engine, and then aggressively harnessed his seat belt.

"You might want to hold on tight. It could get a little dicey," he stressed.

With that, his right foot hit the floor as the engine roared. Tensely we rolled towards the exit, pausing briefly, allowing a familiar black sedan to draw closer, as he systematically checked and adjusted his side and rear mirrors. *Why wasn't he going, I thought, the road was clear?*

"Hang on!" His voiced elevated over the power of the engine.

Nohea dropped the transmission, emergency brake still engaged, and we sat motionless as the tires spun freely. The reek of burned rubber began to creep into the car's interior as a plume of smoke formed like a dark storm cloud around us. The intensifying haze engulfed the rear of the car erasing its virtual existence. He freed the car's brake and quickly accelerated, propelling me aggressively into the recesses of my seat. It took all my strength to rotate my neck enough to assess Colby's condition in the backseat. He'd already made his way to the floor.

The other vehicle chased, but struggled to equal our velocity. The BMW's suspension shifted its weight as we raced around the razor-sharp curves seeking to thwart a possible rollover. I watched as a third car now joined the pursuit. Nohea, not oblivious to our new arrival, continued driving assertively, swerving in and out of traffic.

"Where'd you learn how to drive, NASCAR?" I voiced in sarcasm!

"No, my grandmother," he answered with a smile.

At this point, we were on Highway 30 heading north. The scenic ocean view normally would've been comforting, but as the sheer cliff drop-offs whipped by at 100 mph, it somehow became lost. As the highway opened to a straight passage, I got a decent view of the trailing two cars. To the rear a black sedan, I guarantee the same one from the other day. Directly behind us, an old rusted muscle car blocking the advances of the black sedan, with what looked like a local driver at the wheel.

The highway abruptly bowed causing the wheels to scream in agony as they fought to hold their line. Our pursuers navigated the curve barely keeping control; their hubcaps dislocated becoming an everlasting fixture at the ocean's bottom. The highway instantly tapered to unyielding single lanes, with tight curves, tunnels and no room for error. Nohea shifted gears like a seasoned racecar driver as horns blared from the lethargic passed vehicles. Although youthful, he drove with the composure and skillfulness of a veteran. I wondered where on the island you'd learn such a skill.

"Almost there," he explained with a veteran calmness in his voice. "Once we get through the next tunnel, brace yourself."

We pierced into the darkness of an elongated tunnel, carved from the volcanic rock, with the muscle car on our rear flashing its headlights. Without hesitation, it immediately engaged its brakes, rotating sideways, essentially blocking the tunnel's entrance, causing the black sedan to swerve to avoid crashing. Traffic came to a complete halt in both directions as Nohea sped up, thrusting through the tunnel's exit and around the next bend within seconds. The opposing traffic swiftly becoming congested and on the third curve, Nohea downshifted while simultaneously engaging the emergency brake. The car aggressively rotated 180 degrees, before quickly stopping.

Directly parked ahead, off one of the few scenic plateaus, was a large white trailer that read '*Aina Lani Farms – Fresh Island Herbs*'. As we rolled towards the back of the trailer, its metal doors parted, two men jumped out concurrently pulling down and attaching tire ramps. Nohea, without delay, aligned his wheels driving up into the trailer while the men worked swiftly, returning the ramps, and closing the doors before rushing past us to the front of the cab. Nohea cut the ignition and the brief silence soon became replaced with the hefty crank of a diesel engine. A quick blast of the horn, the hissed released sounds of air brakes, forward momentum and I soon realized what they were doing.

"You are alright?" Nohea asked.

"Yeah, fine," looking back to check on Colby.

"How about you, Colby?" I looked back.

Colby bolted up from the floor onto the backseat trying to make his way to the front. He barked a couple times, as if to say '*I'm Okay*'.

The BMW fit so snugly into the trailer. I was afraid to open the door until Nohea pointed to a shadowed figure emerging from behind a closed door. My eyes adjusted to the low-lighted interior and wondered what awaited me on the other side of that door. I exited the car, making eye contact with the shadow as it increasingly came into focus. A memorable smile beamed, brightening the darkness, Russell. I ran wildly to the front of the car embracing him wholeheartedly as Colby uneasily barked from the backseat desperately wanting to race to my side. Nohea generously opened

Colby's door allowing him access to both Russell and I. His barking stopped, replaced with the continual urge to nudge between our passionate embrace and us.

"What the hell is going on?" I yelled pulling away.

"Just come in and have a seat," Russell encouraged while holding the door.

Colby lead the way into the room while Nohea closed the door as he entered last. The space overflowed with high-tech computers, televisions and other unidentifiable paraphernalia. It was a condensed adaptation of *Best Buy*. I remember thinking; somehow, consumers didn't have access to this technology, at least not yet. This was a transportable stronghold, equipped with a bedroom, bathroom, and kitchen. All the comforts of home. Nohea placed himself in a chair surrounded by numerous video screens with two of the screens displaying live feeds of outside the semi. While passing our pursuers, completely unnoticed, Nohea captured their image and posted it on a nearby computer screen.

"That's the car that followed me the other day," I said, pointing to the black sedan frozen on the screen, "I'm sure of it."

"They've been tracking you ever since landing on Maui," Russell said.

"Who's the man in the Hawai'ian shirt?" I asked.

"An acquaintance of ours," Nohea responded.

"Is he going to be okay?"

"Yeah, no matter what, those guys won't try anything in public," Russell explained.

We pulled around a corner, leaving our chasers in the distance. Russell retreated to a couch, opposite the surveillance equipment but still within its view while Nohea went through a slender entryway on his way to what looked like a small kitchen.

"Miss Jones, would you like something?" His voice radiated from the kitchen.

"A water would be great."

"Mr. Hamilton, how about you?"

"No, I already have something. Thanks, Nohea," Russell retrieved his coffee from the near table. "Please, Erica take a seat. We're safe for now."

"For now?"

I have to admit that didn't sound promising. I sat next to him, immersed in this experience and the contents of the room. Transfixed with the notion, across from me, sat 'James Bond', as more questions came to mind. *Did Russell work for the government? Why were there people after him and especially me? Who the hell were the men following us?* I needed to start getting answers.

"You probably have several questions." Russell said, as if on cue.

"You think?"

Colby jumped up next to me placing his head on my lap as Nohea handed me a water then made his way back to the console. His fingers furiously danced across a holographic keypad as on the screens images toggled across intensively. Periodically freezing, enlarging then transferring the picture to another screen. I watched enough CSI episodes to understand it was form of facial identification software. He was replaying the video of the beach, the chase, zooming in on everyone's faces, while a different computer searched a database for matches.

"I'll try to resolve some of your questions. However, for security reasons and your safety I can't disclose everything. I hope you understand."

Russell took hold of my hand, clutching it with compassion and leaned back to grab a bulky file folder off the end table, sporadically inspecting its contents.

"Let's start first with questions you might have," trying to smooth the tension with a smile.

"Who the Hell are you?" I blurted out.

"Straight to the point, I like that," he said, "let's for now say, I'm your guide on this journey."

"So, this whole love thing is just a game to you?" I questioned, pissed. Nothing I hated more in a man than a liar or player.

"No. God no!"

He reached for my hands, but I pulled away.

"I've been closely watching you awhile. That much I confess. But falling in love with you wasn't part of the operation and has complicated things a little."

"Complicated things. Watching me for a while. What the f—!" He promptly interrupted my tirade.

"Listen, I do love you, more than you'll ever know. However, in my position, we're to remain dispassionate, emotionless, and not personally involved. I broke that rule, and refused to alter those feelings. Please understand there are difficulties we both face, in more than one-way. You need to trust me when I say my heart belongs to you."

He tenderly reached for my hands again, this time I didn't withdraw. Maybe it was the honesty in his eyes, but I knew he was being sincere, and truly did love me.

"I love you too, but I need to know what is going on. Our little meeting at the airport, not an accident, was it?"

"No."

"How long have you been watching me?"

"I don't know to what scope or length you've been watched. I do know my assignment started a few weeks ago."

"So I've been watched for a while! Why?"

"I'm not privy to that information. It's classified. They only told me to observe, make contact, document, but most importantly protect you at all costs."

"Protect me from what?"

"Again, I don't have a response, only speculation, which I don't want to discuss until I have definitive proof."

He began flipping casually through the folder pages as if looking for something specific, either that or he intentionally avoided eye contact, concerned I'd see through his lies.

"What can you tell me? Is Russell Hamilton your real name, do you really work for Dynamic Aeronomics? Let's start with that…"

"Yes, that is my real name and I do work for Dynamic Aeronomics."

"What do you do for them, besides look after total strangers?"

"Like I told you…I'm in promotions. From time-to-time, I've done a few side projects. However, because of National Security issues I'm not at liberty to elaborate on them with you or anyone else at this time."

"So, you work for the Government."

"Not exactly," he hesitated. "My company works for a branch of the Government. That's about as much as I can tell you for now."

"Okay. Then what about the men that chased us in the black car and followed me yesterday."

"Have you ever heard of the Majestic Twelve?"

"No."

"How about the term MIB's or Men in Black."

He searched the folder, finally finding what he was looking for, reluctantly wanting to share, as he awaited my response.

"You mean the mystical UFO guys." I couldn't keep from laughing. "Like the guys from the movies right, you know, Will Smith, Tommy Lee Jones."

"Exactly," but he wasn't laughing.

"Are you kidding? They're not even real."

He handed me a stack of papers, on top, a picture of the mysterious black sedan followed my numerous portraits of men dressed in black suits, clearly surveillance photos.

"You're telling me that these guys actually exist?" I skeptically asked, returning the photos.

"Do you recognize anyone in the pictures below?" He asked before accepting the photos.

"I didn't see their faces, but that's exactly the car I told you about."

He returned the photos to the file folder, and then brought back another set of photos for me browse. This time, there was a new vehicle along with a different set of mug shots.

"Have you ever seen this car or these men?"

"No. Why are these guys MIB's too?"

"No. They're part of a secret organization called The Majestic Twelve." He took back the pictures, then handed me yet another photo, this time a photograph of an individual. "How about this person?"

The man in the picture had similarities, dressed in a consistent theme as the others, but something in that picture bothered me. What I mean, he was dressed all in black except for a hint of a hidden white dress shirt, had sunglasses on, and obviously unaware he had been photographed.

"No, never seen him either. Is he part of the same organization?" I asked.

"No. They all collaborate giving an illusion of solidarity. However, the reality is, if you're contacted by them, all three will have their own unique agendas."

"And they are..." trying to vocal a response.

"The faction referred to as MIB's have two diverse divisions, both working for similar powers within the Government. What I can tell you, one is working to suppress all information pertaining to alien contact. The other, is forcefully pursuing alien technology acquisitions in exchange aiding in their advancing *Alien Agenda*. What agenda and which is which, I can't tell you. They mutually take their professions seriously and I do mean lethally serious."

"Back up a second. You're telling me that UFOs and aliens exist?"

I couldn't stay seated, having to walk around as my brain whirled searching for answers.

"Yes!" Russell firmly answered back.

"Why the Government cover up? Why has no one gone public with this, even you? How long has this been going on?"

I continuously paced with a thousand more questions ready to shout at Russell as Pandora's Box had opened and I wasn't prepared. Who would've been? Russell continued.

"Aliens have lived and visited this planet since its conception, even early man described visits in their cave drawings. Each civilization has its own form of accounts and myths. Part of the MIB's trade is to make sure they stay myths, or at the least discredited facts. They will, have, and continue to pressure people into denouncing what they thought they saw. Silencing them, if you know what I mean should they not comply."

Russell approached, trying to get me to sit down, as shock lightened my face. All this time thinking those UFO people were a bit crazy, including my dear friend Scott, who happened to belong to a group in Vegas. I humored him and his eccentric viewpoints, now I'm discovering his beliefs are fact more than fiction. I eventually returned to the couch, sat down, and finished my water.

"Nohea," I called.

"Yes, Miss Jones," spinning around in his chair.

"Do you have anything stronger than water on this traveling circus?"

Nohea glanced at Russell first, searching for approval and at once, he nodded realizing this was a lot to absorb for anyone. Nohea briefly disappeared into the kitchen appearing moments later with a dark cocktail in his hand.

"Rum and Coke. Very little coke," he said, handing it to me with a wink and a smile.

I took a sip, he was right, more Rum than Coke, but I still shot it back. The burning in my throat didn't even phase me as I handed the empty back to Nohea looking for another round.

"Are you going to be okay?" Russell asked.

"It was just revealed to me we're not alone and aliens exist and you want to know if I'll be okay. Next you're going to tell me that Santa Claus is real and the Easter Bunny is a close personal friend." It was an unnecessary jab, but he got the point. "Why are you telling me all this? How am I involved?" Taking the second drink from Nohea, only this time I planned to milk it with a bit more grace.

"I haven't completely figured all that out. Again, I believe my superiors know, but wish not to disclose that information to me at this time. I only mention this to you because I love you. I'm breaching protocol, putting my life and the lives of anyone who assists me in jeopardy as well. I can't be around you 24/7, so the more you know the better prepared you'll be to handle what might be asked of you in the future. There's an explanation why everybody, including myself call you Ka'iu lani. I didn't believe it until the day at the floral gardens. The shopkeeper reiterated the same name as she presented you that gift. Now I'm convinced this is why all the sudden curiosity has come about you. You still have her gift don't you?"

"Yeah, it's on the sink back at the house," I replied.

"You need to wear it 24/7 for your protection."

Russell scribbled down a note on a piece paper and immediately handed it to Nohea.

"How is wearing a necklace going to protect me from anything."

"Let's just say it's similar to how garlic necklaces protect against vampires. That's all I can say about it right now."

Suddenly a deafening alarm sounded, the computer displays dramatically flashed to life as Nohea hectically typed, frequently arranging the displays. Russell, alarmed, raced to his side.

"What's going on now?" I threw my hands in the air, blindly unaware of what I saw displayed.

"I don't know how they tracked us so quick. They're trying to get a lock on the location." Nohea shot back, now concerned. "A signal is being broadcast from inside this location."

"That's impossible. They swept the truck before leaving. Are you positive?" Russell's vocal tone and facial gestures switched from alarmed to disturbed.

"Look for yourself," Nohea pointed to a satellite map of Maui.

"Erica, did you bring your cell phone?" Russell aggressively seized my arm.

"Yeah, it's in my purse."

"Where's the purse?"

Russell radically scanned the room with his eyes.

"It's still in the car I believe."

He feverously raced out the door, grabbing a small handheld device along the way. He dramatically dumped its contents on the hood having arrived to the purse before me and I watched as he wielded this scanner with precision over all my personal items. As it hovered over my phone, a red light flashed and a high-pitched buzzer sounded.

"Shit," he yelled!

Picking up the phone, he ran to the back of the truck and began unlatching one of the trailer doors. The truck hadn't stopped or even slowed down, barreling across the highway at a high rate of speed. I stood, mesmerized, unsure of what was about to happen.

"They'll have a lock in ten seconds," Nohea's voice yelled with urgency.

Russell struggled with the truck door, as I'm sure its design didn't include opening it from within while driving.

"Seven seconds…six….five…," he continued the count down.

"What are you doing with my phone," I yelled.

Russell vigorously unfastened the door pushing it clear, while trying to avoid falling out the back. As Nohea hit zero,

Russell propelled my phone from the truck like a baseball and at once, it vaporized in midair as a blinding blast of light that seemed to originate from the sky; its unfortunate death. Russell caught his breath as he latched the door shut, nonchalantly turning toward Nohea.

"Are we cleared?"

"Yes. They're not tracking us anymore." Nohea returned his focus back toward the array of video screens.

"What just happened to my phone?" I asked, too shocked to cry.

"They were tracking us with your phone, using your GPS. The phone was on so they probably heard our entire conversation," Russell replied.

"I didn't call anyone."

"You don't have to, they can turn your phone on remotely, even track you if the phone is off and removing the battery does nothing. It's the chip inside." Russell returned to Nohea's side.

"You're kidding?"

"Did that explosion look like I was kidding?" Russell pointed to a satellite screen that Nohea had pulled up. "I was afraid of that…double check it and run a full diagnostic."

Russell waited eagerly for a confirmation from Nohea. About what, I couldn't tell. I watched, trying to follow the screens, however not computer savvy enough to understand all that was happening. God, I wish Scott could've been here.

"That signal's confirmed. Satellite NAS-7," Nohea responded.

"We're in a real mess now." Russell looked at Nohea who shook his head agreeing. "You really must be a threat to them if they want you dead." He glanced at me but with no smile this time.

"Dead?" I frantically replied, not believing what I'd just heard.

"That's right. That beam of energy came from NAS-7; one of the many top-secret satellites capable of destroying targets from space. Its charged, supercoiled, proton cannon has a beam that can be focused on objects the size of a dime or as large as a city block." Russell browsed a printout handed to him by Nohea.

"You're telling me this beam could take out a city block from space?"

"It can take out any object, including a person. It's so precise it could take you out in a crowded assembly without grazing a hair on anyone else around."

Russell fretfully stared deep into my now scared eyes. First, there were aliens, than secret government agencies and now a beam of energy from space intent on killing me. This wasn't turning into a vacation of a lifetime. Nohea handed him a printed report, which he examined, persistently shaking his head in disbelief.

"This doesn't make sense. Why would the NSA target her?"

"Wait, who's the NSA?" I asked.

"National Security Agency," Nohea replied before strong-willing his own two cents, "You know boss, if they heard the conversation the target might not have been her, but you. Everything or should I say anyone else, would've just been collateral damage."

Russell's smile, which always calmed me, replaced with a sense of distress, as he paced back and forth in deep thought. I returned to the couch and an awaiting Colby, seeing he needed time to think. The explosion had frightened Colby, because as soon as I sat down he maneuvered himself entirely on my lap, which was difficult to do for a dog of his size, but he pulled it off gracefully. My view of Russell now blocked by a furry mammoth as I faintly heard Nohea and Russell talking. Nohea's frantic typing overshadowed their faint whispers and Russell's commands. I started to feel the effects of finishing my second drink and wouldn't be getting off the couch anytime soon as my head started to spin. Minutes later Russell rejoined me on the couch, with his file folder.

"I'm sorry you're involved to this level. I shouldn't have got emotionally involved," his face displayed an inner sadness.

"It takes two to tango," I uttered, smiling back.

The smile returned to his face, but only for a brief moment. Russell helped me reposition Colby between us so we could be face-to-face for this delicate conversational topic.

"Who are the Majestic...what did you say, the Majestic 12?"

"The short version, Majestic 12 was formed by President Harry Truman in 1947 to sift through the massive number of UFO sightings and material. Their unofficial job description is to research, contact and preserve communication with extraterrestrial intelligence and at times, are only referred to as MJ-12. They, at the time, only reported to the President of the United States."

"That's it?"

I knew there had to be more, based on his facial expression.

"No, but there's only so much I'm allowed to tell you, as it's classified."

"My life's in danger, you dangle a carrot before the horse, and don't expect me to race off in search of answers. I needed to know, damn it!"

My intent look spoke volumes as he thumbed through the files and after a rather long and drawn out silence, he continued.

"Okay, the following for now is about as far as I'm willing to go for your safety. What you do with it from here is your choice."

"Fair enough," I nodded.

"Besides MJ-12, there's another covert organization created by and reports only to MJ-12 — *The Majority Agency for Joint Intelligence (MAJI)*. They handle, coordinate recovery efforts, study, and communicate with extraterrestrial intelligence. The project is often referred to as, 'the dark side of the moon'. Associates encompass only the brightest thinkers in science, government, business, military, and intelligence organizations within the United States and I stress, only the United States. They're referred to by initials only MJ-1, MJ-2, MJ-3, you get the picture. MJ-1, believed to be Acting Director of the U.S. Central Intelligence Agency (CIA). MAJI works with all local and federal law organizations including NASA, NOR, CIA, FBI, and the NSA, or National Security Agency. Any and all intelligence pertaining to UFO sightings, crashes, and contacts bypass normal reporting procedures and go straight to MAJI. Officially, the Government denies any existence of this organization but, trust me when I say, they are real."

He stopped, paused, and looked up from the pages at me as if he signed my death warrant. I wanted to hear more, but for whatever reason, he wouldn't disclose more information. I still couldn't figure out what was my involvement.

"Why do they want me dead?" I asked.

"That's what I can't understand," his attention fully focused on a pulled file.

"What do you mean?" I inquisitively tried to wrap my head around his lack of understanding.

"They're the ones that appointed me to look after you," his head shook in disbelief.

At the time, I was speechless, as more questions presented themselves with even less definitive answers. I went from an executive secretary to a candidate on some Secret Government hit list all in one vacation. *Could things get any worse?* Somehow, I knew what that answer was going to be and didn't want an answer. Russell motioned, trying to get Nohea's attention away from the computer screens.

"Tell the driver to pull over the first chance he gets."

"Why are we stopping?" I asked.

"We need to get you back to the house. If it's me being targeted you're in jeopardy while on this truck."

"Wait. Don't I have a say in this? I still have questions and need to talk to you about the last couple of nights. I love you and don't want to go!"

Russell got up from the couch offering me his hand for support, which I refused. I was a bit tipsy, but not drunk. He grasped at both my hands and looked openly into my eyes.

"Erica, listen to me carefully. Nohea is going to take you back to the house. Don't talk to anyone. Especially about me, this truck, or even what we've discussed…nothing. As far as you're concerned, this meeting by no means occurred. This is for your safety, but more than that…for the safety of my crew and me. Can you do this for me?"

"Yeah, I'll play along for now, but I still don't understand."

I gave him a friendly hug, and an even bigger smile as he helped me into the car. Colby immediately jumped to the back reassuming his position on the floor as Russell leaned in and gave me a passionate kiss making my toes curl. My passion from the other night reluctantly rekindled now, I wanted even more to dissolve gently in his arms.

"Give me a few days to sort this out," he paused, "possibly try to enjoy your vacation the next few days. You know this is a beautiful island, if you only give into its power."

The truck had already stopped, trailer doors sprung open, the ramps unloaded by the same two guys all before Nohea made his way to the driver's seat. Enjoy what's left of my vacation, like that was going to be possible. I didn't get to explain to him my nightmares from the past two nights, at this instant they weren't nightmares but genuine memories and the only question was how long I could go without sleep. Nohea started the car, as Russell reached his head in the window for another deep passionate kiss.

"Wait! I have to talk to you about these nightmares."

Nohea gradually pulled the car out of the semi in reverse, Russell was still holding my hand, and then motioned for Nohea to stop.

"They're not nightmares. They're abductions," he replied.

"Why are they abducting me?" My eyes were tearing up. "I am afraid to sleep"

"Listen. Talk to no one tonight. It'll be alright. When you get home put that necklace around your neck. As long as you wear it around your neck, they can't abduct you. I promise. I'll contact you in the next couple days."

"How? I don't have a cell phone, remember."

"Don't worry, I'll work that out, just go home and get ready for the marathon. Most importantly, talk to no one, for me. I love you."

His hand reluctantly released from mine.

"I love you, too."

Looking one last time at his face as Nohea went to back out of the truck. I had no idea where we were, but I wasn't driving. Russell briefly waved, then disappeared behind the closed trailer doors and just like that, the truck was on its way. I waved as we made our way around the side of the truck. I knew Russell was watching the video screens and for a moment, a sinking sensation overwhelmed me, as if that might be the last time I'd see him alive. Colby sensed the same thing, leaping from the floor, joining in the good-bye with a hearty bark out the back window. My emotions finally got the better of me as the tear ducts opened, flooding my eyes, and streaming uncontrollably down my cheeks. I knew he was still alive…at least for now. I felt like a widow at her husband's funeral and mourning the loss of fifty years of marriage.

Nohea remained silent the entire ride home as he hoped the backdrop of the surf and the soothing music of Hawai'i would help ease things. I have no idea how long it took us to return to the house; my watch still stuck on 3:30. It was already dark. Having missed the sunset, we'd been gone awhile. I decided once home to record any questions in my journal. I thought it would help to begin making sense of everything. I had access to a computer for research, maybe I would even email my friend Scott back in Vegas. If anyone knew about aliens, abductions, and Government conspiracies, it was definitely him.

Nohea pulled into the driveway and I suddenly remembered the copy of Tracy's folder still in my purse. With all the commotion, I'd forgotten to give it to Russell.

"Nohea, can you make sure Russell gets this folder."

"No problem, Miss Jones," he replied.

He seemed unbothered by today's events, like this was part of his typical day. He was so mature for someone so young. I grabbed Colby from the backseat, closed the door, turning for my temporary home.

"Miss Jones," Nohea called from the car.

"What?"

"I've known Mr. Hamilton for a while now. If he says it'll be alright then it'll be alright. Please enjoy the next few days."

I don't know if it was his tone or the expression in his face, but I believed him. He flashed a smile similar to Russell, slowly rolled up the tinted window, and vanished through the gate. The next two days were going to be hell, while I silently waited for his call.

Chapter 24

Tracy met me at the door with Pakile, like parents waiting up for their teenage daughter to return home from her first date.

"You alright?" Tracy asked, wrapping her arms around me, squeezing so hard I could hardly breathe.

"Yeah, mom." I jokingly replied.

"Pakile said you left a while ago. I tried your cell but there was no answer. I even took a drive down the beach. I was worried sick. I thought something happened."

I didn't know how to react. Russell specifically asked me not to mention him or our meeting. I would have to conjure up another lie, but needed time to construct a plausible explanation. *What would buy me some time?*

"I really have to go the bathroom plus Colby needs supper. Can you hold that thought?"

I didn't have to go, but carried on the charade meticulously.

"I'll get Colby his supper, Miss Jones," Pakile grabbed the leash.

Colby responded to Pakile with a deep threatening growl. Whether a direct response to Pakile or the unwillingness to leave my sight I couldn't tell, but it was a side of him I'd never seen.

"Colby, go get supper," pointing towards the kitchen as he reluctantly accompanied Pakile. "Back in a sec...," to Tracy as I sprinted to the upstairs bathroom, overlooking the fact there was one around the corner.

"Okay, I'll wait for you down here," Tracy, replied.

The motivation for urgently wanting to go upstairs was to recover the necklace. Russell advised me to put it on and not take it off, though I didn't grasp its exact significance. After saving my life this afternoon, I trusted him, but more notably was falling in love with him.

The necklace was right where I left it, in the bathroom. The beauty of the gems glowed fiercely with a greater understanding of their significance. I splashed water on my face in an effort to lighten the puffiness, and then placed the necklace around my neck. I flushed the toilet before nonchalantly making my way downstairs, having to uphold the deception. Colby having had supper flew around the corner, greeting me at the bottom of the stairs. Tracy instantly noticed the necklace.

"That's nice," reaching to examine it.

"Yeah, Russell gave it to me," staring downward at it.

The truth was an older Hawai'ian woman gave me the necklace, but Tracy didn't need to know that, at least not now.

"Did you see him today," with a devilish grin, she asked?

She walked with me towards the outdoor patio, Colby had to go out, I needed a drink, and she continued fishing for answers. Why? It was a beautiful night, but the mysteries of the ocean failed in contrast to the starlit night sky. Maybe, it was because other than vacation, my newfound secrets were weighing on my mind. Russell wanted me to enjoy the next couple of days. To pull that off, I would need the Academy Award Performance of a lifetime.

I was apprehensive about the deceitfulness and deception that was to follow in the coming days. Unfortunately discovering once you start down the path, the harder it is to find your way back to the truth. I anguished over the possibility of slipping up or worse, contradicting a previous deception. I was deceiving everybody around me, including my best friend, all because of a guy I'd only just met. I was falling in love with, yet still knew nothing about; well there goes that fairytale ending.

"So you still up for biking down Haleakalā tomorrow?" Tracy inquired.

Before I got a chance to answer, Pakile had interrupted us with freshly cut fruit and a Pineapple-Mango smoothie. I seized a bite of chocolate covered pineapple, giving myself extra time to ponder the idea, but truthfully just famished. The fruit melted in my mouth like warm sugar. This is why I wanted to come here and Russell was right. I needed to enjoy myself, even if only a few days and I took another long sip of the smoothie. Say what you want about Pakile, he made a great smoothie.

"Yeah, I'm feeling a lot better. Let's do it," I replied.

My smile had returned, maybe because of the escaped intimate hallucinations of Russell. The puncture wounds on my arm a visual keepsake; they weren't hallucinations. I had no cell phone. I hadn't slept in two nights. I was on the verge of a psychotic break, and entrusted with the secret that we're not alone in the universe. Oh, by the way did I mention my boyfriend secretly works for the government and I didn't know whom I could trust? Did I exclude anything? Oh, yeah **SOMEONE IS TRYING TO KILL ME!** This wasn't how I had pictured this vacation.

"We should try to get some sleep. The tour van will be here by 2:30 a.m. to pick us up. We want to get to the summit before sunrise," Tracy dialed her phone and confirmed our reservation. "You think you'll be able to sleep tonight?"

For some reason, I don't know why, maybe it was the necklace, but the idea of sleep was comforting.

"Yeah, I'll be fine," smiling, "sleep's overrated anyways. I'll get enough when I'm dead."

"If you fall asleep biking down Haleakalā, that could be a possibility. Some of those sections have no guardrails with drop-offs thousands of feet."

"Greattttt," my enlightened enthusiasm returned.

"I'm thankful you're alright. Listen. Try to get some sleep. We'll talk tomorrow. Right now I need to sleep."

She gave me another quick hug before making her way upstairs while I waited for Colby to return from the backyard. The sounds of the ocean had made me tired or maybe it was the fresh fruit but, I almost fell asleep in the chair had it not been for the oh-so-familiar gentle nudge at my elbow. Colby sat at my feet begging for a handout. Pakile was nowhere-to-be-found and I didn't want to leave the fruit outside, so picking up the tray I returned it to the kitchen before retiring.

Tracy was right; I needed sleep, even a few hours. I set the alarm for 2 a.m., laid out my clothes for the morning, and wrote a quick entry into my journal with no ambition to write a novel tonight. I opened the window to tranquil sounds of the distant beach as its salty breeze touched my nose and the soft scents of the floral gardens below merging and imbuing my room. I slipped into a short silk nightie that felt great on the skin, pulled back the blankets, and climbed into bed with a single sheet draped over my exhausted body. Within seconds, Colby had sprawled out at the foot of the bed, recognizing the impracticality of a puppy blanket tonight. I was grateful for my shortness, as he claimed most of the bed. His presence at my feet was a comfort.

I hesitated closing my eyes as splintered nightmarish images flashed with uncertainty but today's persistent proceedings were seemingly holding them at bay. The necklace now firmly placed around my neck, twirled through my fingers, the stones illuminating a godly glow from only the full moon's ambient light. I felt like a kid fighting off a bad dream with a flashlight as he hid beneath his sheet from some big bad monster. The only difference, mine were bonafide nightmares.

I played a game, closing only one eye, then both but, only for a second until I finally dosed off, immediately entering a deep slumber. I awoke to the annoying sound of an alarm that clearly had being buzzing for minutes. It was a short sleep but, it was sleep and I awoke feeling refreshed. Normally, a lack of eight hours and I wouldn't be able to function for the day. Yet here it was, six hours over the last three days. At any rate, I had no nightmares or abductions.

December 30, 2009 Early Morning

I opted for a brief shower, quickly dressed and went in search of fresh coffee. Colby, again sensing his uninvited attendance on this trip, decided to linger and snuggled with my pillow on the bed. I gave him a great big bear hug and kissed him on the head before going downstairs. I yearned to climb back next to him and cuddle and he wasn't making it any easier to say no as he softly raised his head and delivered a delicate lick to my cheek. His way of saying '*Go have fun today, mom. I'll be alright*', and that's exactly what I was planning on doing.

Tracy was already downstairs, with freshly brewed coffee in two big thermoses, snacks, and a backpack geared up and ready to go.

"Want some coffee?" She asked.

"Love some," it smelt so good.

"You can put your camera and things in my backpack. I've plenty of room," she uttered, handing me my coffee.

"Thanks."

"Did you sleep?"

"Actually, I did. Pretty sound."

"No nightmares?"

"None that I can remember either psychologically," pointing to my arm, "or physically."

"By the way, how is your arm?"

"It doesn't hurt anymore if that's what you mean. I only hope it doesn't scar."

"It shouldn't but, if it does you'll have a great story to tell your grandkids," she smiled.

"I still have to find Mr. Right first," I exclaimed.

"I don't know…I think you might've already found him."

"We'll see," blushing.

She obviously referred to Russell as Mr. Right. He was more than Mr. Right, he was lust and sexual tension all wrapped up in that tight body of his. He had entered my dreams last night, but the details escaped my recollections. I do remember the dream at times became so vivid it felt alive as we fulfilled our fantasy from the beach. He was a god, taking me to places no other man had gone before. Maybe that's why I slept so sound last night, 'cause I always slept well after sex. Of course, it was just a dream, *right?* Then again, I thought they were only nightmares. Regardless, those types of dreams could happen to me any night, maybe even twice. I'm getting so bad!

We made our way outside, down in front of the gate as we waited for the tour van to arrive.

"Oh, I forgot to leave Pakile a note about feeding Colby."

"Don't worry, I mentioned it to him last night," Tracy replied.

She always remembered every detail no matter how minute, that's what Jim loved about her. On one occasion I asked her about their relationship, she just laughed it off saying he's married. She was right. I on several occasion did meet his wife. Tracy was however constantly extra friendly towards Jim and he reciprocated the feelings. The office rumor was they were having an affair. There was no denial by her either way, so I figured it was her way of saying "none of your business". The truth said, she was right; it was none of my business. However, not many bosses would allow you to stay in their million-dollar house on a private beach in Maui…for nothing.

The lights of the van broke the darkness as it rolled down South Kihei. It had to be them; no one else would've been down here at this hour of the morning. Well, I shouldn't say that now, should I? The bike excursion was a bonus, but in fact, the sunrise atop Haleakalā was what I looked forward to and planned to enjoy. Determined to ignore or at best suppress the past few day's events and take in the next two days. The van stopped, filled with other sleepless tourists daring to brave the night. We must've been the final stop before making the ascension to the volcano's summit.

"Hi, I'm Mika'ele from *Mountain Riders*. You must be Tracy and Erica, my last two of the group."

Mika'ele was a native Hawai'ian with dark tan, cobalt blue eyes, and a smile that lit up darkness of the night. Tracy found him right away delightful, obvious in her physical feminine charm.

"Hi, I'm Tracy," trading a handshake with an Aloha hug.

"Erica," I waved.

"Just jump in, grab an empty seat. There're muffins and coffee if you want some. Made them myself."

We climbed into the van full of half-asleep zombies, sucking down Kona Coffee, and coffee cake muffins. They glared at us, irritated, with an emotionless glare as if we were holding up the trip. Mika'ele, having gone out of his way to pick us up meant everyone else had gotten less sleep than we had and it showed. They resented the outward show as we were both wide-awake, but internally my body still fought the lack of sleep. Tracy let me ride shotgun knowing my excitement for this experience, while she joined the living dead in the rear.

"Okay, ladies and gentlemen sit back and enjoy as it will take us about two hours from here to the top of Haleakalā. On the ascent, I'll point out interesting facts and features of Haleakalā and Maui. We should get to the top about thirty minutes before sunrise. Currently, the temperature at the summit is a balmy thirty-nine degrees, so I hope you dressed warm. If you have any questions please feel free to ask."

With that, Mika'ele turned the van around making for the highway while I wondered if I'd dressed warm enough. I did bring an extra sweatshirt just in case. Tracy handed me my thermos and my favorite, a triple chocolate chip muffin. I didn't need the calories, but figured I'd burn them off on the bike ride down. I sat back and enjoyed the conversation with Mika'ele. I had an amplitude of questions sitting fresh in my mind.

Like, *did he know who the individuals associated with the Majestic 12 were? Who were aliens on this planet? Why was I being abducted? What else was the Government covering up? And, why the hell was someone trying to kill me?* No, I couldn't ask him these questions, he'd think I was crazy. Anyways, someone was already headlong into discovering these answers for me, and he wanted me to enjoy my vacation.

"So Mika'ele, how long have you been doing these tours?"

I asked a reasonable question and expected a practical answer then leaned back with plans to enjoy today. The rest could wait until tomorrow…

Chapter 25

January 1, 2010 Marathon Day

I spent the next few days doing exactly what Russell had ordered, enjoying my vacation! I hadn't heard from Russell since our last meeting and worried, but Nohea promised me everything was going to be alright. I needed these last few days to unwind and get ready for the marathon. Writing in my journal this morning was serving to clear my head before the big run. I erratically wrote down my thoughts of the last few days, rehashing some of the highs and lows.

Since wearing the necklace around the clock, my sleep schedule returned to normal with no more unannounced visitors. I was uncertain of the power it posed but at this point didn't care. If not for that charm, I would've been one sleepless night closer to a psychotic break. At that point, I could see the rest of my vacation spent down a long hallway, in a white padded room, strapped to a bed, and waiting my next dose of Clozapine. Over the last few days, I tried purging my memories of those nights, but to no avail. Tracy wasn't prying, figuring if and when I needed to talk, she'd listen.

I managed to send a brief email to my friend Scott in Vegas highlighting some of the events. He was a member of MUFON (Mutual Unidentified Flying Object Network) and a solid believer in the existence of extraterrestrial life. He was also the smartest person I knew when it came to computers. He had arranged a gathering for me when I returned with some of the members of The Las Vegas UFO Hunters. In his email, Scott mentioned many were experiencers. He said their understanding of the subject matter would be most encouraging to me, especially on abductions.

I can say Tracy was of great help effectively keeping me busy the last few days. If you ever get to Hawai'i, you must see the sunrise from the summit of Haleakalā, although it was chilly at the summits' peak elevation of about 10,000 feet. However, to describe the sun's magnificence as it intensified over the horizon would be futile. In fact, I realized just how insignificant we are on this small rock called Earth, while in awe of the true powers of the Universe. This is one of the few times in my life, I can honestly say, I was speechless.

Of course, later, lacking in sleep, the bike down the volcano offered its own version of awe, the *"Holy Shit"* kind. I managed to navigate down, wanting to stay behind the group most of the way. Tracy was a triathlete, a damn good one, and relentlessly encouraging me to convert from being just a runner. I was an okay swimmer, a decent runner, but biking never was an obsession, even as a child. In the end, euphoric with my experience, as our tour guide Mika'ele was encouraging, educational, and habitually hysterical. I was glad I hadn't opted out, as by far this was one of the most memorable events, I experienced since in Hawai'i.

The day was going so well Tracy and I took an impromptu helicopter charter with *MauiScape* over the Big Island's active volcano Kilauea. Mother Nature, even when violent, is so stunning. Tracy wanted to do a guided hike and view the active lava tubes on our next trip. I wanted to get through this first trip.

MauiScape also included a free private tour of Maui's most scenic highlights along the coast and inland. In all actuality, it wasn't free; Tracy had called in a few favors to get us this private tour. Apparently, MauiScape has links to Jim's company, C.H.A.R.A.

To fly over Haleakalā's summit, and witness *Skyline* observatory from the air, put into prospective the enormity of this extinct volcano. Our pilot explained, Skyline was a Government run facility managed by the Air Force and access required special security clearance. Russell had connection in some way to the Government, so access I didn't think was going to be a problem. He even had suggested taking us to the observatory, but today was the marathon and tomorrow we left for Nevada. I would've liked to see it, but Russell hadn't contacted me and I tried not to agonize over it, although I had hoped to see him before leaving. His company was sponsoring the marathon, and a part of me expected to see him there, but I didn't want to get my hopes up.

The marathon started at 1 p.m. with check-in starting at 11 a.m., so I had time to kill this morning. After jotting down notes in my journal, I spent the remainder of the time on the beach with

Colby. His excitement the other day had prompted me to buy him a Frisbee. We spent every morning, the last few days, playing in the backyard and on the beach. Best investment I've ever made.

As I returned to the house, this out-of-the-ordinary sensation overwhelmed my body. Call it a sixth sense or whatever, but I felt convinced Russell was trying to contact me. Pakile was in the kitchen having his morning coffee and I still couldn't get through how uncomfortable he made me feel. I can't explain it, but since my abductions and the strange light that emanated from his room a few days ago, I avoid him like the plaque.

"Miss Jones, a package came for you," Pakile pointed to the wrapped parcel sitting on the island.

"Thanks."

It was a fairly small box, my name neatly written on its elegant packaging, nothing else, not even a return address. I grabbed it making a hasty retreat to my room with Colby in tow. My paranoia was getting the better of me as I admired it from a distance. I thought about opening it; listening, half-expectant to hear the faint ticking of a clock bomb, like in the movies. I laugh at myself now for that one, considering what had transpired. They had tracked me through my cell phone and could've vaporized me through my cell phone. Let's face it; if their intentions were to execute me, I doubt they'd resort to a simple bomb in the mail. They've since evolved into a more modernized breed of assassins.

Sitting on my bed, I tore into the boxes' wrapping as if it was Christmas morning. Inside were a card and another much smaller wrapped box. The card was from Russell and read:

Erica:

First, I must let know you I'm alright, but will be unable to see you at the marathon today and wish you good luck. On the other hand, I wish to see you tonight. I've enclosed a new cell phone for you and hope you like it. If tonight works for you, open the phone, hit redial and leave me a message. I miss you.

Love,

Russell

My eyes teared up while rereading the card. It could've been the *knowing* he was safe; more likely though was the use of the word *love*. It's been a longtime since a guy's written the words '*I Love You*' to me and meant it, even longer since I believed the same.

I ripped open the smaller box without hesitation, wanting to punch redial. The phone was modern, but technologically had an edge, something I'd never seen in a phone as I gave it a closer inspection. Reflections of my last phone vaporized from space and delayed me hitting redial. Odd, it had no company trademark, even on the back cover. I half expected it to read, "Made in China". I wondered the service provider and if they covered Vegas, something tonight to confirm with Russell. Alright, enough delaying already I hit redial, hoping to hear Russell's voice pick-up, instead a beep, not even a message.

"Russell this is Erica. I'd love to get together tonight. We ought to be home from the marathon after six. I miss you. I can't wait to see you," and hung up the phone.

I couldn't say I love you over the phone. Why? I felt the same way. Perhaps first I needed the answers to all my questions, or just wanted to say it to him personally. At least I was going to see him tonight, a definite motivation to cross the finish line faster.

I joined Tracy downstairs shortly after leaving the phone message, now more than ever geared up to run. I avoided discussing the package or at least its contents and wondered if Pakile had already told her. I was carrying the phone with me in the event Russell returned my call. The traffic was going to be crazy so we had asked Lulani to drive us to Lāhainā and he was waiting for us in the kitchen.

The marathon started on the outskirts of Lāhainā, continued north before returning south, and finished in the heart of Lāhainā's downtown. They were expecting about three thousand runners and after being there a few times, I wondered where they were going to put everyone.

To make a long story short, the organizers did an extraordinary job with the event. The entire course, well thought out with checkpoints, water stops, bathrooms, was one of the best races I'd ever run. The only negative, at least for me, was the humidity, as it hit well over ninety degrees by the afternoon. I did manage to post a new personal best time for a marathon. One reason being, the anticipation of seeing Russell once more. The second I owe to Tracy, who finished over forty-five minutes ahead. She could've waited at the finish, instead she doubled back about three miles to join and encourage me the rest of the way. We crossed the finish line simultaneously, holding hands above our heads smiling. A local newspaper reporter captured the picture, running a small story on us and the event, in addition thoughtfully sending us each a copy. That was the last treasured picture we had together and I cherish it every time I open my fridge.

Lulani picked us up in the limo and as we approached the driveway to the house, my new phone rang. I excitedly answered expecting it to be Russell.

"Hello."

"Miss Jones, a car will pick you up to see Russell at seven," replied a mysteriously intense voice.

"Who is this?"

"A friend of Russell's."

"Where is he? Why didn't he call?"

This spy shit was getting ridiculous.

"Miss Jones, 7 p.m. Please be ready. Sorry, I've got to go," the line went dead.

"Hello, Hello," I closed the phone returning it to my purse.

"What? You got a new phone and didn't tell me?" Tracy questioned.

"Yeah, I lost the other one," failing to disclose the truth.

"Was that lover boy?" She smiled.

"Truthfully, I don't know," telling the truth, "I need to be ready for seven, clearly a car is coming by to pick-me-up."

I wanted to leave it at that, but knowing Tracy's inquisitiveness nature, she was going to press me for information.

"A stranger calls, says a car will be here at seven, doesn't tell you where or whom you're going to see and you're intending to climb on in?" It sounded worse the way she said it.

"Yeah."

I declined to elaborate the meeting was with Russell and at least hoped it would be Nohea chauffeuring me to the location. I didn't recognize the voice and for all I knew could've been the Men In Black. Tracy had a point, what the hell was I thinking. At this point, figuring I'd play it by ear when the driver arrived and cross-examine him before leaving.

"You're either in love or crazy...hopefully you know what you're doing...remember...think before you jump," she slyly remarked.

"I had given up philosophizing on my life days ago."

"Well, at least call to let me know you're alright."

"Deal," I said.

We were both worn-out from the run, but I was motivated and caught my second wind. I hated lying to Tracy but was getting exceptional at it. There was still plenty of time to feed Colby, take him on a brisk beach walk, and be ready for my date. On returning to the house, another delivered surprise package awaited.

It was again addressed with only my name on it, with an inside card written in stylish script that read '*To my Ka'iu lani*', clearly a gift from Russell. It was his code word and this time a beautiful black silk sleeveless Valentino gown. The kind that fell at the knee with a low cutout back designed for braless wear. Also included was a beautiful pair of Prada Patent Leather Sandals with a matching purse. In addition, a pair of thigh high black silk stockings and designer black panties, the kind you'd expect for Valentine's Day. I didn't know where we were going or what his plans were but I knew it wasn't going to be McDonalds. One thing about Russell, for a guy he had great taste in clothes, but what amazed me more was how the whole outfit fit as if sculptured with me in mind. Being petite, I constantly fought trying to find clothes that fit my body.

I'm sure Colby was disappointed with our brief walk on the beach, but my excitement to try on the new outfit overwhelmed me.

I was apprehensive about removing the necklace since it didn't match the outfit and opted to forego it adding it to the contents of my purse, at least for now. One final twirl in front of the mirror as Colby barked his approval from the bed. I had to agree with him, I'd never looked this hot and gave him a gentle peck on his head in thanks, while avoiding his urges to leave his famous drool marks. It was obvious he wanted to come, having spoiled him with my constant presence these last few days. Of course, because of the marathon today, we hadn't had much time together. I left the room before crying to avoid ruining the time spent on makeup.

"Well, look at you," Tracy voiced pleasantly, as I made my retreat from Colby.

"What do you think?" I was spinning like a princess.

"I can say one thing about Russell...I mean your mystery man. He has exceptional taste in clothes." She smiled, downplaying her slip of the tongue.

That meant a great deal coming from Tracy, who had a keen eye for fashion. I envied her for it, but thought, for once in her life, she was jealous of my plans and me. Although, ignorant to the night's agenda, Russell's involvement made it safe, but why all the cloak-and-dagger?

"I'm sorry we aren't spending our last night here together," I addressed Tracy.

"I haven't seen you this happy in a longtime. You deserve this, go have fun." She was being a true friend and at this point had stopped hiding the fact she knew I was leaving to see Russell. "So where is that hunk of a man taking you?"

"I don't know."

"Fine don't tell me," playfully turning her head.

"Really, I don't know. The car is picking me up at seven and that's all I know." The sincerity in my voice and eyes prevailed.

"Why all the secrecy?" She asked.

"I don't know, but I'll call you the first chance I get."

"Promise!"

"Promise," I crossed my heart.

She was acting like an overprotective big sister, but the entire trip was her idea and at the time, we were still best friends so at the very least I owed her a phone call.

"Miss Jones, your ride is here," Pakile's voice echoed over the intercom.

"Okay. I gotta go," turning for the door then turning back, "Do I look okay?"

I needed one last approval. Tracy walked over and lightly embraced me at the door

"You look more than okay, you're beautiful. Now go have a great time."

"Thanks."

With a newfound poise and a big smile, I raced down to the awaiting car.

"Don't forget to call," Tracy yelled from atop the stairs.

Pakile held the door for me; I slowed to show my appreciation still not sure outside what awaited me. To my relief, Nohea stood next to a gorgeous Lincoln Town Car with its rear door ajar.

"Miss Jones, if you would," he said.

"Nohea, where's Russell?"

"Please have a seat in the car," flashing a reassuring smile.

"Okay."

I made my way into the backseat, absent of one Russell Hamilton and gazed through the tinted back window back towards the foyer. Pakile and Lulani watched me go as well as Tracy, who was on the phone. Nohea, upon fastening himself in, nonchalantly turned to study the three, as their eyes curiously tracked us while we continued stylishly down the driveway.

Chapter 26

I tried patiently to sit, as the sounds of Hawai'ian music flowed from the speakers, but had an assortment of questions for Nohea, particularly where were we headed. I was hoping he'd give me the heads up and not sworn to secrecy by Russell.

"So where are we going?"

I blamed the vacant response on the music's elevated volume. I tried again, raising my voice thunderously so to be heard even by the passing pedestrians on the sidewalk.

"So where are we going?"

Again, silence. I was about to crawl to the front when the music lowered and Nohea turned silently, handing me a note that read:

Please don't ask any more questions. I'm taking you to Russell. Please sit back and enjoy the ride.

What was the reason for all this cloak-and-dagger routine? Trusting Nohea, I sat back playing along as we drove roughly twenty minutes almost in circles at times. His continual vigilance in the side mirrors alerted me we had company. He watchfully exited into a sugarcane field by means of an unmarked small road. The radiance of the full moon highlighted the dusty road particles left in our wake. The lack of surrounding streetlights and only the car's headlights as a guide made the road scarcely detectable. Half a mile in, Nohea turned the car calmly to the right unswervingly into the sugarcane field establishing our own corridor. There was no urgency, as if a meticulously planned operation was underway.

"When I stop, please follow me," he explained.

My response was unspoken, but it drastically showed my understanding of the situation. Once we stopped, I continued to tag along through the fabricated small path into what seemed the densest part of the sugarcane. In the distance I heard, one, maybe two vehicles, coming to a halt. At once, doors opened and closed, while gradual shuffling of weighty feet amplified and our pursuers tried closing the distance. As if an optical illusion, we entered a clearing with a two-seated black helicopter stealthy awaiting our arrival.

"Get in," Nohea vehemently shouted while holding the door open.

I watched in bewilderment as he jumped into the pilot's seat.

"Please don't tell me you know how to fly this too."

I'm sure the astonished expression on my face was unmistakable as he began in succession flicking switches. The blades at once rapidly rotated, and within seconds, we were lifting off the ground. As we lifted it became visually clear three cars as well as a handful of men were making their way through the sugarcane. The darkness and density of the sugarcane restricted an accurate facial description. However, the distinctive dark sunglasses, lit by the helicopters landing lights, peered up at us like ants in a field. Once again, with aid from Nohea the MIB's were incapable of apprehending their mark.

"Learn something new every day," I expressed under my breath.

"There are many things you will learn tonight, Miss Jones. Some you'll want to hear and others you may not," he replied, then motioned to put on the headset.

A week ago, I was planning for a grand vacation. Now, flying god knows where, with mysterious agencies in pursuit, to my boyfriend, who clearly knows more than he's revealing. So much for me having one last romantic night on Maui. Putting the headphones on, careful not to mess up my hair, I shifted the protruding microphone to face my mouth.

"Nohea! What the HELL is going on? AND WHERE THE HELL ARE YOU TAKING ME?" My frustration finally peaked.

"Sorry. We were being followed. Plus I wasn't sure if the car had been bugged." He briefly turned in my direction. "We're going to meet Russell at the Skyline Observatory," pointing toward the top of Haleakalā's summit. "ETA, twenty minutes. If you'd like to talk to Russell, rotate the dial ahead of you to 367.3 MHz."

I couldn't wait to hear his voice, turning the dial as directed, but heard nothing but static.

"Hello, Hello Russell," I impatiently waited for a reply.

There was only static, looking at Nohea shrugging my shoulders, when suddenly the faintest voice…

"Aloha, Ka'iu lani. Hope you're enjoying your ride tonight." Russell's voice sent chills up my spine.

"Nohea is amazing, not what he seems," smiling in Nohea's direction.

"You'll find nothing any longer is what it seems," Russell responded.

"I'm slowly figuring that out."

"By the way, how'd you like the outfit?" Pausing, "I hope it fit okay."

Before I could respond, Nohea chimed in over his microphone.

"She's a goddess and a true spirit of beauty," smiling back at me.

At this point, I was blushing, but also wanted to discover why everyone kept referring to me as goddess. I didn't suffer from low self-esteem, but this whole goddess thing was making me feel uncomfortable.

"Mahalo. The clothes fit great, a bit much for romping around a sugarcane field and helicopter ride, you think?"

"Sorry. A necessary diversion. How's the phone?"

"The phone's awesome. I do have a couple of questions though."

"Nohea, what's your ETA?" Russell inquired.

"ETA, about ten minutes."

"Affirmative. Erica, sit back. I'll see you in a few, and then we can talk." His voiced substituted with white noise.

"Russell, Russell you still there," looking at Nohea.

"It's okay. He signed off. He doesn't want anyone tracking us to his location."

Nohea focused his attention as we climbed the southern face of Haleakalā. The dormant volcano emanated at night a truly malevolent aura. The helicopter soared over trees; dangerously close at times, its maneuverability commercially unequaled, with a softness to its whispering blades no louder than wind. The landing lights idle from the ground, we must have looked like a void in the night sky. It took only minutes but felt like days before landing in the observatory's parking lot as Russell waved from the sidewalk.

The blades eased to a stop, as Russell approached the helicopter door, while I eagerly battled to free myself from the damn seat belt. As it released the door opened, Russell effortlessly raised me in his arms and into a warm embrace. I already could feel the passionate embers rekindling into a roaring fire. He smelt summer rain fresh, as if he'd just stepped out of the shower and his tailored formal black tie ensemble highlighted every bulging muscle. The moonlight danced on his highly buffed Armani shoes. Holding on firmly, taking in his dominating embrace, I had an uncontrollable desire to kiss him, and in all honesty wanting to take him right there. Sensing it too, he receded, sufficiently preserving the sexual tension, to admire my body wearing his recently bought wardrobe.

"Nohea was right…you are a Goddess," he affirmed.

"You're looking dashing, too."

I tried not to let my sexual frustration be too obvious.

"Thanks, Nohea," voicing as he passed.

"Mahalo, boss."

Nohea nonchalantly smiled before entering the observatory's front doors.

"Okay, what's going on?" I asked.

"I told you I wanted to show you the observatory."

"Yeah, so why the security procedures and formal outfits."

"You'll see when we get inside."

Offering me his arm we entered Skyline Observatory, taking an easy stroll past the receptionist desk to an extended hallway, ending at a set of double doors marked *Boardroom*. Astonishing, as we entered this room, it had painstakingly transformed into an elegant single table restaurant. Equipped with an ice sculptor, perfectly set sterling silver, China and linen, stylish floral arrangements—even a three-piece string orchestra. Nohea, greeting us at the door had again transformed himself, this time playing Maître D'.

"Table for two, sir?" Nohea invited us in using his best Old English.

As we approached the candlelit table and took our linen draped chairs, the orchestra began playing. The romantic ambience beyond question overwhelmed the room. Never had a man gone through such lengths to impress me before, this was going to be hard to top. I wanted to pass over dinner proceedings without delay to dessert and Russell was dessert. My mind raced, while at the same time, my heart fluttered through my chest. The woman in me wanted to take pleasure in the night, but I couldn't escape the magnitude of unanswered questions. I felt an unrelenting need to get his view on my nightmares.

"I know you've got many questions and tonight many of them will get answered. However, let's ignore that for the moment and enjoy our evening."

He grabbed my hand and smiled. I wanted to enjoy this moment, relish in his company, and stare hopelessly into his eyes. He felt like my future, and I was in love. So the answers didn't come until afterwards, I probably wasn't going to care for the answers anyhow.

We ate dinner, casually talked, and even danced all before dessert. If not for the out-of-the-ordinary start and the peculiarity of dining in an observatory this date would've been perfect. After finishing our dessert, Russell's mood started to shift, his unfathomable thoughts weighing heavy as he contemplated disclosure. The tables clearing a signal that bliss was over and the agonizing reality of the truth was imminent.

"What's wrong?" I sensed his agitation.

"I've a number of answers for you, but also a few questions."

"Great. Where do we start?" I asked eagerly.

"First, I want you to meet someone," he lovingly clasped my hand.

"Who is this someone?" I followed his lead without a choice.

"He's the Astronomer in charge of the SETI program here at Skyline. Are you familiar with SETI?"

"It stands for the Search for Extraterrestrial Intelligence. Right?" my mind recalling a clip from the movie *Contact* with Jodie Foster.

"That's right," leading me up a tight spiral metal staircase, "Careful climbing these stairs."

We had to have climbed two stories of stairs, my ankles feeling the brunt of it with these shoes. At the top, a single white door set off by a simple red lettered sign '*Private*'. Russell entered first, not much room for well-mannered gestures in such close quarters. The door opened to the observation's support deck for the enormous telescope. Technologically sophisticated equipment spread throughout the room's transparent opened walls. The roof of the observatory peeled back slightly as the telescope partially protruded into the open-air. The darkness of the night lit merely by computer displays and the occasional flashing of lit up panel switches. We approached two men in discussion, congregated around a large display screen.

"Erica, this is Dr. Marks and Dr. Williams," Russell explained.

Dr. Marks, an older single man, reminded me of my Philosophy Professor years ago in college. A neatly trimmed, light gray goatee framed his face matching the color of his receding hairline. His wire-framed bifocals sitting on the brim of his nose while a white lab coat embroidered with his name over the top right-hand pocket proudly identified him as Doctor. I guessed single by choice, his passion for his work and his above normal IQ made dating an impossibility or at best unfeasible.

Dr. Williams, a complete reversal of Dr. Marks; clean shaved with a youthful appearance as if still in his late teens, probably a child prodigy. His rebellious thick brown hair tied back in a ponytail revealing his pierced ears. Loose fitting jeans with a Hemp knotted belt, a Hawai'ian shirt and Nike sneakers replaced the dull lab coat. There was a restlessness about him as he chewed the end of a coffee stirrer. It could've been the sleepless nights or maybe his obsession with caffeine, but he was on the edge. Clearly, Dr. Marks indulged him as an equal, as his IQ rivaled, if not topped everyone else in the room.

At first, neither spoke while they sized me up. Maybe I was the first woman they'd seen in months, unable to shake this feeling of a lamb to its slaughter. I reached for Russell who seemed distracted, clearly searching the room for something or someone.

"Where's Samantha?" He asked.

"She's downstairs, she'll be up in a few minutes," replied Dr. Marks.

"Who's Samantha?" I asked.

"You'll see," Russell pleasantly smirked. "Is the presentation ready to go?" He questioned to Dr. Williams.

"Yeah we're ready. Are you convinced this is in her best interest?" Dr. Williams asked Russell outlandishly poised in my direction.

"I told you both she can be trusted," Russell faced me, "she needs to know the truth."

"The truth about what?" My interest peaked.

"I hate to interrupt, but I brought Samantha up."

Nohea arrived through the same door we had, breaking the hidden tension. As he stepped to the side of the opened door, a female Golden Retriever emerged, excitedly wagging her tail while in route to Dr. Marks.

"Erica, this is Samantha," Russell said pointing to a small version of Colby.

She sniffed and grunted in enthusiasm as I reached down to pat her, although a stranger, I was positive she could smell Colby.

"Hello Samantha. Aren't you just a Princess?"

I briefly rubbed her ears before she hit the floor exposing her belly. Colby did this all the time when he was in the mood to snuggle. Nothing like a good belly rub to make your troubles fade away.

"Erica has a golden," Russell expressed to Dr. Marks.

"Well if Samantha trusts you, so shall we," he rolled over a chair, "please Erica, have a seat."

"Thank you," sitting, "now what's this about a presentation?"

Dr. Williams rotated in his chair, pushed a few buttons on his computer, and waited for a confirmation.

"Watch this screen," directing me to an above plasma screen.

On the screen appeared a man from an unrecognized branch of the military, sitting behind a desk in what looked to be his private office. His features, darkly lit, not professionally made, and more along the lines of a VHS home video. The film played gradually zooming into a tight frame around the man.

"If you're watching this tape then my life has been terminated. It pains me to think of the deception both extraterrestrial and within our own Government. My expectation is that this video goes public and doesn't end up silenced such as myself.

Since the beginning of time, Earth has been visited by beings far superior in technology and physical attributes to humans. Some offer help, some come to enslave us and many others watch. Until recently, this UFO phenomenon was nothing to me but a collaboration of delusional conspiracy extremists. That, over the past few months, has proven to be false. To those that have fought for full Government disclosure I put forward my sincere apology, with trust you succeed in the future for the sake of all humanity.

To my dear friends Dr. Marks and Dr. Williams, I offer evidence with this video that you've so adamantly sought. Please understand that your continued involvement may well put your lives in jeopardy. Please continue, if you so wish, with caution. Let my daughter know, in the future, that her father was not a traitor to his people, but a libertarian of truth."

The man, who I later found out was a General, momentarily paused, leisurely retrieving a file folder from underneath the desk. During this time it was visibly obvious the doctors were having a hard time watching, as they turned away fighting back the tears. They either were mourning the loss of their friend or already enlightened with the folder's contents, unwilling to relive those emotions. The General, on reflection, continued with the most undeniable proof of extraterrestrial life I had ever witnessed.

"There are more than two hundred species of intelligent life existing on this planet. Some live daily among us, while others have chosen for their home, the deep-sea and subterranean Earth. Our Government, as well as an alliance of Foreign Governments, is well aware of this fact, and in many cases, aiding their agendas. These species originate from our own solar system plus further outlying galaxies. A number want political asylum from worlds that have collapsed by way of their enemies, others seek to help Earth in her evolution. Worse yet, several are here to enslave and trade us as a commodity throughout the solar systems."

Again, he paused from his disclosure while he removed a catalog of pictures from the file folder.

"I've enclosed a comprehensive catalog of species I've personally interacted and become familiar with, also their known agendas. The paperwork before you details their strengths, weakness, origins, as well as Government agencies possibly involved. Unfortunately, my limited security clearance forbids finding out to what scale of intertwined involvement there now is, and I can only hypothesize. Again, the folders do not document all species so please go with vigilance.

My involvement focused mainly with a species referred to as the Greys. I documented, throughout my involvement, twenty-two separate factions of this species. Although they have a superior technological intelligence, they are but pawns for another race. Again, my security clearance is incapable of accessing details on their agendas. Similar to our religions on Earth, these alien factions each have their own principles. A few have even offered to help advance us far beyond what we are capable of grasping at this time.

Others have a more ominous agenda, which I've speculated on in the enclosed copy. However, most disturbing to me and others in the military is our Government's unwavering participation in their projects and agenda."

He continued, holding up a picture of one species of Greys, which triggered an instant response. I trembled uncontrollably, and then screamed, as those nightmarish eyes penetrated my soul, resurfacing all those suppressed emotions.

"No! No! No! Not again." Screaming, I rolled up into a fetal position on the other side of the room. "Stop! No stop! I didn't ask for this." I hysterically repeated while pointing to the screen.

"Shut the screen off! Shut it off now!" Russell barked.

At this point, I vaguely remembering Russell and Dr. Williams rushing to my side, the frozen close-up of the Grey's face still glaring at me from above on the screen. Finally, Dr. Marks stopped the video image, snatched a bottled water, and rushed to my side, trying to aid the others in calming me down. With the image no longer in view, I stopped trembling and with support was able to get off the floor. Realizing, as I sat in a nearby chair, the absence of my necklace, which shielded me from these memories the past few nights. I frantically searched the room with my eyes for the purse.

"Where's my purse? Where the hell is my purse!" I called, persistently determined to return the necklace to my neck.

Everyone scampered the room in search of my purse. Nohea, at last found it and quickly brought it to me. I swiftly opened it, dumping its contents in my lap with the sole purpose of restoring the necklace. Instantly my body calmed as I quickly clasped it around my neck, whether as a placebo effect or not. At this point, I didn't care.

It took me a few minutes to regain my composure, at which point, I explained my contact with the Greys. I'd in no way mentioned the Greys to anyone apart from Tracy. In a way, it was a release finally to unburden myself from these hidden memories. *Why was it so important for me to see this video? Was it a test? A test I immediately failed, maybe even passed. What has all this to do with me and why did that picture hurl me into such a state?*

"I don't think it's a good idea, at this time to show her anymore," remarked Dr. Marks.

"I agree with you," Russell replied, as the warmth of his soothing hands penetrated mine through his unyielding grasp.

"So, how do we explain the rest of the tape? She needs to hear it," Dr. Williams whispered to Dr. Marks.

Dr. Marks waved him clear, joining him on the other side of the room, where they conversed briefly in private before returning. Nohea, during this time, had exited from sight through a cleverly disguised door found behind a panel bank of computer servers.

"Why don't we shift gears for a bit," Russell commented to the doctors.

"Good idea," agreed Dr. Williams.

Russell slid another chair over next to me, seated himself, trying to get me to focus my attention on his face. His eyes, smile, and essence was totally hypnotizing. I wrote it off as love.

"Erica, do you remember those statues in front of Jim's house?" I nodded '*Yes*'. "The symbols, in particular the etched lettering, correlate to writings discovered in texts that are over twenty thousand years old. Those symbols, and other comparable statues, were discovered buried beneath the largest pyramid in Egypt during the early 1940's. The fact these symbolic statues are at Jim's house is not as great a significance as the fact there are six of them."

"What do you mean by six?" I asked.

"Have you ever heard the name Jim Sparks?"

"No, why?"

"Mr. Sparks wrote a book called "*The Keepers*". In it he details his alien abductions, including what he learned from years of their teachings," Dr. Williams retorted.

"I still don't know what this has to do with me."

"You've been abducted by Greys, which ones are unclear, but you've undeniably been abducted." Dr. Williams continued, "Jim details a number system based on six, which is unlike our base system of ten,"

"The other day, upon passing the sculptures, I had a déjà vu moment. I'd seen those symbols before but couldn't picture the location," I recounted.

"One-way or another you identified with those symbols, maybe because of your abductions, maybe not. There's plenty of additional information our General friend sent us on and off video, you truly need to see," Dr. Marks suggested.

"Maybe another time, not tonight," Russell unyieldingly voiced.

I had been self-sufficient too long to suddenly have a man mediate my needs and it threw me a bit. No matter how protective he was trying to be, no one was going to impede with my pursuit for answers. I loved him greatly, but needed to follow my head, not my heart on this one.

"Give me a minute, and then let's watch the rest of the video." I adamantly expressed. I stood with a little help from Russell as I made my way back to the other side of the room.

"Are you sure you're up for this?" Russell asked.

"Yeah, I'll be fine. I need to know."

"We all need to know," Dr. Williams clarified.

As I sat, once again to be enlightened, a distant sound erupted outside the observatory, one of familiarity. The semi-opened roof allowed the ever-increasing sound of tires excessively approaching over the crushed graveled road. Nohea returned through the hidden panel door with a sense of urgency as he updated Russell with a status report.

"MIB's; no less than two vehicles, one *"Little Bird"*, ETA two minutes. We need to leave now!"

Everyone began collecting the paperwork, including the video, as Russell determinedly dictated orders.

"Nohea. Take the helicopter and draw the *"Little Bird"* out of range over the south side of the volcano. Doctors, you're coming with us."

Nohea immediately vanished, the quickness in his step echoed distantly in the stairwell. Dr. Marks opened the top of his desk drawer and brought back a G37 military issued Glock.

"Dr. Williams, get them out of here! I'll hold them off as long as I can," he insisted.

"They'll kill you, you know that," Dr. Williams responded.

"They won't...they want all that information you're holding...and as long as you have it I'll be safe. Now go, quickly!"

Dr. Marks handed us the remaining folders, as confirmation of his own death danced in his eyes. Nohea had already taken part of the files with him.

"Please take Samantha with you," he asked handing me her leash.

We made our leave only stopping shortly to witness Dr. Marks gearing up for an invasion. There was no doubt as we rapidly bolted down the stairwell, which would be the last time we'd see him alive. The darkly lit sloping corridors circled the circumference of the observatory to an emergency door at its base.

"Okay. Once we go through this door, there's a long steep passageway so be careful," Dr. Williams continued, "it extends from the observatory to a secret door within the janitor's closet at Haleakalā Visitor's Center. Only the two of us know about this passageway so we should be safe," he surely confirmed.

From above, gunshots unloaded as the heroic standoff commenced, the deadly rounds echoed throughout the steel building to the lower levels and ricocheted for a moment until falling fatally silent. We knew the results, hanging our heads in a moment of silence for our fallen friend, before hastily bearing through the narrow rocky cavern.

The center remained closed at night, but it didn't prevent a vast number of stargazing spectators from making the trip, particularly with a full moon. They had gathered on the outside observation deck and I wondered if any had heard the shots or the commotion up on the hill and called for help. We nonchalantly exited the building trying to blend in with the masses. I hadn't noticed the scale of tonight's full moon until now, its sheer size from this altitude was extraordinary. I reached to touch it, almost forgetting the gravity of the situation.

"What do we do now?" I asked.

"My truck is over there," Dr. Williams pointed to his Chevy Avalanche, "they may not even realize we're here. Usually, only Dr. Marks works tonight so we might be safe."

"What about Nohea?" I asked.

"As long as the helicopter got off the ground he'll be fine." Russell explained, nervously searching the skies for a sign.

"What did he mean by *Little Bird?*"

"The Majestic 12 as well as NSA at times uses a Special Operations Light Attack Helicopter known as AH-6 or "*Little Bird*". It's painted black, extremely maneuverable, and mainly used for rapid insertions and extractions, I'm assuming ours." Russell explained.

"Won't they shoot him down?" questioned Dr. Williams.

"They first have to catch him," Russell expressed too confidently, "Nohea is one, and if not the best helicopter pilots I know."

"Yeah, but if they're with the military…"

Russell stopped me before I could finish, turning his head to listen. Suddenly Nohea's helicopter flew over the parking lot, down the canyon, where just the other day, I had watched the most magnificent sunrise. In pursuit, a black helicopter barely visible had it not been for the backdrop of the full moon. Together vanishing, lost to the darkness of the vegetation below. The exquisiteness of this volcano now taking on a new threatening connotation, praying Nohea would be safe and I'd see him again.

"Okay, let's leisurely make our way to my truck," suggested Dr. Williams.

"First take off your ID tag," expressed Russell, pointing to the obvious give away.

"Right," stashing it in his pocket.

One by one, we crossed the parking lot to the Chevy, trying not to look conspicuous. Ever notice the harder you try to disguise yourself the more obvious you end up looking? As we started to enter the truck, Russell detected movement coming down from the observatory. A single car was traveling quickly down Skyline's dirt road, in its wake, an extended dust trail unmasking its true speed.

"Step on it, Doctor!" Russell shouted.

The truck quickly accelerated, erratically almost out of control, tossing us around in the backseat like rag dolls. He was no Nohea. Dr. Williams, I assumed, had no prior experience driving in this manner. He would soon prove me wrong as I turned getting a glimpse of the black car taking chase and quickly closing the distance. I was terrified, having days earlier biked down these roads at speeds no greater than 10 mph, and now the truck raced down at more than sixty. The high-pitched scream from wheels burning rubber told the story, as we snaked our way around s-curves and hairpin turns. The entire time our chase vehicle holding pursuit while occasionally Dr. Williams tapped the brakes to avoid head on crashes with summit bound traffic.

"Are we going to do 'Operation Transport'?" Dr. Williams nervously shouted towards Russell, while trying to keep the truck's trajectory.

"Yeah, I don't think we have a choice. Can you handle them on your own?" Russell asked.

"Yeah, but you might want to take all the files with you and if you don't mind, Samantha, just in case."

"What are you talking about 'Operation Transport'?" I intensely screamed from the backseat.

I held Samantha protectively, as if she was my own, while the curves became tighter. I remembered this piece of the road, as sections dropped off thousands of feet with no guardrails and the idea was nauseating at a leisurely speed never mind recklessly flying along out of control.

"Erica, be ready to exit the truck with Samantha," Russell uttered.

I had no idea what was about to occur and even today I am astounded at the precision and quickness it took, as if performed before or at the very least practiced.

"Right after this next hairpin," Russell shouted, "Erica, get ready."

We took the next hairpin turn sideways just about on two wheels. Ahead of us, a lengthy straightway, that eventually disappeared around a larger section of rocks into another hairpin turn.

"Here he comes," Dr. Williams, voiced.

Russell pointed to a small object heading our way from above the road. It took me a second to distinguish it from the sky, but it was Nohea, with no sign of the *"Little Bird"*. He flew within inches of the truck's roof almost landing directly behind us, while causing our pursuers to lose control. The lack of a guardrail was their final mistake, crashing thousands of feet to their death. As quickly, as he appeared the helicopter sped off out of sight. Looking toward the summit, one more vehicle approached, about a mile back and slowed by ascending traffic. As we made the razor-sharp turn, the brakes intentionally locked, bringing us quickly to a total stop.

"Erica, jump out and hide behind that rock cropping!" Russell yelled.

I did what I was told, pulling Samantha from the truck, making my way to the rocks with Russell bringing up the rear. Dr. Williams continued down the highway with a bursting acceleration while moments later, the second black car rushed by, unaware of our presence with an unyielding determination to seize Dr. Williams.

"Is he going to be alright?" I asked.

"He was in Special Forces with me, he'll be fine." The seeming doubt in Russell's voice and face wasn't encouraging.

"Now what? How do we get down?"

Russell pointed to one of the biking tour group vans up the road, but I was busy watching Dr. Williams' truck screeching down Haleakalā, disappearing into the lower trees. I hoped his sacrifice

199

wasn't going to be in vain. Too many people were risking their lives for me and I didn't know why. Plainly, one of the vans had stopped and was waiting for us to climb aboard.

"Erica, let's go." Russell yelled, refocusing my attention.

I climbed into the back of the van with Samantha as Russell called shotgun. The smell of coffee and muffins jogged my memory, as it took me a minute to realize I'd previously been in this van. It was the same escort we had the other day on our bike tour.

"Miss Jones, nice to see you again. Hope you're enjoying our little island," Mika'ele half joked.

Under normal conditions I'd have been annoyed, but instead, laughed uncontrollably. I wondered how complex the situation was, my own involvement including everyone around me and I questioned the depth of this conspiracy. To say I was suspicious of everything and everyone would've been the understatement of a lifetime. Here I was in love with a man that I knew nothing about, chased down a dormant volcano by government officials that *don't* exist, with information that isn't supposed to be real. Nohea now had the video and I knew several of my answers were on that tape.

We drove into a small little village with Samantha frightened, seemingly missing Dr. Marks. I tried consoling her, my only aid was the lingering smell of Colby still on my person. Mika'ele dropped us off in back of the parking lot.

"Thank you, my friend," Russell shook Mika'ele's hand.

"No problem man, now I only owe you one."

"We're even."

"Be safe, my friend," Mika'ele replied, pulling away.

"You hungry?" Russell nonchalantly asked.

"No, but I could use a coffee."

"Great, the owner here makes a great cup of Kona Coffee."

"What about Samantha?"

Russell pointed to a sign on the door.

ALL PETS WELCOMED THAT ARE LEASHED

Entering the café was a relief, in a way, like being home. I craved coffee, but more prominently, answers. Russell had a great deal of explaining to do, about what or who he really was, my association, the contents of the folder and what remained unseen on that video.

Chapter 27

January 2, 2010

It was early morning, Tracy and I would be catching a plane to Las Vegas shortly after lunch. Russell knew this and instead, ordered our coffee to go; breakfast would have to wait.

We climbed into a different car parked in front of the café. *How many cars did he have?* Hoping this time, I'd make it all the way home in the same one. We weren't on the road longer than five minutes when Russell's phone rang.

"Yeah, go ahead," pausing to listen, "Okay, proceed accordingly." He hung up not missing a beat.

"What was that about?"

Probably pushing it a bit, but what the hell, I'm a woman, which gives me the right.

"Nohea and Dr. Williams are okay. Dr. Marks is dead and Dr. Williams is going underground for a while."

"Is that good news or bad news?"

"Dr. Williams was allowed to escape, but why I don't know. Maybe they hoped he'd rendezvous with us. Anyways, he's going to disappear off the islands and go off the radar screen for a few weeks."

"I'm sorry to hear about Dr. Marks," rubbing Samantha's head, she sensed the lost. "Were you guys good friends?"

"He was like a father, taking me in when I was young, after the loss of my family. My understanding of the galaxy was first learned from him because of the countless nights in that observatory. His General friend was my first drill instructor at Hickman Air Force Base on O'ahu. I've tried to model my life after the two of them."

He spoke with underlying grief, a vulnerability that had gone unnoticed, until now and only strengthened my sentiment towards him.

"How are you and I involved...I mean...not personally...but in this entire mess as a whole?"

"My involvement with you theoretically was to be sternly as an observer. However, I wasn't expecting to fall in love with you and tried convincing my superiors I hadn't." He flashed a smile, grabbed my hand, and gently kissed the back.

"I love you, too," returning the gesture.

"The situation has now taken a turn for the worse. First, with the leak of this video and now with the loss of Dr. Marks. My involvement has gotten personal and I justly believe this was their intent all along."

"So they lied to you?"

"No, just presented enough of the truth to make my own choices while still following orders. Knowing what I know now given nothing at all really. It's your involvement that concerns me the most."

"And my involvement is?"

"Complicated and far greater than you can possibly imagine. I don't what to postulate any meaning until I've had a chance to visit a friend of mine. However, based on your abduction experiences and the contents of the video...well, let us say things will probably get worse before they get better."

"Where's your friend?"

"Nevada."

His turned face unrevealing about trekking to Nevada, unable to distinguish between his excitement and nervousness. Maybe it was the fear of our unknown future, but it wasn't as if I expected him to stay at my place.

"Where in Nevada?" I was secretly hoping southern.

"That I can't tell you, sorry."

"I know, for my protection."

"No, his."

The climate of the highway became our painter's canvas for a short time as our deep thoughts framed a clearer picture. The two of us were approaching from different worlds, but with many current similarities and a clear goal. Although Russell knew more than he led me to believe, we both were in search of the truth.

Samantha licked at my hand, awakening me to her dilemma. I wanted to take her home, but wasn't sure of Colby's reaction to the competition. For the moment, her needs seemingly outweighed my own.

"What about Samantha?" I asked.

"I'll take her. She knows and trusts me. Plus, I've been thinking about adopting since losing my previous Golden."

That was the first optimistic news I'd heard muttered from his mouth in days. If he was telling the truth regarding his dog, then Samantha was going to be in good hands. His demeanor around Colby demonstrated to me his love for Goldens, although, if just a ruse to get into my pants, well that would've been a deal breaker.

Before long, the street's memorable markings woke me from my trance as the gates to the mansion swung clear. The clock revealed enough time for a shower, pack, and to ready myself for the long flight home. The morning sun underlined the frayed condition of my dress, shoes, and purse from last night's events. My body's act in response to the lack of water intake over the last twelve hours; calf muscles began to cramp as yesterday's marathon started to take its toll on me. I hoped it would pass before the plane ride otherwise; it was going to be a painful flight home.

"I'm so sorry about the dress; it was gorgeous."

My voice sadly declared. A princess for the night, but the ball was over and my Fairy Godmother had revoked my rights.

"You did look incredible. Maybe when I get to Nevada we can try again, this time without all the drama."

"I'd like that," smiling as I blushed, "by the way I never did thank you for the phone. What do I owe you for it?"

"Nothing, it's a gift all paid for including service."

"I can't accept that, you have to let me pay at least the monthly bill," my independence showing itself.

"Listen; unlike your other phone this one's special."

"What do you mean special?"

"It can't be monitored, traced, or triangulated back to you or your location, ever!" He was being resolute.

"So no tapped phone calls, GPS monitoring and first and foremost no exploding laser beams from space?" I asked jokingly.

"No, and if there's ever a problem with it hit 735 then pound and a new phone will arrive the next day."

"Now that's what I call service."

I pulled the phone from my purse and gave it a quick once over. In truth, I didn't want another phone after seeing my last one visually targeted for destruction. I trusted Russell's conviction, but I wasn't so convinced.

"I've something else for you. Open the glove compartment."

The glove compartment opened, void of any contents but one; a small wrapped gift box. I swallowed hard, an image of a marriage proposal on the horizon. Sorry, but women of my age fantasize about these things all the time. It was the size and weight of a ring box. The only thing missing was a Tiffany's label.

"Go ahead, open it," he coached.

The gift-wrap peeled back gingerly flaunting a black velvet box. I fought, trying to hold back the tears of joy. Tentatively cupping the velvet in my hands, I debated opening it, while flashes of our future danced in my head. This was ridiculous, how could one little box incite such emotions.

On discovering the contents of the box, a combination of relief, disappointment, and confusion whirled in my mind. I was expecting a ring, instead a single jagged crystal rested amid the velvet and at the time, I speechlessly searched for answers. My wedding plans crushed, replaced with what I thought at the time, an insignificant rock. Had I turned into a heartless, superficial bitch?

Of course, this crystal previously today had mended all my wounds. Knowing what I know now, I should've displayed a greater appreciation for this astonishing gift.

"It's a healing crystal from my people," Russell explained.

The way he said 'my people', escaped me at the time, attributing it to his Hawai'ian Polynesian culture. It was obvious this had spiritual meaning far greater than if he had given me an engagement ring.

"What do I do with it?"

At first, sounding ungrateful, but gradually appreciative of its raw beauty.

"Keep it with you always. Its inner healing powers surpass its outward beauty, much like yourself."

"Healing powers?"

"Yes. If you're ever injured, place the crystal between your two palms and imagine yourself healed. Its powers, along with your inner strength, will heal you." He was serious.

"I don't know what to say."

Actually, I did. YOU'RE CRAZY! However, this was clearly important to him so I played along. This lying was getting a little too easy to create and reflecting back, I'm truly sorry, never again second-guessing his motives.

Russell walked around the car, while I said my goodbyes to Samantha. He was a true gentleman, even holding my door open while I exited with purse, crystal, and file folders in hand. Noticing the files, he stopped me, returning them to the front seat.

"Better let me keep them for the time being. I'll bring them to Vegas in a couple of weeks."

My face, showing displeasure, as the door shut with his thoughts. Inside those folders were potential answers to thousands of my questions. Thrilled he was coming to Vegas, a few weeks couldn't be all that bad to wait. I wanted to pinpoint a date, but without sounding smothering.

"I can't wait. Call me when you finalize your arrangements."

"You'll be the first to know."

Russell leaned in, embracing me, as if for dear life. His eyes penetrated deep into my soul as I felt myself slip away into his. Passionately leaning in, his eyes gradually close, as his heart throbbed with a sexual obsession. Standing on my toes to welcome him, the cramping in my calves vanishing as our lips touched. The rush of power from his essence flowed throughout my body. His robust, commanding hands lifted me like a cloud off the ground while a sense of overwhelming ecstasy rendered our two souls in a single polarity plane. Our bodies currently desiring the same thing, but we knew we had to wait. That moment in time stopped as my life became complete and to say, he was a great kisser, a gross understatement. I'd never been with a guy that stirred vast passion with just one kiss. The power to bring a woman to the brink of orgasm with a simple kiss, I thought in my book, was a dead art form. I'd have to write an updated epilogue for that book.

"Please take care," he said tenderly, breaking the kiss.

"You, too."

"Trust no one, including your friends. Question everything and everyone." He was deadly serious.

"Even Tracy?" I added.

"Especially Tracy!"

The thought that my best friend somehow was involved was disheartening. I witnessed enough last night and during this vacation to distrust just about everyone and everything.

"How about you?" I seriously looked at his face.

"Even me."

That wasn't the answer I was expecting to hear. He kissed me one more time, before making his way around the car to the driver's seat. That thought of being unable to trust even him, was nerve-racking. *Was he trying to scare me?* If so, it worked. Maybe he wanted to keep me on my toes. Maybe, dare I say, telling me the truth.

"I love you and don't ever forget that," he declared, entering the car.

"I love you, too."

I watched him drive away with the electrified expectation of seeing him in Vegas in a few weeks. It was going to be a long flight home with Tracy presumably grilling me with questions. I hoped to avoid any conversation and possibly sleep most of the way. *How could I respond to her questions without the appropriate answers? What if somehow, she was involved?* However, if not involved, any information given could jeopardize her life. The words of advice from my dad as a child echoed to my core. *What a web we weave when we first start to deceive.* There was clearly deception in the air, but it wasn't coming from me, at any rate not completely.

Chapter 28

The gloominess in Samantha's face was still lingering in my mind as Colby joyfully met me at the door. I couldn't wait to wrestle and snuggle his cute puppy head. Colby always found a way to comfort me, his most endearing quality. The house felt vacant and I of course wasn't aggressively going to look for its occupants. Tracy's luggage was already in the foyer, so I made for upstairs without hesitation, jumped in the shower, packed, and before long had positioned my luggage next to hers, void of intrusions.

With time to kill, I was going to indulge Colby with one last rumpus on the beach, but not before taking a few pictures. Reclaiming my camera from the luggage, my first task was stills of the statues outside, then of the Mayan looking piece over the mantel, finally the other miscellaneous art piece of similar origin. I returned to the luggage, exchanging the camera for a Frisbee, to Colby's elation, and was off for one last view of the ocean.

I raced Colby to the beach, sore calves and all, and to my surprise, Tracy was getting in one last tanning session. I didn't blame her. I spent less time on the beach than planned, but the few times I did, they were memorable. Colby ran by her in hot pursuit of his new flying plastic toy.

"So how was last night?" Rolling over on her towel, probing.

I was glad she hadn't seen me enter with my clothes all tattered and torn, otherwise this lie wouldn't have fooled her.

"We had a nice time," retorting with a smile.

"So did he rock your world?"

"No. We had dinner, went dancing, and even spent some time under the full moon and starlit night." I wasn't lying.

"And the rest of the night? I mean you did just get back, right?"

"We talked, he drove me home, kissed me goodnight or more like good morning." I was blushing.

"So, going to see him again?"

Russell said don't trust anyone, especially Tracy. I couldn't tell if she was fishing for information or being a concerned friend. We constantly talked about our boyfriends, why should this be any different. Trying to avoid this conversation would've definitely sent up red flags.

"Well, he wasn't sure, but he might be coming to Vegas on company business."

"Did he say when?" Tracy asked.

"No, said he'd call as soon as the dates where confirmed. He had business overseas and he would be gone for a few weeks. I gave him my number…told him to call when he got a chance."

"Girlfriend, if you let this one get away you're beyond help," shaking her head in disbelief.

Colby had returned with the Frisbee, waiting impatiently for me again to throw it down the beach. It was fun teasing him as his puppy butt wiggled little angels in the sand. I threw the Frisbee and watched his playfulness as he chased the disc towards the water's edge. A part of me wished Samantha had returned home with me, thinking Colby would've loved a playmate in my absence.

"I know. I really, really, like this guy too, but I didn't want to appear desperate."

"There's a fine line between desperate and aggressive and right now girlfriend, you're desperate. Haven't I taught you anything over the last few years? Sometimes being aggressive is okay when you see things you truly need or want, in particular when it comes to tall, dark and handsome."

Tracy sat up staring at me with those 'mother's eyes'. As much as I didn't want to admit it, she was right. I've come a long way since our first meeting, and she's solely responsible for my success today. Without her, I'd never come out of my low self-esteemed shell. So to sit here lying to her over a new boyfriend was tearing me up inside. *I loved Russell, but ultimately was it worth a friendship?* He advised me not to trust Tracy, but in fairness not to trust him either. This put a completely new twist on my life and its direction.

"By the way how's the tattoo healing?" Tracy asked.

The vibrant color arrangement poked from above my jeans waistline. Always wanting a tattoo on my lower back, Tracy offered to pay as an early birthday gift. *I mentioned this earlier in my writings.* After nights of nightmares, car chases, and romantic whirlwinds, I needed to redirect my focus on my vacation and while walking down Lāhainā Tracy pointed out this beautiful tattoo in the window, which I proudly wear today. She at first dared me to get one, thinking I'd opt out, afraid to shatter my innocent image, but that day I felt a bit spirited. The parlor, locally owned, had a fitting name, *Skin-Deep Tattoo Parlor.* The artists inside did breathtaking work and the time they took explaining to me their craft was inspiring. After a little deliberation, Darlene offered to do my tattoo adding her own special touch based on what we'd discussed. I wanted something to remind me of Hawai'i, and the floral gardens shared with Russell. Darlene drew up a V-shape hibiscus floral arrangement using all the colors of the Hawai'ian sunset. Tracy stood in disbelief that I was getting a tramp stamp, but six hours later the proof everlastingly engraved on my lower back. To this day, it is a reminder to fear nothing, no regrets, and the beauty of the Hawai'ian Islands.

"It's healing nicely," proudly dropping my lower back pants to show her.

"I hate to say it, but it looks hot," she smiled.

"Next time maybe you can get one," refastening my pants.

"No! I think I'll leave the extreme stuff to you." She laughed as a beeping came from her watch. "Lulani should be here with the limo to take us to the airport in about thirty minutes. I'm heading back to the house to see Pakile before we go...you coming?"

"No, not yet. I promised Colby a few more tosses."

"Okay. I'll see you at the house in a bit."

She carefully rolled up her towel, putting it under her arm, and making her way up the beach to the house. I tossed the Frisbee once again down the beach as Colby chased. I had promised Colby, but truth be said I didn't care to see Pakile. It was nice; Colby and I on the empty beach, but it would've been nicer if Russell was here as well. I enjoyed my last few moments, the beach, the surf, and my vacation. I would return to the islands, they called to me, and deep down I knew the answers to some of my questions would remain. Colby and I played fetch for ten or so minutes, until he collapsed, exhausted but refusing to surrender, to me, the Frisbee. I enjoyed sitting on the beach with him, his head in my lap, but longed for the comforts of home. Since last night, trying to relax here was impossible, jumping internally at every sound, from a passing car to a person walking by or just staring in my direction. It's one thing to know you are being watched, but not knowing by whom adds a new level of paranoia. I'd always remember this tropical paradise for the good times and the bad, but mostly the passion.

I'm sorry to say, but it was time to go…

Chapter 29

January 2, 2010 The return home to Las Vegas

The goodbyes, at best for me, were pithy with Pakile and Lulani in Hawai'i. Tracy conversely was very emotional, especially with Pakile, even though they'd just met over a week ago. My emotional equivalent earlier that morning had said his goodbyes, although, good-bye felt so absolute, maybe I'll start using the phrase, Aloha.

As predicted, Tracy attempted to inquire exquisitely about my relationship with Russell. Some questions resembled statements and only verified her facts. This caused me to believe she knew more than I thought. Sleep deprived of the past twenty-four hours had clouded my memory, but still positive I hadn't disclosed certain tidbits of information to her. She had at one point access to my journal and might've hypothesized her own theories from my notes. The conversation abruptly ended as my body uncontrollably fell dead to the world the rest of the flight. Except for the sporadic leg cramps, the rest of the flight was uneventful.

Arriving home after ten at night, Vegas time, my body groggy and still working on Hawai'ian time. The nicest feature about the Executive Airport...no baggage lines. In addition, my house was only ten minutes away with no traffic, making the drive doable in my condition. I thanked Tracy for a fabulous vacation as we embraced; in truth, it was exciting, even with the intermittent nightmares. I'm sorry...abductions. The consideration that I'll be sleeping in my own bed tonight was very pleasing.

"Are you going to be okay to drive?" She inquired.

"Yeah, I slept most of the way home and it's just up the road."

"Did you want to go for a run Monday morning before work?"

"I'm going to need a few days to get acclimated to the time difference and a work schedule again," smiling.

"I hear you on that," agreeably voicing on the way to her awaiting limo. "Well then, I'll see you on Monday. If something comes up though, call me, promise?" She waited for my response before climbing into the limo.

"Yes, Mom." I said sarcastically.

She smiled, waved, and climbed in the limo as I approached my dust-covered car in search of the keys. Colby and I both thrilled to be going home. Recognizing we were a short drive away, he barked in circles while dragging me half-asleep to the car. Colby's excessive jubilation kept me alert and entertained on the drive home. We pulled into the driveway, the still house dark, which normally wouldn't have bothered me, but darkness was no longer a friend. Paranoid, I entered the house running room to room turning on every light. My neighbors must have thought I was crazy. *Was I?* Colby had a similar fixation as he tagged along excessively sniffing every corner and door. I assumed it was his way of protecting me from the dark. My hero!

After confirming my solitude, I gave Nevada Power a reprieve, quenching most of the lights. The corner of the kitchen flashed in red as the number three clarified my current messages. Previously, I had my messages forwarded to my cell phone, but that changed after it vaporized. Unfamiliar with my new number and phone I'd stopped sending my messages, so three messages wasn't that bad. I hit play, then proceeded to fill Colby's water bowl.

"You have three messages..." The mechanical voice declared.

Message one..."Hi, Erica this is Scott give me a call."

Message two..."Erica, this is Scott again. I've setup a meeting with some friends of mine based on your email. Give me a call so I can give you the scoop."

The next message is the one that made me think twice about returning home to a house all alone.

Message Three..."Miss Jones," uttered the deliberately altered computer voice which sounded male. "You should be more careful with your acquaintances. What you know will die with you," it paused for effect, "If you tell anyone, you commit them as well you to death. Sweet dreams."

I expected one of those long Halloween laughs at the end, but it never came as the timestamp of the message showed it had arrived moments before. The message's content and underlying tone didn't trouble me as much as the "*Sweet Dreams*" element at the end. That for sure had put a damper on getting a good night's sleep. I wished right then for a gun to put under my pillow while I slept.

I wanted to call Russell, but knew he was going to be out of contact for a while…then my cell phone rang, causing me to jump on the counter as if I'd seen a mouse. The phone read *incomplete data* and I now hesitated to answer, but did anyways.

"Hello." A definite fear attached to my voice.

"Erica, you Okay. This is Russell."

"I was going to call but…"

"Just wanted to confirm you made it home without incident."

Even over the phone, his smiling voice was gratifying.

"Yeah, a bit nerved from this strange message left on my machine," playing it back for him.

"Listen, you're fine. They're only trying to get a rise out of you. Trust me, if you were in harm's way I'd already be there by your side."

I sat in the kitchen, daydreaming, as his voice became my lover, wanting to climb into bed, the phone on my pillow and listen as he softly whispered me to sleep. The crazy thing is I believe he'd have done it willfully.

"Erica…Erica…are you still there?" His voice raised in tone.

"Yeah, I'm sorry just tired."

"Listen you'll be fine, just wear the necklace."

"My friend Scott wants to meet sometime this week. What should I tell him?"

I'd forgotten to bring up Scott and his UFO group to Russell. I had hoped to heighten my knowledge of the subject from them, but I still wanted Russell's suggestion on how or if I should proceed.

"Who's Scott?"

"He's a good friend and part of a local group; the UFO Hunters. In addition, he's a prodigy on the computer. You don't mind do you?"

"No," there was a pause, "tell you what, let me know when you're going and I'll see about flying in and go with you. How's that sound?"

There was a casual excitement in his voice, intrigued to meet this group. I had hoped to see him, but not so soon. Of course, I questioned his intentions, per his order. Was he coming to see me or to do recon on Scott and the UFO group?

"That's great. I'd really like that," I replied.

"Okay. Call me from this phone after you confirm with Scott. In the meantime, go get some sleep. I'll talk to you soon."

"I will, promise."

There was a slight pause as if he'd hung up so I began to close the phone until his voice resounded loudly.

"Erica, by the way did you notice the surprise left for you?"

"What surprise?"

"Go check in your sitting room."

In all my fearful confusion of turning on lights, I'd overlooked a new addition to the furnishings. Positioned in the far corner of my sitting room, was a beautiful Koa Wood Rocker similar to the one I'd fallen in love with on Maui and on closer examination it wasn't similar—it was the one. Somebody had some explaining to do...

"It's beautiful. How'd you get it here so fast? By the way, how'd you get into my house? Never mind. I don't want to know right now, but you have plenty of explaining to do when you get out here, mister."

"What can I say? I love you," happiness surging in his voice.

Nothing's more romantic then when a man says he loves you without a prompt.

"I love you, too," I answered as the line mutually went dead.

I sat in the Rocker for a few minutes thinking of Russell. The chairs comfy cushions, tenderly rocking almost putting me to sleep but still in disbelief I'd at first overlooked it. It made me wonder what else I might have ignored and with that, did another comprehensive sweep of the house.

I hesitated calling Scott so late, but knew he was one of those computer geeks up all hours of the night playing on-line games. I needed to confirm a time and date for Russell as soon as possible. The phone rang several times before finally being picked-up; this was the norm. Scott was heavily into conspiracies and Government cover-ups regarding UFO's, and even more paranoid then me, convinced his every move tracked by the Government. The reason for his delayed response was the time it took to route his calls through his various computers to elude tracking.

"Hello, this is Scott."

"Hey, this is Erica, what are you up to?"

"Just playing *World of Warcraft* on-line. You just get back from Hawai'i?" He asked.

"Yeah, did you get my email with the pictures?"

To save time before leaving Hawai'i I quickly emailed him the pictures. Thinking I was being witty; using a terminal at the airport to avoid detection. In hindsight, that was the worst thing I could've done for him.

"Yeah, I emailed them to my friends. We should have some information for you when we meet. I sent the possible dates to your email."

"I haven't checked my email yet."

"Well how's this Thursday. Say some time after 10 p.m.?"

"Why so late?"

"Remember my group runs a weekly radio show called Higher Vibrations and the show doesn't finish until ten. I figured we'd meet them at the station after since everyone will be there." His excitement for this stuff overwhelmed his voice.

"Alright. That'll work. Do you mind if I bring a friend?"

"I don't have a problem, but some of the other members get a little jittery around new faces. You can never trust the Government."

"I know what you mean." A week ago, I'd have laughed at him; tonight, I agreed wholeheartedly. "He's kind of my boyfriend…well I mean…Hell…He's my boyfriend!"

It was uncanny talking to Scott about guys because in high school the two of us tried dating, but found we were better off as friends. The date was awkward, having been friends years prior, and when we kissed goodnight it felt like kissing a brother. Therefore, we came to a mutual decision we were better off as friends, but it still didn't change underlying emotions.

"So it sounds like you had an extremely pleasurable vacation."

Scott's voice stressed and lingered on *extremely* and *pleasurable.*

"It had its moments."

"Hold on, Erica."

His voice silent on the other side of the phone, but in the background his keyboard keys danced frantically. At first, I thought, how rude to drop our conversation for a video game.

"Listen Erica, someone is trying to trace this call from your line, definitely Government in origin and they're good, really good. Listen, Thursday night at the radio station."

Before muttering thank you or asking if he was going to be alright, the phone went dead. This happened constantly with Scott and normally I'd have downplayed the situation. Now with what I knew and had previously experienced, it was not so easy. I debated calling back from my cell, but knew he wouldn't answer an unfamiliar number.

My body was craving sleep even though my mind wasn't. Colby had buckled down at my side already in dreamland evident by his constant twitching. However, once I made my move for the bedroom he hurriedly awoke racing to my side, leaping on and to the middle of the bed before the light even flicked on.

"You better save room for me, you bed hog."

Here I was, late at night, tired, and lecturing a dog about bedroom etiquette and from his dopey expression, he didn't care. He folded full-size fluffy paws over his snout, hiding his deep brown eyes from me, while a generously unending sigh beckoned and moments later, he was back to dreamland.

I changed into a nightshirt, emptied my purse's contents on the sink, and became once again aware of the crystal Russell had given me. It seemed quirky at the time, putting it underneath my pillow for added protection, but I'm glad I did. The following morning it returned to the same purse, where it remained until this morning when it completely healed my wounds. Not so quirky now, I thought.

Chapter 30

I glanced up from the lined pages, checking the time. I'd been writing as if my life depended on it, and I guess in a way it did. At first, when I started this morning my handwriting was legible, now nearly through an entire notebook, it resembled more or less a doctor's script. I'd hoped someday soon this written substance could be transcribed professionally, if not by me at least someone willing to risk their life for disclosure of the truth.

There was still plenty of time before I had to meet Detective Wilson and I had most of the prior events documented meticulously. I intended on sharing copies of my notes to Scott, Mufon's Director, and all the members of Higher Vibrations and a select few in the media. I'd read about Robert Lazar, his claims to have worked at Area 51, and his reasons for going public. It was those reasons, including the fear for my own life that prompted me into taking such drastic measures. My hope, after recent intimidating battles, that this journal would save my life and the lives of many others in the future.

The thought of another cup of coffee, enticing, but it hadn't roused me enough to make a fresh pot. I was midway to the most illuminating disclosure so far and not wanting to waste time, I decided to revisit the story on paper.

Alright, where was I? That's right...

I called Russell the following day giving him the details of the meeting. We didn't talk long, but he verified he'd call from the air and asked if I'd pick him up at the airport. He'd arranged to stay at City Center on the Strip. However, with a little arm-twisting I convince him to stay at my house, not that he needed a whole hell of a lot of convincing.

The next few days were about as normal as they get. Wake up, go to work, come home, and go to bed. I hadn't gone running since returning, in a way subconsciously trying to avoid a one-on-one with Tracy. We got along great at work, both so hectically catching up on misfiled paperwork that interaction was rare. I often wondered what if anything our bosses would do in the event either of us quit. I knew both of them were lost without us catering to their needs the past week.

Scott emailed me several times that he'd found some answers, but never elaborated in detail, occasionally throwing in added questions. He said he was saving the whole lot for our meeting Thursday and was being either vague in his line of questioning or cautious, afraid someone was checking his emails. I felt watched; at home, in my car, even at work, but couldn't support the claims. The sporadic anonymous phone calls, deathly silent on pick-up was about it, and I chalked it up to telemarketers and wrong numbers.

I intermittently researched the net on experiencers and their abductions with mine, nonexistent since Hawai'i. Mostly because of this necklace that never left my neck, especially at night. Scott warned me about the dangers of researching online. Explaining the mountains of misinformation gathered from ill-conceived reporting. However, he stressed, most damaging facts cleverly calculated, orchestrated from deep within Secret Government factions. Over the years, he had managed to hack into most sites determining and tracing their origins. He candidly counseled me that my web surfing was probably noted; as well as he'd have definitive answers on Thursday. That was comforting to hear considering some of the interpretations posted in blogs and on websites scared the daylights out of me.

I awoke Thursday morning with butterflies in my stomach amid expecting to meet Scott and finally receiving answers, but mostly I yearned to see Russell. At work, Tracy mentioned joining the girls and her at Prive for our monthly Thursday, "Girls Night Out", which had completely slipped my mind. I lied, explaining my need to return home, while character-acting symptoms of a migraine. The girls bought it, but somehow believing Tracy didn't as the disgust on her face a dead giveaway.

Driving home that night, south on Highway 15, momentarily in my side mirrors appeared a black sedan similar to the ones in Hawai'i. My hands tightened around the steering wheel, my heart raced, as sweat dripped from my bridge of my nose, frantically searching for visual confirmation. I tried to downplay it as the variety of cars in Vegas and an overactive imagination worried about tonight's assembly. The balance of the drive, I varied my speed, while constantly inspecting my mirrors for company. A faint speck, barely remaining in view long enough, followed, mimicking my actions. Within streets of my house, the dot enlarged as the sunlight reflected across a highly glossed metallic grill perched elegantly in front of a black reflective sedan. I slowed to a halt, afraid to head towards my dead end street. The sedan rapidly approached, only slowing to pass, the driver rolled down his window, long enough to curse a few choice words in my direction about woman drivers. Taking a deep breath, realizing how foolish I was being I headed home, letting his comments slide.

I'd forgotten my cell phone this morning at the house so I was in a rush to check for messages. He hadn't called with an arrival time or airport. There was McCarran International, Executive, plus a handful of other privately owned airports that could accommodate his plane. As thorough as he was, I betted on Executive Airport because of its relative closeness to my house, but didn't want to assume anything. I arrived home having to wait a minute, as Colby needed supper. I checked my phone and sure enough, Russell had left a message not more than ten minutes ago. Dialing, I listened for the sound of his voice message.

"Flying into McCarran International airport back gate. Plane arrives at eight. Will be waiting on the tarmac. Tell security your clearance code…Ka'iu lani." He was brief and to the point.

How funny, he used the Hawai'ian name given me as the security clearance code. Then again, how many others would've known that name code? The clock boldly displayed 6:30 p.m., still plenty of time to take a quick shower, with the airport not far away. I'd spent the entire week cleaning, not that it needed it, just for him. I must be in love.

I arrived at the airport's backside entrance, checked through security with my pass code, and not surprisingly, Russell stood on the tarmac faultlessly dressed in his masculinity. The landing lights of the plane backlit him and even from a distance, the outline of his body screamed sex. My headlights struck him straight on highlighting his perfectly cut suit, his silken hair down, blowing in the wind, reminiscent of a modern day romance novel. Guys with longer hair than me never turned me on, but for some unknown reason, his did.

I stopped the car a few feet away. Unable to control my urges, I jumped out, running, and leaped into his arms. His muscular build lifting my tiny frame off the ground, my legs tightly wrapped around his waist. We kissed, two lovers alone in the dark. Our body heat unloaded around us like lightning, as the cool Vegas night temporarily suspended the inevitable to come.

"God I missed you," taking in his smell.

"Missed you, too," he said.

His hands explored my womanly body in ways no man had done. I couldn't stop kissing the warmth of his face. I unlocked my legs, sliding my feet to the ground, his rigid excitement to see me, unmistakable. I thought about rescheduling our meeting to another night, heading straight home to do a little personal investigating for myself. I had no idea how long he was staying, but I wished he'd never leave.

"We probably should get off the tarmac," he said. As little by little, he lowered my feet back down to Earth.

"Yeah…you're probably right…I'm sorry," fumbling for the right words.

"Do we have time to eat?" He asked.

I was thinking dessert and he, my whip, cherry-topped sundae. Then I looked at my watch, realizing I hadn't had supper yet either I change the tune, just a smidge.

"Sure. Their radio show starts at eight and finishes at ten. The station's about twenty minutes from here. What are you in the mood for?" Hoping he said me.

"Do you like Sushi?" He questioned.

"Love it. I know the perfect place."

"Great. I'd like to get to the station early. I'm curious to hear their broadcast. If that's okay with you?"

"Why not."

We loaded his luggage in the car, which seemed like a lot, so I assumed he was staying for more than a couple of days.

"So how long are you staying in Vegas?"

"That really depends," as he climbed into the car.

"Depends on what?"

"Answers," he decisively communicated his thoughts!

I agreed, wanting answers too, and Scott assured me he'd have the answers for us tonight. I only hoped they didn't lead to more questions, but somehow knowing they always did.

This was Russell's first trip to Vegas, so I drove to the restaurant by means of the downtown strip. On a Thursday night, this was a possible alternative, but I would've steered clear, had it been the weekend. The weeknight traffic was slow but tolerable. However, on the weekend it was absolute gridlock because of unfamiliar out-of-towners.

There was an incredible Sushi restaurant not far from the radio station. It was an unseasonably warm night for January, in the low 70's, which was rare. Russell suggested taking our order to go, sitting under the stars with the top-down, and listening to the radio show from the parking lot. It was a romantic gesture considering the remote location of the station. Russell's charisma seemingly always made the worst circumstances blissful. I brought my journal, burdened with hundreds of questions for Russell, Scott and his friends as well as explicit questions directed only at Russell whom I wanted answers to now before meeting strangers. Granted, not all were strangers, but enough to warrant concern. Russell's present interest, besides me, was the context of the radio show, as he listened intensely to Scott and his friends, waving off questions until after. I was fine with it, waiting this long for answers, what was another hour away anyways?

Scott was the Executive Producer, more the behind the scenes guy with no ambition to be one of the personalities. Having never personally listened to the show I sat in amazement. As I said before, Scott was a good friend, but I thought this UFO thing was a joke. The show's topic tonight, DUMB's (Deep Underground

Military Bases) and the Governments that deny their existence. On the air were a former Base Commander and Major General in the Air Force who had worked at one of these bases and had even seen alien bodies. The dialogue was attention grabbing to say the least, but the real show was happening outside, as Russell's facial reactions told a different story. He often jotted down notes of particular so-called facts, alternating between shaking his head in disagreement and snickering under his breath as if knowing fiction from truth.

The show was wrapping up so I gathered my journal as Russell gathered his black brief case and we headed towards the station doors.

I turned to him before entering the station, "So what did you think of their show?"

"Let's say for every bit of truth there was twice as much deceit. The thing is could you tell the difference?" He smiled.

I stopped him at the door, "So the guy was lying?"

"No, not completely. He was just giving his point of views with facts interwoven between bits of fiction."

"What do you mean?" I grabbed at his arm.

"Remember when I told you to trust no one?"

"Yeah, even you."

"Even me," he laughed, "sometimes, the easiest way to hide something is to leave it in plain sight."

I kind of understood where he was going, but I didn't have time for a theoretical discussion. I knew Scott was still learning about Russell, and unsure of the knowledgeable people waiting beyond those doors.

"Promise me you won't embarrass Scott in front of his friends." I was begging him.

"Erica, I trust you, so consequently I trust Scott and his friends. However, given my past and experience, you may find it's them not as trusting towards me."

With that, Russell opened the door, allowing me to enter the station, where answers to some of my questions awaited. I hoped!

Chapter 31

KLAV was tactically located atop an isolated mountaintop and overlooked the Las Vegas valley. The signal, though powered down at night, still covered the entire Clark County listening audience. The view from within the studio helped deter from the lack of an interior design and absence of today's modern broadcast equipment. The studio's yellow tinted ceilings, black and white dusted wall photos, and retro furniture showed the age of a day when radio ruled. From the reception area, through a glass window, you could watch the show and its hosts. The contents of the studio crammed into a room, scarcely large enough for a closet, with an engineer older then the station, perched over an analog production board. Signs of modern technology came only from a small LCD screen that networked the Internet's podcast, Skype, and live chat room. Over the past few years, the show had developed a worldwide Internet following in the thousands.

Scott met us at the appointed reception desk, which was little more than a small table with an undersized handwritten note taped to the front in a congested part of the hallway.

Scott was my age, attended the same high school, but traveled in different circles. He moved away briefly to attend MIT, graduating with a Master's Degree in Computer Science in an unprecedented three years. To say he was one of the brightest in his field wouldn't justify his accomplishments. Companies on the cutting edge of technology tirelessly tried to recruit him, including Microsoft, IBM, Intel, even the Federal Government's Military. By the time he was twenty-seven, he was already a self-made millionaire from the multiple websites and technology he'd developed, selling to the highest bidder. His appearance, by no means, gave you an idea about his wealth. His long brownish hair with a hint of gray pulled back in a ponytail extenuated his pronounced frontal receding hairline. His left ear pierced, on display a Hearts on Fire Diamond that would make any woman jealous. He wore glasses, with thin black frames dating back to the 1950's. His daily wardrobe of choice was casual to extreme casual.

Tonight it was a customized black collar polo shirt from his on-line store promoting Government Conspiracy. Over the front pocket, embroidered, was his name as well as the show, while the back boldly read, 'UFOs—Plausible Deniability—Enough Said'. His jeans hung loosely over his small-bodied frame, held-up only by an over tightened black belt. His vintage white high-top basketball sneakers were his trademark. I don't think he even owned a pair of dress shoes. His outward reflection, a cross between nerd and someone who'd never escaped the 80's fashion trends.

"Erica, glad you could make it," embracing me with a hug while sizing up Russell.

"Scott, this is Russell Hamilton, the man I told you about."

Scott shook his hand, his jealousy evident with the crossed glanced he shot in my direction. He knew we could only be friends, even though he wanted more, so at times he acted more akin to a protective older brother.

"Listen, when the show finishes, we'll enter the studio, and I'll introduce you to everyone. I must tell you they get a little jumpy around military types."

His stare focused on Russell as if he knew a bit more than anyone else knew including myself. I'd confirmed Russell's involvement, either in the past or in the present, with the military, but he still had questions. It was clear Scott knew a great deal more than he was telling me. Russell nodded his head as if to say silently, "touché".

"Everyone here uses code names to protect their identity. They referred to me as *"The Code Breaker"*. Please don't use my name, Scott, while we're in the studio. They're a finicky group and can get a little paranoid at times, but with good reason once you've learned their stories."

I'm sure my face had the same puzzled looked as Russell's or we were both trying not to laugh. Maybe this wasn't such a good idea after all, I thought. What the hell, I needed answers and Scott said they had them. *How bad could it be?*

"No problem Scott," I spoke as he turned, his eyes voicing his discontent. "Sorry, Code Breaker." A low chuckle escaped from underneath my breath as my smile turned stern.

I'm going to give a brief recap of the main players that were at this meeting and what we discussed. In retrospect, I'm thankful that no one used their real names, fearful now for their safety more than ever. Although the group has a robust membership, the nucleus consists of about ten; four of them were at this meeting.

First, the *"Russian"*. Although a U.S. citizen since the early 1980's, his Russian accent still very much pronounced, thus I figured the name. He was of average height, slightly overweight, short graying hair, which matched his goatee. He was casually dressed, but I could've pictured him teaching calculus at an Ivy League school. His understanding of the UFO phenomenon paired with his own abduction story was extraordinary. I could've sat and talked to him for hours comparing notes about our own unique experiences.

Second, the *"Patriot"*. A retired Vietnam Veteran scarred by years of surgeries to fix his ailing battle scars until at last, confined to a wheelchair from a botched surgery on his hip. His eyes appeared older, his body worn out, disguising his true age, an assured sign of his surreptitiously decorated combat profession. His image best matched an older version of Tom Cruise's character in *"Born on the Fourth of July"*. When he talked, his fervor for politics, religion, and the subject of UFO's masked his physical limitations.

Third, the *"Assassin"*. A widow, habitually quiet, but you could sense a wrath inside waiting to unleash as her long blonde hair tucked nicely under a baseball hat. She dressed young for her age. The eyes glistened with youth, but the face under beige tinted concealer, matured by unanswered questions from her husband's obscured death. His UFO knowledge could've led to his premature death. As his shortened career within an unknown government agency was unknown to her. Regardless, I felt for her in more ways than one, picturing myself likewise soon mourning for the loss of Russell.

Fourth, the *"Mechanic"*. His hefty width was only equivalent in stature to his personality. He had the appearance of a test pilot straight out of the 60's, with the typical brown leather bomber jacket, sunglasses, and Government issued wristwatch and clean-cut hair. His outsized hands, covered with aged-calluses told stories of his livelihood. His enigmatic obsession was the historical documentation, and creation of the Secret Government Agency dating back to Roswell. His favorite subject was anything concerning "The Majestic 12". His understanding rivaled that of Russell, which impressed me from the start and in a passing conversation mentioned his provisional involvement with Area 51. At the time, thinking it was accidental, but in hindsight, it was deliberate. Why, I still don't know. I only mention this because of Russell's facial reaction to the slip. It was intriguing, as if scanning his mind for some sort of image authentication.

I arrived with an open mind eager to unearth answers or at the very least get support from others who've had comparable experiences. I left as a believer with a new intrinsic drive to discover the buried truth.

We congregated in the studio around a small arched broadcast console, our chairs inches apart in the cramped room. The studio goes automated after their show until the morning talent arrives at six. Once seated, *Code Breaker* booted up his computer, while the *Mechanic* removed a baton from his jacket, meticulously performing a symphony from all corners of the room.

"What's he doing?" I asked while leaning into Russell.

"He's sweeping the room for bugs. You know, listening devices."

"All clear!" The *Mechanic* barked, returning to his seat next to the *Russian*.

"The room is in lock down," replied *Code Breaker*.

"What do you mean lock down?" I asked.

"This room has limited soundproofing so we've put an extra electronic energy field around the room. This should prevent anybody from recording or listening to this conversation," explained *Code Breaker*.

"What are you worried about?" Russell asked.

"Erica, do you remember the other day when you called me and I said your call was being traced?" The *Code Breaker* questioned.

"Yeah," secretly disappointed I didn't have a code name.

"The signal was Government issued, not standard, but High-End Military Government crap. Interesting was, the trace originated from Rachel, NV."

I've lived most of my life in Henderson, never venturing too far from the city. I mean sure, Las Vegas, the occasional business trip to Reno, a few times skiing in Tahoe, and a few outings to Hoover Dam via Boulder City, but that was about it.

"What's so special about Rachel?" I asked.

The look on everyone's face including Russell's was bewilderment. How could you live in Nevada and know zilch about Rachel? No one answered right away, all still in astonishment.

"Did I miss something?" I patiently waited for some kind, any kind of response.

"Rachel's home to Groom Lake…Area 51," Russell finally professed, smiling.

As a child growing up, there were rumored stories circulated all over the news about Area 51. How, according to our Government, it didn't exist. The reports of supposed aliens working alongside humans on reverse engineering captured crafts. The topic was a big deal for a while in 1989 when Bob Lazar went public, but it had since died down. Although Rachel was a short drive outside Vegas, it had never caught my interest.

The *Mechanic* then went into direct details of his working out at the site, including what he saw and didn't see. He talked about his Q Security Clearance, flights called 'JANET' (Just Another Non-Existent Transport), mysterious white buses and descriptions of the base. Russell was clearly fascinated with his in-depth knowledge and its inner workings.

"So do you still work there?" I inquired.

"That's classified," he snapped sternly.

An awkward stillness engulfed the room as if I'd touched a nerve and in hindsight shouldn't have asked that particular question.

"Erica, the fact someone was going through grand lengths to trace your call…shows the information in your presence has significance," continued *Code Breaker*.

"What information? I came here looking for answers."

"The answers you seek might just get you killed," chimed The *Patriot*.

"Well it wouldn't be the first time I've had my life threatened. Right, Russell?"

I turned to Russell for support, what I got from him was entirely different as the genuineness in his face was deadly.

"Truth can be a deadly game, Erica. They were just trying to scare you. Trust me! If they wanted you dead you wouldn't be here."

"Spoken like a man in the game," retorted The *Patriot*.

Russell was uncomfortable discussing what he did or didn't know and if he was in the game. He wasn't going to divulge this in front of total strangers. Maybe alone I'd get answers from him, but not here, not like this.

"Anyway," the *Code Breaker* pressed, "we were able to dig up some information for you."

"Well I made a list of...," The *Russian* piped in, cutting me off in midsentence.

"Listen to what we have first, and then we'll entertain your questions." He leaned towards me with an Iron Curtain strictness in his eyes.

"Erica, we each have a few things to say and will go around the room. If at the end, you still have questions we'll address them at that point. Fair enough?" The *Code Breaker* voice.

"Fair enough."

I waited, absorbingly listening, while taking detailed notes for my own future references, as each one had their own competence on the subject matter. The *Assassin* talked about MIB's, Top Secret Projects, covert agencies, and how I was involved. The *Mechanic* discussed Majestic 12, NSA and Area 51's probable associations. The *Russian* detailed his abduction, which had many similarities to my own. He explained possible scenarios of why Government, and possibly alien entities, had been targeting me as well as their likely hidden agendas. The *Patriot* revealed a potential course of action, which included an appointment in Rachel, NV. Finally, the *Code Breaker* talked about my personal records, and different agencies that had accessed them; the how, what and why's. How some files were red flagged, others removed and altered all for what look like legitimate reasons. The problem was none of these agencies were genuine, only facades for veiled government agencies, which even he hadn't been able to track down the source. He also mentioned that every one of my files now linked to a new military program that could track my precise location via GPS. Therefore, that's why they had to secure the room.

The entire conference lasted for hours, but felt like minutes. I sat, paying attention to every nerve-racking detail, occasionally making notes, checking off answered questions, and adding new ones. The information was scrupulous, but still left me with serious questions I needed answered.

"So can I ask my questions now?"

"You may hand us your questions," the *Russian* replied.

Looking up from the pages of notes with a room full of eyes, I awaited my next move. In truth, I didn't want to hand them my notes. The questions scattered among the many pages with no clear order and this was the only copy. I checked my watch, stalling for a moment, as I wasn't going to take the time to organize and rewrite them now having to be to work in the morning.

"Can I email them to Sco−," almost slipping, "To Code Breaker?"

They looked around the room at one another for confirmation.

"Yeah, that will be fine," agreed *Code Breaker*.

"I do have one question before we go," I paused while the others stood from their seats. "Why me? Why now? Why the blood work and medical experiment?"

Alright, more than one question, but under the circumstances, entitled. The members froze, as if posturing for an oil painting. Their individual body language, each expressed personal theories, while their eyes shifted around the room as if in a chess match, awaiting the next move. No one wanted to be the first to articulate his or her beliefs without concrete evidence to support the claim. Finally, the *Russian* removed a pen and notepad from his pocket, and feverously wrote. The only sound within the room came from hard-handed pen strokes contacting paper as time slowed while I tolerantly watched and waited. Everyone knew his intention; their bewildered faces watching his every move as he carefully creased the document and slid it across the table at me.

"There's a man called *"Phoenix"*. None of us has actually met him in person, but he does supply us with inside information. He contacted our group a few years ago and is an exceptionally reliable inside informant. If you need questions answered, make contact with him. He may or may not respond," he shrugged his shoulders, "I've enclosed the drop site and protocol on that piece of paper. Don't lose it as we'll never give it to you again."

With that warning, the other members continued to gather their belongings, and then exited the room. The more I tried to find answers the more I felt trapped in an episode of the *X-Files*. The words of *Fox Mulder* echoing in the back of my head *'The truth is out there'*. Maybe fiction was more real than I wanted to confess. My eyes prodded Russell, seeing if he had any questions, but he wasn't getting the hint.

"Russell, you have any questions?"

"No, not at this time. But I'd like the opportunity to come back and chat at a later time," he was rigorously all business.

"That would be acceptable. Just coordinate it with Code Breaker," replied the *Russian*.

With that, meeting adjourned, everyone making for the door after a brief moment of handshakes and embraces. I lagged behind hoping to talk to Code Breaker, I mean Scott, privately.

"That was insanely intense," I uttered to Scott.

"I told you they can be, but they know the material," Scott talked while packing up his computer. "Listen, Erica. I need to ask you something, but I didn't feel it was appropriate in front of the group."

"What is it?"

"I need to get into Jim's office so I can get access to his personal computer."

"What do you want to know? Maybe, I can ask him at work tomorrow."

"No you can't! I need to get access without his knowledge, understand?"

"You want my help to break you into his office?"

My voice cracked under the illegal undertone of his request. Especially considering Jim was a good friend, having helped get my current job, plus closed the deal on my home. On top of everything else, allowing me to stay at his beach house on Maui only weeks ago. The last thing I wanted to be, especially in today's job market, fired.

"I don't know, Scott," apprehensiveness in my response.

"Let me handle that Scott," Russell expressed.

"What do mean let you handle that?" I questioned his motives.

"It's best you don't know the details, that way they can't trace it back to you. You know…plausible deniability." Scott got a good chuckle from that line as Russell reached for his inner jacket pocket. "Scott, here's my card. Call this number tomorrow and I'll arrange everything."

"Alright," skeptical, but Scott took the card, nonetheless.

I don't know what bothered me more, my boyfriend agreeing to and orchestrating an illegal breaking and entering or my best friend encouraging and engaging in these activities. I needed to reevaluate my life, friends, and acquaintances. Maybe that's what the unidentified caller had tried to do, warn me.

"Excuse me for one second," Russell grabbed his phone, dialing as he left the room.

"Interesting boyfriend you have," Scott smirked.

"Tell me about it. I should say the same about your friends."

"Listen, I know enough to respect them, but I don't trust them. You should do the same with your boyfriend."

"You're jealous," hitting him on the arm.

"No." There was fear in his eyes in which I'd never seen. "Listen, whoever's involved, their security clearance is higher than that of the President. Much, much higher."

"What do you mean the President…of the United States?" Once again, I questioned his information.

"What I'm saying is exactly what Russell said earlier. If these people want you dead then you're dead…end of story."

Scott walked me to the car where Russell was waiting for me. Russell was still conversing on the phone, but I wondered with whom?

"All I'm saying, as a friend. Be careful." He paused looking around as if someone was listening. "Contact Phoenix, but wait until I've had a look at Jim's computer."

"What is so damn important about his computer?"

"Erica, you have known me your whole life. If there's one thing I know, its computers. If my hunch is right, most of the answers you seek are embedded somewhere in Jim's computer." With one long lost lover's stare he hugged me, whispering in my ear, "Just be careful."

Scott had parked on the other side of the studio, so after a short embrace, he left, and continued abruptly to it. I'll never forget the look on his face. He was right, he knew computers, and there was nothing he couldn't do with them. He did have a misunderstanding with the FBI about some trumped-up charge of hacking into the CIA personnel files. I never believed it, but then again he told me it was their way of trying to get him to work for the Government. When no evidence came forth, the jury found him not guilty and ordered the Government to drop all charges and seal his records. Scott never talked about his short stint in a Federal Holding Facility, but said the Government got what they wanted and didn't even pay him for his time. I think that explains his personal vendetta against Government Agencies in the search for transparency.

Russell finished on the phone by the time I made it to the car. I don't think he wanted me to hear the conversation.

"Can we head home now?" I was tiredly awaiting his verdict.

"Yeah, but I'm going to need to head out shortly after we get there."

"What for?" Catching myself, "I know, the less I know the better-off I am."

If it weren't for him being so damn sexy, I would've told him to go get a room. There was something about him, maybe it was his mysterious ways, but no doubt the sexual tension between us was unbearable and I was optimistic that tonight we'd continue where we left off on the beach. However, once again my enviable fantasies put on hold because of *business.*

"Listen, I'm really sorry," pulling me into arms, "I'll be home before you leave for work and we can at least have breakfast together. I'll even cook." He kissed me ever so softly on the lips.

"Deal."

Reluctantly, I broke the embrace in exchange for the driver's seat of my car. I started the car, pulled out of the dirt lot and made for home. I wasn't going to get much sleep; nonetheless, I would get more than Russell would.

"Do you need to use my car?"

"No, there'll be a car at your house for me when I get there."

"I never told you my address, how the—never mind I don't want to know."

It dawned on me he must have already had it. He had to; as that is the only way he could have got the rocker inside. Anyway, we drove the short distance back to my house, only briefly stopping to take in the breathtaking aurora of the distant Vegas city lights. Along the way, I pointed out landmarks to aid in his navigation of the city. Then again, I didn't think he needed help; more than anything, he was humoring me.

Sure enough, we pulled into my driveway to an idle truck with a military tagged license plate, no driver, and keys in the ignition. Maybe that's whom he had called. Where and why he had to leave, I didn't know and wasn't going to push for an answer, at least not yet.

With the newfound keys and his luggage in tow, he followed me into my home. I'd hoped to share my room, among other things with him, while he was in town. However, once in the house, requesting the guest bedroom, reining-in his internal sexual urges while on the surface appearing gentlemanly. As much as I wanted him in the same bed, I understood. That's my story and I'm sticking to it.

Colby instantaneously remembered Russell, his tail wagging with excitement and encircling his legs at a dizzying pace, finally sitting, awaiting his touch. Russell lightly tapped Colby's head, his unique calming effect clearly worked on the both of us. I knew he had to run off shortly, but that didn't change my craving desire for him now. I wanted to wake in his naked arms, roll over, and kiss him good morning, but that fantasy as well as others would have to wait for yet another day.

"I'm really sorry about this," he reiterated.

"I understand. I think," hugging him.

His towering magnetism leaned down, engulfing my petite frame in a passionate embrace, and then we looked genuinely into each other's eyes, as our lips locked deeply into a kiss. Although brief, it was timeless. Once more, he was leaving me on fire with no way to quench these flames. If I slept tonight, my fantasies would run rampant, that was certain.

He grabbed his black briefcase and devoid of hesitation, made for the waiting truck. I followed in his moonlit shadow, secretly wanting him to stay.

"Remember breakfast, I'm cooking."

He climbed in, the red amber glow of the taillights rapidly vanishing from sight.

My only wish, breakfast, served hot and in bed!

Chapter 32

Here it was already six in the morning as I leaned over dazed in search of the snooze button not recalling setting the alarm before bed. Colby, without fail, always had me up by four-thirty for his breakfast. I will say, although short, I slept sounder last night than I had in a while. If it not been for the smell of fresh bacon and coffee coming from the kitchen, I might've returned to the warmth of my pillow and been late for work.

I wanted to scuttle out to see if Russell was cooking, but I knew. I instead at once jumped into the shower and dressed for work. It's one thing to wake up next to someone. It's another for only one of you seen with bed head, but I had to admit, the aroma of fresh bacon was almost worth the risk. Colby's face, as he wiggled his way into the bathroom, agreed. Plus, from the content look on his face, he'd already had breakfast, including a side of bacon. I readied in under twenty minutes, a new personal best, but then again it was Casual Friday. How tough was a pair of jeans, blouse, and black dress boots to put on.

Russell picked up breakfast, cause except for coffee, and the occasional dish of cereal; I wasn't much of a morning breakfast person, unless you included Dunkin Donuts as a major food group. I turned the corner for the kitchen, trying to refrain from jumping into his arms. It was more of the casual, been married for years, persona I was reluctantly trying to pull off. There he was, cooking, still in the same suit, minus the tie and jacket from last night. There's something sexy about a guy knowing his way around a kitchen and Russell was cooking up more than breakfast in me.

"Morning Sunshine," he said, grabbing a carton from the fridge, "how do you like your eggs?"

"Scrambled," even with a shower half-asleep and needing that first cup of coffee to jump-start my brain.

"Coffee's next to your plate," he said.

He'd even remembered how I liked it. He was worth keeping.

"Have you been up all night?" I asked.

"Yeah, I got in a little while ago. I fed Colby so you could sleep a little longer."

His calming personality must transcend past humans to even the fury four-legged variety. Colby goes crazy even when I come home from a run in the morning, never mind strangers.

It's amazing how refreshed and alive he appeared, even in the dim light of the morning. I swear this guy never sleeps. Then it hit me. I never gave him a key to get back in the house.

"How'd you get in the house?"

"I've done more than just promotions in my time," smirking.

"Kind of figured that out already," sipping from my coffee, "but seriously, how'd you get in?"

"I got a great education, Master's Degree in fact, courtesy of Uncle Sam and the Air Force. I was part of the Special Forces."

He slid breakfast in front of me, a ploy to change the conversation. Things weren't coming together as fast as I liked and his past was still a mystery. I took a few bites then continued the casual interrogation, wanting to see how deep I could dig.

"So, do you still work for the Air Force?"

"Did my time, but honestly, you really never retire. I still have many good friends who are active." He was being loosely illusory.

"You mean Nohea?"

"Nohea works for an entirely different "Classified" special branch," he pulled a seat next to mine.

"And that would be…"

"An Above Civilian Classification," he articulated with authority and a warm smile.

"In other words, none of my business."

"For the time being and your safety, yes."

I would heed those warnings many more times over the coming days, but the way Russell expressed it to me that morning wedged a divide in my mind. We broke eye contact momentarily as he proceeded to give Colby strips of bacon. Colby had found a new best friend. I didn't mind, gave me a break from his morning slobber routine on my pants.

"You know you're spoiling him, right?" I was trying to break, even if for a moment, the uncomfortable tension in the air.

"Yeah, but he's such a great dog. He reminds me of Orion."

"Orion?"

"My Golden that passed away."

"Sorry."

"He had a good life. Was my best friend for almost sixteen years."

Great. One awkward conversation, right back into another and I needed to find a new gear to shift to, as the thought of Colby dying was too tough to face right now. He was young, so I planned to have many more good years. The last thing I wanted now was to think about my life without him.

"So, where'd you go last night?" I asked.

"I had to meet someone from Dynamic Aeronomics. They were going on vacation this morning and I needed their keys. Plus, I arranged things for Scott for tonight."

"What do you mean tonight?"

"You said you didn't want to know." He was slowly nibbling on his bacon, the entire time intently expressing a devilish grin. He knew I wanted to know, but wanted to hear it direct from me.

"You're really going to break into Jim's computer tonight?" I wasn't surprised, okay maybe a little.

"If, what Scott thinks is on his hard drive, I agree. We needed to get access to that computer."

"What do you think is in his files?"

"Let's say if I'm right, you're gonna have all the answers you wanted." His gaze noted my response.

"Well that's good then, isn't it?"

"I'm helping your friend Scott for two reasons. The first, to help answer your questions, second…," he pondered, "if we find what I think we might find, your friend's life will be in jeopardy."

"What do mean 'jeopardy'?"

I put down my fork, deeply staring at him, my eyes searching his for a completely definitive answer.

"I mean these people will stop at nothing to silence him and anyone he tells!"

His eyes penetrated mine all the way through to the back of my subconscious. He was letting me recognize the seriousness of the situation. Scott knew this, and tried expressing his concerns the other night and that's why he sought to do it so bad. The entire time I was equating it to a pissing contest between the two of them over me. Sometimes, while running after the truth, you miss the caution signs along the way. Russell was going to protect him, if he could, the best way he knew how. The same way he was looking after me. I figured that if I went along, that would keep the both of them honest. I mean, people were already trying to kill me.

"Then it's decided," returning to my breakfast.

"What's decided?" Russell's voice resigned.

"I'm coming tonight too."

"No way! Out of the question," his head was shaking in disbelief.

"Listen, people have been watching me and trying to kill me since I arrived on Maui. I have keys, security clearance, and nothing better to do tonight. So what's your problem?"

Russell knew how stubborn I was becoming since we first met. He also knew I was right, if they could stroll into the building devoid of alarms that would solve a significant part of their plans. Although, I don't think security concerned either of them that much.

242

"Okay," turning towards me, "but we do it my way." I got the feeling Russell didn't like to give up control that easily.

"Fine. Your way," I smiled.

He moved from across the table to my side, finishing breakfast, while enjoying small talk about Vegas' weather. I had to go to work as the hands on the clock showed I was running late. Time with Russell always seemed to stand still, while the rest of the world flew by. I prayed traffic was going to be light for a Friday.

The plan was simple. Scott was to meet us at the house around eight tonight. It was a Friday so everyone left early, but sometimes Heather and Jim stayed late to finish paperwork for the weekend. The price you pay to have your name on the door. Plus, Jim's main appointments were always on the weekend, so he liked to have everything ready before Saturday. We would go together, use my security access, and stroll in and out before anyone even knew. Easy right?

I ran out the door with another cup of coffee in my hand, leaving Russell, a person I still knew nothing about, in a way, a perfect stranger, alone in my house. Sometimes love is blind. Anyways, Colby would keep him honest. Then again, for bacon and a belly rub, Colby would let you take the stereo and television.

I tried to remain focused at work, but whenever Jim walked by I felt guilty and I hadn't done anything yet. I didn't know his connection to all this and was even questioning Tracy's involvement. She was Jim's right hand man, so to speak, but what, if anything did she know?

The second hand hit five and I was out the door before it made another round. Tracy confronted me in the parking lot because I'd been avoiding her all week. I suppose she was picking up on it and wanted an answer.

"I've got to go out of town this weekend, but are we still on for a Monday morning run?" She asked.

"Yeah, that'd be great," avoiding direct eye contact.

"So, heard from Russell yet?"

"Yeah, I talked to him this morning."

I wanted to get home to Russell, but didn't want Tracy to know he was in town.

"So, when's he coming to Vegas?"

"Sometime next week, but he wasn't exactly sure on the date." I was mastering the art of deception.

"Can't wait to meet him again."

Looking back now there was something in the way she phrased it that bothered me, but at the time I couldn't put my finger on it.

"I gotta run, Colby's expecting supper," I stumbled to unlock my car door.

"You and that dog of yours."

She smiled, shaking her head as she disappeared into the darkness of the garage. Traffic was dreadful for Friday night; then again, this was Vegas. You'd think I'd be used to it by now. Maybe the rush to Russell's waiting arms made it seem worse than it really was. I wondered if Russell had been home all day. *I doubted it.* Would he have gone probing through my house? *Maybe.* What were Scott and Russell so worried about on Jim's computer? *Good question.* My mind was racing the entire trip home, but the thought of returning to someone besides Colby was comforting.

I turned onto my street, as brief excitement changed to disappointment on noticing the absence of Russell's truck. Where'd he go? Here I am, less than a month into the relationship and already worried, questioning his whereabouts. Tracy often commented part of my problem was the negative I found in everyone and everything. I grudgingly convinced myself he was at work, being there was an office in Vegas and the main reason for him making the trip. It can't always be about me, I thought.

Colby met me at the door as normal, almost knocking me to the ground in excitement, but also greeted by the familiar flowery scent of the Hawai'ian Islands. On the dining room table was a gargantuan, but beautiful arrangement of flowers; a varied patchwork of colors I'd not seen but at the Floral Gardens on Maui. Attached was a small handwritten note.

"Thought you would worry where I was so, these are for you. I had to go down to the office to do a little work. See you in a bit.

Love, Russell."

How does he keep doing that, always knowing what I'm thinking? I started to wonder if he was a mind reader or just truly my soul mate. There was another scrumptious smell emanating from the kitchen and again, another handwritten note attached to the face of the oven door.

"Didn't know if you would have time, so I also made supper. Should be ready shortly just wait for the oven to beep."

I flicked on the oven's light reassuring what I already knew from my nose. The smell of roasted pineapple, mixed with the buttery smell of fresh cut almonds, drizzled with an unidentified cream sauce over a large whole chicken. If you're a woman reading this…Guys like this do exist. If you're a guy reading this…TAKE NOTES! The oven beeped moments after feeding Colby. He hesitated to eat, something he never does, the famished look in his eyes told the story. He wanted my supper.

"You're not getting any, so don't even think about it."

His low pitch whining at times can be so charming and add to that, his uncontrollable drool dangling from the corner of his mouth, well let's say we both had a really nice supper.

I was getting nervous waiting for Russell and Scott to show up at the house. I knew Russell could handle himself, he'd proven that already, and I had seen Scott take on certain Government agencies with his mind alone. *So why be nervous about tonight?* I had two men in my life and feelings for both, past and present. They were risking their lives to help me find the answers, which I thought we'd have after tonight. Maybe it wasn't about them as much as the guiltiness of illegally breaking into Jim's office. Of course, there's always that underlying thought—I loved them both.

Chapter 33

I waited in the sitting room until quarter of eight, Colby snuggled tight by my feet, feeling my anxiety and still no Russell or Scott, not even a phone call. The phone, at this point, was in my hand about ready to call Russell when it rang; no number or name, again.

"Hello," I nervously spoke.

"Erica, this is Russell. Is Scott there yet?"

His voice sounded distant as the signal struggled to cross the miles.

"No, not yet. Where are you?"

"I'm running late. I'll meet you at the office, hitch a ride with Scott."

"Anything wrong?"

"No, I'll see you in a bit. I need you to do me a favor though," sounding rushed.

"What?"

"There's a black tote on my bed, can you please bring it with you?"

"No problem. I'll see you in a bit."

"Okay."

Before I could inquire about anything else, the phone call slashed dead, almost as if deliberately disconnected. It was just my nervous tension getting the better of me again, at least that's what I had convinced myself of at the time.

It wasn't easy making out Russell's request as either he was out of cell range or there was electrical interference of sort. I could almost feel a light static charge tingle against my ear. The noise environment behind his voice resembled that of a train platform and I could hear what sounded like an abundance of conversations as a backdrop. I couldn't withdraw enough of the dialect to establish the language, but it wasn't English.

I headed to the guestroom to grab his tote with a part of me wanting to be inquisitive, but somehow knew he'd know, he always knew. Since arriving, I hadn't entered the room, giving him his privacy, but of course, it wasn't as if he's spent much time here. The room, unchanged from normal, as if he had dropped off his stuff for appearance, the bed undisturbed, bathroom absent of personal toiletries, towels spring fresh and didn't even appear used. I wondered if he ever slept and there, in the bed's center, exactly where it should be was the black tote.

The bag didn't weigh a great deal, further tempted; I nearly opened and inspected its contents. The only problem, on the outside zipper was a High Tech LCD lock. *Never seen anything like that before,* I said to myself. I grabbed the bag and simultaneously the doorbell rang, causing me to recoil away from the tote. It took me until the second ring to distinguish the sound and it had to be Scott. Grabbing the bag, I jogged towards the front door trying to calm down, Colby followed along the way.

"Just a second," I yelled while checking the peephole for a familiar face.

"Scott, go to the garage, I'll meet you there."

"No problem," his voice barely rising over Colby's incestuous barking.

Frantically gathering my things, I hit the lights, did a mental checklist of everything needed, and made my way, tote in hand out to the garage. Colby's expression spoke volumes, but Scott was waiting, so I hurriedly kissed his head.

"I'll be back soon. Watch the house," muttering from behind the closing door.

The garage door opened to a laughing Scott.

"I see Colby still remembers me."

"Yeah, he always protects me from the bad men," snapping back.

"Touché," he looked around, "Where's Russell?"

"He's going to meet us there."

He always loved enraging me for no reason, like it was a game and almost pleasurable. Probably his one and only blemish, but for me that was huge, plus tonight I insolently wasn't in the mood for jokes. He'd spent so much time with his computers that at times lacked the social aptitude. Tonight, he was out to prove to me just how good he really was at hacking. Plus, I had a feeling Russell and him were having some kind of macho male contest over me and I had to admit, I was flattered. Scott knew he didn't have a chance with me; besides, physically he wasn't Russell.

I walked towards his so-called car; the light from the closing garage replaced by the moonlight showed a primer stained Charger with a hint of an underlying yellow tone. This aged salvage wreck showed more work down to its facade then the women of Beverly Hills, the front bumper dented and hung on for dear life, and never mind the absence of a rear bumper. Nevertheless, it did have two front seats, but even from this short distance, I could see the back lacked one. The bent radio antenna was classic. I half expected the original eight track still in the dash. As I said before, Scott was rich, but you'd have never known.

"Do you want me to drive?" I asked.

"Are you kidding? I've seen you drive. I'll take my chance with this baby."

He stroked his hand over the hood of the car as if it was some kind of high-end sports model.

"The door's not gonna fall off when I open it, is it?" I felt dirty just looking at it.

"No, but I'll have to open it from the inside."

He climbed in, slid over and opened it as I stood there, waiting, shaking my head in skepticism, as this was a death trap by any standards. Nevada was liberal in car safety but this was ridiculous. Climbing in, tossing the tote between us, I clamored around the bucket seat praying I could find at best a seat belt.

"What happened to your other car?" I nervously inquired.

"Someone stole it the other day."

"Why? Is your other car as sporty as this?"

"I don't know. Maybe they liked the color."

"Rusted over primer spots is not a color," I added.

"You're just jealous," he said grinning.

"There are many things about you that might make me jealous but your car…not one of them. Can we just go?"

He recognized the urgency in my tone and with modest prodding, the car started, erupting into a billow of smoke. Slowly the engine roared, as we jerked forward while he found the right gear.

"Well, we know why Al Gore thinks there's Global Warming, don't we?"

"Laugh now but this baby can do a hundred and eighty."

"The thought of you even doing seventy in this bucket of bolts scares the crap out of me."

"So you think of me a lot then?"

He tried to flash a "Russell" smile towards me as we pulled down the street, but couldn't pull it off. I was going to have to send an apology to my neighbors and HOA for the noise violations. If we were trying to be stealthy, this wasn't the way to travel.

It didn't take us long to get to my work as Scott, wanting to make a point, hit a buck twenty on the fifteen north. I believe my nail marks remain set into his door panel. The lot was vacant for the most part this time of night as Scott drove around towards the back while I kept my eyes focused for Russell's truck. Nothing. The car grinded to a halt and I do mean that literally. We were going to give Russell five minutes, and then I'd get Scott into the building so he could start doing whatever he needed to do. My ears hadn't stopped ringing from the un-muffled engine and barely heard the phone ring from my purse.

"Hello, this is Erica."

"About time you get here. Could you make any more noise on the way in?" It was the familiar voice of Russell.

"Where are you?" My head scanned the lot.

"I'm already inside, waiting on you two."

"What?" I was puzzled. "Never mind, I won't ask."

I hung up the phone, walked to the front door, searching for my ID the entire time shaking my head. It shouldn't have surprised me. Told you...pissing contest.

"Aren't we going to wait for Russell?" Scott asked.

"He's already inside," my voice muttered in astonishment.

"Wow. He's good."

Scott followed me inside, analyzing every glide my security card made through the various readers, three just to get to the elevator. I always wondered why we need so much security and every time I brought it up the answer always, the same—*we had sensitive financial information regarding high profile clients*. Granted, we had clients that were worldwide leaders and dealt with my boss because of his discretion, but still. Once in the elevator Scott began humming nonchalantly to the Muzak.

"Do you mind?"

"What can I say...I love this tune," he smiled, "by the way, this is some high-end security for such a small company."

"What do you mean?"

"Let's say I've been in military bases nearby with less. Kudos to your boyfriend if he got in here undetected."

The door buzzed to our floor and not a moment too soon because Scott had shifted from a hum to singing the words.

"Sixth floor women's lingerie...stocking...bras...and my personal favorite, panties."

"Knock it off. Can't you be serious for one second?"

"I am being serious. They are my favorite."

We crossed the hall to the main office and one last checkpoint, except for Jim's office. Scott began inserting what looked like earplugs into his ears. I didn't question him at the time, thought it was his way of blocking out my endless petty concerns. Russell was already inside, light on, computer booted and talking on his phone. He abruptly got off and let us in, as his face shot Scott an uncharacteristically conceited glance. Scott walked by, hand extended, with what looked like a wad of rolled cash, nodded and continued to the computer. If I didn't know better, they had a side bet on Russell gaining access without my help. Scott looked unquestionably impressed by Russell's ability, as it showed in their exchange, but nothing he did lately was shocking.

"What was that all about?" I asked, but knew they wouldn't answer, at least not the truth.

"What was what about?" Russell shrugged.

"Scott, what's going on?"

"Nothing. Your boyfriend's getting me a great deal on a new car. Now have a seat, be quiet, and watch the master at work."

Russell pulled up a chair, trying to hold back his laughter. In a weird way, they almost seemed like friends and as I took a seat, it dawned on me this was the first time I'd seen Russell in something that wasn't a designer suit. Dressed head to toe in a tight fitting black ensemble, his hair tucked neatly under a cap. Black, theoretically slimming, but on him it seriously defined his sculpted rock hard muscular body and if the aim was Black Op Military—nailed it. I wanted to question him on it and he sensed it, but felt this wasn't the time or place.

After hooking to Jim's computer a few pieces of his own equipment, Scott sat down and began the process of hacking the files. I didn't know what I should do, being out of my element.

"Did you bring my bag?" Russell asked.

"Yeah, it's right here."

Russell grabbed the bag, used what almost looked like a remote car starter, but with a blue laser, pointed it at the bag, and the lock freed itself. Scott glanced away from the display momentarily to watch. There wasn't much in line of tech equipment Scott hadn't seen or played with at some point and the look on his face screamed new toy...I got to get me one of those. Russell unloaded the bag of goodies, not your run-of-the-mill Best Buy specials, while Scott's eyes returned to the monitor screen and the daunting task ahead. I had to admit, being a tech virgin, as Scott would say, but Russell's toys had the tang of sophisticated military hardware.

Scott actively typed away; occasionally swearing at the screen, then would talk dirty to it, apparently his way to get it motivated. Someone in a bordering room might've mistaken it as if he was getting lucky and in a way, he was hoping. I recognized his confidence trying to prove his aptitude with computers. Russell removed a miniature black box with an attached USB cable from his tote, walked over to Scott, and placed it next to the main frame.

"What's that?" Scott questioned.

"A plan B," he reasoned.

"What...don't think I can get in?" Scott stopped typing, turning to Russell.

"No. I have no doubt that you can get in. I'm more worried about what might happen when you do."

Scott was as confused as I was. Did Russell know something that we didn't? The imagery of my cell phone vaporized flashed in my head as Russell gazed honestly into my eyes. I got the message he was trying to convey.

"Just get us in, Scott. Russell knows what he's doing."

Scott turned back, frantically typing, trying to achieve access. His velocity increased as Russell busied himself attaching cables from the suspicious box to Scott's minicomputer. I watched with admiration at Scott's skill on the keyboard. The frequency at which he toggled and navigated through the maze of code was unearthly. It was akin to watching a master sculptor, such as Gian Lorenzo Bernini; chip away at a slab of marble unearthing a masterpiece. His ability to turn zeros and ones into his own work of art was nothing short of extraordinary.

"Is there anything I can do?" I asked, feeling useless by now.

"Are you familiar with Jim's filing system?" Russell inquired.

"Tracy trained me before I went to work for Mr. Grant. I'm assuming she does all of Jim's filing the same way."

"Great, go over to the filing cabinet and see if anything jumps out or seems irregular."

Russell pointed to a set of three file cabinets on the far wall and I made my way over there unsure what I should be looking for, and then turned back.

"They're all locked."

Russell nonchalantly walked over, grabbed a pair of miniature picks from a hidden Velcro pocket on his upper left arm and within seconds they were all unlocked.

"There you go," returning to his prior position, as if no big deal.

I knew there was more to Russell than meets the eye. That's part of his allure and the whole *James Bond* persona he represented. I tried to remain focused, while perusing over the various files, as the many names of high profile clients, including Hollywood celebrities, was intriguing. *What was I looking for?* It didn't take me long to find something. Near the back of the first drawer was a file with my name on it. Odd I thought, considering I worked for Mr. Grant. I removed it but was hesitant to open the thick manila folder.

"I think I found something," turning with folder in hand.

On the surface, my family tree, personal timeline of my life as well as some kind of investigated background check. I dug deeper into the file. It had many pictures from my childhood to present, even a baby picture of me in the hospital taken with my original birth parents. The person holding me looked vaguely familiar, but I couldn't place my finger on where I'd seen him before. The problem was all the text both handwritten and typed was in an unknown language–at least unknown compared to anything I'd ever seen. At first, I thought it was various shorthand, but on further review, it wasn't and I knew shorthand. I offered it to Russell, as his raised eyebrows detailed the importance of this find.

"What does it say?" I asked.

"I'd have to ask a friend," he took the file from me.

"We can't just take the file, can we?"

"Don't worry Jim won't be in till Monday I'll have it returned by then."

I stood, baffled at his comfort with this executed espionage plan and returned to dig something else up from the cabinets he could steal. The room fell silent as Scott's fingers stopped typing.

"Erica, does Jim have pets, kids, or a wife? Anything that might help crack his access code," he waited with fingers at the ready.

"No kids that I know of, but his wife's name is Samantha." I went back to checking the files then remembered, "Wait he does have a Golden Retriever named Chloe. If that helps."

Once again, Scott's rampage against the keys returned breaking the silence and I continued going through the folders stumbling on one labeled in big red letters...CHARA.

"Try CHARA," yelling back in a low tone to Scott.

"Nope," his voice frustrated.

I flipped through hundreds of additional files when I came across *Action Deep Lien*. I opened it, again finding similar writings to my folder and on a hunch voiced across the room; not expecting a confirmation in any form.

"Try Action Deep Lien!"

"Bingo! That's it...were in." Scott's voice, though excited, hinted to disappointment that he hadn't solved this puzzle on his own.

We gathered around the now feverously scrolling computer screen. Scott had switched his focused assault towards the minicomputer searching the contents of all the drives.

"What are you doing now?"

"He's looking for any encrypted files on the hard drive," Russell's voice answered for Scott's, as he leaned in for a better look.

"That's right," Scott seemed taken aback at Russell's familiarity of this process, especially considering this was Scott's own program.

We patiently waited about ten minutes as the minicomputer aggressively scanned the drives. Scott spent the time explaining in detailed technical terms what his program was looking for and the complexity of writing its code. The information transcended my knowledge of computers. Heck, I was glad in the morning when my computer turned on at work. However, Russell seemly captivated, often exchanging personal recommendations with Scott. The two guys unknowingly having a male bonding moment.

"There, that's what we're looking for," Scott excitedly pointed.

"Is that the only file?" Russell asked.

"Yeah, but it's an awfully large file. It's almost a third of the drive."

"Can you get into it?" I questioned.

"Let's see," he coolly clicked on the folder.

Those words would come back to haunt me because within seconds the file opened scrolling through pages on pages of weird numbers and symbols. However, seconds later the entire second floor lights simultaneously flicked on and the alarm started wailing a deafening, almost paralyzing high pitch tone.

"I was afraid of that."

Russell immediately reached for a toggle switch on the mysterious black box then looped a USB cable to the back of Jim's computer. I had all I could do to remain conscious as the sounds of the alarm penetrated my hand-cupped ears. I wonder now if that was why Scott chose to wear the earplugs.

"Can you make a copy of the file?" Russell asked Scott loudly, yet calmly.

"Yeah, but it's encrypted and without Jim's computer we may not be able to open it."

"Just make the copy," Russell directed.

"What's going on?" I anxiously voiced.

You couldn't hear, but the glowing blue and red lights flowing like beacons from the parking lot below suggested the influx's of our neighborhood police. I felt like a common criminal, yet in a way I did have clearance to be here, but didn't want to try to explain.

"The file tripped the building's alarm," Russell answered as he gathered what he could while Scott finished the copy.

"I've never seen a file encrypted with this type of security. Whatever is on this disk we're not supposed to see it." Scott responded with apprehension.

I managed to get to the window and see the brigade on approach to the building; a half dozen police cars. They had already hit the parking lot while a procession of others sped their way down this small road towards the parking lot. Perplexing, was seeing a variety of military vehicles shadowing the first responders.

"I have clearance. I'll just say I was working late," turning back to my cohorts.

"Are there military vehicles with the police?" Russell asked, but I knew he knew.

"Yeah, about half dozen or so."

"Military. Shit, what the hell is on this disk?" Scott screamed.

Scott had dealt with the military before and it wasn't a pleasant experience. He told me stories of hacker friends that vanished without a trace after trying to tap in to government's computers. His own story happened after he was stonewalled filing for information through The Freedom of Information Act. He was looking for documents on UFOs. Scott decided instead to find his own truth and hacked into the CIA's supercomputer. Although he avoided convictions by unwillingly helping the military with a few issues, rarely did he discuss his personal involvement, promised with threats of his own untimely demise.

"What are we going to do? I mean how are we going to get out of here?" I asked.

"File download complete," Scott explained.

"Grab everything." Russell harped making his way to the door pointing skyward. "Make your way to the stairs and head for the roof."

"What are you going to do?"

"Make sure no one can trace this back to you," Russell's eyes shot at Scott.

Scott understood the commands and jesters, grabbing at my hand pulling me towards the stairs. There were numerous floors between us and the roof as the stairway door closed leaving Russell behind. I thanked the *Lord* I'd worn sneakers. It seemed like seconds into our ascent when Russell bolted by, ultimately bridging the gap to the roof first and for such a muscular man he moved with the speed and agility of a cheetah.

Scott and I hit the last flight of stairs not knowing what to expect at the top. Below, the sounds of military issued boots pounded at the stairs. The ghostly sounds of M16A4 rifles, locking and loading while commands, *"shoot first ask questions later"*, echoed in the lower stairwell. We emerged to the roof with a new form of urgency and a large black helicopter, similar to the one Nohea had flown in Maui, idling in front of us.

"What the...," Scott explicitly shocked.

"Go, go, go." I screamed pushing Scott in the back.

At this point in my life, little was starting to shock me with Russell.

"Hurry and get in before we have company," Russell pushed.

He motioned to the open side door of the helicopter. I stopped halfway to wait for Russell, but he was busy doing something to the door, so I quickly matched strides with Scott, entering the helicopter first to find a familiar face.

"Miss Jones, nice to see you again," Nohea said with a smile. "You might want to hurry up as we don't have much time," pointing to a radar screen with numerous blips entering from the extreme right of the screen.

We strapped ourselves in as Russell dashed towards the helicopter, taking his seat alongside Nohea, turning towards us as he motioned Nohea to take off.

"Hang on; this is going to be a high-speed flight."

I'd flown twice on a helicopter, both times in Hawai'i, but this flight was something out of *"Top Gun"*. We accelerated off the helicopter pad with such force it felt more like a missile launch than a helicopter ride.

"Can we go back? I think I dropped my stomach back on the roof." I cried sarcastically.

I noticed our pilot and copilot were too busy up-front to laugh, but Scott thought it was funny. He always got my strange sense of humor.

"Since when did we join the Special Forces?" Scott joked, still trying to shake the white from his face.

"We're clear." Nohea declared directing his comments to Russell.

"Okay. Boys and Girls, everyone's still got their fingers and toes." Russell turned to us laughing.

I swear this guy got off on this stuff. He was enjoying himself, even at our expense.

"We're going to touch down in a few minutes," he explained.

I didn't want to know where, but I assumed they planned this all along.

"So this was Plan B." Scott piped into Russell.

"Actually this was Plan A all along," grinning, "Scott we're going to need a secure location to decode that disk you made. Any ideas?"

"I have all I need right here," tapping on his black bag.

"Alright then. Once Nohea drops us off we'll head for Erica's house."

"Won't they trace us back to my house? I did use my security card to get in, plus the video cameras."

"No. I took care of all that before leaving."

I didn't want to ask how, Russell always thought one-step ahead of everyone, and I figured he'd already planned for that little detail.

"So, Nohea how do you like Vegas?" I was trying to bring some levity to the situation. Not like the two up-front needed it, just all in a day's work for them.

"The city looks great at night from the air." He turned to Russell for reassurance. Why, I don't know.

"Scott, are you going to be able to decode that file?" I needed to know if this was all worth the risk.

"Yeah, the algorithm looks simple, but I'll need some time to find the key."

"The key?" I questioned.

"Although locked with high-end security, the file itself is one based on a simple code of numbers with a base root of six. Once I unlock this base, it should lead me to the embedded file locked-in its main program. At that point, I should be able to translate the information into a form we can easily read." He paused, shrugging his shoulders. "In theory, of course."

"What?" I turned to Russell. "There's that number system of six again," he knew what I was referring too.

Scott noticed my all too familiar stare sitting across from him, but this time it wasn't what he thought, as it addressed Russell for confirmation.

"Anyway," Scott continued, "it looks as if the key is nothing more than an anagram of the original text code. It will just be a matter of finding the right combination."

"I don't understand."

"If I say, for example, *into full homes*, what comes to mind?"

"A house that is filled?"

"No. Shuffle around only the letters—*into full homes*."

"I don't know…*elf homo sunlit?*"

"Right idea, but wrong combination. It's *The Moon Is Full.*"

"So all we have to do is find the anagram for what?"

"It looks like from the access code *Action Deep Lien.*"

"So how difficult is that going to be...what, a few hundred different combinations."

Scott took a second to type a few things into his phone.

"How long do you think it will take?" Russell turned from the front to ask.

"It depends on the number of combinations and if there're any extra roadblocks along the way." Scott's facial expression changed slightly as he tilted his head from the phone. "...and actually Erica there are 71,429 different combinations or variations of this anagram."

"Great. Plus extra roadblocks?" I rolled my eyes.

"Yeah, whoever encoded this was good. I mean damn good. Although the code is simple, our computer's binary code is based on zeros and ones not six. So even if I get into the file and if I can't find their cipher key, I'll still have to write a code to translate the original transcript in order for us to read it."

You could tell his brain was already going a mile a minute. If there's one thing we both loved, it was pleasure from brainteasers. However, for me I could've done with a little less drama.

It didn't take long to arrive at some out-of-the-way vacant strip of desert. I made out the shadow of Russell's SUV in the distance as we landed. He had planned this all along, probably making his way in via the roof and I bet security wasn't even aware of this obvious hole in the building's defenses. Of course, how many people had the funds for a helicopter or the desire to break and enter such an irrelevant office? I knew of one!

"Are we still on for Project Deep Core?" Nohea asked Russell.

"Yeah, as planned." Russell appeared low-key with his reply.

"See you in two then, boss." Nohea turned towards Scott and I. "Hope you two have a nice night. Miss Jones, again a pleasure to see you."

"You too, Nohea. I think."

We climbed out of the helicopter, heading for the truck as Nohea, with a quick salute, once again took flight. The absence of running lights allowed for the illusion in the night sky of a black void. Its silhouette highlighted only by the moon and swiftly weakened as it turned, melting away over the mountaintops like the wind.

According to Russell, we were only twenty minutes away from my house. I'd never been on this side of the mountain, of course, there was no reason to, but he was right. Scott immediately went to work trying to crack the anagram as soon as we got home.

It wasn't late but I still felt tired from the day's stress. I wanted coffee and figured everyone else could use some as well. Colby was quiet with everyone and spent most of the time at Scott's feet in the office. Traitor, I thought to myself. I made everyone coffee, sat down next to Russell in the kitchen hoping to get some answers as we waited for Scott to work his magic.

"Seriously Russell, you're not a promoter specialist for your company, are you?" My face couldn't get any more serious.

"Yes and no."

"Cut the bull…I need to know."

He paused searching for the right words to explain who and what he was. This was going to be good.

"I worked…"

"You mean work," cutting him off midsentence.

"No. I worked years ago for a private security firm, eventually I ended up employed as an independent contractor for a branch of the military." He wanted to finish with no interrupting questions.

"What branch?" I persisted.

"I don't know," He read the reservation in my face, "Really…I don't know. Now just let me finish," taking a sip of coffee. "We both started in Special Forces and that's where I met Nohea. Our unit was part of an elite covert extraction company and our projects were 'Top Secret', frankly, they were 'Above Top Secret'. Both of us hired to coordinate security measures by this firm because of our unique abilities. They called the project 'The County Club' and dealt with privately arranged meetings for a select group of people. You know them as The Majestic 12. During that time, your name crossed my desk many times. When given the chance to meet you, I couldn't resist. I just didn't, don't think, my superiors considered we'd have formed this kind of bond."

"What do you mean by 'Above Top Secret'? I keep hearing this being mentioned."

"It's for security clearance that even exceeds accessiblity to the President as well as all known government branches. My unit, for all purposes, didn't exist. If you know what I mean. Remember before when I said *Plausible Deniability*."

"Fine. How come my name kept coming up and how do I figure in all of this?"

"I have a theory on that but don't want to alarm you until after we decode what's on that disk."

"Humor me." I finished my coffee, headed for a second one, and considered making this one a little stronger.

"I don't know if you'd believe me, even if I told you."

"Try me!"

"Alright." He paused to collect his thoughts. "Here it goes…Thirty Thousand years ago an alien race altered the human genetic codes, thus advancing your evolution by thousands of years. Their singular purpose was to create a slave race to aid in the strip mining of your abundantly specialized minerals from deep below in the Earth's crust. About three thousand years ago another race of beings intervened and was trying secretly to free your people. Thus, an intergalactic underground war has been raging for many years on your planet. In July of 1947, in the Mesosphere, during one of these secretive battles, a ship or saucer was shot down and crashed…"

"You don't mean Roswell, New Mexico?"

"Exactly! Now this is where it gets complicated. The people of this planet weren't and are still not ready for full disclosure about their history and the future of their world. Both species had been careful about revealing themselves and their technology. However, the military, with its progress, had descended on Roswell faster than the aliens could descend and recovered the downed ship. Then, the President of the United States as well as your Military Generals decided to cover up the story until they reversed engineered the technology. During the following years, one species attempted and succeeded with contacting your Government, eventually signing an undisclosed treaty. This allowed them select, undisclosed genetic testing on humans, in return for their advanced technology. Then another race, tried to warn leaders of the world about their deception, but self-indulgence for power and their supreme weapons overshadowed the truth. Since then every sighting, abduction, and resulting crash is easily trumped-up as fake in order to continue this line of deceit. I can't begin to describe the rank that this now extends, just what I've learned and been privy to."

"So you're telling me little green men created the human race?"

"No, I'm telling you that little Grey men had a hand in man's evolution. I'm also telling you that other species have had a hand in man's technological advances."

There was a long pause as I tried to read his face. If this was his idea of a joke, he wasn't holding back the punch line, or was he?

"Come on Erica…think about it for a second. A few thousand years ago, you were living in huts, a hundred years ago, you learned how to fly, fifty years ago, you went to the moon, and now your technology is advancing faster than your civilization. In the last sixty years, you've advanced a thousand times faster than the previous three thousand years…coincidence? I think not."

"So our Government knows what's going on?"

"A fraction of your Government is privy to this information. Again, *Above Top Secret.*"

I got up, restlessly walking around, trying to absorb his statement, as my head frenziedly shook with disbelief. Scientifically it made some sense, but Theologically—confused. If it's true, then my Catholic ideology is a farce, in fact religion in general a sham. In addition our own evolution, it seems had gaping holes.

"How do I play into this whole charade?" I asked.

"While altering the genetic makeup they noticed a strange anomaly if you will. Some, men and women, had a hidden dormant gene, that when triggered, immunes them to these species' mind controlling devices, usually, making these humans far superior. This gene is unique to certain people of this planet. One race in particular, taking note to this anomaly, attempted to crossbreed with humans. In effect transferring their power and activating this missing gene. If my corrections are right, you have this gene and power, only you are unaware of the potential it poses."

"So all these abductions, including mine, are nothing more than science experiments, trying to find a missing gene and we're the lab rats?"

"No. Some species are just inquisitive about human sexuality. Some are trying to educate and advance your knowledge of the universe. However, yes, some are trying to find persons carrying this unique gene in order to genetically alter it out of human DNA before too many become...to put it bluntly—*activated*."

"So, I don't understand how suddenly I am involved. Until last week I'd never had an abduction or at least I don't remember it."

"There are two factions of Government sharing the same information. One faction is trying to find a way to implement this gene into everyone like a vaccine. While others are trying to help erase this gene so it never sees the light of day. In return, they'd gain more technologically advanced weapons."

"Yeah, but how'd they find out about me? Was I just a random choice?"

"No. This has more levels than you can grasp, but I'll try to simplify. You know how over the years you gave blood, in addition, years ago you tried to help a friend with a bone borrow transplant, plus occasionally you donated plasma?"

"Yeah, so?"

"That's how they found you. See a sample, every time you gave blood, plasma, or bone marrow were automatically sent to a central Government lab. All results are then DNA tested, cataloged, and filed. Subjects that fit into active carriers are then flagged and surveyed."

At this point as you read, you, in all likelihood, are thinking the same thing I was. *That's the last time I do that.* Of course, I realized it didn't matter now because they already had all the information they needed anyways. That extra shot of Bailey's to my coffee was looking good right about now, but instead I decided to take a break and check on Scott. Russell didn't say anything else, only followed me into the office.

"How's it going?" Russell asked Scott.

"With over 70,000 combinations it might take awhile. If you want, take a look through the list I printed and see if anything pops out at you."

Scott grabbed an encyclopedia of paper newly printed off the floor, smiled as he handed me the paper-weighted list, pausing to notice the flushness had drained from my face.

"What's the matter, you look like you've just seen a ghost?"

"Yeah, the Ghost of Evolutions past," grabbing the papers from him.

"The what?"

"Never mind…I'll tell you later. Just break this stupid code and let's see what's so damn secretive on this disk."

I started scanning down at the pages upon pages of printed numbers that looked nothing like an anagram with only one burning question. *Was this even worth it?* In my depressed stupor I almost tripped over another printed pile of paper.

"What the hell is all this?" I collected some of the fallen pages.

"Sorry, that's the code I'm writing to decipher the cryptograph of the original message. Just in case." He replaced the compilation I lost when I tripped with another. "Here's the possible anagrams of the original password. I told you it could be a slow process."

As Scott returned to the keyboard, Russell and I pulled up a chair and began thumbing through the pages of anagrams. We looked through pages about an hour before one line literally jumped off the page at me. Could it have been that simple? Sometimes if you want thoroughly to hide something, all you need to do, put it in plain sight.

"Scott, stop!" I yelled.

"Did you find something?" He asked.

I had to double check what I was seeing, and then pointed it out to Russell, who shook his head in approval.

"Try, '*Alien Deception*'."

I waited watching Scott enter every flicking character on the screen as it played in slow motion from every angle. I'd thrown the challenge flag out and waited for the referee to confirm my convictions.

"That's it!" Scott shouted.

Scott stopped typing as the screen went black, then flooded with pages on pages of the same text that filled my files as well as the files for *Action Deep Lien*. Scott frantically grabbed a fresh ream of paper and hit screen print.

"Do you think you can decipher the text?" Russell asked.

"Yeah, I'm gonna have to write a simple program based on a value of six to find the key. It'll take me some time, but I can't do it all here. I'll need to use my main frame back at the house."

"Okay. Why don't you get a few hours of sleep here and keep Erica company. I'm going to meet someone and show them this hard copy. We'll meet over at your place, say nine tomorrow morning?"

Scott, as a friend, had slept over in the past and it didn't bother me. However, what troubled me more was my boyfriend, who'd been here now for two days, and hadn't spent one night. How he functioned on such little to no sleep was beyond me. I'm sure as part of Special Forces Training he learned to handle being sleep deprived. Yet, never looked tired? I knew Scott delighted in the idea of staying the night, but he would've preferred to go with Russell or at the very least, home, to start breaking the code.

"Why don't I go with you or, at the least, drop me off at my house on the way?" Scott asked of Russell.

"No!" He snapped back. "You're staying here with Erica, at least for tonight." He grabbed the newly printed pages, made toward his room then returned with his infamous black briefcase.

"Well, you heard your boyfriend. Guess tonight we're sleeping together," he grinned.

"You wish. You got the couch!" I walked out of the room.

"Just kidding," he laughed following me to living room, but I knew better.

"Alright. I'll see the two of you tomorrow morning at Scott's house."

Russell leaned in to kiss me with one eye on Scott. I could tell he wanted to say I love you, but didn't want to put Scott in an awkward position. I felt the same. He ran out of the living room to the front door as if there was a fire, only seconds later to poke his head back around the corner.

"I love you Ka'iu lani." His eyes fixated on mine.

I don't know why but momentarily I hesitated, "I love you, too."

"By the way Scott…great work tonight." Russell expressed with approving thumbs up, and then quickly disappeared around the corner. He was good at that.

I was waiting for a smart-ass comment from Scott. Instead, I got the unexpected as he stood up, put his arm around me, and in a friendly gesture reassured what I already knew.

"He really does love you and would do anything for you. I can tell. Don't let this one get away."

He wasn't sad or jealous, but a father figure, glad to see his baby girl finally leaving the nest. I knew if Russell ever tried to hurt me, Scott would be there to pick up the pieces because he always has.

We walked to the kitchen, finished the coffee while reminiscing about our past, the past of humanity and the future of us all.

Chapter 34

I managed to sneak in a few hours of rest. Knowing Scott was nearby was a comfort, although I would've preferred Russell. There was something to be said about having a man in the house—no offense towards Colby. I emerged from my bedroom, silently after a quick shower, hair still damp, to get Colby his breakfast. I thought Scott might still be asleep; instead, he was frantically working on his computer, unwavering in his quest to solve the key. I knew how Scott's mind worked; he'd probably remain sleepless until he solved it. I've seen him at times; eyes pried open for three days straight playing on-line games. On-line Gamers considered him a God, referring to him only by his nickname, '*Slayer*'. *Slayer*, *Code Breaker*, to me he will always be just Scott, a good friend for life.

"Did you get any sleep?"

"A little, but this stuff is just too damn interesting."

"I know what you mean."

"No. Come see what I mean," pointing to two pop-up menus. "The stored information here is in a three-dimensional matrix, unlike our two-dimensional writing." His eyes remained fixated on the computer screen.

"I don't get it."

"Okay try and picture this, we write in a two-dimensional space so what you see is what you get. This information is encoded three-dimensionally. So, picture this cup." He lifted his coffee cup from last night. "If you look at just the front of the cup and read it that is our dimension. Now, picture that same writing but every time you turned the cup, new information appears. That's what we're dealing with. No one, at least no one on this planet, writes like this."

We talked last night a little about my recent experiences and information Russell revealed to me about the Government. I intentionally censored most of the information, figuring the less he knew the safer it might be for him and as a friend, and sensing my fear he didn't push for answers. In time I'd tell him and he was fine with that…for now.

"I got to get back to my mainframe at home with this information." Scott stressed.

"We can leave now if you'd like. Give you a head start before we meet Russell."

"Great!" He assembled his possessions and in seconds was ready and heading out the door to the car with papers falling behind like a breadcrumb trail.

"Let me see if Colby needs to go out first." I yelled to him, as he was already in the car.

Scott lived on the other side of town, North Las Vegas, in a small townhouse. It wasn't in the nicest of neighborhoods, but again he didn't like to flaunt his prosperity. His condescension for materialistic wonders was at times, so endearing, but as a woman, I'd never live over in that area of Vegas. It dawned on me, in our haste for Scott's home neither of us ate breakfast. It was a little before eight when I pulled up to the front of his town home, needing something in the form of food and sure he could've used no less than a quick coffee fix.

"I saw a Dunkin Donuts just up the street, my treat. What do you want?"

"The usual," He juggled his handful of gear out of the car.

"Back in a few. Be careful."

"That's my middle name."

His warm, friendly smile, hazed over from his breath entering the valley's unusually cold air.

I never got the chance to say thank you for being a friend. It's funny what runs through your mind after a loss. Things you wished you'd said others you didn't, and just stuff in general. I'll miss him.

I started to shed tears, the loss of a true friend is not something I'll take lightly again and as painful as the next few paragraphs will be to me they have to be written in Scott's memory. He was a true unsung hero to humanity that people of this planet will probably never know about.

I waited inside Dunkin's for my bagel and Scott's egg sandwich, while the screaming sounds of fire trucks raced by down the street. At that exact moment in time a gut-wrenching feeling manifested in the deepest pit of my stomach. A premonition if you will of an ominous sensation of death and destruction. I left my order, rushing out the door as the world slowed, in pursuit of the emergency vehicles.

It didn't take long for the physical to surmount the mental as my hands began to shake and my breathing quickened. In the not too distant Vegas skyline appeared pillars of flames and plumes of smoke engulfing into the morning's blue sky with only one probable locality. My car sped back to Scott.

I parked across the street in shock watching in horror as the parking lot overflowed with the commotion of emergency vehicles and personnel. Scott's entire complex was ablaze. I wanted to run over, but my legs paralyzed with fear, already knowing as tears flowed like rivers down my cheeks, the chest tightened with anxiety as my hands uncontrollably shook. The bastards killed him! I got my best friend killed. Looking back towards the fiery inferno through tear-blurred vision, a recognizable face hastily raced through the gathering crowd towards my car, Russell. Somehow, instinctively, I mustered the strength to meet his outstretched arms in the middle of the street.

"Thank god you're alright," he screamed, as his arms became a pillar of strength around my body.

"They killed him. The Sons of Bitches, they killed him. Didn't they?" My voice screamed over the commotion.

"They're saying it was a gas leak," Russell wiped the tears from my face with his hand.

"Do you really believe that?"

"No."

He didn't need to say anymore as a black sedan, similar to what was in Hawai'i; drove passed us slow enough to ensure we'd notice, while Scott's burning building reflected off the highly tinted glass. I understood the significance. We were next.

"Come back here you bastards; you missed me again." I yelled as Russell held me back, wanting to chase them down the street.

"Don't," he expressed, pulling me back into the comfort of his muscular arms.

I stayed watching, with a frozen stare, for most of the afternoon while the fire extinguished. They pulled only one body out, charred beyond recognition and its only identifier it was Scott, positioned around the lifeless neck. A gold heart friendship necklace I gave him as a gift years ago, inside a single picture of him and I hiking. He never took it off and there it was, covered in ash lying atop an unrecognizable blackened dead man's chest. I stopped the paramedics and agonizingly removed it and as if it was the hand of a child held it gently between fingers. I knew this charm physically wasn't Scott, but now it was all I had left of our friendship. Russell helped me to my feet as the covered body wheeled away to an awaiting ambulance.

The townhouse had nothing left to it, but the smell of melted silicone parts and burned bits of outdated furniture. All the information we'd worked hard to retrieve last night had melted away. All that remained was Russell's hard copy and after talking with Scott this morning I didn't know how much that was going even to help.

When I look back now, that was the first time I'd met Detective Wilson. He was understandingly caring then, trying to get what information he could without upsetting me. I told him the truth of why I thought Scott was murdered. Well not the truth, only cautiously advised him that I didn't think it was an accident. I asked if he'd check into it. He probably thought I was having a tough time dealing with the loss of my friend, but humored me with *I'll look into it*.

Russell spent the entire day silently comforting me, at a loss for words. He expected something like this would happen but not so soon, and worked hard at all costs trying to avoid such a confrontation. As a soldier, you train to be emotionless on the field of battle and I could see this in Russell's eyes. I was getting a crash course and had failed. My head filled with planning funeral arrangements. I was the closest to family Scott had and I wasn't going to let him down again. I needed to call my boss because there was no way I was going to make it to work Monday.

Russell eventually drove me home. The rest of the night dragged by as, I sat in front of my fireplace staring at the picture inside the pendant, tissue in one hand, my other on Colby's head in my lap. Russell sat in the room for support, but knew I needed space, at least tonight. Someone was going to pay for Scott's death. I personally, was going to see to it and no one was going to get in the way, not even Russell.

I couldn't write another line. Those emotions a painful reminder of how far I'd come and how far I still needed to go. I grabbed the heart-shape pendant still around my neck trying to hold back another wave of tears.

"Shit!" I noticed the time.

The morning by now had vanished and the balance of the story needed to wait. Detective Wilson was expecting me at one. I had a prepared signed alibi for him, not by choice, which still needed verification down at the station. This was the second time in less than a week Detective Wilson was going to interrogate me about a deceased friend. Somehow, I didn't think this was going to go as well as it did the first time. One friend dies it could be an accident, a second friend dies and they label you a possible suspect or worse, serial killer. The truth is I was the only suspect they had, but I didn't think they had any proof. The thought of spending the rest of my days in prison, unable to see Colby or Russell every morning was heartbreaking and unpleasant. Although a part of me now felt vindicated for Scott's death. Russell had assured me that I'd never find myself behind bars, but if it happened, he'd watch after Colby as he's now watching over Samantha. *How does one's life suddenly become so complicated?*

Chapter 35

I left the house headed for the police station, with darkened purple, puffed tired eyes. If I didn't feel remorseful, I at any rate looked the part. I didn't even get out of my neighborhood before picking up that oh-so-familiar dark shadowed tail in my rearview mirror. This time, I figured it was the local police making sure I was heading for the station. However, the color and model soon erased that idea. After a while, it's like your own shadow, you know it's there so why bother checking.

I safely arrived a few minutes early, with my alibi written down and cemented firmly in my mind; equivalent to a get out of jail card, or at least, hoped. Before entering the main lobby, I did a double check behind me…yes my escort was still there. I wondered if they'd visually appear in the station if things went south for me. I thought; I'm on my own on this one.

I felt like a celebrity on entering, minus the red carpet, everyone looking up from his or her mundane tasks to catch a glimpse of dead-woman-walking. Even the receptionist didn't need an introduction knowing right away, who I was. After a brief silent gawk in my direction, the room returned to its normally congested behavior.

"Hi, I'm looking for Detective Wilson." I tried not to announce myself loudly.

"Yes, Miss Jones, he has been expecting you. Just take a seat over there. He'll be with you momentarily." She said.

I'd never been in a police station and wanted to break for the door. I can tell you living in Vegas I'd more or less expected to see a row of slots on the wall, instead there was the dread of society. As much as I hated to gamble, the comfort of pulling on a one-arm bandit would've been a much-needed distraction. I was uncomfortable waiting for the detective, being as much fun as waiting for my OBGYN. I respected our men in blue in this city for this was one job you could never pay me enough to do and they did it well.

I instantly recognized Detective Wilson from the other day as he made his way through the security doors motioning for me to join him. He didn't say a word to me as we made our way down to his office, only the intermittent glance over his shoulder, sizing me up, but that was enough.

Not your emblematic Vegas cop, he loomed barely over six feet and weighting in under a hundred-eighty pounds. He was basically a stick with a badge. His physical features dwarfed in comparison to his heartfelt charisma and passion for his craft. The image of a once-handsome man chiseled away from the twenty plus years on the force. He was African-American and his facial features resembled that of Morgan Freeman. I always liked him as an actor, maybe that's why I felt so at ease with the detective.

I sat down in a hard wooden chair, across from him, separated by a desk, engulfed under piles of ongoing cases. I thought 'You could really use a secretary'. Cuts in the department and everywhere in Vegas were taking their apparent toll. He straightened his tie as he leaned forward; the rusted springs from his career chair chilled the air. He motionlessly read the opened file, trying to find the right words to phrase his first question. I watched enough CSI to know they wanted to watch you squirm for a little first. It's only when they talk fast and first that they really do have enough evidence to convict. If he had substantial evidence I wouldn't be sitting here, but in holding, so I figured I'd break the ice. Noticing the picture on the wall behind him of a beautiful woman and two kids, I'd try to get on his good side.

"Is that a picture of your family?" I asked.

"Was, she and the kids left me over a year ago." He held up his left hand. The ring's absence had almost completely tanned.

"Oh, I'm sorry." That worked well. I thought now he's really going to be pissed.

"Don't be, it was my fault." He paused turning to look at the picture. "This job became more important to me than them."

His face laced with lines of regret and I essentially felt sorry for him. You could see how this job could drive a wedge into any family. The daily thought of never knowing if your spouse would return from a day's work.

"Listen Erica, let's cut the bullshit." He turned and closed the file.

"Okay."

"I have two people dead within a few days of each other. The only common thread is they were friends of yours." He paused for dramatization, "makes me not want to be your friend, if you know what I mean?"

As I went to respond, he stopped me in my tracks with one finger.

"Just listen!"

He got up from his desk and made his way in front of me as he perched himself on the only clean edge of his desk. If he'd have had any bulk to his physical presence I might've felt intimidated. However, this bad cop image didn't fit him at all.

"I had a visit from a General Samson this morning who swears you were with him last night and told me to drop all, if any, charges. I don't like people telling me how to do my job, particularly pompous, take-no-for an answer, in-your-face, Generals." He leaned in closer, the light-yellow stained teeth highlighting his speech. "Especially, when the leads we have in both these murders seemed conveniently and continually to trace back to you."

I thought it was interesting he was calling Scott's death a murder, 'cause at the time, they were calling it a gas leak. I thought otherwise and asked him to check into it, maybe he did. I found it also interesting that a General I'd never met was pleading my case.

"First, I don't know any General Samson. Second, I thought Scott's death was an accident." I questioned his motives and evidence.

"We thought so too, at first. Then there's this little thing we like to do called an autopsy. Ever heard of it? Anyways, the DNA pulled off the burned body doesn't match that of one Scott Parker. Truthfully, we don't know whose body we have at the morgue. According to the report, the body had been frozen and apparently dead for well over a year. Can you explain that?" He was looking directly at me for an answer that I didn't have.

"No." I quietly muttered.

A part of me was suddenly overwhelmed with the hope Scott might still be alive, but another, confused. *If it wasn't Scott's body, whose body burned in that townhouse and where was Scott?* Images of the men that had been following me, torturing him for information filled my brain. I think my facial expression told Detective Wilson everything he wanted to know. From that point, the conversation shifted gears.

"Are you telling me that you believe Scott is still alive?" I asked.

"You tell me," he barked back.

"I don't know, wish I could."

"Erica, I like you, but I need answers. So stop playing games with me. I don't care if your friendly, high-and-mighty General wants you cut loose. I'll stick you in holding and conveniently lose your paperwork on this desk for a few weeks. Get my point?"

"Well I did do up this statement," fumbling around in my purse for the letter.

He walked back around the desk while reading the letter, his neck muscles bulging over the tightened collar. The redness in his face showed the heightened levels of his blood pressure. He sat down, added the letter to the file, effortlessly closed it, and added it to the mountain of paperwork to his right before popping a much-needed nitro pill.

"We both know that this is bullshit and not worth the ink on the page." He reached for a pad of paper.

"I wish I could help, but I can't."

Then he did something totally unexpected, writing briefly on a notepad while lecturing me on my civic duty and constitutional rights. The detective, then without missing a beat handed me the note, briefly holding a finger in secret to his lips before continuing his barrage of my rights. It read simply, '*This room is bugged, please play along*'. He smiled hoping to gain my trust. I didn't know what he had in mind, maybe this was a sick ploy to get me to talk. I only knew that for some strange reason at that moment I trusted Detective Wilson and would try to oblige his request, if I could.

"They told me not to ask you any questions, but I'm going to anyways." He finished writing something else on the pad of paper and handed it to me as he asked each question. "Do you know why Tracy was out on Highway 375?" The pad read, '*Is your life in danger?*'

I understood what he was trying to find out and how so I played along the best that I could.

"No, I don't know why she was out there." The whole time shaking my head yes.

"Do you know anyone who would've wanted your friends dead?" The paper read, '*Does this have to do with Area 51?*'

"No, I can't think of anyone." Again, shaking my head yes.

"Do you know anything about the robbery at your place of employment the other night?" He took a little longer writing this time. The paper read, '*Can I meet you later at your house, in private?*'

"No, just what I read in the paper." Again, shaking my head yes.

"Do you want some coffee?" He walk towards the brewing pot sitting in the corner, adorning the wall his many department and military recognition of honor awards for bravery in the line of fire.

"No, I'm kind of coffeed out." I grabbed the paper and quickly jotted down the following:

Thanks for your help. I'm being followed and my house watched so please be careful. I don't know if I can answer your questions, but I'll try.

He sat down and casually viewed my written reply. "Well, this shouldn't be a problem." That was his response to the question but he continued. "Based on what I've seen and have for evidence, I can't hold you, yet," emphasis on '*yet*'. "But don't make any plans in the near future." He smiled.

I don't know if he was trying to earn my trust in order to coerce a confession out of me or maybe he knew more than he was leading on and not willing to tell me in the office. I had a feeling, my life, no matter where I went anymore, wasn't going to be private.

"Is that all Detective?" I stood from my chair.

"For now, Miss Jones. For now." He stood up, walked over showing me the door. "I'm guessing you can find your own way out."

"I think I can find it," reassuring him with a smile.

That was it. The door closed behind me. For a second everyone's eyes raised again, until I took notice, than like good little workers, they put their heads down returning to civic duty.

I wanted to get back home and finish my journal. Russell promised me he'd be back tonight for supper. Maybe, I'd shift my worry on what to cook for dinner. Although an illusion, to imagine I had a normal relationship might help take my mind off things.

I noticed my shadows were no longer in the parking lot. I knew, although unseen, they were still out there somewhere. I decided to take the highway home, instead of the side streets, as the time on the dash assured me, I'd missed rush hour, so why not.

I wasn't on Highway 15 South for more than five minutes when my side mirror picked up the fast approaching image of a large black Escalade. Here we go again I thought and as the Flamingo exit passed, I caught another hint of an Escalade merging right, onto the highway. The two shadowed my speed of sixty-five for a few miles and I let them. Finally one passed only to pull directly ahead and in, controlling my advancing speed while the other pulled tightly up to my bumper, tapping it slightly, enough to make me aware of its presence. I accelerated trying to widen the distance, but the leading SUV wasn't moving. Again, it matched my speed this time hitting the rear with added force. I sickened with the thought that they intentionally were trying to run me off the road. The vehicle backed off enough to pull alongside my driver's side door. I couldn't see through the darkened windows, but I knew their plan and I wasn't going to let it happen.

I broke abruptly, falling in behind the second SUV, driving a car that was no match in size or speed, but I might have a chance with maneuverability. I broke for the far left lane speeding up and swerving in and out of three lanes of traffic. Maybe, if I was lucky, Detective Wilson had a tail on me or at the very least; someone would pull me over for reckless driving. However, after a few miles I soon realized that was a false hope. I was so preoccupied with the

SUVs I'd totally forgot about my other shadows. They aggressively chased, but reserved their distance as if they were filming for the nightly news.

My exit was still a ways to go, but if I could keep them guessing and over to the left long enough, I might be able to shoot off the South Point Exit last second. The limited traffic ahead under protest made room for us as we sped down the now merging lanes and each time they attempted to ram my driver side door, I increased or decreased speed just enough for them to miss. I was setting them up. With the off-ramp fast approaching, I gave one more look over my left shoulder and noticed the back passenger side window rolling down as the muzzle of a high-powered rifle slowly emerged. My life flashed before my eyes as I realized I wasn't going to make the exit. No sooner had that thought entered my mind than the grinding sound of metal on metal woke me out of that death trance. It seems that my other shadows had hit the SUV with such force they essentially pushed them ahead of me at an unbelievable speed. I saw my opening, within seconds, I slammed on my brakes, firmly turning the steering wheel towards the exit with all my strength with hopes I'd miss the Jersey barriers. The car banked, its low profile scraping at the surface below as the tires screamed to meet the demand. The second SUV tried to follow and met a-not-so-friendly, immovable Jersey barrier. In my side mirror, the truck slowed as it made its way through the air, pieces of concrete shooting out around it like fallen stars. The final destination its roof, as it slid across the off-ramp and down the embankment.

The convertible sounded like a dragster as I pulled off the exit, around traffic and through the red light down Silverado Ranch, with a ticket the least of my worries right now. I ran another two lights, though no one now in pursuit before finally slowing, eventually pulling over onto a siding to catch my breath. My life was getting more and more exciting by the minute.

I feverishly searched my purse for a piece of gum when I came across the note the "*Russian*" had given me the other night on how to contact "*Phoenix*". He said I might find the answers to my questions through him. So out came a pad of paper from my purse and I began writing a list of questions. My hand was still shaking, but each letter I made legible by boldly printing in large, crisp, capital letters. The first question, *"Where the hell is Scott?"*

The note carried with it two sets of instructions. One, the drop off point with location and instructions, while the other a pick-up point. The first line, GPS coordinates, which fortunately my car had thanks to a generous gift from Tracy for my birthday. When construction in Vegas was unmanageable or days like this it was a great feature to have. Something that never gets old in Vegas, construction. The line under the GPS coordinates read, *"Drop the letter in the box that shouldn't be there"*. *What the hell was that supposed to mean?* I finished my letter, sealed it in an envelope addressed to Phoenix, and typed in the GPS.

The directions took me to the older end of Henderson near Boulder Highway. I pulled on to a dead end street, thinking how fitting, as my trip came to a close. A few sparsely spaced houses set across from a run down trailer park. The pleasant female voice stating, *"You have arrived at your destination."* What destination? I scanned the desert terrain for some evidence of a box.

Then at the far end of the road, as it transitioned into a dirt trail, I became aware of what they were referring to, an outdated, faded blue USPS box, sat in front of a tree, overrun by underbrush. It had to be what the *"Russian"* meant, considering streets here had their own community mailboxes. The only location ordained by these boxes anymore was in front of the post office. I pried back the rusting top door looking for any evidence of a pick-up time to the faded white lettering *"Seek the Truth"*. This was it. It had to be. I dropped in the letter and listened as it echoed in the emptiness of the surrounding metal. I surveyed the surrounding area for signs of *"Phoenix"*, but knew he would never show his face and enlighten me with the answers. The answers weren't here anyways, that was an entirely new location and would wait for another day. I drove off heading for home with lists of newly unanswered questions. *If Scott wasn't dead, where was he? When would I see Detective Wilson? Were the MIB's trying to scare or kill me?* The most important thought that came to mind; *what was I cooking Russell for dinner?* I had to start getting my priorities straight.

Chapter 36

I stopped on the way home to get a whole chicken with plans to cook for Russell. I wasn't the greatest chef by a long shot, but it was one of the few dishes I cooked well. Plus, with a two-hour cooking time, it'd give me enough time to wrap up writing the past few days in the journal.

Colby greeted me at the door with an out-of-character, agitated enthusiasm but for once, no one was inside or outside the house, at least for now. However, I still did a casual walk-through in order to set my mind at ease as it had become habitual. While in my bedroom, I decided quickly to change for comfort even though Detective Wilson had plans on dropping by some time tonight. I'd hoped he'd at least call first. Nothing beats the feel of fleece jammies and a long plush micro-fiber bathrobe. I popped in the chicken, grabbed my notes, and set in the kitchen to complete my thoughts.

Journal continued:

The following days after Scott's death, my body wandered around in distress to the point of complete nausea. If it wasn't for Russell that first night, I don't know how I would've managed. He gave me space, and I spent most of the night in front of the fireplace, mourning. I sensed something was on his mind, that he needed to share, but wanted to wait until I was ready and when I couldn't cry anymore, I fixed myself tea. I loved coffee, but drank tea when my body craved the mental unwind. Russell's eyes guided me to him on the couch. I descended down into the couch and Russell's awaiting arms with my freshly brewed tea warming my hands. His hands gently brushed the bangs from my eyes and as our eyes met, I could see his challenge at suppressing his thoughts slowly coming to an end.

"What is it?" I asked, sniffling back the tears.

"Nothing," Russell replied, his eyes breaking contact with mine.

"Listen, there's nothing you can tell me now that'll make me feel any worse…so have at it."

"Well," Why does bad news always follow a long pause, "I think your friend Tracy works for the Government…more precisely out at Groom Lake…Area 51," he cautiously watched my reaction.

"No! You're wrong. She works for Jim Charleston!"

"That's a cover. In fact, Jim's entire company has ties to numerous high-ranking officials that date back well before the Truman administration. Actually, Jim Charleston, officially on paper, doesn't exist. I did a routine background check on him and his file was inaccessible, even for me, coming back "Above Top Secret". So did Tracy's."

"Great, this day keeps getting better and better," muttering under my breath.

I reached out my hand demanding to see the file for myself. Somehow, it wasn't going to surprise me, but I still needed to see it. Their antecedents rolled out in front of me in an intricately woven computer schematic. Although at first, still in denial, much of the information seemed inconclusive to me.

"Are you sure? There isn't much information here," as if I needed to question his motives.

"Listen, I can confirm it, if you're up for a trip."

"A trip! How?"

"Get dressed, we're going for a drive," closing the file, "and you're gonna need someone to watch Colby, we'll be gone all-night."

With my curiosity about maxed out, I made an immediate call to my neighbor's teenage daughter. I always hired her to watch Colby, giving her free run of the house, with never a problem. She in no way had a problem with Colby and he didn't care either way. The reality of it, she spoiled him even more than I did, if that's even possible. I collected my things in an overnight bag within minutes. I wasn't going to work tomorrow, so casual was easy to coordinate and as soon as my puppy-sitter arrived we jumped in Russell's truck and headed out on the road. It shortly dawned on me that during my rushed pursuit for the truth I never asked the location.

"So where're we going?"

"Rachel," he sternly replied.

"Why?"

"We're going into Area 51."

Over the last few weeks, I'd done research on my abductions, looking for answers. Area 51, as well as Patterson Air Force Base, kept frequently popping up, sending out red flags. I knew we weren't going to stroll up to the front gate and ask for a visitor's pass. I doubted we'd even get to the front gate without being stopped, even if Russell somehow had security clearance. Surely, there's no way they'd let me, a civilian in, that's for damn sure.

"Trust me," he turned and smiled. I hated when he did that.

It took a little over ninety minutes to make our way out to Rachel. Russell, the entire route took precautions so no one followed, but in all likelihood, they were somehow watching. To say this place was remote, well let's just say you have to make the drive yourself to understand its solitude. Surrounded by mountain peaks and the occasional sheered cliff that sliced through history, each layer a different story; the road extended almost indefinitely towards the valley floor's distant horizon.

We passed through several small towns before hitting Highway 375, conveniently renamed in 1996 "*The Extraterrestrial Highway*". Bordering where the 93 North branched off was an old, decrepit casino, a precursor to the modern day Vegas. Its outdated, broken neon and fluorescent bulbs laid rusted, kneeling in silence to the vacant desert surroundings. Its glory days replaced with roadside billboards littered with various symbols depicting the famed Green Alien Head. My personal encounters with these celestial beings contrasted this smiling, hand waving, welcoming features pushing burgers and jerky. The road to Rachel at this point was still sixty plus miles and gradually climbed through Hancock Summit, snaked around breathtaking rocky vistas, before descending into the lower valley. The spectacular views hit home its remoteness, if you like mountain and desert backdrops. Russell stopped abruptly after hitting the summit, as I quickly became nauseated. Russell's historian knowledge of this area was impressive considering he'd never been to Nevada or at least that's what I was lead to believe.

"I thought you said you'd never been to Nevada?" I questioned.

"No. What I said was I'd never been to Las Vegas."

"Oh, it's all in your point of view, young Skywalker," I respond in my best Obi One Kenobi voice.

"What…Oh, *Star Wars*…I get it," he laughed.

If anything, Russell found my nerdy responses laughable. I was half joking, but a part of me wanted the truth, particularly from him. However, there was a seriousness in his face that overwhelmed his facial features.

"I don't think you grasp the seriousness of what we're going to do," as he turned, my smile evaporated.

Before entering Rachel, we passed on our left, a remote dirt road, nearly invisible except for the flaked silver backside of a twisted stop sign. The road extended like a steel beam for miles, finally merging into the outlying mountain's base. If not for Russell pointing it out, I certainly would've missed it as we flew by doing seventy. That was the point.

"That's Groom Lake Road, the main entrance to the base," he explained.

"There's no sign. I'd never would've known it was there," turning over my shoulder for a better view of this road to nowhere.

"Exactly!"

We drove a few miles, further passing milepost twenty-nine, gradually slowing as we passed this old, off-white, shabby mailbox that extended from another unlabeled dirt street. Russell, pointing out the multitude of cars stationed in wait along the highway. The occupants had gathered around this box like an altar, eagerly awaiting their chance for a picture.

"What's up with the mail box," laughing at the day-trippers, "They've never seen a mailbox before?"

"That belongs to the Rancher Steve Medlin who lives over-the-hill. It also marks the sight of many UFO sightings. Probably the most photographed mailbox in history. It used to be black before Steve changed it out, if I recall sometime in ninety-six and it is one of the best spots along the highway to view the airspace of Area 51. Steve likes his seclusion and hates all this attention even to his mailbox."

It sounded like there was more to this story, but he wouldn't lead on. You know that whole, *'Plausible Deniability'* thing. My nausea was getting worse, besides I was hungry and hoped for a *Subway*. However, as Rachel's flatness appeared down the road that quickly was ruled out of the equation.

We pulled into Rachel's remote town a little before noon, made a left on to the remote graveled road marked Old Mill Street. Shortly before the turn was what I'd call my now favorite sign in the world, it simply read:

Welcome to Rachel humans 98 — Aliens?

Among the sporadic newly built homes, the town appeared as if dropped from a tornado, leaving the remains of a southern trailer park. A few dozen scattered homes marked only by the makeshift fences that held horses in the front of their yards. If you wanted to get away, off grid and disappear from society this was undeniably your spot.

"You hungry?" Russell asked.

"I could use something," but what, as I quietly thought, scanning the miniature town.

"This place has great burgers, plus the owner is a sweetheart."

We immediately came to a halt, parking in all places, openly before a tow truck with a "UFO" hanging from its tow. I thought, great an "Alien" themed local inn and tourist attraction, plainly the only one in town. Russell mentioned staying the night, as the truck's engine gave way to outside forces stirring. He paused, as if returning home, the bearer of bad news, reaching for my hand, as he craved silent moral support. We watched two obvious locals, dressed in camouflage gear, exit the inn, and mount their ATVs. They were clearly studying us as they passed, slowly but surely by our truck before speeding down a narrow private path in a dust storm cloud.

"Listen Erica, be careful what you say here," Russell professed.

"What do you mean?"

"Some of the locals work out at Area 51. Who? I couldn't tell you. For all I know even the owner might have ties. Just be careful what you say, how you say it, and whom you say it to. And for safety reasons don't give anyone your real name," he was serious.

"I'll play the perfect, little, curious tourist. Okay!"

"Fine."

Russell knew the tone in my voice. I got a little spirited, especially lately, when told what I can and can't do or say. On top of that, I was hungry, and still wasn't feeling able bodied, not quite premenstrual, but close. The wind whipped around, creating mini-dust devils that chased one another over the flattening terrain. The fine dust particles pelted our face like hypodermic needles as we ran into the *Little A'Le'Inn.*

The inn's few modern features overshadowed in seventies mosaics that overflowed the doublewide renovated trailer space. A sort of welcome home vibration emitted from the history laden walls. I couldn't help myself as the montage of pictures that wallpapered most of the interior walls called. The random pictures uncontrollably chilled my core, while the amplitude of alien commercialism returned my humor. If not for the authenticity of my particular circumstances, I would've bought one of everything efficiently shelved. Tourists stood out, sitting at tables, gawking over their newly bought merchandise, while believers exchanged individual stories of personal encounters. I wanted to sit and share, but Russell's firming grip on my hand told me otherwise. A few locals, intermixed, silently ate except for the rare, raised-eyed chuckling. Their response to downplaying the base's speculated theories as if they knew the truth and wanted to expose its misguided followers.

Russell aggressively but politely led my way to the front counter. The grooved revolving chrome plated fountain stool reminded me of my childhood hangout. They easily out-aged the employee that tended to us as soon as we sat down. Their limited liquor selection atop the bar broke up our image, as it reflected from the adjacent mirror. An intermittent chill pierced my spine from the constant entering traffic. Russell had picked these seats purposely, as the only windows set to our right disclosed a clear view of incoming parking lot vehicles. The emergency exit a quick jolt to the left if needed, and I was gradually becoming attentive of his preciously premeditated way of thinking. The attendant, kind, with a silent smile, handed us a menu before embarking to check on other patrons.

The menu was standard, but with a perversion in its creative use of alien terminology to name the fast food. One of my many weaknesses was the draw to the cholesterol infused snacks and the delicious fried grease smell lingering from the backroom's kitchen didn't help matters. The smell, triggered years of a suppressed addiction and the idea of ordering a salad with water further slipped to the recesses of my mind. I looked to Russell for guidance.

"So what do you recommend?"

"My favorite has always been the *Alien Burger with Secretion.*"

"The what?" I shrugged being too lazy to search the menu for a definition.

"You know…burger with cheese," smiling.

"Oh."

"What can I get you?" Tony, our young server returned.

"I don't know…how about an *Alien Burger* with a Coke."

"Do you want Secretion?"

"No," replying abruptly as the thought conjured up impure thoughts with Russell sitting next to me.

"And you, sir."

"The same," his smiling eyes were on the same impure page.

"Okay. I'll be right back with your drinks and it'll be a few minutes for your burgers." Tony spun, bringing back our cokes from the lower cooler before continuing to the curtain drawn kitchen.

"You know this is the first burger I've had in about two years." I addressed to Russell.

"Then you're in for a real treat," taking a sip of coke.

"What do you mean by that?"

"Nothing."

"You don't really plan to stay here tonight do you?"

"We are and we aren't."

"Oh. That clears it all up," basking in the missed metallic taste of Coke.

Russell lowered the tone of his voice to a hushed whisper. "Nohea's got a trailer here and we'll join him later. However, for appearances we came, we ate and we'll leave. Understand?" He gave me a trivial wink of his right eye.

"Got it," returning to caffeinated goodness.

"Just take in the atmospheric energy of this place."

"Weird choice of words."

"Not really. Close your eyes and see and feel the room with your inner mind."

"Right."

"Try it...," he insisted.

I decided to humor him, laughing uncontrollably the first time, and after some added prodding, relaxed my eyes listening to the flurry of sounds echoing around. I soon could hear voices that weren't vocal, the nausea intensified as I tried to control the impulse to heave. A tingling sensation of warmth crawled up my spine like the morning Sun. There was something in the room, an energy...no, multiple energies talking to me all at once but I couldn't distinguish them from the ambient noise. The harder I focused, the further intense this feeling of throwing up permeated from my stomach to my mouth. It reached its tip, my eyes sprung from the trance quickly probing the room for relief. Across the crowded inn was my reprieve, a door labeled, *Women's Restroom*. A frequent visitor suggested to his friend as I ran past, '*She must've had the Alien Burger*', laughing at the same time. I might've believed them had it not been further from the truth. I stood over the sink hurling cold water on my face in an attempt to suppress the approaching taste of coke that fermented in the back of my throat. My body vibrated internally a blissful tone of tranquility and I don't know to this day how to describe that short-lived moment, except to say a sense of clear simplicity overcame my being.

After the urge to vomit subsided and I collected myself, I returned to Russell. I traversed the tables, walking across the shallow room returning to the false privacy of my stool as every patron's eyes fixated on me. I felt great, better then I'd ever felt in my life. Tony had fetched our meal in my absence and I instantly drew to its greasy bouquet without hesitation and engulfed myself in its sinister deliciousness. The taste of meat against my pallet was warming. I should've felt guilty but reflected within, *'you're going to die of something someday'*. Russell watched in amazement as I made quick work of the burger. It didn't stand a chance.

"You alright?" He asked.

"Never better. I don't know what just happened, but Wow," wiping the medium rare juices from my chin.

"You opened yourself up to possibilities," he retorted between bites.

"Whatever it was, I'm definitely energized, that's for sure."

Russell motioned for the check, "Let's get out of here, and take a short drive."

"Alright."

He effortlessly tossed down payment including a significant tip. If I didn't know better, it was hush money to Tony. The service was good, but even as big a tipper as I was that exceeded the maximum. He grabbed my elbow in an attempt to hasten our departure to the truck. The sandstorms had subsided, replaced with a frigid current of air marking snow advancing from the mountains. I climbed into the truck with Russell's help to the return of my nausea. How soon we must say good-bye to the good times. Russell entered, immediately starting the truck, as two of the local patrons exited to note our departure, only returning to the warmth of the inn once we'd returned to Highway 375.

"Where're we going now?"

"Heading back to Coyote Summit," Russell mentioned, his eyes relentlessly glued to the rear mirrors of the truck.

"What's wrong?"

"Too many prying eyes and ears."

"You would know."

"You should start knowing too," turning sternly.

"Sorry."

"I'm sorry, too. I need to explain a few things to you before we meet with Nohea."

"Alright, I'm all ears."

He pulled up to an outcast overhanging Coyote Summit only accessible with four-wheel drive. The cloud-covered sun felt warm, until I realized the heat came from the blowing vents and was warm. I felt like a teenager again, on a date, parking in an attempt to hide my guilty pleasures from my parents. This was the first time since Russell had arrived in Vegas that we were totally alone and I wanted him, he knew it and he wanted me too.

Chapter 37

I rarely in my personal relationships was ever aggressive, especially when emotions moved into a realm of intimacy. However, around Russell, there's always a desirability silently drawing me into him. He had something on his mind and so did I. Something I'd wanted to do since the first day our eyes met. He turned towards me, my body melted, as his eyes privately undressed my body. At last, our lips met like opposing magnetic poles, my hands pressed against the sculpted firmness of his chest as his heart beat rose matching the intensity of his breath. Like a tiger on the hunt, I pounced from the passenger to the driver seat, straddling him, at last settling my inner thighs around his waist. The windows rapidly layered with a thin film of condensation, as the cold outside separated from the sweltering inferno from within. The released energy from under my skin by irrepressible firings of my cellular synopsis was intoxicating. Then, as spontaneous as it had started it abruptly ended, with Russell lifting me from his lap, returning me to the solitude of the bordering passenger seat. My body involuntarily lunged towards him in a futile attempt to subdue my prey. Those advances repeatedly halted by a stern face atop a throbbing piece of meat, rejected, having once again come so far. I faced the agonizing reality my lustful desire would go unsatisfied.

"No! Not like this," Russell again pushed me away.

"What?" Brushing the hair from my flushed cheeks, "What's wrong?" I tried to catch my breath.

"This can't happen. Not now and not this way." He sat buttoning his shirt.

"I want you…don't you want me?"

"Erica, I love you more than you'll ever know," returning his hands to the wheel, "but I don't want our first time to be like this."

I had to confess, I admired his sense of principles, but my hormones raced through my blood and morality was not an option. He gently wiped away a small circle with his hand from the front windshield as his face stared to the outlying mountaintop as if to draw strength. He was serious and this wasn't going to happen, finally succumbing to my frustration.

"Listen," grabbing his hands, "I understand…I think." Still frustrated as my breathing equalized. "Whenever you're ready, I'll be here."

"I love you." He turned gently kissing my hand.

"I love you, too," returning the gesture, "just don't wait too long, if you know what I mean." I smiled, reassuring my want to stay.

"It's not what you think."

"What is it then?"

"Nohea should be here shortly. We'll discuss it then." He hit the clock radio confirming the time with his watch.

"Nohea's meeting us here?"

"Yes. We need to switch vehicles before returning to Rachel and the trailer behind the Inn. They've already seen this truck."

"What do we do with this truck, just leave it here?"

"Actually, that was the plan."

Okay, I wasn't going to make love to my boyfriend and I was gradually coming to terms with that, but to discuss our sex life in front of Nohea I thought was a bit inappropriate. I needed to start getting some answers before Nohea arrived.

"Alright then, start talking. I love you, but all this CIA spy shit is getting a little too much right now."

"Just wait until tonight and most of your questions will be answered. I promise," he tried flashing one of his famous smiles.

"Sorry, but that's not going to cut it this time. Talk!"

He could see I wasn't going to waiver from my convictions, not tonight. He reached behind his seat feeling for his little black brief case, bringing back a file folder, and then handed it to me.

"Look at it."

There were pictures of Tracy and Jim entering what looked like a secure facility checkpoint. The setting was desolate, a gated road to nowhere as alongside their car high-ranking military personnel stood. I wasn't an expert, but I was slowly becoming one and I could make out the polished stars adorning the shoulders. Also included were pictures of ground sensors, aircraft, military vehicles, hangers and a highlighted detailed satellite map of a base. The map dissected into three, boldly circled, and labeled in white over the terrain was Area 51, S-4, and Deep Core.

"What's this?"

"That's a picture from the back gate of this base taken less then twenty-four hours ago. Also, details for you to memorize in the event we separate while on the base."

"Wait just a minute." I sat in attention firmly back into my seat. "You're going to try to break into a top secret military base. No way...you're crazy...you've lost your mind." I struggled to find the words for—**Insane**.

"Getting in...that's the easy part. Getting *you* out might be the rough part."

"What do you mean me? No way in hell! I watched a piece on YouTube about this base that Scott had sent over, they shoot and then ask questions later, and if you survive, you might conveniently become extinct. No way am I stepping foot on that base."

I handed him back the file, opened the door, climbed out in search of fresh air as Russell quickly followed to the ridge of Coyote Summit. Once again I became immediately nauseated.

"Erica, get back in the truck and hear me out."

"You're out of your flippen mind," I muttered.

I stepped forward almost falling because of a freshly covered ground of snow. In my tempered disgust, I hadn't noticed the giant flakes that had accumulated and now still fell like oversized down pillow feathers. It hardly ever snowed in Vegas, but the higher elevations of this valley were prone to it during this time of the year. I wondered how long we'd been in the truck. It felt like minutes, but the sun falling rapidly over the secluded mountain and now doused by the low hanging clouds told a different story. I was freezing and on added prodding by Russell, I started to return, craving the warm sanctuary of the truck. Through the now thickening flakes, headlights approached from the lower dirt road advancing to the rear of Russell's truck.

"Don't worry; it's Nohea," checking his watch as Nohea approached, "Right on time!"

Nohea looked out of his element, his Hawai'ian tanned body assaulted by the falling snow's whiteness.

"Hey boss...Miss Jones, a pleasure...Nice day, huh?" Nohea replied with his arms extended, head to the sky, allowing the snow to pool in his hands and over his face.

"No, not really," I snapped back.

"You told her didn't you?" Nohea shouted towards Russell.

"Kinda' had too."

"She took it better than I thought," Nohea smiled as he passed by me, recovering our bags.

"Well...," Russell raised his shoulders en route to the new car.

"You didn't tell her everything, did you?" Nohea cautiously opened the rear door for me.

"What do you mean, *'everything'*?" My voice yelled from behind the tinted glass.

"No!"

Russell lingered shortly outside the passenger door in the snow while Nohea made his way to the driver's side. I think they both were waiting for the initial shock as well as the colorful four letter superlatives to subside. They both entered simultaneously, cringing to a never-ending barrage of questions stubbornly hurled from the passenger seat. Nohea, without a word, slowly but surely turned the car and headed towards Rachel, while Russell waited patiently until the need to catch my breath, before finally breaking his silence.

"Are you done now?"

"Done. I'll give you done," reaching over to hit him on the shoulder.

"When we get back to the trailer I'll explain everything."

"You'd better. Both of you."

I could see the silly smile present on Nohea's face in the rearview mirror as he turned to Russell. The same face my dad made to mom when I did something wrong, but too funny to correct. That's all I could see, as each window was so heavily tinted.

"Think this is funny, Nohea?"

"No, Miss Jones, not at all," his childish smile trying to hide, but it was ever so present.

"How the hell can you see out that window?" I asked.

Russell interrupted, "Don't worry, he's fine, we'll be at the trailer in a few minutes. How about some music?"

"Whatever."

I sat back stewing over the lack of information given to me, having come to expect it from others over the last few days, but not from my boyfriend. Of course, I kept calling him my boyfriend. It wasn't as if it was official, but he never corrected me, so I assumed he was okay with the title.

The car stopped outside one of the trailers. It was barely visible from within the car's interior, since what little daylight there was, had now disappeared. I tried to open the door but it wouldn't budge.

"Sorry Miss Jones, they only open from the outside back there." Nohea immediately exited, getting my door.

"Thanks, Nohea."

"No problem," offering me a hand, "our trailer is right here in front; number four."

I don't know why, maybe it was my sexual frustration, or my vehemence towards the two guys, or the newly fallen snow, but I hadn't noticed the car Nohea had arrived in, until now. I turned, my facial expressions preceding the gut-wrenching words trapped deeply within, as Russell instantly dropped his bag, ran to me, and covered my mouth with his vast hands, muffling my screams. I kicked as he dragged me like a rag doll into the trailer, Nohea swiftly in pursuit restraining my legs while our bags silently sat on the ground in the gathering snow.

Chapter 38

This was the feared lifetime scenario you always hoped to evade as a woman. Nohea closed the door, briefly releasing my legs, as I thrashed about trying to regain some sort of leverage. I knew the odds of overpowering the two of them would be next to impossible, but I wasn't going down without a fight. Nohea again, with added difficulty this time, restrained my legs. Russell clutched my upper torso, tightening like an anaconda before the kill and I strained to breathe, my lungs restricted, the world around me dimming.

"Erica...Erica stop! Just relax!" Nohea's voice rolled up my legs from the floor.

My FUs, unequivocally explicit, though muffled, aiming to kick him away with a free foot. The years of self-defense training lost to the heightened adrenalin rush.

"Erica, listen," Russell whispered in my ear, "it's not what you think. We're not going to hurt you, please just stop."

Russell tenderly brought my thrashing body to the floor, his hand still restricting my vocal ability, as Nohea managed to subdue my legs with his entire weight, which crushed my capacity to uphold the fight.

"Erica! Listen," Russell's voice rose, "Ka'iu lani! Listen!"

At this point, any attempt to struggle was a waste of energy. I needed to clear my mind and hope a future opportunity to escape would present itself. I focused transversely on what looked to be a framed UFO photograph, how poetic, trying to level it within my mind. Its slight unevenness hung on dark reproduced wood paneling walls, my body's muscles gradually unwound, lessening to the point of limp, as both Russell and Nohea steadily released the intensity of their restraints.

"Ka'iu lani, Ho'amalu ia makou pauloa Ka'iu lani kamali'i wahine!" Russell's assertion dissolved my focus. "Promise me, if I release my hand you won't scream or try to run," he whispered in my ear.

Russell tried repositioning himself in an effort to achieve eye contact, cautiously maintaining his hand over my mouth. I didn't want to look him in the eyes, afraid that would only enrage me more.

"Erica, please…let us explain. You're in no danger here; I promise you," he quietly pleaded, "remember, what I said. If they'd wanted you dead, you'd already be dead."

My eyes, at last lifted to his, as an internal calmness overwhelmed my skin. I don't think it was what he said as much as the honesty present in his eyes and the singular tear that cascaded down his cheek. My eyes' dilation as well as the festering onslaught of matching tears corroborated my clear intentions.

"You have to promise if I remove my hand you won't scream or run, just listen to what we have to say." Russell gazed deeply into my eyes awaiting a response. "Promise me," his hand's tension relaxed over my mouth.

I could shake my head in concurrence now that he'd lessened his embrace. Russell and Nohea both, apprehensively, released me from their hold as I scurried away to a far corner, like a mouse, positioned between the seventy's television stand and sofa. I pulled my knees to my chest, wiped the panic driven tears from my face, and sat in a fetal position.

"Don't come any closer, either of you!" I fought through the tears.

"Nohea, go get the bags," Russell turned to ask.

My eyes shifted towards the now unfastened door, picturing myself leaping to freedom. I knew I'd never make it, so opted to bank my energy for a later date. The kitchen was next to me, but not knowing if or where the knives would be, I sat, remaining vigilant. Nohea had quickly returned with our bags in hand, and disappeared down a narrow hallway. He relieved himself of the bags into individually, privately locked rooms, at the far end of the trailer.

The impression seeing an identical sedan to one that had followed me in Hawai'i as well as driving away from Scott's burning townhouse was too much to stomach. The whole time, my boyfriend was playing for the other team and I was just his pawn. The range of ways I was about to die drifted around my mind.

"You're not going to die and we're not playing for the other team." Russell responded without missing a conscious beat.

"Stop right there," motioning with my hands! "How the hell did you know what I was thinking?"

"I've always known," Russell inched close, "and if you'd let me I'll explain."

His features expressed his heartfelt intentions as by now he'd closed in enough to reach out a touching hand.

"Erica, dig deep inside those emotions of yours. I love you and have no reason to hurt you. Please, take my hand and have a seat on the couch."

In the background, Nohea feverishly arranged Russell's computer on the coffee table while laying out multiple file folders, maps and miscellaneous, out of the ordinary devices.

"Boss, we're all set over here." Nohea confirmed as he passed behind, on the way to the kitchen.

"Thanks, Nohea. Erica please, come."

This time as he reached for my hand, devoid of thoughts, I instinctively extended mine. I could feel his warmth, but the coldness of the corner had already penetrated my spine. Keeping his distance, he escorted me to the far end of the couch. I could see the snow had stopped through transparent curtains of the rectangular picture window, as a thick cover dosed over the back lot's various vacant trailers. My adrenaline had stabilized as the trailer's aged and draftiness became increasingly felt.

"Nohea, turn the heat up a little and make us some fresh coffee. It's going to be a long night." Russell smiled, reassuring his intentions.

"Already on it, boss." Nohea confessed from the outdated kitchen.

"Are you ready to learn the truth?" Russell maneuvered his wireless mouse across the coffee table.

"The truth, right," I huffed back in disbelief.

"Erica. That car outside we borrowed and I need it to carry out what we've planned for tonight."

"Right…borrowed," I nodded my head in disbelief.

"Stolen…if you'd like, Miss Jones." Nohea boldly stated as he doled out coffee while shadowing Russell.

The smell was intoxicating, the steam rising from the rim, dancing in seduction. I hesitated accepting it, subconsciously fearful it might be tainted, but eventually succumbing, encompassing my hands around the toasty warm mug. The heat flowed up my arms as it drew to my nose. It smelt like coffee as I inhaled the dark aroma while my senses searched for any out of the ordinary lingering deposit.

"We didn't put anything in it," Russell watched from the opposite end of the couch.

"How the hell do you keep doing that?"

My lips dove for the rim wanting, to settle there for the night as my mind raced with questions.

"I'll explain everything as soon as you're ready."

"Oh, I'm more than ready."

Nohea pushed up the reclining sofa from across the room while Russell finished examining the neatly laid paperwork. You would've thought he was about to give a billion dollar pitch to an Angel Investor, at this point it might have been an easier sell.

"Where to begin…," Russell questioned aloud, flipping through his computer files.

"How about the fact you're able to read my mind. What are you…clairvoyant?" I declared.

Russell glanced over at Nohea, who just shrugged his shoulders as if to say—*Your call.*

"Okay. Yes, but the ability to read minds is actually, being telepathic, which both Nohea and I are. This transcends through our family history, dating back generations. All males, who choose to accept this endowment, can channel it, thus becoming extremely skillful. That's why we're so sought after by our employer."

"Who do you work for? It's not Dynamic Aeronomics is it?"

"No, it is, but we have another employer."

"And," I motioned for an answer with my free hand.

"Both of us work for a faction of the Government called The Majestic 12 Council."

"I thought you told me that these guys were after me."

"They are...in a way...it's complicated...but not the faction we work for. Seemingly, there's an internal power struggle going on and a rogue group has infiltrated our secret organization. Their intents are unclear and we've, Nohea and I, been reactivated as moles to unearth the truth."

"Well that explains everything. So this whole wanting to be my boyfriend, is just part of the infiltration?" This was the second time I'd called him on our relationship and my pissed voice expressed the frustration.

"Yes...I mean No...I mean. As I said before, at first yes, it was, but no, I didn't plan to fall in love with you! I can't stress that enough."

"That's comforting to know," I cynically replied.

"He's telling the truth, Miss Jones. Listen, we have much to cover before going in tonight." Nohea chimed in.

"Nohea, it's okay," Russell motioned to lower the intensity.

"Why are we, but especially me, going in anywhere?"

"For you to understand, you must see with your own eyes. Plus, we need to recover something and can't do that without your help," Russell explained.

"See and recover what?"

"Where you came from and your potential destiny."

"What do you mean *where I came from?*" I shifted in my seat.

"Do you have any recollection of your birth parents?" Russell asked.

"Some. They died when I was young."

"Did they ever give you anything, maybe a keepsake of some sort?" Nohea asked.

"No. Not that I recall."

Nohea looked over at Russell, as if this path was now a dead end. Russell remained unspoken as he searched through the stacks of paper on the coffee table. He finally, fixated on a photo that seemed cut from *Archaeologist Monthly*.

"Does this picture appear remotely familiar?"

The picture was a small necklace replica of the artifact that hung in Jim's house on Maui. I clearly recall that one piece as was blindly drawn to it, but I couldn't remember why. I had the strangest sense of déjà vu while standing and admiring it.

I need to note here, hating to break the continuity of the story. The necklace, identical with the picture I was show and questioned about by the MIB's, had the thirteenth symbol. At the time, while being interrogated, I had completely forgotten Russell had showed me its picture and steadily started to understand their concerns.

"Yeah, Jim has a larger copy of that on his mantel in Maui."

"Did you touch it?" Russell asked.

"God, No! Why?"

"I'll get to that in a minute," Russell shuffled further into the papers, "how long have you known Jim and Tracy?"

"A few years. Tracy introduced me to Jim, who helped get me my current job. Why?"

"Do you remember when I told you I thought they worked for the Government?"

"Yeah," grabbing the pictures from Russell's hand.

"Well, they don't just work for the government, but at the base...Area 51," he paused, unsure how to voice what was on his mind.

"Just say it," sensing his apprehension.

"Do you recall the conversation on Maui about the diverse categories of Alien species and their involvements within our Government and that some have their own agenda? Well, Jim and Tracy are...Reptilians...and have been working here on Earth for some time."

His voice had rapidly spit the information out and now he waited, watching my expression. I sat at the end of the couch, glazing over the pictures, drinking my coffee to its end trying to justify a response. I wanted answers, but these were pardon my French, *horseshit*. I chucked the pictures back to Russell in disgust.

"What the hell is this...Mind Game Night?"

I stood, hesitated, and considered breaking for the door, but instead made my way in search of another cup of coffee.

"I told you she wouldn't believe you unless she saw it with her own eyes," Nohea leaned back in his chair in despairing satisfaction.

"That's fine. Nohea, we've got to give her some time," Russell rebutted.

I pondered those very questions while the coffee poured and I searched the cabinets for a bite to eat.

"The chips are in the top right cabinet," Nohea's voiced cried.

"Thanks," reaching for the chips, detesting his sudden retort.

I resented their genuineness that they both read minds, it creeped me out. Particularly Nohea's perceptiveness when it came to my intimate fantasies about Russell. I returned with the chips, a full cup-of-joe, and more questions; this time choosing to sit closer to Russell.

"Let's say I believe you...they certainly don't look like reptiles."

"No, Reptilians," Nohea corrected me.

"Reptile…Reptilians…whatever," grabbing a handful of chips, salt, and vinegar, my favorite.

I waited restlessly, as you do when watching a B-Rated horror movie. I mean, you knew the effects were going to be bad, almost laughable, but hoped the story line would improve…and boy did it. Russell presented me with a delicate, wafer thin, microchip and a picture.

"They use an apparatus comparable to this to cloak their true identity. Human minds work on diverse but like frequencies. In fact, everyone's thought-vibrations are as individually unique as a fingerprint or iris scan. All they need to do is dial it in and they can change your visual perception anytime and anyplace."

The pictured gadget, as well as the microchip in my hand, wasn't large, maybe dime size, thinner than a strand of hair and could be placed anywhere on their person, even imbedded in their cell phone. I continued to read the fine print below the picture:

One can make this device inactive in two ways:

> 1. *A strong magnetic current that either shorts it out or alters your magnetic energy (Aura) flowing around you.*
>
> 2. *By retraining your mind, to separate the conscience from the subconscious at will.*

"Let's say this is true," skeptical at best. "What do they want with me and what do my birth parents have to do with this?"

"Your dad was part of, *The Intergalactic Federation of Light*, and had been combating this race of Reptilians across the galaxy for ages."

"So you're saying my parents were aliens?" This was now verging on the implausible.

Russell continued, "No. Just your dad. Your mom was human and had no idea about your dad. It was her unique genetic code, along with your dad's, that created you. Kind of a unique hybrid of the two. You're one of many hybrids that occupy this planet. Some unaware, the majority apathetic of how special they are and refuse direct involvement."

"So what am I supposed to be some intergalactic super hero?" I rolled my eyes expressing disbelief.

"Not in the frame of reference that you're referring to, but yes, you could say that," Nohea interrupted.

"Your abilities will become increasingly noticeable over time if you choose to take the path. You've already the power to heal, yet are unaware of its importance. Have you ever wondered why you've never been sick?" Russell questioned.

I'd never thought about it, but in all my years, not so much as a sniffle, even as a child. While others suffered from the flu, I thought *I'm not going to get sick* and the symptoms never manifested. I credited it to nothing more than mind-over-matter or just plan luck.

"Okay. So, you said if I choose. What do you mean?" I asked.

"You have a sort of symbiosis with *The Intergalactic Federation of Light*. They can't intervene in the matters of other star systems without first a formal invite. That's why they've not contacted you or directly involved themselves with Earth's path towards destruction. However, if you willingly and wholeheartedly invite them into your subconscious, they'll help you. If you choose not to get involved, which is freely your choice, express your wishes and be done." Russell explained.

"So how many others on this planet have opened themselves up to such an invite?" Hoping Russell would elaborate.

"None!" Nohea leaned forward.

"None! I thought you just told me there are others?"

"There are many who've heard the call, but none willing to take the next step. And if someone doesn't step-up soon I'm afraid Earth will be lost to the Reptilians and everyone on this planet will become their slaves or..." Russell's face flushed with a cold intensity.

"Or what?"

"Food!" Russell's voice agonizingly shot.

I got the food part and those images were frightening, as a nature documentary of a lizard eating a cricket played in my mind, but I was still unclear on the whole, slaves' scenario.

"What do you mean slaves?"

"Your Government, or should I say a faction of it, right now works with the Reptilians and the Greys and these Greys are slaves to the Reptilians. Over the millions of years, they have lost their ability to reproduce and shortly, they'll become extinct. At that point in time they'll need new slaves to assist in strip mining planet Earth, as well as future ones. Currently, they're helping your U.S. Government build a space weaponry system."

"Yeah, *Star Wars*," I interrupted.

Russell continued, "What your Government doesn't know or won't admit to, is its true intended purpose. The Reptilians have helped advance this planet's technology tenfold over the past fifty years. Giving you cell phones, GPS, and advance satellite imagery. The weapon will coordinate all these electronic gadgets into a single direct array energy beam. Its pulse sent around the planet will ultimately disrupt Earth's electromagnetic poles causing an immediate pole shift. When that happens anyone not wearing their own self-generating magnetic generator in all sense of the word…will have their memories wiped clean. At that point, the Reptilians can easily take over the world with no resistance from any military or person."

My attention and lackadaisical smile had vanished, replaced with horrific fear. If what they were saying was true, I didn't see what help I was going to be, now or in the future. Russell and Nohea could both read my mind and were sure they understood the metaphors playing like *Dawn of the Dead*.

"I don't understand how I'll be able to stop this."

The coffee and chips at this point had lost their flavor.

"If we can get you into the base and show you the truth then you'll believe. Then at that point, get our hands on your father's necklace. His light energy stored inside should transfer to you once you put it on. Then we get you out…hopefully…with them unaware of your presence or all hell is going to break loose."

"What about my dad?" I asked.

"That's a story for another time. I promise to tell you, but right now we need to focus on the details of getting into the base."

Russell brought forward the file he tried showing me earlier.

"Are you in?" Nohea's unsure look waited for a reply.

They mutually watched profoundly, as if trying telepathically to read my heightened feelings. I busied my mind in an effort to block their infringement, allowing my subconscious to linger on their question at hand. It must've worked, because the blankness on their faces demonstrated they were falling on deaf thoughts. I relentlessly believed growing up there had to be more to my simple life, as if preordained for greatness I guess I was right. I hadn't considered, "saving the world", as appearing that high on or even on my list. If this meant I'd learn about my real mom and dad, no one was going to stop me. Anyways, I still had a score to settle with the people who torched Scott's townhouse.

"I'm in, where do we begin?" I boldly announced to the relief of both men.

Chapter 39

I wish all facts of our little trip could be revealed. However, by Russell's request, for my life, several details were removed before publishing this book. I'll try to clarify shortly in this story, but for now let me return to that night just before leaving Rachel for the base.

My head was spinning from the hours and hours covering the covert operation ahead. Russell and Nohea were unwavering in detailing their mission as well as possible contingency plans should something go astray. For them this emerged like a day's work but terrified me out of my mind.

I exited the puny, airplane-like bathroom that separated Russell's bedroom from my minute room. This trailer's design was built for short-term needs not expanded comfort. Russell was adjusting the many chevrons that adorned his manly chest. The gold stars reflecting off his dark blue Air Force uniformed shoulders as his newly reflective polished shoes, a black liquid gloss, appeared out of place against the aged carpet.

"What do you think?" I said. Spinning ever so slowly clockwise like a model on a runway.

"Looks like you've found a new calling," Russell expressed.

He was referring to my identical uniform, but of the female persuasion. I wasn't one for skirts, especially during cold winter nights, but this was straight military issue; naturally lacking the ranked insignia. I had my hair pulled back, tossed lightly into a bun, and gently tucked underneath a military cap. My look, in an odd way fit, yet I felt extremely uncomfortable portraying something I was not. A creation of conservative upbringing taught to respect the military.

"Not sure if I like the skirt," tugging at it, trying to get it to drape just right around my hips.

"You look great. Just remember what I said," Russell cautioned.

"I know. I know. Walk with confidence and don't fidget."

Nohea peeked in around the corner wearing similar gear minus a few stars. I'd never seen him so dressed up, trading his Hawai'ian prints for solid blue and looked extremely dashing, if I did say so myself.

"We've got to go, boss," drawing attention to his watch.

"I'm ready. You ready?" Russell glanced in my direction.

"As ready as I'll ever be."

We each snatched up a small military issued nylon tote. The guys labeled it *a lifeline* in the event we found ourselves separated. It was filled with all kinds of so-called goodies of the likes I'd hoped wouldn't become necessary. The thought of getting into that black sedan still scared the hell out of me, but it was a prerequisite for our plan to work.

To say that base's security was top-notch would've been a gross underestimation of the truth. Russell enlightened me that from the moment we crossed over Hancock Summit they'd constantly recorded our presence. Legally, the Government didn't have the right, but as I was finding out, we no longer had any Constitutional Rights. One reason for me feeling sick was a steady bombardment of signals from both LRAD (Long-Range Acoustic Device) and HAARP (High Frequency Active Auroral Research Program). Some people were seemingly more sensitive than others were to their rays, especially if calibrated for a specific internal agenda. After a while, your body gets use to them, although I knew he wasn't telling me the truth because I still felt sick. We got in the car, Nohea driving, Russell and I in the back as guests. Nohea's eyes glued to the rearview mirror and us, obviously waiting for something.

"Erica, there's one more thing," Russell cautioned as he reached into his pocket.

"There always are with you two."

"This is slightly more serious."

At this point Nohea turned his focus from the mirror to offer me a bottled water, which quickly united with a blue horse pill from Russell's hand.

"What's this for?" I asked.

"Remember when we discussed the outer limit security and the camouflage dudes."

"Yes. How could I forget?"

"There was one thing we didn't mention," Nohea chimed in.

"And…"

"They don't just carry automatic weapons, infrared, and sonic devices…they also have as a minimum one telepathic person with them at all times."

"Great. They'll be able to read my mind."

"That's what this pill is for," Russell compellingly handed me the water and pill.

I don't want to linger on this, but it did take a little prodding to convince me to down an unknown pill. I trusted them, even though Russell harped continually to trust no one, including him. Apparently, their ability limited to only conscious thoughts, unable to reach deep into your subconscious. This pill, until I'd learned on my own, would keep my subconscious mind from displaying our plans hopefully long enough until we got safely on the base. Reluctantly, I downed the pill as Nohea immediately drove us towards our destination, the back gate of Area 51.

Within minutes, the effectiveness of the medication was becoming clear, aware of my surroundings, but in a faintly dazed state. It's the kind of sensation you suddenly get awakening from an intense dream only to find yourself returning to a sound sleep. I was aware of what was going on around me, but my mind couldn't separate if I were dreaming or awake. To this day, I believe they didn't want me to recall or reveal the procedure for getting on the base undetected. When asked later, Russell wouldn't elaborate or clarify fact from fiction. I desperately wanted to include details but feared repercussions of handing out classified information. In reality, afraid of circulating misinformation, while mixing the truth of what happened to what I imagined. I'll say this; we made it to the base without incident, that's for sure.

I'd been to Nellis Air Force Base multiple times for their air show and, as the effect of the pill gradually wore off, Area 51 on the surface didn't appear any different from Nellis. Of course, it's not what's on the outside, but what's on the inside that counts; my mom forever drilled that into my head. Funny what you remember in times of stress.

We parked in a bordering lot wedged between a nearby hangar and communications building while the effects of the pill slowly disbanded. They wanted to ensure I was in absolute control of all my faculties and able to perform my required duties. The base, even at this hour, bustled with activity, although most of the staff had returned home via JANET flights to McCarran International. This wasn't our goal; instead, a collection of concealed hangars, a few miles south from here was our objective. A dry lakebed on the map labeled Papoose Lake, better known as S-4. It was only safe to continue once they mutually and effortlessly could read my mind.

"If you can read my mind now, what's to stop someone else from doing the same?" I asked.

"No one is allowed to, within S-4 base limits, to use their telepathic abilities," Nohea explained.

"How the heck do they enforce that?"

"They don't have to…if you're caught, accused, and found guilty; you're put to death, no questions asked. That's incentive enough for anyone. They essentially have sophisticated sensors within the buildings that can pick-up on those transmitted brain waves." Russell replied.

"Plus, we're hoping to avoid as much physical contact as possible." Nohea stated.

At this point, I was getting a little skeptical, as the entire thing sounded like a dreadful sci-fi plot. However, I soon discovered fact can be stranger than fiction and they weren't kidding about a great many things.

"We good to go, boss?" Nohea's soldier eyes appearing in the review mirror.

"Yeah, we're good." Russell turned away his mind confident of my ability.

The gravel kicked under the car like hail as this small road snaked its way around the valley's dry lakebed. The tinted windows made it difficult to get bearings, as the road seemingly headed nowhere. Irregular flashings of distant lights descended from set-in mountain structures and flowed around us as if lost in a canyon. Russell called my attention to an array of radar towers flashing on the outlying hillside.

"See that revolving structure?"

"Yeah."

"That's Project Deep Core's entrance."

"I don't see anything but a small hill."

"Exactly, but at the base of the tower is a simple shack with an elevator that extends thirty levels below ground level."

"What's Project Deep Core?" I asked.

"A story for another time, right now we're heading to that hillside and the S-4 facility."

"You're excellent at leaving a girl hanging."

Russell understood these aimed frustrations were at him personally, not professionally. He grabbed my hand, kissed the top while flashing a smile that sent shivers pulsating throughout my body.

"Sometimes the best things in life are worth waiting for…"

"You guys need a room," Nohea barked from the front.

"That'd be nice," my sexually frustrated voice responded.

The exchange lasted less than a minute, typifying my current as well as near future life. Stress filled with moments of livability you'd cherish for a lifetime, no matter how short. It was almost enough to make you borderline insane.

The sedan followed the makeshift road like an old friend as it gradually became a firmer surface, not quite dirt, but not asphalt either and expanded while hugging into the hillside. At the far end, tucked ever so slightly against the rocks, appeared an entrance to a miniature lit building.

"Is this S-4?" I asked.

"Yes, but the hangar side of it. The base itself, located below ground within numerous sublevels," Russell explained.

"Hangars?"

"Nohea, stop the car for a second, and roll down the windows," Russell ordered, "Erica, look closely at the side of this mountain."

I scanned the sloping terrain, not sure what to look for as my eyes adjusted to the outside surrounding moonlit night. After tracing the road's surface to the steep hillside, it ultimately came into focus, nine massive rectangular sections, of rockless voids, separated equally by natural rock. The molded, cold steel hangers were a perfect match to the surrounding foreground. My eyes strained to identify where they began and ended, although we sat less than twenty feet away.

"Boss, look." Nohea pointed to light gradually streaking from beneath the furthest hangar like beams of a sunrise.

"What is it?" I asked.

"They're opening one of the hangars. Nohea, you'd better get us moving. You're in for a treat Erica. Remember, control your emotions."

We leisurely rolled forward as the last of the nine hangar doors folded into the mountain. Its opening created a day-glow-blue fluorescent aura around the black sedan. Nohea immediately raised our tinted windows. However, perfectly centered and still visible was an unknown craft reflecting the moonlight in its mirrored smooth surface.

"Is that what I think it is?" My voice's astonishment prevailing.

"What do you think it is?" Russell asked.

"It looks like…like something out of this world…a UFO"

"It's whatever you want it to be," Nohea said.

"So it is a UFO?"

"No! He said it's whatever you want it to be," Russell reiterated.

I wasn't going to get the truth from them, at least not a straight quote, that much was sure, so I reached for my cell phone to make the next big YouTube sensation. Russell politely grabbed my wrist shaking his head in disagreement.

"Erica, you can't," politely prying the phone from my palm.

"Why not? People need to know the truth!"

"They're not ready for the truth. At least not yet. After tonight you'll understand."

I recovered my phone from a hesitant Russell, as the car jerked to a stop around the left corner of the opened hangar. I wanted to run, touch it, and see for myself its authenticity. A flash of intense vivid light emanated around the corner shooting out across the desert landscape into the night sky. Before, *'what was that'*, entered my mouth, the hangar lights doused, sealed once again, behind the steel plated facade.

"Erica, please remain focused on what our plan is…for your sake and ours," Nohea stated with a reserved urgency in his voice.

"Right, sorry."

"Remember Erica, follow our lead, and don't look around otherwise they'll stop you and ask questions. I can't stress this enough. You have to give off the appearance you've done this a thousand times. Got it?" Russell's stressed voice lingered while reaching for his briefcase.

"Yeah, got it."

"Take this, clip it on your right breast pocket."

He handed me my own white, nameless, neatly laminated military ID. Listed in audacious print, **MAJ 12**, and a yellow one-inch square that sat atop a lengthy bar code. It made me feel like a commodity, especially after what Russell explained about our Birth Certificates and their Stock Market exchange rate. Again, off topic. A story I think for another time. Right now, I had to remain focused. Still, there was something eerily familiar about these ID's but at the time I couldn't put my finger on it.

Our bags remained in the car to evade any suspicion, except Russell's black briefcase. The building's display outside lacked importance, but its internal safety measures resembled TSA airport security measures on steroids, minus the groping. If you'd made it this far, odds were your security clearance checked out, but they weren't taking chances. Nohea went first with Russell pulling up the rear. I was to mimic Nohea to the letter, something we'd covered to exhaustion back at the trailer.

A soldier unemotionally greeted us on entering. He, along with his many co-workers, dressed in flat-black tight fitting jumpsuits. The legs tucked deep inside their black calf high boots that glistened with deadly secrets. The only visible color, a scarlet red beret neatly placed atop their freshly buzzed hair. No ID or insignia detailing branch, only two firmly attached patches over each pectoral muscle. The first was an undersized bluish white triangle. In its center, was the symbol of the *"all seeing eye"*, similar to the top of the pyramid on the back of the one dollar bill. What did that have to do with the military? The second was a large 'carat' figure, symbolic of a pyramid, with a vertical slit slicing it in half. Displayed to the left and right of its apex were two floating full moon shaped planets while at its base a strange highlighted font. The entire black image set off against a sky blue background. Again, oddly familiar but I struggled, maybe because of the lingering effects of the pill, to pinpoint time and place. I'd seen this before, that was definite.

Individually, we advanced through a full-size rectangular metal detector; however, I don't think they were scanning for metal. After that, a handheld ID scan before walking into the intrusive full body scanners. Then a brief wait, before going to the final secured door, as confirmation of your identity danced throughout the many computerized displays. Each of us finally had to submit to a retina scan as well as a digital fingerprint reader. It sounds complicated and time-consuming, but took only minutes; more than I can say for the airport. My face remained emotionless throughout the entire procedures as if it were no more than a nuisance. Russell's advance faintly ceremonious as the soldiers constantly saluted his presence. *Don't trust anyone, including me*, echoed in my mind.

Once through the final checkpoint my breathing returned to normal. The long, white, almost hospital like, décor hallway, paralleled what I personally labeled, *Hangar Number Nine*. The lights were dim, with little activity, and reminded me of an empty auto shop. There were no mechanics, but various men and women dressed in white lab coats gathered around flashing screens with heavily used clipboards. I caught myself staring, something Russell absolutely stressed to avoid at all cost.

"Erica, keep your eyes forward...shoulders back...and relax." Russell's whisper flowed over my shoulders.

I wasn't going to react, instead I refocused on what I could see within my limited peripheral vision, as my eyes straightened, matching Nohea's briskly paced walk. We advanced, gaining access through a series of double doors, each time having to swipe an ID. Then we passed a barrage of laboratory testing facilities. The transparent glass revealing darkened workstations until tomorrow's return. The vast wall lined with sophisticated servers still churning out colossal amounts of data, presumably from the day's previous test results. It wasn't easy, formulating accurate details from the images that passed the recessed corners of my eyes.

Finally arriving at the elongated tunnel's end, my eyes fixated on the left wall and its larger-than-life number set in the stone, Level 1. Again, déjà vu encompassed my body as the elevator doors retracted. My mind, so focused, wouldn't allow a recall of that recessed memory. There were seven level buttons, the first two easily accessible. However, levels three through seven had two keyholes, one on the left and right of the level's button. I assumed you'd need further security clearance to access those lower levels and one of the keys from the emotionlessly armed security guard that accompanied us down to level two. No Muzak, only the elevator's mechanical sounds, and I fought back the urge to hum Scott's song he so cheerily admired the other night.

Scott, I missed him so much, especially tonight. I wish he'd been here to see this facility. He fought for years, trying to unveil this base and it cost him his life. The body they pulled from his smoldering townhouse wasn't his, or so they say, but I knew otherwise. My hand sunk deep into my front skirt pocket, squeezing his charm, recalling in a flashed timeline our friendship until his face faded, erased by the fiery loss. I longed to be optimistic while fighting back the tears, but those days are gone and this wasn't the time or place for a meltdown. It was crucial I pull myself together, for more than my life was at stake now.

Level 2 opened, mimicking the hallway of one, but that was as far as it went for similarities. The floor plan became an intricate labyrinth with hallways extending almost indefinitely in all directions, with a defined circular pattern. If you didn't understand the layout, you could wander for days only to pass by the same unmarked door repeatedly. Unlike the larger lab rooms on level one, these were offices. The softly lit halls helped hide the repetitiveness of the unmarked suites.

Nohea eventually halted at a door on his right, motioning me back, as Russell promptly swiped his ID, changing the electronic lock light red to green. Nohea prompted me to follow Russell through the opened door into a familiar looking room. I'd seen this setting somewhere before, but where? It was too many cases of déjà vu for me to consider it a coincidence anymore.

"Erica, have a seat." Russell motioned to a brown leather couch along the far wall.

"Great, these heels are killing me." I eased into the soft leather, removed the heels, and began massaging the balls of my feet.

The guys went to town neatly ransacking the file cabinets and desk drawers like a stealth thief; only working more rapidly as if they'd had fluency with the office's content as they desperately avoided disturbing the original scene.

"Boss, I don't think it's here," Nohea softly shouted.

"It's got to be," Russell replied, while continuing his search of the desk drawers.

"What's got to be here?" I asked.

"Power." Russell briefly looked with determination.

"If it's not here they've already found and moved it." Nohea pulled up a seat next to me on the couch while Russell reclined in the executive patent leather chair.

"It's not here," Russell, said, "It must be on a lower level."

"Yeah, but which level?" Nohea's face showed concern for the first time since I'd met him.

"There's only one way to find out," Russell rose from the chair.

"How come I don't like the sound of that?" Returning my heels, I stood up following Russell on his brisk rush for the door.

"Because we weren't expecting this and it wasn't in our contingency plan." Nohea's voice, because of his closeness, raised the hair on the back of my neck.

If you learned anything so far, you know Russell always had a plan and always knew what's happening next. I don't know how, but he knew and it astounded me, but also terrified me. The fact he for once, was at a loss for a plan, worried me to death. I do mean that literally, as even Nohea's reaction to the change expressed the same.

"What now, Boss?" Nohea moved quickly to Russell's side.

"We've got to go down to level three."

"And Erica?"

"She'll be fine."

"What's on level three?"

"Nothing!" Russell paused, turning back to reiterate his point. "Erica. I am sorry. Listen, it's more important than ever you don't speak unless spoken to and follow us closely. I'd hoped to get us in and out without exploring lower levels. The fact they moved the item we seek means they know our intent or at best know you've figured out your significance. If we play our cards right, we still might get out of this facility alive," glancing at Nohea then back to me, "All of us. No matter what you see below you must, and I can't stress this enough, remain calm and don't say a word. Promise me!"

"I promise."

For the first time, fear glazed his eyes, let me rephrase that…not fear but an apprehension, for my life. My vet displayed the same uncomfortable glance in her eyes when she gave me the news that my previous Golden Retriever needed to be put down.

Whatever warranted such an inauspicious look belonged to the contents of the lower levels and I was about to find out.

I didn't say another word on the way to the elevator. I wanted to…I wanted to say *'Fuck You All'* and leave. However, it wasn't a viable option anymore; having made my bed, I now had to lie in it. I was still unclear on a great many details. Let me clarify that for you. I had a mass dose of reality thrown my way in a short time period and as absurd as the explanation sounded, I was bit by bit realizing it was indeed fact. Scott's warnings over the years fell on my deaf ears and now I wished I'd been a little more astute.

The elevator door opened to a different guard occupying the cubicle's rear quarter, this time an M-16 harnessed around his right shoulder. My heartbeat elevated with such intensity, the rhythm played taps in the recesses of my ears.

"Level Three." Russell's smooth toned expressed.

"Key please, sir." The guard vigilantly watched us all while retrieving his own key from around his neck.

Russell dug into his collar revealing its twin, a sterling silver key, it's ragged cut grooves sending reflected beams of light shooting around the elevator like meteors in the night sky. Simultaneously they inserted and turned the keys as the level three light illuminated. The doors closed, I felt encased in a coffin struggling for air as we transcended deeper into the belly of the beast. I thought they must've excavated the entire mountain's subfloor for this facility. Of course, maybe this wasn't a mountain to begin with, considering of late that things weren't what they seemed. The elevator halted, the doors glided open, while Nohea's body blocked my initial view. I believe now that was intentional. Russell removed the key uncharacteristically hurrying me out of the elevator allowing the door instantly to close.

What I remember from that point is the guys whisking me down a hallway to another office, my shoes floating across the rock-slated floor; equivalent to the Secret Service's job to President of The United States in the event of an emergency. My increasing uncontrollable seizures would've been a problem if identified by passing staff. Russell and Nohea understood this risk, and we couldn't go back. I regained some sense of controllable stability once lying down with Russell pushing water, and Nohea applying a cold compress to my head.

"Erica, do you hear me?" Russell's fingers snapped. The sound throbbed, but dwarfed in comparison to the current nightmare that flooded my conscience.

"What the hell is this place?" I already knew the answer.

The ghost-pain from the triangular scare marking my upper arm was a present reminder of that unwilling visit. Clearly, on exiting the elevator the molded rock wall formations had hit a cord. My memories, no longer able to focus on the mission, returned like a tsunami. The images of my abductor's experiments returned with full force. I'd definitely been here before just not this level. Clearly, a fact intentionally omitted during the hours of absurdities expressed while prepping for this mission.

Russell walked around the room in comfort as if it was his personal man cave and I later discovered that in fact it was his office. Returning to a scene that represented such horror petrified me. Russell sat at the end of the couch gently massaging my legs and feet. The feel of his hands through the nylons should've been erotic, but wasn't. His eyes wanted to read what I was thinking, but in this environment, he couldn't. There was a clear hole in his plan, an opening that had me in fear for my life.

"You knew about this place and didn't tell me." I pulled my legs away from his hands, pushing the cold compress along with Nohea away from my head.

"Yes," Russell responded.

"All you can say is, yes?"

"What do you want me to say?"

"I don't know," bouncing up, pacing feverishly around the room. "Shit...Shit..."

"Erica," Russell reaching for my hand.

"Don't you touch me or so help me god I'll scream."

"You scream and we're all dead." Nohea's head tilted from the floor.

"Right now, that doesn't sound half bad."

As much as I loved him, his continued lack of disclosure infuriated me to my core. My blood pressure boiling to the point my skin began to crawl. I wanted to bolt for the door, but knew there was no way to get to the surface without that key and I jumped as the phone next to me on the desk rang, its red light blinking in rhythm.

"Hello," Russell answered, "Yes Sir. No, I'm here with Nohea. If you insist." He returned the phone to its receiver, paused; his eyes stared at me, searching for the right scenario, and with a computerized displayed emotion. "Erica, we don't have much time. Get in the bathroom and hide. Don't come out until one of us comes for you."

"I'm not going anywhere but home without answers," I stubbornly voiced.

"I don't have time to explain, but if you value your life, and ours, just do it. Now!"

There was something he wasn't telling me, but no matter what, I wasn't ready to die, not without avenging Scott's death. I hurriedly made my way to the full-size bathroom and no sooner resolving to the chilled toilet seat than a knock came from outside.

"Enter," Russell barked to his guest.

I was curious and hoped to catch even a glimpse of our mysterious visitor through the crack in the door jam. However, all I could see was the back of Russell's firm body. Normally not a bad sight, but I wanted to see the reason for my rush to secrecy.

"General, nice to see you again," Nohea saluted.

"You too, Colonel."

"General," Russell extended his hand to our guest.

"Russell. You don't mind if the Major General sits in on this one?" The General replied.

"No, not at all. What can I do for you?" Russell asked.

Russell finally sat back in his chair, but by then the General's face had already moved past my limited view as his left shoulder peeked momentarily around the chair's silhouette revealing a circle of five stars. I turned my ear towards the crack trying to catch every word that flowed in on the softened, recycled cold air.

"It seems your little pet project is getting out of hand." The General's voice was deeply harsh like a Drill Sergeant and barked with a lifeless aged tone.

"I don't know what you mean?" Russell's voice rebutted.

"If you don't tighten her leash we'll do it for you," the General paused, "Just like we did with Mr. Cooper and, that ever so troublesome, Scott Parker."

I had to control myself from breaking through the door. It wasn't going to do me any good. This was his playground and he had the bat and ball, nevertheless I knew now who killed Scott, as I fought back the tears.

"General, that won't be necessary. She's not a threat."

"Not now, but if she ever figures out who her father was, she could be, and we can't have that…now can we?"

"No, sir."

"So, I expect a full report on my desk within forty-eight hours." The General expressed.

"Yes, sir." Russell rose for his chair in unison with the General.

"Good. Then we understand each other. If she or you do anything to affect this pending Treaty…well, let's hope it never comes to that. Right?" The General's voice, though calm, was prevailing in his threat.

"Understood."

I tried catching one last glimpse as they made for the door, but once again, Russell blocked my view as salt-and-pepper hair showed from under two visor caps, but only from the back.

"Nohea. Russell. Good day." The General's voice terminated as the door closed in his wake.

"General. Major General." Both Nohea and Russell voiced to an empty room.

I returned to the coldness of the toilet seat waiting for someone to enter. It was dark and lonely but gave me time to think. I couldn't distinguish the dialogue between Russell and Nohea, and felt I'd had enough prying for one night. I refocused on my newly found memories. That's when it hit…the previous room we were in…I had seen it before, the General in the video at the observatory, that was his office. The puzzle started to fall into place. However, I still had questions and the person with those answers sat on the other side of the door. As if on cue, Nohea opened the door inviting me out of the darkness into the light.

"Who was that?" I asked.

"Never mind, that's not important," Russell stated as he feverishly typed on his computer.

"I think someone threatening to kill me deserves an answer, plus he killed Scott." I loudly voiced.

"Keep your voice down, Erica," Nohea hushed at me.

"Fine. The room we were in was the General's from the video wasn't it?"

"Yes." Russell blasted at me hesitating to continue his thought.

"So, who was he?"

Russell paused, unsure if he should continue, "He was your father. Your biological father."

I had to sit, my legs buckling from the truth, as it wasn't the one thing I expected to hear tonight. In the background, a printer zipped through its scheduled cycle, cutting the silence like a knife.

"What?" I questioned, not knowing what else to say.

"Your father worked for this base. In fact he was one of its principal reasons it exists," Russell stressed, his body turning to recover the newly printed page.

"I thought you said my father was some sort of extraterrestrial."

"He was part of the original race of Nordics that met with Eisenhower back in the 50's. He went undercover working inside the newly formed Majestic 12. Only a select few knew he wasn't of this planet…and even fewer knew his true reason for being on this project."

"How come you didn't tell me?"

"Erica, until a few moments ago I didn't know how deep this conspiracy went and to what extent. Your father was working to gain inside knowledge on the Grey's plans for the Nordics. They tried to warn Eisenhower but his General Advisers were more interested in receiving advanced weapons technology then *Enlightenment*."

I wanted to return back upstairs to his room. *I don't know why?* He wasn't there, but a part of me now felt like he was. That explained my calmness while in his room and my heartfelt familiarly while watching the video. I finally was able to put a face with my true origin.

"Boss, what now?" Nohea inquired.

"We go get that medallion and get the hell out of dodge…for good."

"Do you know where it is?" I asked.

"With the Major General escorting the General I'd venture a guess and say level five in the archives room and waiting to be filed…I hope." Russell's face wasn't optimistic at all.

"You don't sound convinced."

"Erica, level five is not a place for you." Russell voiced.

"Sorry, but been there done that…"

Russell wasn't amused at my attempt to lighten the mood. He was right; it wasn't a place for me in more ways than one. Mainly, due to his fear they would identify me and thus blow this whole operation. Whatever his plan was, for the safety of us all, I would obey.

"I want Nohea to get you back to the car. I'll meet you there in a few." He apprehensively looked down at the printed page before addressing Nohea. "Get her to the surface. If I'm not at the car in say ten minutes leave without me."

"No way. We came in here together, we leave together." I stressed.

"Nohea, that's a direct order." Russell set the paper on his desk.

Nohea reached for my arm pulling me towards the door but I managed to wrestle away from his grip, running to embrace Russell. A part of me felt like I'd never see him again. Also, I wanted a look at that printed page. It was at that point I'd never question him or his true motives again.

The letter read as follows:

Dear General of the Air Force Cliff Patterson:

Please accept this letter as a formal notification that I'm resigning from my position effective immediately. Thank you for the opportunities you have provided me during my time here. I've the utmost respect for you and your goals for this project.

Regarding operation "Dawn", you'll find a completed file sent to you via certified mail in the coming days. Erica Jones is and will remain under my protection. She is no longer a threat to you or your project and I kindly request you to resolve any and all future contact. In the event project "Dawn" continues or Erica Jones is harmed, I've arranged with Wiki Leaks to release all known documentation. This also applies to Nohea and me.

Sincerely,

General Russell Hamilton

Russell held me longer, as if wanting me to finish reading the memo, before Nohea tried to pull me away, but not before passionately kissing the man I loved. He was giving up everything for me, which said it all. I fought Nohea briefly before he lifted me off my feet heading for the door. Russell's eyes called *I love you* with no sign of *goodbye*. Deep down I felt the same.

"Nohea get her out of here. Now! Erica…," Russell paused.

I shook Nohea off as he sat me down to open the door. I had to regain me composure if we were to get out alive, straightening my skirt, tucking in my shirt and adjusted my cap.

"Russell I know…see you in a bit," I voiced with a newfound reassuring smiling.

It didn't take long for us to reach the surface and exit the facility. I kept waiting for the alarm to resound while armed guards shot first asking questions later, but everything went fine. Nohea slid into the driver's seat while I called shotgun. He set his watch for ten minutes as we eagerly watched the entrance doors. I don't know who, him or me, watched with uncertainly more as each minute digitally ticked away. Ten minutes came and went to the sound of aggressive beeps begging for freedom. I pleaded for Nohea to give him an extra five minutes, but like a good soldier, he took his orders seriously. I didn't cry, or talk the entire ride back to the trailer. Nohea, giving me my space as again the chemically induced memories were vague. I knew I'd see Russell again, I don't know why, but I knew.

We arrived in Rachel to a trailer with its door wide open. The limited amount of snow that had drifted inside advised our intruders weren't long gone, if at all. It was still dark, the sun not due for a couple more hours. Nohea asked, more like ordered, me to stay in the car until he double-checked the trailer for intruders. The thought of no Russell and a looted trailer wasn't reassuring enough for me to stay the rest of the night, at least not in Rachel. I wanted the comfort of my own home and a friendly face, particularly one with plentiful fur. Nohea agreed and collected our possessions, what was left of them, while I changed into something practical. He then drove me to Russell's truck still parked up on Coyote Summit.

"Remember, straight home. Stop for nothing and watch for cattle. They'll do a number on you, even in that truck." Nohea loaded my personal belongs.

"What about Russell?"

"He'll be fine, Miss Jones. I promise." The uncertainty in his eyes glowed in the darkness of the night.

"Are you following me home?"

"I'll catch up; I need to take care of a few things back in Rachel."

I wasn't scared anymore. That point had come and gone a long time ago. I was ready for a fight, especially with that General. I pulled back onto the Extraterrestrial Highway heading towards

Vegas unaware that fight was coming sooner than expected and from an unexpected source.

Chapter 40

Between my adrenaline and the sporadic vibrating cattle guard, the drive home was going smooth. The lack of an illuminated road only made my hands tighten harder around the wheel. The dash's green lights wrongly washed my tired skin tone, while my mind periodically shifted to thoughts of Russell and his safety. He was alive; I could feel it deep inside. The canyons and narrow passage over Hancock Summit sent chills down my spine. The viewable drop-offs from earlier in the day appeared as black abysses void of life and for the first twenty or so miles, I was alone in this desolate desert. There were over the horizon the periodic flashes of brake lights but I still felt alone. I constantly watched my speed over the crest, leery of stray cattle that called this road home.

My heart raced on the way down while riding the brake as a single pair of headlights rapidly approached. Maybe it was Nohea, maybe not. My eyes rapidly switching from side mirror to the task of navigating the descent, as there was no place to pass until we hit the lower valley floor, which was still miles away. The vehicle closed extremely fast without losing control. I would've never navigated this course at such speed, even during the day.

The car fell in behind, almost drafting, its headlights tucked neatly out of sight into my bumper. Russell's truck handled like a tank and I longed for the maneuverability of my car. My only comfort came from its heightened frame. Nohea's signal was simple; three flashes of his high beams, watching, as we hit the valley floor, but the signal never came. Maybe nothing I thought, just another recreational driver. I tested my theory slowing well below the posted speed limit and waving them around in an attempt to get them to pass, they never did. I was still a long way to Vegas and stopping wasn't an option, especially out in the middle of nowhere.

I knew the outer part of Ash Springs wasn't far away and at least there, I'd find remote pockets of civilization. The nearest gas station sat on the city limits and was the only safe place I felt prepared to stop. After driving miles under the posted speed it was evident, they weren't going to pass, for whatever reason, as they eventually withdrew from my personal space. I tried to forget and concentrate on what my life was going to be like starting tomorrow. *Would Russell still be part of it? Should or how would I get the message out to the world? What part did the people around me play in this whole conspiracy, especially my best friend Tracy?*

I was coming up on the junction of Highway 93 South near the old Casino. The outline of its sign and infrastructure floated against the moonlight like a ghost ship. A simple horseshoe turn and the sanctuary of Ash Springs would almost be in reach. The truck crawled to a halt at the stop sign while noticing the trailing lights had fallen even further back to almost a stop. See...worried about nothing.

My focus was on the turn, checking for oncoming traffic and I didn't notice the instant acceleration in the side mirror closing in. I remembered the sound of the air bag exploding in my ear as it protected my forehead from a certain fracture. The metal on metal resonance ripped apart from the rear axle of the truck. A second jolt forward engaged the side air bags as the truck aggressively spun ninety degrees. This was no accident, but a blatant attempt on my life, made to look like an accident. I mustered enough strength to open my dazed eyes as a set of cracked headlights froze in the distance waiting for signs of life. My head's throbbing pain, dwarfed with the ghastly noise of burning rubber and ever-growing beams of light heading for the passenger side door.

The truck, its contents were strategically targeted for destruction. My arm shielded my eyes from the projectile shattered glass. The lights again pulled away, awaiting movement, ready to engage in yet another assault. The coldness of the air was a wakeup call to the grogginess. I needed to get out of here, but the truck wouldn't restart. The remote engine's revving was deafening, its frame, highlighted by the backdrop of the full moon now that its lights had expired. I had to focus or this was going to be my last night on this planet.

I don't know why, but I reached for the glove compartment in hopes Russell kept a gun as they always did in the movies, and this seemed more and more like one. Sure enough, locked and loaded. I wasn't much of a gun person, but my dad was an avid member of NRA or should I say my step-dad. This wasn't a rifle, but they worked on the same simple principle, they killed whatever was in front of them when fired. The iciness of the steel warmed, as blood from my gashed head lightly dripped down, in search of the gun's safety. One clip, sixteen shots, I hoped it would be enough.

The car's shadow, this time with the help of my adrenaline, came swiftly into focus. There were two people in the vehicle, but the only one I cared about right now was the driver. I fired; my finger pulsed on the trigger as my arms fought the recoil. The pain, deafening from its pressurized reverberation as I emptied the entire clip into the driver's front window, a choice I'd soon regret. It worked, as the car swerved down an embankment originally marked for my grave.

My head rang worse than any migraine I'd ever had and I searched the compartment for another clip, but there wasn't one. Maybe the crash had disabled the passenger. If not, I was shit-out-of-luck. I again tried to start the truck, nothing. I reached for my cell phone and rapidly dialed Nohea but no answer. I hit the last number to dial Russell; the phone rang as my back gave way to an opening door. The phone dropped from my hand as my shoulder blades smashed against the graveled pavement and Russell's voice faintly called to me through the pain. My fingers scraped at the dirt, arm extended to its limit, the phone only inches away until kicked by a pair of vaguely familiar three inch stilettos. My eyes scrolled up the lean legs, tiny waist, and unforgettable lost facial features.

"Tracy?" I questioned, agonizingly trying to get to my feet.

"You Bitch!" Tracy fired. "Just couldn't leave well enough alone...could you?"

"Me...what the hell are you talking about." I gathered myself erect using the truck as my crutch.

"You and your so called boyfriend," pacing like a prowling tiger as she contemplated going in for the kill. "I should kill you right now just for fun."

"How's your driver?" Sarcastically laughing as blood spit from my mouth towards her shoes.

"Just as good as your friend Scott," She laughed. "Seen any gas leaks lately." This time the laugh got sinister, almost joyful.

"It was you? Son of a Bitch…it was you!" I wanted to lunge at her but my strength hadn't fully returned and the ringing in my ears hadn't decreased in volume.

"You're just like your father…thinking you can save the world. Look what good that got him. He's saving the world alright, as sod for the trees."

Her pacing quickened waiting for the right moment to pounce. If Tracy had one attribute I positively hated, it was her incessant need to ramble when making points. I needed more time to collect my strength but knew I was no match for her, even though outer signs showed she'd suffered some injuries in the crash.

"What do you know about my father?" I questioned.

"What, your boyfriend didn't tell you?"

"Just that he worked at S-4…same as you."

"And here I was thinking he cared for you."

As she sneered, I caught a flash of razor sharp teeth escape the corner of her mouth. My hazy eyes struggled to focus in on her face as she was definitely sneering, but something was different. I strained my bloodshot eyes trying to elaborate on the missing details. It was no use, at least not yet.

"He doesn't care for me…he loves me."

"You're a lab rat experiment to him. Remember the men in white coats from your abductions…he's one of them."

"I don't believe you," fighting back the tears.

She was good at playing head games. I'd seen it enough over the years with her ex-boyfriends. She was trying to weaken my spirit and it wasn't going to work, not this time. Her confidence strengthened, gradually encroaching towards me, as I played the wounded deer while trying to draw her closer into my personal space. My only chance without a weapon was my lethally trained hands, but she needed to be closer. If I struck first, it might give me the upper hand. In a fair fight, no doubt, she'd take me, but this was life-or-death. We never got the chance to spar while in class, however tonight we were going to find out who was the better student.

"Russell authorized every little test, right down to ones we didn't feel were essential." Her grin closed in as I dug my heels into the loose particles of gravel. "I think he got off on watching you squirm…I know I did."

"You always did."

My fingers on my right hand folded forty-five degrees leaving my palm exposed.

"Recognize this…?" Tracy questioned.

She had pulled a badge from her pocket and I recognized it instantly. It was same badge on the lab coat in my abduction as well as the same one adorned by the Reptilians deep in the underground caverns. Tracy didn't look Reptilian, but she could've been using a cloaking device similar to the one Russell had showed me. However, if Russell was in on this plot the entire time, the information given might also be inaccurate. The adrenaline percolated like a pot of coffee waiting for the beeps to signal it was ready. A few steps closer and I'd launch in an offensive. A little "*Shock and Awe*" of my own. My Sensei privately demonstrated that one timely, upward thrust to the nose could disable your opponent, even kill them, and I was about to test his theory.

"Sorry can't see it; my eyes are a little blurred from the so called accident." My poker face looked her straight in the eyes trying to draw her in one-step closer.

"Take a good look," stepping ever so slightly forward.

I felt the rush of power extended from the earth below, up my spine, down my shoulder to the waiting open-faced palm. My arm a coiled cobra about to strike as the clarity in my eyes returned long enough to launch the first and hopefully last offensive. I felt the wind cut as my palm ripped through the night, contacting the bridge of her nose. There was no pain, as my arm became stronger than steel, extending its shaft through to an axis point beyond the horizon. Her head snapped back and her body now airborne, propelled feet away and landed harshly in the gravel. I'd amazed even myself at the power unleashed uncontrollably on my friend. Tracy's body lay motionless with no signs of life while my rush subsided and the situation's reality along with its pain returned. I gathered my remaining strength wanting to witness the destructive wrath and verify I'd succeeded with my goal. The image I found lying feet away no longer resembled that of my friend, but more of a reptilian substitute. Although the shell had changed, it was hard to erase years of friendship and I wanted to drop to her side, hold her, and apologize. *For what?*

Here I was with no vehicle, no friend, and hurting with the weight of the world on my shoulders, understanding no one would believe me. I needed Russell more than anything now…my phone, where was my phone. I hobbled back to the truck to retrace its whereabouts when over the rise I could make out distant headlights approaching. I prayed it was someone that could help, but my darker side feared it was the military. I had little left so I began to drag my left leg towards the approaching lights while fighting the numbness that crept up my right arm. Blood fell like tears down my bruised cheeks.

The truck came to a stop a few feet away, its lights highlighting the true extent of my injuries. I wanted to drop to my knees in pure exhaustion, the high beams blinding what little vision I had left. The doors on both sides opened as strong silhouettes cautiously approached. I heard a comforting voice carry through the stillness of the night air, but it wasn't what I wanted to hear.

"Erica, look out behind you!" Russell yelled.

"It's not that easy Bitch!" Tracy whispered in my ear as she raked what felt like claws down my back.

I fell to the ground screaming in agony. I assumed she was dead but now I was going to pay for that assumption with only modest strength, at best, to fight anymore.

"Russell, help," I screamed.

"Back away," Tracy picked me off the ground like a rag doll. "She's mine and there's not a damn thing you can do about it."

I could see Russell and Nohea gingerly approaching, fearful for my life. Tracy's now Reptilian arm, though petite, was commanding and wrapped dangerously around my neck and I felt lifeless as she tossed me around like a piece of tenderized meat.

"Russell, help!" I screamed again.

"Erica, listen to me carefully," Russell yelled.

He froze in his tracks while trying to get my attention, afraid Tracy might become rash. I tried to remain focused but my body was giving up, drifting in and out of conscious dream state. The massive amount of blood loss was causing my body to shut down nonessential functions and I felt my legs going limp as well as my arms.

"It doesn't matter Russell. She attacked me first. Galactic Laws dictates I've a right to this kill." Tracy licked the side of my ear taking in the blood.

"Erica, did you attack her first?" Russell pleaded.

"Yes," I dazzlingly responded.

She had struck the truck first, but in some twisted reality it wasn't her driving, thus my predicament.

"Told you lover boy. Maybe, I'll eat her right here in front of you," she licked my other ear.

"Boss, we can't do anything. You know what the Treaty says. If we interfere you risk triggering an Interstellar War," Nohea cautioned.

"I know what it says," Russell snapped back.

Russell gradually reached out for me, or at least it felt that way in my mind as Tracy slowly tightened harder while I began to gasp for air.

"Before she dies, do you want to tell her the truth of whom you are or should I?" She adjusted her grip turning my head, lifting my body. The scales sliding under my chin awakened me ever so slightly. "Take a good long look." My legs dangled, as the now muscular hands formed a noose, her Reptilian face now completely replaced that of Tracy's. The blood dripped off my nose ever so slightly in front of her face and she quickly lapped it up with her forked tongue. "Now take a good look at your boyfriend." She had shifted from Human form to full Reptilian. The deadly scales closed in tighter around my neck. If there was joy in killing, I was seeing it firsthand. "Tell her the truth Russell and I might let her live."

"The truth about what?" Russell questioned.

"The real reason you're here and what you want with her. I want for her to hear it with her own ears from you."

I don't know if Russell had sent something to me telepathically or just imaged my own unlikely escape, but his body language had abruptly changed. The aura around him started to glow, as I took in the last of my shallow breaths waiting for the big confession.

"Erica," he paused, "Tracy I can't, and you know I can't."

"See how much he loves you. Then I'll tell her." Tracy's voice deepened in pitch as she lowered me into her arms.

"Elika, Ho'amalu ia makou pauloa Ka'iu lani kamāli'i wahine," he passionately called out to me in the night.

My eyes fixated on his glowing face as the darkness encroached and I felt the sluggishness of my own heart as its blood pooled around at my feet. That name, that Hawai'ian name, that face, that smile. Yes, that smile, yes, yes that loving smile. I'd seen that trusting smile before.

"Your boyfriend is…," Tracy began.

Russell interrupted, "Erica, get down, now!"

I flung my head back as hard as I could with one last chance for freedom. It was with enough force that Tracy's grip lightened, dropping me to the ground in my own blood while a beam of light shot across the sky above me dilating my eyes, rendering them useless. I wanted to run to the light and end this misery, but it squarely had hit Tracy in the chest. The dwindling brightness vanished as fast as it had arrived. I collapsed every inch of my body begging for forgiveness and before blackening out, my bludgeoned head sprawled beneath the starry sky, watched as Tracy's body convulsed next to mine. Her eyes no longer hazel-green, but reptilian yellow, flashed vertical slit lids as she took one last breath of Earthly air. Two male figures, now nothing more than shadows hovered above me as the stars morphed revealing a bright white light surrounded by three distinctive bluish-purple orbs formed in a triangle. Its image seemingly dropped like a veil, overshadowing my limited peripheral vision as the blinding light gave way to the faintest of voices.

"Nohea, take care of this. I'll get her back to the house."

"Boss, what about Tracy? You know The Intergalactic Council is not going to like this."

"So be it..."

Russell's voice softened as the world around me shot from a bright heavenly light to darkness. My last thought, I was on my way to heaven.

Chapter 41

I awoke in my bed, the clock's neon face painfully beaming into my eyes. I knew my memory was drastically searching for the truth, but fell victim to another void and unexplained missing time. The digital display clicked adding an extra minute, still sixty short at the very least. Maybe this was all a dream. I tried sitting, even my hair hurt. Nope this wasn't a dream. My head searched, but not far, for the softness of the pillow while even its delicate pressure hurt causing me to cringe, at any rate the ringing in my ears had stopped.

"Good, you're up," Russell joyfully expressed.

Exiting the bathroom he knelt at my side with cold compress in hand, the white cloth blotted with patchy dried blood, which I assumed, was mine and tenderly applied the moistened towel to my forehead.

"Is that my good linen?" I painfully smiled.

"Well, at least she didn't kick the crap out of your sense of humor," he replied.

"Says who?" I tried turning my head to shift views. "Do I look as bad as I feel?"

"I don't know…how bad do you feel?"

"I don't think there's a part of my body that isn't bruised."

"Well you're in luck…purple's the new winter color this year."

I tried to laugh but my ribs hurt even with shallow breaths.

"Don't make me laugh, it hurts too much." I felt Russell reach for my hand, gripping it with a tenderness that reassured his love for me. "Thank you." A single tear rolled down my cheek. He gently wiped it before it hit the pillow. The saltiness still burned in its absence. "Is she dead?"

"Yes," he wanted to look away as the pain strained his face.

"What happened? She was going to kill me...then there was a flash of white light. That's the last thing I remember...well almost."

"Let's just say fate intervened," his eyes locked onto mine.

"It was you. You saved my life."

"All I did was prolong it; you still have a lot to offer."

I was tired, everything hurt, yet I wanted to wrap my arms around him...make love to him.

"I guess this is the only way I can get you into my bed." I found the strength to squeeze his hand.

"I'm just glad that someday I'll get that chance." He leaned in with a gentle kiss, my lips bypassed the pain long enough to enjoy his softness. "You need your rest."

"Can you stay?" My lower lip trembled.

"I can't...not tonight."

"But what about...," he interrupted, hushing his finger over my mouth.

"You're safe...for tonight. I have a few loose ends that need addressing and it has to be done tonight. I'll have one of my guys stay till the morning."

You're safe...for tonight wasn't the reassuring answer I wanted to hear, but it would do. My body wanted to shut down, reboot and rebuild as I leisurely drifted into dreamland. Russell's image dematerialized as if a figment of my imagination. I craved sleep and little by little found comfort rolling to my side as a familiar face awaited, those dark brown eyes saddened with his inability to keep me safe. He gracefully crept to me, the best that a dog that size could do, exceptionally vigilant not to touch my bruised body. His tongue, as if to console me, ever so gently touched the tip of my nose and I managed enough movement with my arm to drape it over his shoulder. I drifted off to sleep with happy memories of the most faithful dog I'd ever owned now watching over me. His promise to me, I'd have a good night sleep. The one and only thing I trusted.

Chapter 42

I closed my journal gratified the writing was finally over, as my mind couldn't recall anything more. Colby's head nudged my elbow in agreement. It was time for him to eat and I had to check on supper.

The chicken had another half hour and still no call from Russell or Detective Wilson. I'd hoped the good detective would've graced me with his presence before Russell returned, as he was the last thing I felt like explaining. I don't know if I could have anyway. I mean, what if Russell turned out to be General Samson? That would've been game up.

I went to the bathroom to freshen up after letting Colby outside. He didn't what to break from my side, but his bladder won that battle. I did a quick wardrobe change again as thoughts of Russell entered my mind. My body had healed amazingly fast with the help of that crystal and I only wished it worked so well mending mindful memories. The agonizing loss of a friend was a hard void to fill, even though she turned out to be a *Royal Bitch*. My mind drifted through those memories oblivious to the ringing doorbell. If not for Colby's insistent barking, the daydream might've continued for a while.

I let Colby in as he raced for the front door. His gesture, one of playfulness not defensiveness as if he knew who was on the other side and wanted to play. I peeked through the door to a fishbowl view of a dozen red roses and without asking *who's there*, flung it open, and wrapped my arms around my new life.

"Keep at least one rib intact," Russell charmingly spoke.

"Sorry...God, their beautiful."

Colby's excessive energy nearly knocked the floral vase arrangement from Russell's hand.

"Nice to see you too, Colby."

Our embrace broke with a little help from wonder dog. Colby's outstretched front paws landing mid-waist on Russell while his trademarked signature drool hit thigh high.

"Colby, down," raising my voice, tugging at his collar.

"Don't worry, he's fine. By the way dinner smells great."

We walked into the kitchen with Russell entertaining Colby long enough for me to put the roses on the dining room table. The lingering aroma overpowered the smell of roasting chicken and somehow was a comfort. The last few weeks were just a dream and this was the life I longed for, that's what it felt like.

I explained my meeting with Detective Wilson and his insistent intent on paying me a visit tonight. Russell swore no involvement with the detective and he didn't know a General Samson. We had time to kill (*Not really a good pun considering past events*) so Russell asked to read my journal, apprehensive at first, but I thought it only fair, considering it did involve him. Truthfully, he was telepathic and I naturally assumed he already knew the contents.

Russell was a fast reader and rapidly scanned every page, only occasionally looking up with a slight blush confirming the parts involving him, but more importantly us. Oh well, he knew my intent towards him, something I didn't hide well. He finished reading, closed the journal as the buzzer for the oven called. He didn't say anything, at least about the journal, as his conversation shifted to the simplicities of life. We had a great dinner by candlelight and a lovely conversation about life. Anytime the conversation shifted to the past few weeks he quickly steered it to the present. Russell wanted this night or at least moment, to be as normal as possible. It felt surreal and I was in love.

The meal ended and I was hoping for dessert. Maybe, whip cream with a side of Russell. He reached across the table and our lips met. The fire from Maui had returned, although I don't think it ever left. The table's inconvenience melted away as our bodies entwined and stumbled to break away from the kitchen with the bedroom seemingly miles away. He effortlessly lifted me from the floor to the counter as my legs refused to unwrap from around his waist. He smelt amazing, like fresh baked chocolate chip cookies from the oven. The kind you ate while hot, and he was sizzling.

I was about to surrender my body, giving into the ecstasy I'd so longed for over the past few weeks when the phone rang. I fumbled for the volume as his hands explored the inner sanctuary of my soul. The machine eventually clicked on and although low, it wasn't off.

"Erica, this is Detective Wilson, pick-up." I avoided his first request my body arching. "Erica…I know you're there I have a man outside." The thought of someone looking in from the street got my attention and Russell's.

"Yes, what!" My voice snapped as I struggled to slow my breathing.

"I wasn't interrupting anything?"

"No, just ran to get the phone," wanting to say *hell yes*.

"Good, I'm on my way there. Let's say…twenty minutes."

"Great," I said in apathetically agreement.

The phone and my libido instantaneously went dead. I thought what does a girl have to do to get laid around here. I stopped to check Russell's reaction, as he agreed with a smile, knowing he'd heard telepathically what I said.

"Listen, Erica," Russell professed while helping himself to a glass of water. "Do you plan to show anyone…in particular Detective Wilson that journal?"

"Not yet, but I think the world needs to know…don't you?"

"The world's not ready for the truth," Russell replied.

"What do you mean?"

"I wish I could give you the details, but you only know half the story." Russell returned to the table and my journal, casually flipping through the pages.

"Half the story, what do you mean half the story?"

"In time, you as well as others will come to know the truth. In the meantime, for your safety and mine I have to censor out some of the information you've written."

"Fine, but it won't change what I already know. It'll still be inside this head," knocking lightly to my scalp.

"It's safer in your mind than on paper. Trust me."

I watched as most of the information explained to me while in Rachel received a heavy dose of the bold black sharpie as pages on pages becoming as black as night with only a trace of irregular simplified words showing through. All the information on chemtrails, Planet X, underground bases, secret alien treaties and their agendas effortlessly erased, but not from my mind; even details about 9/11 and the Apollo Moon Landing, were all gone. The true details about names of government officials and the trillions on trillions of dollars that have masterly gone unaccounted, all gone. Someday everyone would know the truth, including myself.

"Why keep any of this then?" I asked.

"It makes for a great book don't you think?" He recapped the pen dousing its smell with the truth.

"Maybe, but no one will believe me."

"That's the point, *Plausible Deniability*." He returned the book with his devilish smile. "By the way I have a little something for you."

He reached for a ring size box from his pocket as once again I filled with a committed expectation. I seriously doubted this was another crystal, although with the power I gained from it, would have also been a welcomed addition. However, both dwarfed the object that I was about to set my hands on for the first time. I didn't say a word as the box's golden beauty brilliantly revealed its luminosity, drawing me in like the summer sun.

"Is that what I think it is?" My hands electrically reached.

"None other," Russell removed it, "here hold it."

This had been our goal at S-4 and at the time, it seemed so trivial. However, as my hands savored in the power and my body absorbed its gradual light energy I quickly realized the weight of the situation. Russell reached for the charmed medallion and carefully clasped it around my neck. My eyes filled with the memories of my birth parents, especially my dad and his passions.

"It's beautiful."

"Like you," Russell wiped away the single tear rolling down my cheek. "Your dad would be proud of you right now."

"Why were they all so afraid of this?"

"Your dad had a powerful light energy, as you will someday discover, the longer you wear that around your neck."

"I still don't understand."

"Erica…,"

A familiar ring interrupted Russell's continuation of my family history. Detective Wilson was right on schedule. I hid the journal as Russell offered to take Colby for a walk, allowing me time to talk to the detective. Russell wanted to avoid a situation in which he might've had to explain himself to the good detective. Anyways, Colby seemed more than eager to go with Russell. When it came to a walk, once he saw the leash nothing else mattered.

Chapter 43

"Detective Wilson, welcome," I opened the door.

"Erica," he nodded.

Colby was too excited, eager for his walk, to pay any attention to the detective that now stood in my kitchen. Russell avoided eye contact at first until the detective offered him no choice.

"Hi, Detective Wilson and you are?" He openly extended his hand.

"Russell...Russell Hamilton." Russell was fighting Colby's excitement. "Pardon me if I don't stay, but Colby's a bit eager to go for his walk."

Russell walked past me, paused as if to say the hell with it, kissing me as if longtime lovers.

"Have fun with Colby." It sounded questionable coming from my mouth.

"You too." Russell's voice echoed from the closing door.

"Detective, have a seat, please."

"Thanks."

It took a few minutes for him to settle in, the entire time trying to read my expressions. I'd gotten good, good at hiding my emotions, except when it came to Russell. He flipped through a few pages of notes before finally putting his right hand down, pen still in hand.

"Start from the top," I stated, trying to be funny.

Detectives clearly don't have a strong sense of humor.

"We've gone down that road. Let's try something different starting with, who's Russell Hamilton?" His voice was firm.

"He's my boyfriend, sort of...no...I mean...yes...he's my boyfriend." That came out wrong.

"Which is it," his face unamused.

"Boyfriend."

"Can you explain why the body we pulled from Scott Parker's house wasn't his and whose body it was?"

"No I can't. That body was wearing Scott's necklace." I pulled it from my pocket. "Plus, I haven't heard from Scott. If he were alive, he would've called. I know he would've." My eyes teared up which wasn't a hard sell as it was the truth.

"Can you explain to me, why when I called Nellis Air Force Base, they have no record of a General Samson? Heck, even the FBI doesn't have a dossier on him." His blood pressure was rising as the visually building pressure tightened around his wrinkled eyes.

"As I told you at the station, I know nothing."

"I have two of your friends, dead. One, burned beyond recognition and turns out to be a John Doe. The other, found dead out on 93 South in a deliberately torched SUV. The truck registered to a Dynamic Aeronomics. The DNA found under her nails was female and she didn't die of any fire."

"No." I interrupted when I should've kept my mouth shut.

"No. Apparently, her body had received a jolt of electricity equivalent to that of a bolt of lightning. Funny thing is there were no storms or strikes last night. Any ideas?" His eyes expressed it not as a question.

"Not one. Really not big on theories. I prefer facts. Do you have any?" I was starting to get cocky.

"Well let's just hope the DNA doesn't come back the way I think it might." He smiled while writing himself a brief note. "Wait till you hear the kicker. The coroner called on my way here to tell me Tracy's body is missing."

"Missing!" My heart skipped a beat.

"Yeah, m-i-s-s-i-n-g, missing. Wouldn't know anything about that would you?"

"No."

"Well let's try something you might know about…This Russell Hamilton wouldn't by chance work for Dynamic Aeronomics?"

I didn't have to say much as my body language told him everything he needed to know about that question. It deserved an answer, no matter how absurd. He was only going to ask Russell when he got back anyways and as my mind raced for a snappy comeback, the doorbell rang again. Saved by the bell I thought. I must've locked the door instinctively and poor Russell didn't have a key. Not yet, not like he need one anyways.

"Excuse me, Detective."

"By all means."

The walk to the door slowed, struggled with the thickening air, at least in my mind that's how time appeared, but it was happening in real time. Drawn to the door impulsively, I opened it without checking, something I rarely did, and my heart coming to a standstill as Jim Charleston had aggressively pushed it open. It slammed against the wall causing one of my only Lassen paintings to hit the floor shattering glass at my feet. The aggressive pushback of a chair as well as a safety release from a Glock 9 mm flowed from the kitchen. Standing next to Jim was Pakile, Lulani and they weren't here to bring the 'Aloha Spirit'.

Detective Wilson's years of being a desk jockey had finally caught up to him as he prematurely turned the corner. Lulani rushed in pinning my petite frame to the wall.

"Everybody hold it right there," Detective Wilson flashed his dusted off 9 mm and tarnished badge.

Before his command had even comprehended in my ears, a thin beam of ultra-white light emanated from Jim's open hand sending the poor detective's gun in flight. His astonishment eventually turned to fear, as terror of the unknown will do that to you. He froze motionless, his hands extended to the ceiling, but his eyes frantically searched for his only source of defense. Out of the corner of my eye, I saw it smoldering some feet away and so did he.

"Don't or the next blast is going to be directed to you," Jim adamantly confessed.

346

"Detective please, don't do it," I pleaded with him.

"That's right, Hoʻolohe iā ke Kaʻiu lani kamāliʻi wahine," Pakile softly voiced as he approached me with a newfound youth.

"What did he say?" Detective Wilson directed his question to me, while lowering his raised defenseless hands.

"He said something about Sacred Princess."

Lulani adjusted his weight, shifting my arm behind my back to the point of almost breaking it, easily forcing my feet towards the detective. Jim had already made his way to the detective recovering the gun along the way.

"How primitive," Jim leered putting the gun in his pocket. "See Detective, she's under this grand delusion that she's a hero to mankind, a soon to be short-lived career choice, I'm afraid to say."

"Erica, what the hell is going on?" The detective asked.

"Yes Erica, do tell," Pakile circled me like a shark. "That's right, you don't know, now do you?"

I'd never felt terror like what I now sensed around Pakile. His eyes absent of life, clouded with the blackest of revenge. Russell was out walking Colby, so my only hope was to stall long enough for the cavalry to arrive.

"I know enough!"

Fighting Lulani as he raised me to my toes while Pakile stopped, his delicate frame didn't seem so delicate anymore as he slapped me right across the face. His hand stimulated the tenderness from the other night.

"You know nothing!" He slapped the other side of my face, both cheeks now matching my deepest blush.

"Then enlighten me," my voice tenderized by the slap.

Pakile continued to pace about, reeling in his pleasure from my abuse to the point of erotic excitement. He stood before me, staring up ever so slightly, as Lulani had finally reached the full extension my toes and arm could take. Pakile raised his hand as if to slap my face again only to stop short, his elderly hand reached deep inside his jacket pocket as his image flickered like a fading candle before ending on a disturbing morphed reality.

"What that hell…" Detective Wilson's face whitened if that was even possible.

I had seen this image before in my worst nightmares and in reality. This one now stood at almost nine feet before me in a long flowing robe. His tail hovered inches above the floor. Where once stood a frail old man was now an enormous pissed off Reptilian. His voice deepened, his Hawai'ian slang replaced with one of royalty and a more suited, raspy lisp. My eyes fixated on the new Pakile, one of strength and pure rage as the vertebrae in my neck cracked in stress as Lulani helped reach eye contact. Detective Wilson's vague muttering was falling on deaf ears, as I had my own problems.

"Been taking your Viagra I see. Do me a favor try not to relieve yourself on the floor. I just had them done."

Not to self, Reptilians don't find us funny. At all!

Pakile unleashed the back of his muscular hand this time raking it across my face. His scales shredded the softness of my cheek like coarse sandpaper as once again blood dripped down, pooling to the floor at my feet. He bent over, his eyes fixated on the freshly drawn blood, as his warm breath smelt of past deaths still decaying in the recess of his mouth. I wanted to offer him a Tic-Tac, but figured he'd add a matching scar on my other cheek. His forked tongue searched the air tasting for the metallic iron in my blood. It settled on my cheek for a taste as if my blood was a fine wine. He let the savory juices linger inside his mouth, as his saliva became alive calling for more as he returned to his erect stature.

"Good enough to eat, if only you taste as good as your father." He sharply fixated his eyes down. "I'll try not to dirty your clean floors."

I definitely didn't like the way he phrased that last line, but I especially didn't like that fact of now knowing how my father died. Had I known him, really known him, my sadness would've overwhelmed me. However, to mourn his faint memory now would've been ill advised.

"If I'm going to die anyways, I want to know the truth. Anyways, why so pissed? Is it because I took out Tracy?" I managed a painful grin in an attempt to stall for more time.

Pakile's hand, in a blur, crossed my other cheek, this time drawing more than a little blood, the pain so forceful it at any rate made me forget my arm was about to be twisted off like a chicken wing.

"Let me have her for five minutes," Jim's voice echoed.

"No!" Pakile commanded with authority. "I see you're wearing your family's Coat of Arms. I assume a gift from your boyfriend?"

"What's it to you?"

"He'll get his in due time for interfering in Intergalactic Laws. Anyways, I'll enjoy adding it to my collection on Maui."

"Over my dead body!"

"That's the plan," he moved in closer.

Had it not been for the repetitious nature of Detective Wilson and his persistence in regards to Tracy, I wouldn't be alive today. Throughout Pakile's little tirade the detectives' questions went unnoticed, but somehow his voice reached us this time.

"What about Tracy?" Detective Wilson loudly questioned.

"Not a good time, Detective," I chimed.

"You see, Detective," Pakile twisted his bulky weight towards the detective, his tail intentionally grazing the side of my head. "Erica killed Tracy, who happened to be one of our Princesses and furthermore next in line for the throne, to be exact."

The detective's face searched for anger towards me for deliberately lying to him. However, under the circumstance his eyes wrote it off as a legitimate act of self-defense.

"So, that explains why you're here."

I tried shifting my body away from Lulani, but the constant pressure on the back of my calves twinged with the preliminary onset of cramps. Pakile whipped back around leaning in for one more lick. "No, it doesn't. Not only was she royalty, but Jim's daughter as well as Lulani's sister."

"What does that make you?"

"Kupuna kāne," he voiced.

"Sorry, don't speak Hawai'ian...lizard or whatever you just said."

His head lowered. My eyes forced an answer, as his eyes gradually met with mine, the deep slits, dilated, temporarily washing away the yellow.

"Grandfather!"

His face overshadowed mine as he demonstrated restraint, his jaws wanting to bite my head off at that very moment with one lethal snap.

"Oh shit!" I turned my head to avoid his razor sharp teeth.

"Oh shit is right, little one."

He smiled, revealing the multiple layers of teeth. The front door was still open and I felt a chill run up my spine and stay. The kind of chill you feel when someone is watching you. Death was around the corner and I'd run out of time and so had Detective Wilson. There wasn't going to be happy ending after all.

Chapter 44

What happened over the next few pages took place in real time in seconds. I've tried to recreate the pace of the events by limiting this chapter.

From around the corner came the sound of the cavalry played not with a bugle but with a single bark. Lulani's attention diverted from me to the approaching Colby, releasing his grip. Pakile noticed my release and attempted to swing his hefty tail trying to knock me to the floor; however, the strain on my calves had taken its toll causing me to collapse. Pakile's misjudged target only succeeded in hurling Lulani across the room.

Detective Wilson grabbed at Jim, wrestling him towards the kitchen. Jim hadn't morphed into Reptilian form and this was going to be the only advantage the detective was going to get. I rolled across the floor towards the front door as Pakile's massive foot punished the tile, cracking it in two. Russell was coming, he had to be coming and entered pursuit alongside Colby both leaping over my immobile horizontal body. I was right. Thank god, I was right.

Inside Russell's fisted hand, a beam of light illuminated the air and knocked Pakile off his feet as his hefty body sank into the floor. Colby was relentlessly barking and had positioned himself between the action, Lulani's lifeless body, and me. He gave up no ground as I relentlessly massaged the knots out of my calves, trying to find a way to stand and help. Colby's body was shielding me from harm, but also blocking my view of everyone else's status.

Lulani was down and from the power of Pakile's strike, out for good. Detective Wilson was around the corner and out of sight, but his unrelenting resistance was loud and clear; a good sign if he could maintain the upper hand and avoid Jim's transformation to a Reptilian. Russell was cautiously standing over Pakile, who even lying down dwarfed Russell in size. I couldn't tell if Pakile was still alive, although his body wasn't moving, though at one point last night, Tracy's wasn't either.

From the kitchen, two shots fired and I only hoped Detective Wilson had pulled the trigger. Jim emerged around the

351

corner bleeding, but not dead. His eyes obsessed on me as if he was on a suicide mission. He wanted one thing and one thing only—me dead. Two more shots fired from the kitchen catching Jim in the upper arm and back, his adrenaline heightened and his body barely flinched as the shots ripped through his flesh.

"Jim, stop, or I'll fire," Russell yelled.

A spherical glow once again germinated between the closed and tightly gripped fist of Russell. Pakile's tail flinched. I noticed it, but didn't have time to warn Russell as it swatted at him like a fly, pushing him airborne through the glass slider into the backyard. Pakile snickered with annoyance in my direction before aggressively giving Russell chase as the first attack had left him only dazed.

Jim now had the only chance he was going to have to kill me. Two more shots fired from the kitchen this time grazing his lower leg and upper torso. Colby stood his ground refusing to back down, his teeth ready to go toe-to-toe with Jim, as my legs, despite knotted with cramps, found the strength to stand. At this point running wasn't an option and neither was walking.

I'd lost track of Russell and Pakile. I was defenseless, unable to handle my own weight, all the while trying to anticipate Jim's next move. Colby leaped side to side extending his paws in the air, as if he was a shadowboxing Grizzly bear, trying to shield me from Jim. The sound of a beaten body hitting the floor originating from the kitchen didn't improve my predicament. Jim remained out of Colby's reach, and with his right hand retrieved a device from his pocket and directed it in my vicinity. The outside commotion intensified, for now I'd take that as a good sign. Jim cut short his approach, instead opting to shift his right hand from side to side in an attempt to align me in his crosshairs. Colby countered each offensive gesture quicker then he followed a cookie. The frustration in Jim's face was becoming apparent.

"Enough!" Jim's voice vexed.

A beam of light meant for me deflected, the smell of smoldering fur instantly permeated the room as Colby's lifeless body hit the floor with a bone-cracking thud.

"Noooooo!" I screamed.

"Annoying little dog. Now it's just you and me, princess," Jim sinisterly laughed.

His approach was slow and methodical with no intention on killing me with that weapon, wanting to experience the last breath coming from my crushed windpipe as his razor sharp teeth sunk deep into my skin. This man wanted revenge in the utmost way. I can't say that I blamed him, I did kill his daughter and as Colby laid there in front of me, lifeless, I too had a reason to fight, and he wasn't getting me that easily. *Could I do to Jim what I did to Tracy?* I was soon to find out.

He moved in at last, morphing into his true Reptilian self, while the continued hums of laser fired from outside. Jim straddled Colby, the last obstacle before being in reach of his goal. Colby, with one last heroic breath locked his snout onto his leg. Jim shook him off like a flea, his body landing across the room, but not before leaving a permanent impression in the wall. I had to remain focused. I was going to get only one shot. I felt my heel dig in, my fingers roll exposing my palm and the metal stiffness starting to form in my elbow.

One more step, just one more step you miserable excuse for a species, I thought. In midstride of his last step, a white beam shot from the patio, nailing him square in the back. I watched as the beam picked him up, propelling and embedding him against the far wall, before vanishing. Russell sprinted between the broken doorframes with his body heavily damaged from Pakile's abuse. Russell alive meant only one thing, Pakile was dead and now so was Jim. Russell ran over clutching me in his arms as I collapsed.

"Are you alright?" he asked.

"Yeah, thanks to you and Colby...Colby...Russell, take me to him."

Russell lifted me off my feet to Colby's side. His breathing labored with a cauterized hole above his chest the size of a soft ball. His hind legs both shattered as extruding bones showed no need for x-rays, as blood ran from his eyes like tears. He was beyond a vets help as his tongue gently licked my hand as I held him. His way of saying "I'll be alright I'm just glad that you're safe". I nestled my nose into his neck, the putrid smell of burned flesh now replaced that loveably baby power smell. He was my hero; I repeated it repeatedly into his ears as the sound of his breathing weakened. I knew this day would come, but not now and not like this.

"Erica," Russell tried to get my attention. "Erica!"

"What!" I screamed through the tears.

"Do you still have that crystal?" Russell crazily asked.

"Yeah it's in the bedroom on the dresser. Why? Do you think it will work?"

"It's worth a shot."

I didn't want to leave his side, but time was of the essence and I knew exactly where to find it as my body found new strength. I dashed to the bedroom where the stone on the dresser called me, then rushed back to Colby's side. Russell had delicately moved him to a blanket on the couch. I pulled the crystal from its pouch.

"This is going to work," I voiced to the heavens.

I grabbed the stone, gently tucking it between Colby's front paws. His furry, overgrown slippers did a good job of hiding the crystal. I feverously rubbed my hands together to generate heat before encompassing my hands over his paws. Nothing, the stone wasn't illuminating like it had done earlier for me and Colby now struggled with every breath, as his chest barely had the strength or will to rise and each pant gargled. Russell positioned himself around me; his arms mimicked mine as his large hands engulfed Colby's paws and mine. He tenderly kissed my bleeding cheek.

"For luck."

"For Colby," I answered.

The crystal ever so slightly began to radiate, with intermittent beams of light, splitting Colby's fur. I never wanted anything so bad in my life, but for my one true friend to have a second chance on life. I snuggled down into his fur, my ear to his, praying for a miracle. If there were a God, he'd answer my prayer. Right? RIGHT!!!

The Hawai'ian Language

To help in your journey and to enjoy this book in better detail, below is a brief explanation of the Hawai'ian language. This includes the names, locations, and phrases used in this book. When possible, the correct pronunciation, as well as its literal meaning and brief description have been included.

A reminder that this is a work of fiction. Names, characters, places, and incidents either are products of the author's imagination or are used fictitiously. Any likeness to actual events, locales, persons, living or dead is entirely coincidental.

The Hawai'ian language is a graceful, soothing, and pleasant-sounding language that has a soft flowing nature to it off the tongue. The sounds tended to invoke breathtaking sunsets, with cascading waves and a soft breeze touching your cheek under a palm tree. Hawai'ian shares its roots with most Polynesian languages and uses many common words. Today, Hawai'ian is spoken as an everyday language only on the privately owned island of Ni'ihau, a.k.a. *"The Forbidden Island"*, to the locals. You shouldn't be intimidated by Hawai'ian and with some simple ground rules; you'll realize that pronunciation is not as hard as you might think.

The Hawai'ian alphabet has only twelve letters. Five vowels: *A, E, I, O* and U, as well as seven consonants, *H, K, L, M, N, P* and **W**. The consonants are pronounced just as in English, with the exception of **W**. It is often pronounced as a *V* if it is in the middle of a word and comes after an *E* or *I*. Vowels can be long or short. Long vowels are usually written with a macron (ā, ē, ī, ō, ū), but if no macron is available, a circumflex (â, ê, î, ô, û) can be used instead.

Vowels are pronounced as follows:

A – pronounced as **a** in *above*, if stressed **ā** as in *car*.

E – pronounced as **e** in *bet*, if stressed **ē** as *ay* in *pay*.

I – pronounced as **ee** in *bee*, same if stressed **ī**.

O – pronounced as **o** in *sole*, same if stressed ō.

U – pronounced as **oo** in *moon*, same if stressed ū.

 Glottal stops are represented by an upside-down apostrophe ' and are meant to convey a hard stop in the pronunciation. The word for glottal in Hawai'ian is 'okina. So if we are talking about the type of lava called A'a, it is pronounced as two separate A's which would sound like "ah-ah" in English.

 Diphthongs are two letters that glide together. They are *ae*, *ai*, *ao*, *au*, *ei*, *eu*, *oi*, and *ou*. Unlike English diphthongs, the second vowel is always pronounced. Stress the first letter and end with a short *a*, *e*, *i*, *o*, or *u*.

Continue to 'Words' next page…

Below are words used in this book, how to pronounce them and their meaning. Enjoy!

Aloha (ah-low-ha): Hello, good-bye, or a feeling or the spirit of love, affection, or kindness.

Elika (e-li-ka): Hawai'ian for Erica meaning, ever ruling, lone ruler, or island ruler.

Hawai'ian (hah-wa-yan): A native inhabitant of the Hawai'ian Islands or Hawai'i's Polynesian language.

Heiau (hay-ee-ow): Pre-Christian, a place of worship or rock shrine. This word references a freshwater pool found in *Wai'anapanapa State Park*.

Hula (hoo-lah): The storytelling dance of Hawai'i.

Ka'iu lani (ka-ee-oo-La-nee): Refers to the lovely or sacred one; also name of Hawai'i's last princess.

Kamakawiwo'ole, Israel (kah-mah-kah-vee-vo-o-lah): Was a musician, singer-songwriter and a native of Hawai'i until his untimely death due to his weight in 1997 at the age of 38. His music increased in popularity after his death. Known locally as Bruddah Iz.

Kamāli'i wahine (ka-mah-lee-ee wah-hee-ney): The first word means child but can also refer to Prince or Princess; wahine means women or woman; however, the two words together mean Princess.

Koa (ko-ah): Tree used for canoes or island furniture.

Kona (ko-nah): Meaning leeward or dry-side of the island; is a district on the Big Island of Hawai'i and has an ideal growing climate for coffee. Thus is referenced in this book as not only a location, but as a coffee brand.

Kukui Nuts (koo-koo-ee): The meaning of the word is 'Enlightened'. The Kukui is the state tree of Hawai'i also known as the Candlenut Tree. The oil of the nuts in ancient times was burned for light, thus the meaning of *'enlightened one'*. The nuts are polished and used in leis. In ancient Hawai'i, Kukui Leis were reserved only for royalty.

Kupuna kāne (koo-poo-nah kāh-neh): Meaning Grandfather.

Lei (lay): Necklace of flowers, shells, or feathers. Each island has its signature lei flower, The Lokelani (small rose) Lei is the lei of Maui.

Lulani (lou-la-nee): Meaning is "highest point in heaven".

Mahalo (mah-hah-low): Thank you.

Mele (meh-leh): Meaning "song".

Mika'ele (mi-ka-ele): Meaning *"one who is godlike"*. Hawai'ian for Michael.

Nohea (no-heh-ah): Handsome, of fine appearance.

'opakapaka (oh-pah-kah-pah-kah): Hawai'ian pink-red snapper fish.

Pakile (pah-kee-leh): Meaning is kingly or royal.

Pele (peh-leh): Meaning is lava. Also, known as the Volcano Goddess.

Continue on to 'Phrase' next page...

Below are phrases used in this book, how to pronounce them and their meaning.

Hoʻolohe iā ke Ka'iu lani kamāli'i wahine (hoh-oh-loh-heh ee-ah keh Ka-ee-oo-La-nee ka-mah-lee-ee wah-hee-ney): "listen to the sacred princess".

Aina Lani Farms (aye-nah lah-nee): The first word means "*land or earth*"; Second word means "*heavenly*". Together they mean "*heavenly land*". This is briefly mentioned as a logo on a semi-trailer in the story and was used completely factiously. Although, there is an Aina Lani Farms on Maui and they grow "*Fresh Island Herbs*" there is no correlation.

Aloha Au Ia'Oe (ah-low-ha ow e-ahh-oye): "*I love you*".

He ipo no ke po (heh ee-poh no keh poh): "a lover for the night".

Hoʻamalu ia makou pauloa Ka'iu lani kamāli'i wahine (ka-ee-oo-La-nee ka-mah-lee-ee wah-hee-ney): "protect us all sacred princess".

Ke Ka'iu lani kamāli'i wahine (keh Ka-ee-oo-La-nee ka-mah-lee-ee wah-hee-ney): "the sacred princess"

No Ka ʻOi (no-ka-oy): Meaning '*the best*' or '*number one*'. The locals refer to Maui as this; Maui No Ka ʻOi.

Continue on to 'Locations' next page…

Below are locations used in this book, how to pronounce them and their meaning.

Haleakalā (ha-leh-ah-kah-lah):   Meaning *"house of the sun"*. Haleakalā is Māui's highest peak, a dormant volcano and one of the tallest mountains in Hawai'i.

Pools of 'Ohe'o (oh-hay-oh): Known as the 'seven sacred pools' and is located inside Haleakalā National Park just outside Hana. The stories behind the pools are a work of fiction, but breathtaking.

Hali'imaile General Store (ha-lee-ee-maee-leh):   Found in Hali'imaile on Hali'imaile Road in Hali'imaile. It's constantly voted as one of Māui's best places to eat. Although real, the author took liberties with the interior décor and menu creating a work of fiction. Any resemblance to the actual persons or locals, living or dead is entirely coincidental.

Hana (ha-nah): Meaning *'work'*. Also, a small-town on the east side of Māui.

Hawai'i (hah-vy-ee): Although associated with all the islands, is technically one of the eight, and the youngest. Also, known as the *'big island'*.

Honoapi'ilani Highway (ho-no-ah-pee-ee-lah-nee):   Route 30. This highway starts in Wailuku, extends through Lāhainā, and ends in Honokohau Bay, which it then continues as Kahekili Highway. The two highways total a spherical expedition around west Māui.

Kahului International Airport (ka-hoo-loo-ee): The largest town on Maui and to the north and host the major airport, mall and ports.

Keawakapu Beach (kay-ah-wa-ka-poo): Meaning *"the sacred or forbidden Harbor"*. Keawakapu Beach is the last beach on South Kihei Road and is roughly a half-mile long. This is a very popular space for both tourists and locals. There are numerous multimillion-dollar homes that sit back off the shore, but the beaches are still public and tend not to be overwhelmed. This happens to be a very dog-friendly beach as many walk their dogs daily, but a leash is required. The northernmost parking lot is probably the least secure of the three parking lots for Keawakapu because the Wailea Patrol doesn't patrol that section. In this book, Jim's house, sits off this beach and it is completely fictional. Although, this book does reference parts of this beach the author took considerable liberties in its description.

Ku'au Inn (koo-ow): This is a beautiful Bed & Breakfast, run by locals, located in a small beach village of Ku'au on the North Shore of Māui.

Kula Botanical Gardens (koo-lah): The meaning is *"open meadows"*. Kula Botanical Gardens is a family owned and operated garden located in Kula and a district of east Māui. In addition, its home to 2,000 species of indigenous Hawaiian flora and fauna. Established in 1968 by Warren and Helen McCord as a display garden for Warren's landscape architecture business, the garden has evolved into a tourist destination that draws thousands of visitors every year. The garden is located on the slopes of Haleakalā totaling approximately eight acres and includes colorful and unique plants, astonishing rock formations, a covered bridge, waterfalls, Kio pond, and aviary. The author took enormous freedom with the exterior as well as interior décor to create a work of fiction. Any resemblance to the actual persons or locals, living or dead is entirely coincidental.

Lāhainā (lah-high-nah): Meaning is *'cruel sun'*. Was Hawaii's first capital and sits on the west side of Māui. The main attraction to the town runs along Front Street.

Makawao (mah-kah-wow): Meaning is *"beginning of the forest"*. It is a town found on Māui and marks the beginning of a vast rain forest on the northeast side of Māui. Known for its local eateries, cowboy-like culture, and local laid-back atmosphere.

Mala Ocean Tavern (mah-lah): Meaning is *"garden or plantation"*. It is located on, the well-known, Front Street of downtown Lāhainā on the water.

Māui (mow-ee): Meaning is *"valley isle"*. Is the second largest of the islands and known for its large isthmus between its northwestern and southeastern volcanoes as well as the numerous large valleys carved into both mountains. Its main feature is the dormant volcano Haleakalā.

O'ahu (o-ah-oo): It has no confirmed meaning in Hawai'ian but is often referred to as the *"gathering place"*. This is the third largest island and home to the state's capital of Honolulu.

Okolani Drive (o-ko-la-nee): Forks off South Kihei Road and continues to Piilani Highway. Found on the western side of Māui can connects you to Keawakapu Beach.

Pipiwai Trail (pee-pee-why): Found above the Pools of 'Ohe'o and is a four-mile round-trip hike. The highlight is the Waimoku Falls. This is part of the trek to Hana.

Pu'u Kukui (poo-oo-koo-koo-ee): Known as *"the mountain of light"*. This is the highest peak of west Māui's mountains with an elevation of 5,788 feet. It is also one of the wettest spot's on the planet, receiving an average 386 inches of rainfall a year.

South Kihei Road (k-ee-hey): This is a road found in Ma'alaea, Māui and extends north to south along Keawakapu Beach. In the book, Jim's house if fictionally based on this road.

Wai'anapanapa State Park (why-a-nah-pah-nah-pah): Meaning is *"glistening waters"*. It is a 122-acre park found in Hana.

Wailea Blue Golf Course (why-leh-ah): Meaning is *"water of Lea"* and pays tribute to an ancient Goddess. Wailea is the town, Keawakapu Beach, is located in as well as this golf course. Russell's company's house is mentioned as residing near this location.

Waimoku Falls (why-moh-koo): This is a combination of two words; wai meaning *"freshwater"* and moku meaning *"island"*. This magnificent 400-foot waterfall drops down a sheer lava rock wall into an awaiting pool and is spring-fed. It's the climax to the Pipiwai Trail in Hana.

About the Author

Tina Marie is a successful business owner turned writer and lives in Henderson, Nevada with her family, including her unique Golden Retrievers. Her love for family equaled only by the love of the Golden Retriever Breed. A lifelong experiencer, who believes we are headed for an ascension into a higher vibrational frequency.

Sir Colby, an inspiration, doing what he does best…Sleeping!

Please take a moment and help save a Golden today.

Golden Retriever Rescue Southern Nevada -- *www.grrsn.org*

To contact Tina Marie Caouette:

Tina Marie Caouette

tinamarie@tinamarieentertainment.com